# Praise for Sarah Price

"The Plain Fame series gives a unique insight to some of the harsh life challenges that artists face when trying to balance fame and their personal lives. These books tell the story from the artist's perspective. Highly recommended!" —Aton Ben-Horin, Director of Worldwide Rhythm & Pop A&R, Warner Music Group

"*Plain Fame* has a unique story line that will keep you up late at night hiding under your blanket with a flashlight, trying to squeeze in one last page before you head into La La Land. Yes, it's that good! I love that I loved these characters so much. They are as different as night and day . . . an Amish girl and a famous pop star brought together by an unfortunate accident involving a limo. Or was it unfortunate? Some may say it was fate pulling these two together like a magnet to metal. The only thing for certain is that their lives are about to be forever altered . . ." —Sue Laitinen, book reviewer for DestinationAmish.com

"Once again Sarah Price does not disappoint. I have enjoyed every book that I have read by her. *Plain Fame* is a little different from your normal 'Amish' novel. Readers who don't normally read Amish novels will like this one, as it, in my opinion, is more about how fame affects someone rather than being just an Amish novel." —Debbie Curto, book reviewer from *Debbie's Dusty Deliberations*

"Amish Christian romance like none other—Sarah Price opens both her characters and her readers to new worlds. This love story could easily become a classic as two lives from opposite cultures collide, creating intense conflict and romance. *Plain Fame* was my introduction to Sarah Price and the beginning of my Price addiction."
—Lisa Bull, blogger of *Captured by My Thoughts*

# Plain Choice

## The Amish Classic Series

For a complete listing of books, please visit the author's website at www.sarahpriceauthor.com.

# Plain Choice

*Book Five of the Plain Fame Series*

*Sarah Price*

**Waterfall**
PRESS

Text copyright © 2016 Price Publishing, LLC

Published by Waterfall Press, Grand Haven, MI

www.brilliancepublishing.com

Amazon, the Amazon logo, and Waterfall Press are trademarks of Amazon.com, Inc., or its affiliates.

ISBN-13: 9781503933217

ISBN-10: 1503933210

Cover design by Eileen Carey

Printed in the United States of America

*Three years ago, I first "met" Alejandro and Amanda.*
*They evolved into real people for many of my readers (and for me, too).*

*The inspiration came from my own "celebrity crush" on worldwide superstar Pitbull. After writing the first two books, I met him. The day was May 31, 2013—the very day I was diagnosed with breast cancer. He inspired and comforted me during a very difficult period in my life. Writing these books kept my spirits high during the complications of my treatment.*

*So I dedicate this book—and the entire series—to Pitbull.*

Gracias, *amigo.* <3

# About the Vocabulary

The Amish speak Pennsylvania Dutch (also called Amish German or Amish Dutch). This is a verbal language with variations in spelling among communities throughout the United States. For example, in some regions, a grandfather is *grossdaadi*, while in other regions he is known as *grossdawdi*. Some dialects refer to the mother as *mamm* or *maem*, and others simply as *mother* or *mammi*.

In addition, there are words and expressions, such as *mayhaps*, or the use of the word *then* at the end of sentences, and, my favorite, *for sure and certain*, that are not necessarily from the Pennsylvania Dutch language/dialect but are unique to the Amish.

The use of these words comes from my own experience living among the Amish in Lancaster County, Pennsylvania.

# Chapter One

Amanda would have never expected that the one thing she didn't want to give Alejandro was the one thing he would take: his freedom.

Two weeks had passed. Two long weeks with no word from Alejandro. He hadn't contacted her, and despite her desire to reach out to him, each morning she merely looked at the cell phone on her kitchen counter, willing it to ring.

It didn't.

Now, as she stood on the small hill at the back of her family's farm, wiping the sweat from her brow, she looked around at the familiar surroundings. They felt surprisingly foreign, as foreign to her as visiting Colombia, Brazil, and Argentina had felt.

How, she wondered, did I end up back here, caring for Isadora and separated from Alejandro?

The sun had barely crested the horizon. The full impact of its powerful heat was still hours away, but she needed a moment's break to catch her breath. Perspiration glistened against her forehead and down her neck. Even her back felt damp. Her dress, a simple floral pattern that brushed against her knees, did not keep her cool enough given the work that they were doing.

Up ahead she saw Jonas and Harvey working the team of Belgian mules that pulled the plow through the dry dirt of the fields in preparation for planting corn. As the mules pulled the plow, the earth parted behind the moldboard, dividing it in a smooth, fluid motion and leaving behind a narrow trench. It was like watching the ocean as it rose up in gentle waves, the only difference being that the footprint of the plow left behind neat rows of tilled soil whereas the ocean waves rolled onto the sand and then back to the sea.

The ocean.

She shut her eyes. The first time she saw the ocean was in Los Angeles. Alejandro had taken her to the beach just outside the city proper. She had never walked on sand that was so soft nor had she felt the gentle push and pull from waves. In Miami, the ocean was something she saw on a daily basis from the rooftop patio of Alejandro's condominium. She could stand at the wall and watch it for hours, the rise and fall of the water mesmerizing her as it pushed toward shore.

She took a deep breath as if she could smell the salt air. Instead, she smelled the fresh scent of dirt, a more familiar, if not as pleasant, scent.

She wondered if Alejandro was in Miami or Los Angeles. Certainly he had not yet departed for Europe. In the two weeks since he had left, she had done her best to remain unemotional and calm. She knew Isadora needed stability, not drama, in her young life. The farm provided that for Isadora. What she hadn't counted on was Alejandro's reaction. While Amanda tried to wear a brave face, on the inside, her emotions churned, going from heartbreak to humiliation and from angst to anger.

As hard as she tried, she could not shake the image of Alejandro leaving on that morning. It was seared in her memory. The coldness with which he'd spoken to her and the dismissive way in which he merely turned and walked away conflicted with everything she'd learned about her husband. She could not wrap her mind around the idea that she had been deserted. Where had everything gone wrong? she wondered.

"You all right, then?" a deep voice said from behind her.

Amanda shifted her attention from her inner sanctuary to the man behind her. She tried to smile as she turned to Harvey. Her arms wrapped around her waist, as if that would help her hold things together. Amanda nodded her head. "*Ja*, just fine," she said.

He placed his hand on her shoulder, a gesture that caused Amanda to look away. "You don't have to be out here, Amanda," Harvey said. "We'll do just fine the two of us. 'Sides, Izzie will be looking for you shortly."

Again, she nodded her head. "I know."

"But you do what you have to," Harvey said, a soft expression on his tanned face.

She managed to smile at him. After all of his kindness to her and her family, it was the least she could do to let Harvey know how much she appreciated his compassion.

Two weeks, she thought as she watched Harvey walk back to Jonas, who was adjusting the harness on one of the mules.

It was hard for her to face the truth: her husband had left her on her parents' farm and gone off to continue his own life, separated from her and their daughter, Isadora. After all that they'd been through, she couldn't comprehend that their marriage might actually be over. So much had happened in the year since they'd met—from the accident in New York City to the onslaught of paparazzi in Lancaster to the whirlwind romance that took her to cities she never even knew existed: Las Vegas, Los Angeles, and Miami.

And then they had gotten married in autumn.

She'd known that marrying Alejandro would not be easy. It wasn't that she didn't love him. That had never been the question. But the South American tour had been especially hard for Amanda. On a continent where she could not communicate culturally or linguistically, their differences had emerged in full force. In his interactions with the sophisticated and exotically beautiful women that always appeared magically backstage and with his friend Enrique Lopez, another Latin superstar, Amanda had watched Alejandro transform into Viper, the womanizing international sensation who charmed everyone he met. His nights began to linger into the morning hours and between all of his interviews and obligations, she rarely saw him. Gradually, she found herself spending more time alone than with him.

Neither of them had been prepared for the arrival of Isadora, his five-year-old daughter from a long-ago one-night stand with a Brazilian woman. Amanda had known about the daughter. Alejandro had told her about the child when they first met. But because he had no relationship with the daughter or the mother, Alejandro never mentioned them again. Frankly, Amanda had forgotten about it.

So when the Brazilian government worker arrived with the child, explaining that Isadora was headed to an orphanage if Alejandro and Amanda did not take her, the shock of suddenly becoming parents had overwhelmed both of them.

"Amanda?"

She looked up at the sound of her name carried on the morning breeze. Jonas was waving to her, beckoning her to help them.

Obediently, and grateful for the interruption to her racing thoughts, she hurried down the field and joined the two men.

Her brother-in-law stood by the larger of the two mules, examining a piece of leather. "*Ach*, it's broken, I reckon."

Amanda peered over his shoulder at the tie strap. The ring that held it to the trace carrier, the piece of leather across the mule's rump that kept the plow attached to the harness had, indeed, torn off. "That's not *gut*," she said. "I don't think I remember Daed having an extra one."

Harvey took off his hat and wiped his brow with the back of his arm. "I can run over to the harness shop, fetch a new one." His offer would save them time. As a Mennonite, he drove a car. It would be much faster than Amanda or Jonas hitching a horse to a buggy and riding over. "Amanda, you want to ride along?"

She was about to decline, but Jonas nodded his head. "You haven't left the farm since Alejandro left. Might do you some good."

She was too surprised that Jonas had mentioned Alejandro to turn down Harvey's offer. It was the first time Jonas, or anyone besides her sister, Anna, had said anything about her husband. It just wasn't the Amish way to pry into someone else's business, especially if it involved marital problems.

The morning that he'd left, her family had quietly accepted Amanda's explanation for Alejandro's abrupt departure. She told them that he had meetings and she hadn't wanted to leave yet, especially with Isadora's progress adapting to her new life in America. Despite her puffy eyes and tearstained cheeks, they simply listened to her, nodded, and never asked another question about him.

Later that morning, in the privacy of the *grossdaadihaus* where Amanda stayed with Isadora, Anna had inquired further. When Amanda burst into tears, sobbing into her hands, she shared the entire story. She told her sister about the South American tour, the truth about Isadora's appearance in their lives, about Alejandro's rebuffing the child and leaving her in Amanda's care, and the final hours of their time together.

As any good sister would do, Anna listened and then embraced Amanda, holding her while she cried. Afterward, the rest of the family seemed to look at her with a sense of pity, something Amanda detested. But they never asked any questions. When it came to matters of the heart between husband and wife, they wouldn't interfere or probe for more information.

While grateful for their unspoken support, Amanda disliked the cautious way that they treated her, as if she were a fragile doll, ready to break at any moment. Her only relief had been Isadora, who asked only once where "Papi" had gone. When Amanda explained that Papi had gone away on business, Isadora had never mentioned him again.

"Ready, Amanda?" Harvey asked, the broken tie strap and trace carrier in his hands.

She nodded and followed him as he walked across the field toward his car parked behind the barn.

The number of paparazzi camped out by the entrance to the farm had declined since Alejandro's leaving. With Amanda staying on the farm and no news to report, most of the photographers had moved on to something—and someone—else in the hopes of capturing their moneymaking photos. A few remained, and when Harvey drove past them, they eagerly snapped photos of Amanda riding in the car with him. She ignored them, for once unaffected by their intrusive lenses and knowing that at least one of the photographs would make the tabloids and social media news by evening.

"You'd think they'd give up," Harvey said as he drove down the road.

Amanda shrugged in a casual sort of way. "You'd think so, but they don't."

"It's invasive."

She smiled as she looked out the window. She liked how straightforward Harvey spoke, never saying too much but always willing to speak his mind in a quiet and calm manner, without any drama. "They hardly bother me anymore."

He nodded as if he understood.

Feeling as if she should fill the silence in the car, Amanda explained, "Those few photographers are nothing like the paparazzi at the airports and arenas. The Englischers sure do have a propensity for enjoying gossip about their favorite celebrities, I reckon."

Harvey chuckled under his breath. "No different from the Amish grapevine, wouldn't you say?"

She smiled. "*Ja*, I reckon so."

Even though the Amish community shunned all worldliness, allowing access to the advances in the outside world only when permitted by the bishop of each church district, the Amish were human beings and spread stories as much as non-Amish people. The only difference was that the Englischers had access to technology, so news traveled slower among the Amish communities.

Amanda remembered when she first returned to Lancaster with Alejandro. Women in Lititz, as well as surrounding towns, had known about her arrival with the famous singer, Viper. Not long after the paparazzi located her parents' farm, Alejandro had left in the hopes that they would follow. But the reporters stayed behind. For the next few weeks, the gossip among the Amish grapevine had focused on the prying lenses at the end of the photographers' cameras, all on account of Amanda. On the few occasions she'd managed to leave the farm, she knew that the Amish people stared at her. The younger ones might have stared at her in awe, while the older ones scowled and scorned her. On more than one occasion, the bishop had arrived with a tabloid in his hand, angry that so much attention was focused on their community.

"Just worse, I imagine," Harvey added.

"Much worse."

Harvey cleared his throat and glanced at her. "Ever think about calling him, Amanda?"

She shook her head. Harvey knew better than to ask that question. Only once had she gone against the unspoken rule from her upbringing about a woman reaching out to a man. That had been when Alejandro first left her after the accident and the bishop wanted her to leave the community, perhaps to return to Ohio to stay with family. Amanda had resisted; she didn't want to be shuffled from Amish community to Amish community, nor had she wanted to interfere with her sister's budding romance with Jonas. So Amanda had approached the media that lingered by the driveway and spoken to them, hoping against hope that Alejandro would receive the message.

He had.

And he had come for her.

She leaned her head against the headrest and watched as they passed farm after farm. With everything turning green at last, she couldn't help but take comfort that at least she wasn't in Los Angeles, surrounded by tall buildings and congested highways. She'd probably be spending her days alone or, at best, sitting in the studio as Alejandro recorded another new song. She thought about her friend Celinda, a young singer she'd met last autumn. Amanda wondered if they would have caught up for lunch or shopping had she gone to California with Alejandro. Of course, according to the tabloids, and confirmed by Alejandro, Celinda was in the midst of a separation from her longtime love, Justin Bell. Amanda couldn't help but wonder how Celinda had coped with the devastating discovery of his indiscretions.

At the harness store, Harvey got out of the car and hurried around to open the door for Amanda. She hadn't even realized they'd pulled into the parking lot.

"I'm so sorry," she said as she started to get out of the car. He held out his hand for her and she accepted it, looking up at him and managing to thank him with a soft smile.

It was a fortunate day when Alejandro had arranged for Harvey Alderfer to work on their farm. He had become like a brother to her and an uncle to Isadora. Without Harvey, Amanda knew that the farm would have fallen into disarray before Jonas arrived. But now that Jonas was fully entrenched in the community after moving there from Ohio, the two men managed the farm without need of much assistance. Still, when the four walls of the kitchen felt like they were closing in on her, Amanda often escaped outside to lend a hand.

"You all right?" he asked.

She nodded her head and looked away. The sting of holding back tears forced her to blink several times. She would not cry, she told herself. Do not cry.

"I'll go in. Why don't you just take a seat on that bench yonder?" He pointed toward the shade of a large, overgrown tree.

With misty eyes, she nodded her head and obediently walked to where he had pointed. Sitting on a bench that was long overdue for a fresh coat of paint, Amanda watched a car pull out of the parking lot. But her mind was elsewhere, across the continent and in the arms of her husband. She smiled, her first genuine smile in weeks, as she shut her eyes and remembered the feel of his touch on her bare skin.

It was a memory she was beginning to fear would eventually fade.

When Alejandro awoke, the sun had not risen yet. He had appointments with the recording company first thing in the morning and then needed to work with the choreographer and dancers on new routines for the European tour. With only days until his departure, he felt as though he was on autopilot, simply moving through the day and responding to the reminders from his smartphone and from his manager, Geoffrey.

Shuffling from the kitchen to the bedroom of his apartment, he stretched his arms over his head, feeling the tightness in his neck and shoulders. The stress of the upcoming tour combined with the added strain of his separation from Amanda weighed heavily upon him. He almost dreaded the former, but being busy preparing kept him from thinking too much about the latter.

He missed her. That was something he had anticipated when he made up his mind that space was what she needed. Leaving her had been the hardest thing that he'd ever done. Her face, her tears, and her pleas haunted him at night. He found himself taking a strong nightcap each evening to avoid struggling with sleep. Many times, especially at night, he'd longed to pick up his phone and call her.

But he knew he couldn't.

Despite all the awful things that his former manager, Mike, had done to disrupt his relationship with Amanda, Alejandro was now starting to see the wisdom behind his actions. How could he have expected Amanda to adapt to his lifestyle? With her Amish upbringing, she had handled it as well as anyone could have expected. And when Isadora was thrust into their lives, she had taken to the role of mother better than any other woman would have.

The only problem was that he didn't want children. Not yet. And dragging a small child on tour with them was not only taxing but also inappropriate. The late nights, the constant travel, and the people who surrounded him—it was just not an environment for a child. While the idea of a family appealed to him, he had come to realize the timing was just not right.

And then Isadora had arrived.

In all honesty, he hadn't thought about his Brazilian daughter in years and he had never expected to meet her. Now, five years old and basically left all alone, Isadora Daniela da Silva was suddenly a very real part of their family. When she arrived at their hotel before their departure from Rio de Janeiro, Alejandro had barely been able to look at the child. She was born of lust, not love. Yet Amanda had immediately taken over her role as Isadora's stepmother and had quickly come to the same conclusion as Alejandro: a music tour was no place for a child.

When Amanda left Rio de Janeiro, his first feelings of anger at her abandonment were soon replaced with enlightenment regarding the situation. His alter ego, Viper, would always be a playboy in the minds of the fans, even now that he was married to Amanda, the involuntary darling of social media. Just as Mike had predicted, the fans wanted controversy, not love. Just as Justin Bell had played the media with his relationship to Celinda Ruiz, and social media gobbled it up, Alejandro realized his fans wanted the return of the old Viper.

Perhaps they'd merely wanted to see how such a situation would pan out, a philandering Viper with innocent Amanda. He had no intention of giving the public what they wanted. His love for Amanda was unquestionable. Even before his rise to fame, everyone had always wanted something from him. People surrounded him with ideas and schemes, trying to become a part of the story. His story. Alejandro had learned long ago to proceed with caution to ensure that his reward far outweighed anyone else's.

With Amanda, he had finally learned how it felt to be loved and supported with no expectations in return.

He ran the faucet to fill the Keurig water reservoir. Coffee. That's what he needed. Something strong to jump-start the day.

As he waited for the liquid to pour into his mug, he leaned against the counter, rubbing his forehead. He wondered what Amanda was doing at that moment. Perhaps sharing breakfast with Isadora? Or milking the cows with Jonas and Harvey?

He grimaced when he thought of Harvey. For the past two weeks, he'd tried to abolish the memory of watching Harvey carry Isadora and hearing the soft banter between Harvey and Amanda. When the media first published photos of Harvey protecting Amanda from the paparazzi a few months earlier, Alejandro hadn't given it a second thought. The photographers had wasted no time in speculating about a possible relationship between the two, but it was a thought Alejandro easily dismissed.

But when he watched them together and saw the ease with which they worked as a team, it made the pieces of the puzzle come together: What if Amanda was not meant to be his wife? What if all of this was God's plan for her to return to the Amish community and find a husband more aligned with her past?

His phone vibrated and Alejandro broke free from his thoughts. He looked around the kitchen to locate his cell phone. It rested on the counter near the stove. He hadn't remembered placing it there. When he glanced at the clock and saw that it wasn't even six thirty, he sighed.

Probably Geoffrey confirming that a car would be waiting downstairs for him in forty-five minutes.

He reached for the phone and answered the call. *"Dígame, chico."*

"Alex! You're up already?"

*"Sí, sí,"* he responded. *"Claro,* G. What's up?"

There was a brief pause on the other end of the phone. For a moment, Alejandro wondered if the call had dropped. When he heard Geoffrey clearing his throat, he knew something was going on, something that his manager hesitated to tell him about.

"You asked me to alert you if there was . . . uh"—another hesitation—"any word from Lancaster. My guys just saw photos hitting the social media circuit. I wanted to let you know."

Alejandro took a deep breath. If Geoffrey was calling him, the photos were not good news. Geoffrey would not bother him with photos of Amanda hanging out the laundry or sweeping off the porch.

"You want me to send you copies?"

Alejandro nodded, even though Geoffrey could not see him. Behind him, he heard the hissing noise of the coffeemaker finishing the brew for his coffee. He didn't need it anymore; he was wide-awake. "Send it to my private e-mail, *sí.*"

"There are more than one, Alex."

Bracing himself for the worst, Alejandro hung up the phone, set it on the counter, and started pacing. He kept his hands clutched behind his back, his thumbs tapping nervously. Other than that, he tried to maintain his composure as he waited for the digital photos to arrive. Geoffrey's voice had said it all. Whatever was being sent was likely the one thing he did not want to see: his wife assimilating back into the life of the Amish. Still, he knew that it was her choice. He had given that to her, the gift of choosing which life she wanted.

When his phone made a noise, Alejandro picked it up and prepared himself for the e-mail. One tap of his finger on the link and the images began to display on his screen.

His heart fell.

The photos confirmed his suspicions. As he swiped through them, seeing Harvey Alderfer talking with Amanda on the crest of a hill, Harvey opening the car door for her, and Harvey guiding her through the parking lot of a store, Alejandro knew what her choice would be. When he saw the final image, the one of Amanda staring up at the Mennonite man, he shut his eyes.

Maybe he had known from the beginning that she belonged there, with her family and community. If it wasn't Harvey, it would be someone else who would accept her for who she was and who she should become: a hardworking farmer's wife and doting mother. He had fooled himself into thinking that he could settle down into the role of loving husband.

"*Ay, Dios mío,*" he muttered, clicking the phone so that it shut down. He shoved it into the pocket of his robe and stood at the counter, both hands pressed down on the granite top. With a lowered head, he took several deep breaths. He didn't want to leave her. Losing Amanda would be the single most difficult thing he would ever do. He knew that. His fans would greet a divorce with mixed feelings: some supporting the decision because they missed the old Viper and others hating him for leaving Amanda. But she deserved better. She deserved happiness.

He knew that he needed to think through the decision before making a final choice. He knew she loved him. There was no reason to doubt that. The only problem was that he loved her more, and from the look in her face in that final photo, he knew that his love was not enough for her. Now, if he could only get her to come to the same realization.

# Chapter Two

Her cell phone lay on the counter, fully charged but completely silent. Amanda stared at it as she stood there, tapping her fingers on the Formica countertop. The screen remained black, a slight reflection on the glass. For a moment she almost reached out for it, but just as quickly she withdrew her hand.

It wasn't the first time she'd thought about contacting Alejandro during their separation. All of her life she'd been taught to let God handle difficult situations: *Cast your bread upon the waters, for after many days you will find it again.* Without doubt, this was one of those times. Another week had passed, and with each new dawn she felt a heavier weight inside her chest. There were times when she was working in the garden that she would stop, turn her back toward the house, and silently cry, weeping for the unknown, wondering whether Alejandro would return for her.

At night after she tucked Isadora into her bed, Amanda sat in bed reading the Bible by the light of a flickering flame. She took comfort from the verses, particularly the story of Esther. Over and over again, she read that story. The affinity that she felt for Esther embodied her desire to find a way back to Alejandro. Esther was strong and smart;

she understood how to handle the king, a man who adored her and, it seemed, whom she adored.

But unlike Esther and the king, Alejandro had *left* her. His parting words lingered in her memory: *We have choices in life, Amanda. You chose to leave the tour with Isadora despite your love for me, and I am choosing to leave you here because of my love for you.*

Oh, how those words haunted her, especially at moments when she stood alone in the kitchen, staring at the phone as if willing it to ring.

"Knock, knock."

Amanda looked up and forced a smile as her sister, Anna, walked through the door, leading Isadora behind her.

"Mammi!"

Breaking free from Anna, Isadora ran to Amanda and hugged her legs. Laughing, Amanda knelt down and, after extracting herself from Isadora's arms, returned her embrace. Her stepdaughter's dress, a pretty replica of an Amish dress but made from a soft blue floral print, smelled like lavender. Her long dark hair hung in a thick braid down her back. As Amanda held her, she felt the end of it brush against her arm.

If anything could make Amanda feel better, it was the joy that Isadora gave to her each and every day.

Pulling back, Amanda rejoiced to see the light of happiness glowing on Isadora's face. What a perfect change from when Amanda first saw the child wearing an old dress and shoes that didn't fit. Despite her grandfather's best efforts, Isadora's face had told the real story, one of insecurity and inconsistency. Now, after six weeks in Amanda's care, Isadora presented herself as a joyful child with balance in her life.

"Izzie!" Amanda said cheerfully. "Did you go out to see the kittens, then?"

She nodded her head. "*Ja*, kittens."

"Nice fat kittens this year," Amanda said, running her fingers over her stepdaughter's stomach, which made Isadora laugh. "I reckon they'll be right *gut* mousers."

Isadora made a face, apparently not liking the idea of the kittens eating the mice, which, according to the five-year-old, were "*muito* cute." It had taken Amanda a few days to realize that Isadora was combining Portuguese with English to express her thoughts about the very cute field mice that often scurried through the barnyard.

"Oh, she loves those kittens, Amanda," Anna said as she moved over to the table and sat down, one hand resting on her enlarged stomach. "The little orange one likes to chase a little string Izzie found in the barn."

"Is that so?" Amanda exaggerated an expression of surprise. "Did the kitten play with you?"

"*Ja*, orange kitten."

Standing up, Amanda gave Isadora another hug. "Then I think you should name that kitten, don't you think? Now you go on and play a spell. We'll come up with a right *gut* name for that kitten before we say prayers tonight."

She watched as Isadora did as she was told, practically running to the far side of the room where her toys were. Not once had Isadora defied her. If Amanda asked her to do something, she did it without question. Now she flopped onto the floor, lying down on her stomach, and began to pick through her toys, settling on the wooden animals that Harvey had made for her. Amanda watched for a minute, her heart swelling with love for Isadora.

Turning toward her sister, Amanda realized that Anna, too, had been watching. There was a glow about her face, a sparkle in her eyes, that Amanda noticed as she sat down at the small table next to her.

"You're smiling with your eyes," Amanda said, hoping that her voice did not give away the pain that she still felt in her heart. Even with Isadora making her so happy, it never seemed to fully disappear.

"Am I now?" Anna smiled. "I reckon I am. She's such a blessing, *ja*?"

Amanda felt the conflicting emotions of love and despair. "She's a blessing indeed," Amanda agreed. "Some days I don't know what I'd do without her." Yet that, too, was a bittersweet thought. There was an uncomfortable moment as Amanda wondered if Anna also understood the irony of the position Amanda was in.

At last Anna spoke, changing the subject to something less distressing. "I have news, Amanda. *Gut* news! I felt the *boppli* kicking today."

Amanda swallowed, a moment of regret washing over her: her happiness for her sister was overshadowed by the sorrow she felt herself. The kicking of a child within her womb was something Amanda knew she was unlikely to feel. Alejandro had made his position about children more than clear when she thought she might be pregnant before their departure for the South American tour. His reaction to Isadora's appearance had only confirmed it: a large family—maybe any family!— was not something he desired.

Besides, from the way that things were now, Amanda worried that he might never contact her at all. He had been adamant that he was not giving up his career and that she belonged on the farm. If Alejandro was so convinced that they were wrong for each other, what could she do? There was no point in chasing him or trying to convince him that things could work out. Ever since the tour in South America, their relationship had been nothing more than tension and a clash of cultures that had created an ever-growing chasm between them. The unexpected arrival of Isadora had only solidified the distance between them.

"That's *gut*," Amanda said, blinking her eyes as if she could forget her thoughts. She tried to focus on her sister. "I should like to feel that when it kicks again."

"It feels like little butterflies!" Anna laughed as she rubbed her stomach.

When Amanda didn't respond, her eyes returning to watch Isadora, Anna reached across the table for her hand. "Amanda," Anna said in a soft voice. "You've said nothing about Alejandro since he left. It's been almost three weeks. You say that my eyes are smiling, but your eyes are filled with hurt."

"Stop," Amanda whispered.

"*Nee*, your eyes tell the truth, Schwester. Now it is time for your mouth to do the same. What has happened? Has he contacted you?"

The truth was one thing that Amanda could not say. Not out loud. If she did, she'd have to confront the blackness that clouded her heart and kept her awake at night. She longed to be a family, to experience the joy of raising Isadora with Alejandro, to see his mother—the formidable Alecia—melt with love when she saw her granddaughter. Even more, she longed to feel the butterfly flutters of a life forming within her womb. But these were things she could not say. So, instead of speaking the truth, she merely shook her head and said, "I miss him."

That was as close to the truth as she could admit.

"*Vell*, of course you do! He's your husband!" Anna gently squeezed Amanda's hand. "Mayhaps you should join him."

Amanda shook her head once again, fighting the swelling emotions that tightened her throat. She could not cry in front of Anna. She knew that, if she did, Anna would suspect that she was hiding something. Just a little more probing and Amanda would not be able to stop herself from blurting out the entire story.

"*Nee*, Anna," she replied, glancing over her shoulder at Isadora and blinking her eyes, hoping that would keep the tears at bay. "Alejandro's world on the road is no place for a child." With her tears contained and the hold on her throat loosening, she managed to look back at her sister. "Or for me either, for that matter."

"Is it truly so awful, then?"

Amanda hesitated before responding. She formulated an answer in her head before she let herself speak. "It's just very . . . different. It's a little too bold for me."

"Bold?"

How could she explain this to Anna? The women. The crowds. The parties. It was not a world that her sister, or anyone from her family, could comprehend. And how could they, when she could barely understand it herself? "Worldly, I reckon," she said slowly. "South America is a beautiful country, but it is so different from how we were raised, Anna. Days are long and nights are even longer. And on tour there is little sleep and constant traveling. The people are everywhere and there is no privacy."

Anna laughed. "You mean like here? With those people stealing our photos?"

Amanda would have laughed with her sister, but she couldn't. *"Nee,"* she said. "It is worse. At least on the farm we can move about somewhat safely and without interference. But traveling with Alejandro . . ." She paused and thought for a moment.

The memory of the women in Rio walking past her and calling her *pobrecita* came to mind. They had been mocking her, as if she was too ignorant and unworldly to understand what they wanted from her husband. But Amanda knew. Alejandro had told her all about those women when he first brought her home from New York City after the accident last summer.

Sex. It was all about sex. Those were the kinds of women whom Alejandro had slept with in the past—the type of women with whom Viper had enjoyed the carnal joys of lust instead of love just because he could. They were most probably of the same class as Isadora's deceased mother.

Anna caught her breath. "Oh, Amanda," she whispered. "I cannot imagine what you must have experienced." She held up her free hand as if warding off something dangerous. "Don't even try to explain it further!"

"I wouldn't do that." Not to Anna or anyone in the family.

"You were right to not go with him, then. It is better to stay here until the tour is over, I think."

"Traveling with Alejandro is too hard on my sensibilities, I reckon," Amanda said at last. "The one thing that I learned was that success in the music business comes only with sacrifice of self, and I'm not willing to surrender that part of my soul."

"And he is willing to, then?" Her sister looked horrified.

Quickly, Amanda shook her head. "It's not like that, Anna. And I don't want you to judge him."

"I would never judge another person," Anna replied softly. "I just don't understand."

And Amanda wasn't certain she could explain it. Some things in life had to be experienced to be understood. "One of the things that I've learned is that we are very insulated here, Anna. Even in Ohio we were sheltered from the outside world. And that world is not always very pretty and definitely not simple." She ran her fingers along the edge of the tabletop. "He had a rough childhood, and the only thing that saved him was music."

Even though Anna nodded, Amanda knew that her sister didn't fully understand.

"He doesn't know any other life, Anna," she said. "How can someone sacrifice their soul if they know only one way to live?" She frowned. "I think of that often, Anna. If a child is born into a life and is taught how to live that life, like Isadora, and is never exposed to the Word of God . . ."

"I don't think I care for this discussion," Anna whispered.

"I felt the same way, Anna," Amanda admitted. Those women who wanted to have sex with Alejandro were sinners in Amanda's eyes and according to the Bible. Yet if no one showed them the light and truth of Jesus, what would happen to them on Judgment Day? "But it is something I have to think about because I am married to a man who sins . . . at least according to our beliefs and values."

"Then why?" Anna asked. "Why did you marry him?"

Amanda bit her lower lip and shut her eyes. No matter what Anna felt for Jonas, or any other Amish woman felt for her husband, there was no amount of explaining that could convey the intensity of emotion that she felt for Alejandro. When he lifted an eyebrow or gave her a half smile, when he stared at her over the rim of his dark sunglasses, she felt as though electricity ran throughout her body and butterflies fluttered in her stomach. Just one glance from Alejandro made her knees feel weak, and when he pulled her into his arms, it took her breath away.

Time had done nothing to extinguish the flame of passion she felt for that man.

"I love him," Amanda said at last, opening her eyes and staring at her sister. "I love him in ways that there are simply no words to express."

Amanda sensed Anna's visit was ending, and for that, she was thankful. She could not fight the tears much longer. Anna started to get up, withdrawing her hand from Amanda's and placing it lightly on her stomach. As she rubbed it, she glanced at Isadora once again. "Mayhaps he'll see that his old life is not good and he needs to change for his new life."

Amanda wasn't so certain that would happen, but she didn't say anything.

"I best get going now. Mamm needs my help with Daed. We'll see you at supper, *ja*?" Anna didn't wait for an answer as she headed toward the door that led to the main house. "Oh, I almost forgot why I came over in the first place!" She laughed absentmindedly. "Harvey asked if you might help with the milking? Jonas isn't back yet from his errands. Mamm and I will watch Izzie."

Amanda didn't need to be asked twice. Working in the dairy helped her forget everything that burdened her. For the few hours that she helped with chores, her mind was kept busy while her body worked.

"Izzie," she said. "Go with your *aendi* now."

Isadora looked up from her toys. Her eyes traveled from Amanda to Anna.

"Mammi Lizzie made fresh cookies," Anna said in a soft, sweet voice.

"*Ach!* Anna! Not before supper!"

"Just one won't ruin her appetite," Anna retorted and held out her hand for the child to take. "Right, Izzie?"

The little girl grinned and nodded her head emphatically. "One."

Amanda managed a real smile. She held up her pointer finger and said, "Just one, then. But you dare not have more than that, Isadora."

Anna and Isadora walked hand in hand to the door. After they disappeared through the dark opening, Amanda stared after them, her mind wandering for just a few moments. She wondered if she would have left the South American tour if it hadn't been for Isadora. Perhaps she would have stuck it out, hiding her unhappiness over Alejandro's behavior change, which had become even more pronounced after Enrique had joined up with the tour.

Enrique Lopez.

Almost as famous as Alejandro, Enrique lived the lie that had been Alejandro's past. She had witnessed it firsthand when they had the week break in Argentina. Instead of flying back to the United States, Alejandro had rented an estate, or, as they called it in Argentina, *una estancia*. While the house and grounds were beautiful, so were the dozens of women who hung around the pool all day and the house all night. With dark, pecan-colored skin and thick black hair, each woman was more beautiful than the next. And Enrique was not afraid to tell them that.

His lie was fidelity. He could offer no one a relationship, just a moment in time. But the women did not seem to mind. In fact, they seemed more drawn to Enrique because of his commitment to infidelity. Witnessing that side of stardom and success had given Amanda a glimpse into her husband's past that made her worry about the future.

As she walked toward the dairy barn, she caught a glimpse of the paparazzi that still lingered at the end of the farm's lane. When Alejandro left the farm, the media began to descend upon the Beiler family once again. But as the days continued to drag on, one by one the major reporters and photographers began to leave for other more profitable assignments. A die-hard four of six remained behind, hoping to catch that one photograph of Amanda that they could sell to the entertainment programs on television and to the tabloids.

Harvey must have been watching her from inside the barn. He stepped outside of the entrance door and shifted his hat back on his head. "Still out there, eh?"

Amanda sighed. "*Ja*, still out there."

"They must be pretty committed to stay for so long," he said. "Maybe they'd like to help us milk the cows."

For a second she thought he was serious, his comment was so dry. But when she realized he was joking, she couldn't help but laugh. In her mind she could visualize their expressions if she were to approach them, letting them have an uninterrupted moment for their photograph before inviting them into the dairy to help with mucking the cow pen and kneeling by the cows' udders to milk them. It felt good to laugh. She realized she hadn't since Alejandro left.

"Wouldn't that be something?" she replied, still smiling.

***

Alejandro stood at the window, his hands behind his back, and stared outside at the crowded city street beneath the building. Los Angeles. It was a city of endless hope, broken dreams, and an occasional rising star. Having started his ascent to fame in Miami, he had been fortunate enough to bypass the journey that so many aspiring entertainers took through the city of angels. It was a difficult journey that often ended with the same tale of talented people waiting on tables or taking temporary jobs to make ends meet. They arrived in Los Angeles convinced that they were the next Taylor Swift or Viper. But there could only be so many superstars, and as Viper had learned early in his own career, remaining on top was almost as difficult as getting there

His early years had been struggle after struggle. He sang in clubs, often getting into fights with rowdy patrons who'd drunk more than their share. His approach to music was different, and in those early years he never thought he'd be the next great anything. He just knew that rapping was poetry but with a beat behind it. He quickly learned that a lot of Miami natives liked his form of poetry and, to his benefit, began demanding more.

A few years and four albums later, he found himself the opening act for Big James, the leading hip-hop rapper at the time. Now, after seven years of long days and even longer nights, Viper was the leading hip-hop rapper. On tour, Big James opened for him. The irony was not lost on either performer.

Throughout his own career, Alejandro saw countless people struggling to make it big in the music business, many of them hoping that Viper would take them in under his wing as a protégé. But Alejandro knew better than to sacrifice his time and success by giving pieces of himself to others. The music business was about making money, not friends.

"The car's here," Geoffrey said as he walked into the room.

"And so it begins again, sí?" Alejandro sighed. After a stop in New York City, he would take an early-morning flight to London for the first date of his European tour. He looked away from the window toward his manager. "Any news from Lancaster?"

Geoffrey stopped looking at his phone and studied Alejandro. His face had an expression of concern. "Alex, if you don't mind me saying—"

"I do mind, G," Alejandro interrupted him in a curt tone. "I asked you a simple question. Have you heard anything?"

"Just call her."

"I said I mind your opinion, Geoffrey!" Alejandro snapped at him. He glared at his manager, pausing to reach into the front pocket of his suit jacket to withdraw his sunglasses. "A simple answer is all that I need."

"No," Geoffrey responded at last. "No word."

Satisfied, Alejandro slid the sunglasses onto his face and straightened his shoulders. "That's all I asked."

And with that, he exited the room and walked down the hallway toward the elevator.

For the last few days, the papers had been eerily silent. While the last few photos they'd published had focused on Amanda and hinted at an inappropriate relationship with the hired man, Harvey, when questioned about their separation, Alejandro remained silent. Speculation ran the gamut: Alejandro left her because he fell in love with a woman in South America, or Amanda left him because she caught him with not just one woman but two. When Harvey's photo began to enter the stories, the focus of the media shifted from Alejandro as the culpable party to Amanda.

One statement from Alejandro could have stopped the gossip and speculation, but he refused any and all interviews as he prepared for the European leg of the tour. He spent his time meeting with the label executives about his next album and with his recording team to outline the songs. Alejandro could work on lyrics and music while he traveled, creating new beats on his laptop, even while his team remained in Los Angeles.

For more than three weeks, he had tried his best to stay focused and keep himself busy. No matter how hard he tried to convince himself that he could forget, if only for one day, each night when he went to bed, regardless of the hour, it was always Amanda he had on his mind.

He would lie in bed, tossing and turning as he thought about the South American tour and the even more disastrous trip to Lancaster at the end of the tour.

No amount of keeping busy could prevent Alejandro from seeing the image of Harvey Alderfer carrying Isadora, and of watching her run past him straight into the arms of Amanda.

Amanda belonged in Lancaster. And Isadora did, too.

His lifestyle did not lend itself to being a father or husband. He should have known that before he married Amanda. But there had been something about her that made him believe that, if ever the possibility existed, she was the one who could change everything. After all, she wanted nothing from him, and that was something he wasn't used to.

"Viper!"

The elevator doors opened into the lobby. A horde of people waited for him just outside the entrance. Reporters. Always the reporters.

Making certain that his suit jacket wasn't mussed and his eyes were hidden behind his sunglasses, Alejandro straightened his shoulders as he exited the elevator. His black Manolos clicked against the marble floor as he walked past the security desk and exited through the open doors. The crowd of reporters pushed up against him, closer than he usually permitted reporters to get to him. A security guard rushed after him and began to shove people away from Alejandro. But he didn't seem to notice. Instead, he continued walking toward the waiting car parked at the curb.

"Is it true that Amanda left you?"

"Who's the man at her parents' farm?"

"Why did she leave you during the South American tour?"

The barrage of questions continued, but Alejandro ignored every one of them. He focused on getting from point A to point B. He refused to allow distractions to delay him, especially distractions from the media.

"Viper, is it true that you're getting divorced?"

He stopped walking, hesitating just long enough that the security guard bumped into him and the media began to swarm around him once again. Without thinking, he turned around toward the reporter who had asked the last question. He snatched off his sunglasses and with glaring blue eyes sought out the reporter, fully aware that the others were busy recording him and taking his photograph.

"A divorce?" He narrowed his eyes and glowered at the reporter before him. "Don't you have something better to do?" he asked as he took a step forward, his body invading the reporter's personal space. "My private life is none of your business. Neither is Amanda's."

"Is the divorce because of your daughter?"

From behind him, Alejandro heard someone else call his name. He glanced over his shoulder and saw Geoffrey fighting his way through the crowd. Knowing that he had only seconds before Geoffrey stopped him from responding, Alejandro leaned forward. He stared into the face of the inquisitive reporter, his nose barely inches from the other man's. The flashing anger in his eyes caused the man to try to back away, but with the other people behind him, there was nowhere to go. Alejandro glared as he hissed between clenched teeth, "There is no divorce."

"That's it, people," Geoffrey yelled, shoving someone away from Alejandro and grabbing his arm. "Back off, everyone. Let Viper get going. He's got a plane to catch."

Slowly, Alejandro backed away from the reporter and, in one fluid movement, slid his sunglasses back onto his face, shielding his eyes from the reporters. As he moved toward the car, he maintained a purposeful stride in the hopes that the camera did not catch the real emotions he'd felt at that one word: *divorce.*

He loved her. And he had left her. But he never imagined that the marriage would end in divorce. Now, as he climbed into his car, his face turned toward the tinted window as Geoffrey sat beside him,

Alejandro had something else to contemplate. Was a divorce the next logical step at freeing Amanda and permitting her to live a plain life, free from the complications brought on by marriage to him?

# Chapter Three

"Mamm!" Anna said in a hushed voice. "The bishop's here!"

Sitting at the kitchen table, Amanda looked up at her sister's announcement. There was a panicked tone in her voice as she looked from the window to her mother. Amanda had heard the sound of the approaching buggy, but the gentle noise seemed so natural that she hadn't given it a second thought. Until she heard Anna.

All morning Amanda had been helping her mother and sister bake pecan pies for the fellowship meal that would follow a women's gathering at a neighboring farm on Wednesday. Isadora liked to play with the dough, and using a small rolling pin, one that Amanda had used as a child, she flattened out several pieces of dough for her own tiny pie tin. Making the pies with her sister and mother almost made Amanda feel as if she were truly home again. She half expected her brother, Aaron, to come running through the door to announce his latest discovery, whether it was a nest of small blue eggs from a robin or a snake sunning itself on a rock.

But Aaron was dead, and this was not her home. Miami was her home. With Alejandro. And with Isadora.

Now, Anna was standing on her tippy-toes staring out the window at the gray-topped buggy that had pulled into the driveway just a few minutes ago.

"The bishop?" Lizzie hurried to the window and peered over Anna's shoulder. "I wonder what's happened."

"Why does the bishop showing up mean something bad must have happened?" Amanda asked in a dry tone.

"Oh, Amanda!" Lizzie scolded as she quickly scanned the room to make certain it wasn't untidy for the bishop. "Now's not the time to get sassy."

Amanda's only response was a quick eye roll, to which Lizzie responded with a disapproving click of her tongue.

Regardless of what Amanda had said, she knew that her mother was right. The bishop was a busy man, with upwards of twenty-five families to minister to in his church district. On top of that responsibility, he also had to maintain his livelihood, which, in their bishop's case, was as a shopkeeper. With so much to do, he rarely made social calls just for the sake of merely extending pleasantries.

"Oh help," Lizzie muttered, giving the counter a quick wipe down with a dish towel. "I do hope nothing's wrong."

Her mother's fretfulness irritated Amanda. Even before his footsteps sounded on the steps to the porch, Amanda knew that whatever had brought the bishop to their doorstep most certainly had to do with her. During each of her trips home, the bishop had made it his duty to come to the house with the sole purpose of reminding her that she might still be Amish by birth, but she was no longer Amish by choice.

With her mother and Anna quickly putting away the freshly washed bowls they had used for baking, Amanda sighed. She stood up and glanced at the clock. Not quite two o'clock. Isadora wouldn't wake from her nap for another hour. With no reason to avoid the bishop, she wiped her hands on her apron. "Reckon I best go invite him inside," she said in a low voice as she began crossing the kitchen floor toward the mudroom.

Before she could reach for the doorknob, the door opened and Jonas walked inside, followed by the bishop. Jonas glanced at Amanda and then quickly averted his eyes. That expression solidified what she already knew: the bishop was bringing her bad news indeed.

"Good day, Lizzie. Anna." He glanced over at Elias and nodded his head. "How's he faring today?"

Lizzie wrung her hands. "Just about the same, Bishop. Not much difference, except I noticed he's eating less."

The bishop walked toward him and leaned forward. "You need to eat, Elias. Don't be giving Lizzie a hard time about that, you hear?"

Disgusted, Elias rolled his head to one side and stared out the window.

Straightening, the bishop looked over at Amanda. "You wouldn't happen to have a free moment now, would you?"

Respectfully, Amanda nodded, her eyes shifting for just a moment to look at Anna. They exchanged an unspoken communication: Anna urging her to remain respectful, and Amanda conveying the dread she felt at being called upon by the bishop. Without a further moment's delay, she followed him outside so that they could talk in private.

His black boots, scuffed at the heels, walked slowly down the walkway that led away from the house and toward the barn. He kept his hands clutched behind his back, and she noticed that his shoulders were stooped. There was something else, a limp as he walked. He had aged in the past few months and, for a split second, she felt regret that her presence in Lititz seemed to constantly create unnecessary stress for the man.

"Amanda," he began slowly. "I saw you at church last Sunday."

She waited for him to continue as she walked alongside him. He had greeted her with the customary handshake when he entered the room, his eyes glancing down at the child that clung to her dress.

"And with a child, *ja*?"

Ah, Amanda thought. So this is what his visit is about. "*Ja*, my stepdaughter."

"I see."

They walked a few more paces in silence. Overhead, a blue jay flew into the branches of a tree and one of the older barn cats tried to climb the trunk to catch it. When that failed, the cat sauntered away, its tail in the air.

"As I have come to understand it, you have returned and intend to stay for a while, *ja*?"

"I . . ." She hesitated, uncertain how to respond. She knew what he wanted her to say, that she was leaving and would take Isadora with her. After all, the bishop had made his position clear to her numerous times in the past. The truth was, Amanda didn't know what she intended to do. She stopped walking, and when he realized that she was no longer beside him, the bishop did the same.

She couldn't help but wonder who was talking about her—and to the bishop no less! It wasn't as though she had any friends left. Those with whom she used to socialize at school and during her *rumschpringe* were either married and had moved into a new church district or were merely avoiding her for fear of developing a worldly reputation among the church members. Amanda understood their reasons, and when she reflected upon the matter, she realized that, had she taken her kneeling vow, she would have probably done the same.

Besides, she remembered all too well how the members of the community reacted when Alejandro first stayed at her parents' farm. The gossip that traveled through the Amish grapevine, the looks from other Amish people at the market, and the intrusion of the paparazzi on her parents' farm quickly made Alejandro an unwelcome visitor in Lititz, Pennsylvania. Now that she was married to him, she fell into the same category.

The bishop gestured for her to continue walking with him farther away from the house. She presumed that, whatever he wanted to discuss, he didn't want anyone to overhear.

"It has come to my attention that this husband of yours—"

"Alejandro," she interrupted, hoping she had masked her irritation that, after all of this time and the numerous interactions she'd had with the bishop regarding Alejandro, he still insisted on calling him anything but his name.

The bishop made a noise acknowledging her. "Alejandro, then. It has come to my attention that he has left you here and that there is strife within your marriage."

Once again, she was left with a dry taste in her mouth. How the bishop knew such intimate details, she could only imagine. While the Amish grapevine spread stories almost as quickly as social media among the Englische, this information most likely came from another source. She suspected the tabloid newspapers and magazines were the culprits as they'd certainly carried stories about Viper's departure to Europe without Amanda. From the way the paparazzi continued to stake out the farm, Amanda knew her presence in Lancaster was well known. However, she worried about the content of those stories. They were usually blown out of proportion and in some cases were outright lies.

"Alejandro is in Europe, *ja*," she said in a measured tone.

The bishop nodded his head, indicating that he already knew that fact. "Will you be joining him or returning to Miami, then?"

She bit her lower lip. If only Alejandro would reach out to her. Without that first step, she knew that there was little chance of salvaging the marriage. He had, after all, deserted her. With each day her hopes faded, especially now that he was on tour. She knew from experience the temptations that he would confront. Without her by his side, would he succumb to the seduction of his former lifestyle?

"Given time, I imagine so," she finally said.

The bishop inhaled deeply, his eyes wandering across the fields still devoid of growth. Soon they would be green with the beginnings of the corn they'd planted just the previous week. Spring was a beautiful time on the farm, and the bishop seemed to take a moment to absorb it.

"You must know, Amanda," he said, his attention still turned elsewhere, "that I was not fond of your decisions. You have made a lot of choices that have impacted many people."

She remained silent, waiting for his lecture. Perhaps he would even go so far as to point out the obvious: whether she admitted it or not, her husband had clearly left her behind when he went on tour. And that was not the sign of a healthy marriage.

"But God has reasons that we do not always understand. I believe quite strongly that this is your chosen course, the life he wants for you." He paused, and in that brief respite he turned toward her. "I wouldn't dare question his authority. Whatever is happening in your marriage with this Englischer, I cannot pretend to have the knowledge to provide guidance, Amanda. I can only turn to Scripture: *the wife is bound by the law as long as her husband liveth.*" He looked at her with a stern expression. "That is not man's law but God's law. Man has a choice: follow the law of God or the law of sin. The decision is yours, Amanda."

She clenched her teeth and fought the urge to reply.

And then he said something that surprised her. "But that is not why I am here, Amanda. You are, after all, an adult and you know what you are doing." He started walking again, this time toward his buggy. The door was already open, so he reached inside and handed her a plain brown envelope. "I wanted to leave this with you. I feel strongly that you should see these, Amanda. I believe it will assist you in making your decision." As he placed the envelope into her hands, he made eye contact with her. "Remember, it is your choice as to which law you would follow."

When she took the envelope from him, it felt heavier than she thought. She glanced down at it and started to peel back the flap that sealed it.

"*Nee*, Amanda," the bishop said gently, stopping her with his hand. "I would recommend looking at the contents in private."

She waited until the bishop left, the package still in her hands. Her curiosity was countered only with dread. Whatever was inside the envelope was not of a pleasant nature. She knew that without looking. She suspected that the bishop had given her a collection of news stories about Alejandro being in Europe without her, photos of him with other women, tabloid stories that would bring her to her knees.

With dread building inside her chest, she clutched the envelope and turned to the house. It was better to wait to open it until later in the evening, when no one else was around. The bishop had warned her not to open it until she was alone, and she didn't want to risk getting upset in front of her family.

"Amanda!"

Harvey jogged from the barn toward her. His skin glistened from working in the dairy where the air did not circulate; on warm days it became hot and humid.

She tried to smile as she greeted him.

He took off his hat and with the back of his arm he wiped at the beads of sweat on his forehead. "Jonas isn't home, and I wondered if you might help with the milking this afternoon," he asked. Then, with a grin, he added, "Mayhaps Izzie would help, too. You know, she's learned how to squirt the milk into the cats' mouths."

"She has, has she, then?" Amanda smiled at the thought. Growing up on the farm made for wonderful memories. She remembered when her father had taught her the same trick. How she had loved to tease the cats, who sat in a row when she milked, anticipating the sweet treat of fresh cows' milk. "When she wakes, we'll come out then."

Anna and Lizzie stood in the exact spot where Amanda had left them. They stared at her with unspoken questions on their lips and wide eyes. When Amanda volunteered no information, her mother glanced at the envelope she held.

"Everything all right, then?"

Amanda nodded at her mother. "*Ja*, right as rain." She avoided their inquisitive gaze and gestured toward the door that led between the main house and the *grossdaadihaus*. "I best go check on Izzie. We'll be helping Harvey with the evening milking anyway."

Once inside the *grossdaadihaus*, she left the envelope unopened on her kitchen table. For a moment, she contemplated opening it to read through whatever horrible things had been printed in the media. She didn't even want to envision the photos.

Just as quickly as she thought of opening it, she decided to hold off. If she knew nothing, she could say nothing. By the morning, no one would inquire further about the matter. Instead, they would continue with their own pleasures, the simple things in life such as baking or gardening. Only Amanda would be left with the burden of whatever contents the envelope contained. There were times when knowledge seemed a heavier burden than unknowing bliss. She suspected this was one of those times.

So it wasn't until four hours later, after Isadora had gone to bed, that Amanda sat at the table under the light from the overhead propane lantern and contemplated the envelope. She studied it and speculated about what the bishop had found. The very fact that he had taken the time to bring these items to her attention spoke volumes about how much their relationship, which had once been so volatile, had evolved over the past year.

But now it was time. She dreaded opening the envelope, for she knew whatever was inside was going to cost her plenty: emotionally, spiritually, and psychologically. She prayed for stronger balance in the ongoing conflict between her upbringing and the life that she had married into. As of yet, God had not answered that prayer.

Her fingers trembled as she slid open the sealed flap of the envelope. Tilting it, she poured the contents out onto the table. As she had suspected, it was filled with articles from tabloids. She shuffled through them, staring at the articles and photos, the feeling of a horrible lump increasing in her chest.

"Oh help," she whispered, her fingers reaching out to touch the items, moving them apart so that she could take them all in.

The bishop had performed a great service by bringing these items to her attention in such a confidential manner. She let her fingers touch the different photos. The headlines didn't surprise her. Each one implied infidelity, betrayal, and divorce. What did surprise her, however, was that the photos and articles were not about Alejandro. Instead, they were about her: photos of her on the farm, photos of her in town, photos of her in the car. And all of the photos showed Harvey by her side.

As she sat there contemplating the meaning of the stories, she thought back to when Alejandro had come to the farm after the South American tour. When he'd arrived, Harvey had walked outside the barn with Isadora in his arms and a smile on his face. Amanda remembered how Isadora barely greeted her father, practically avoiding him as she ran inside to be with the rest of the family. And Amanda remembered how in the middle of the night after having made love to her—what she now recognized as his parting gesture, a gesture that spoke more of his love for her personal happiness than his own—he had left before the sun had fully crested the horizon.

Suddenly, everything became clear.

After the disastrous South American tour, when Amanda had left with Isadora, Alejandro must have been more than hurt. His lifestyle was too much for her, and when he came to Lancaster to retrieve her, he'd likely seen her with fresh eyes.

She knew now that he had left her because he thought Lancaster was the right place for her and perhaps even for Isadora. By leaving her in Lancaster, he thought she had the opportunity to return to her culture and religion. The tabloids had run with the story of Amanda leaving Alejandro and returning to the arms of Harvey Alderfer, a man much better suited for an Amish girl. After all, the sole purpose of tabloids was to sell papers, and what sold better than a sordid story of sin and sex?

Disgusted, Amanda pushed the papers away and leaned back into the chair. Her mind raced, whirling with random, untamed thoughts. If she had felt horrified at first, she now felt nothing but anger. Wasn't it Celinda who'd told her she should believe nothing in the media? Hadn't Celinda warned her that there were parts to be played—a form of pandering to the public—that necessitated giving the fans the stories they wanted? It was an unspoken contract: stars provided fodder for gossip to the public so that the public could live vicariously through them.

"If they want something to talk about," she said out loud, "they shall have it."

Alejandro greeted Enrique with a friendly bear hug, clapping him on the back and laughing when Enrique did the same.

"*¡Amigo!* Good to see you!" Alejandro said, holding him at arm's length.

They were in Madrid, getting ready for the first series of European concerts. With Enrique as his opening act, Alejandro knew the tour would sell out. Enrique appealed to the same audience as Viper, but he also appealed to younger women. By teaming up on tour, both expanded their reach. And since they often recorded songs together, the pairing was well received onstage.

"*¡Sí, chico!* Good to be back on tour." Enrique sank into the sofa in Alejandro's suite, crossing his one leg so that his ankle rested on his knee. He wore a simple outfit: ripped jeans, a white T-shirt, and construction boots. With his boyish good looks and naturally dark skin, he never had any trouble with the ladies. "I stay in one place for too long . . ." He didn't finish the sentence, but he didn't have to.

"You just arrived?"

Enrique nodded. "Just arrived from Las Vegas. Ten days at the Colosseum. Hail Caesar!" He looked around the hotel suite. Alejandro spared no expense in procuring luxurious comforts when he traveled. Enrique looked slightly impressed. "You hit the arena today?"

"Earlier, *sí.*"

In fact, Alejandro had spent the better part of the day there, overseeing the equipment setup and ensuring that everything was fully operational. With the gap between the South American tour and the European tour, there were new stagehands on the crew, and Alejandro wasn't about to take any chances. Four nights in Madrid needed to run smoothly to ensure the crew knew what they were doing, especially since they had to dismantle, travel, and set it up again in Barcelona for Tuesday. Alejandro was a businessman and not about to risk failure at any step of the tour.

"So I'm doing a club run tonight. Joining me?" Enrique smiled.

Enrique's reputation had eclipsed Alejandro's. Not so long ago, the two of them had traveled together, performing around the world and leaving shattered hearts along the way. They spent one day in a country before flying to another with memories of hazy nights and pretty women who were willing partners in just about anything imaginable and even things that weren't.

But Alejandro had given up those days.

Alejandro shrugged. "Not my scene anymore, man."

Enrique rolled his eyes. "Your old lady isn't even here! Come on, Alejandro. Just like the good ol' days."

But Alejandro remained firm. After all, running the club scene with players like Enrique was exactly how Isadora came to be. For a brief second, the image of his daughter's face flashed in his memory. He wondered how she was adapting to her new life. But as soon as he thought of her, he shoved the image into the back corners of his mind. She was fine with Amanda, better off than in his own care or in an orphanage.

"Nah, I got some beats I'm working on for a new song," he said, gesturing toward his laptop. "Some of the guys are coming over to work on them with me."

Enrique let his head fall against the back of the sofa as he groaned.

"Got a morning meeting and then a run-through with the new girls," Alejandro said. The truth was that he was meeting with Movistar, one of the largest brands in Spain for telecommunications. They were finalizing an endorsement contract that would be rolled out in fourteen Spanish-speaking countries. With his appeal to the younger audiences, Movistar was chomping at the bit to sign him for an advertising and promotion campaign. If the money was right, Alejandro would be happy to sign just about anything. "Need to be in top form," he added.

"The great Viper!" Enrique slapped his hand against his leg. "I wouldn't believe it if I hadn't seen it myself. Chained at the ankle."

"You talk too much," Alejandro said, only half joking as he moved across the room to the bar. He poured himself a drink and glanced at Enrique, silently asking if he, too, wanted something. "You know this life, Enrique. If you aren't working, you're dying."

"Clubbing is working!" Enrique insisted. "Hanging with the locals, dancing with the Spanish beauties. *¡Ay, mi madre!*" He moved his free hand as if shaking water from it. "Have you seen these women? Each one is more beautiful than the next! It's my duty to integrate myself into their society." He reached up and accepted the glass that Alejandro handed him. "You, of course, haven't noticed any of them, no?" he added in a mocking tone.

"I noticed," Alejandro admitted. Unlike the South American women who dripped sexuality, the Spanish women exuded sophistication. "I'm just not interested."

Enrique shook his head. "I don't get it, man. Here I was thinking it would be like old times, even those last weeks of the South American tour. But if you're gonna be into the work scene, why didn't you just bring her?"

Alejandro stiffened, unwilling to share his personal woes with anyone, even Enrique. He had learned years ago that personal issues needed to be kept private, shared with no one. If he did, it would create a surefire leak to the press. And any hint of gossip would spread like wildfire. Some entertainers used that to their advantage, like Justin Bell and Celinda. Their on-again, off-again relationship was constantly in the media, with fans speculating whether the latest breakup was the final one or if the glamorous Hollywood couple would get back together once again.

That was not for Alejandro. Not now, anyway.

When it came to Amanda, he preferred maintaining his privacy. No one needed to know anything about his decisions or his reasons.

"You don't know what you're missing out on, Viper," Enrique said. "These women are . . ." He made a howling noise. "Hot!"

Alejandro made a face. "You can get that anywhere."

"And I do!" Enrique laughed.

Shaking his head, Alejandro rolled his eyes. "You just don't get it, *chico*. There's something deeper out there. I have that with Amanda."

"Say all men when they first get married," Enrique quipped. "Look, man, you can't stay with one woman in this business! No one can."

"*I* intend to."

"Then she won't. Trust me."

Had anyone else made such a comment, Alejandro would have quickly escorted that person out of the room. With Enrique, however, he knew better than to take him seriously. No one could doubt Amanda's fidelity to him.

The irony, of course, was that Alejandro wanted to give her the space to decide—on her own—whether she had made a mistake in marrying him. With Harvey Alderfer in the picture, there was the chance she might suddenly realize that she had. And from the looks of the tabloid photos, it might not take long for that awareness to hit her.

Enrique glanced down at his cell phone. "Hey, I heard a rumor about Celinda Ruiz. Is she meeting up with us?"

Alejandro nodded. "Geoffrey will let me know next week. Hopefully, she can join us for a few shows."

With a mischievous grin and a sparkle in his dark eyes, Enrique growled playfully. "Now that's one I'd stay home for . . . at least for a few nights."

"She's ten years younger than you!"

Enrique gestured toward Alejandro, a playful reminder that the age difference between Amanda and Alejandro was even greater than that. "And your point is . . . ?"

"I'd be careful there, Enrique. Don't forget that between Celinda and Justin, their fan bases would slay you if you start toying with her. Set your sights elsewhere, or you'll get public backlash, *chico*."

"*Ay*, Viper! Giving me fatherly advice?" He shook his hand as if trying to shake off a bug.

"Not fatherly. Just professional, man."

"*Sí*, *sí*, such a professional now." The way he laughed made Alejandro glance over at him, a scowl on his face. He didn't need any reminders that Enrique's fame had helped Viper rise to the top of the charts. The few songs they sang together had broken Viper into mainstream music stations. But Alejandro knew that Viper remained on the top of the charts—for hip-hop as well as pop—because of his songs and collaborations with other artists, not to mention his business prowess.

"You talk too much," Alejandro said in a low voice, warning Enrique that he was crossing a line. "Don't you got somewhere to be, Enrique? I got work to do and you're going to kill my vibe."

Enrique jumped up from the chair and headed to the door. "You change your mind, you let me know, brother! This little *chico* can always find a woman for a friend."

"Get outta here!"

It wasn't until Enrique left, eager to hit the Madrid clubs with his entourage, that Alejandro stood at the window of the hotel, staring out into the night. With his drink in hand, he wondered what Amanda was doing at that very moment. So many times he'd thought about contacting her. He wanted to text her, to call her, even to send someone to fetch her. But as soon as he thought about doing so, he remembered South America and he remembered Isadora. Amanda had made a choice, a choice to leave him and return to America so that she could be a mother to his child. When Alejandro had seen her that day in Lancaster, and realized that Amanda needed to remain on the farm, to be near her family and to have religion back in her life, he had known that leaving her there was the right thing to do.

If only it *felt* like the right thing to do.

He felt empty inside, his heart devoid of any emotion. He was tempted to succumb to the darkness of depression.

But he refused.

By throwing himself into his work, he managed to temporarily forget his heartache and the pain of abandoning Amanda. The next six weeks would be busy with recording his new songs and meeting with European companies that wanted him to become their brand ambassador. And, as always, he had interviews for radio and television, as well as with print reporters. It was enough to keep him busy and focused on his professional future, the perfect distraction from his private life.

# Chapter Four

In the morning, just as the sun was rising, Amanda slipped out of bed and hurried to the kitchen to brew some fresh coffee. She needed it this morning, for she had barely slept the previous night. In her mind, she saw the photos with her standing close to Harvey, often looking up at him with a questioning look upon her face. If Alejandro had, indeed, seen the pictures, he surely would think that there was an attraction between them. That was, after all, what the media was suggesting.

And hadn't that been what Alejandro had suggested when he left?

Still, something began to formulate in her mind. Alejandro was a master of manipulating the media. Hadn't that been the very reason that, last summer, he'd returned to Lancaster to fetch her? His goal had been to give the media what they wanted so that they would lose interest in the story and Amanda could return to Lancaster on her own, in peace and, most important, without the paparazzi following her. Only it hadn't happened that way.

Not only did the media refuse to lose interest, but Alejandro and Amanda had fallen in love.

During their brief courtship, he had continued working the media, including kneeling before her at an award ceremony after presenting her with an engagement ring. When it came to the face he showed the public, everything was a show and each show had sold-out tickets.

Somewhere between midnight and dawn when she arose, Amanda began wondering if his leaving her behind was part of the performance. From the moment that idea crossed her mind, she could no longer sleep. She remembered what Celinda had told her about some of her breakups with Justin and about not believing the tabloids or gossip channels. Sometimes, Celinda had told her, the celebrities manipulated the media as much as the media manipulated the stories.

Suddenly, Amanda knew exactly what she needed to do: fly to Europe.

She was already on her third cup of coffee when Isadora padded down the stairs and ran across the floor to Amanda. Throwing her arms around Amanda's waist, Isadora buried her face in her lap.

"Did you sleep well last night, Izzie?"

"*Ja*. I dream of the kitten."

"Dreamt. You dreamt of the kitten," Amanda gently corrected her.

"I dreamt."

Amanda smiled and rubbed Isadora's back. "Good girl. Now, how about some breakfast before we go walk down the lane a spell?"

Amanda brought a chair to the counter so that Isadora could stand on it and help her with the cooking. Of course, Isadora's version of helping was not always very helpful at all. But Amanda encouraged her, showing her how to whisk the eggs and put the bread on the rack for toasting on the stove top. Despite almost a third of the eggs splattering on the counter and floor, Amanda managed to salvage enough to make enough scrambled eggs for the two of them.

When they sat at the table to eat, Amanda shut her eyes and said a quick prayer, Isadora bowing her head as she mimicked her.

"Now, Izzie," Amanda started slowly, "I must tell you something. Can you listen to me while you eat?"

Isadora nodded her head as she tried to scoop up some eggs with a fork.

"Mammi needs to go on a trip," Amanda said. "I need to go see Papi."

The eggs fell back on the plate as Isadora stared at her with wide eyes.

"You'll stay here with Anna and Jonas." She looked at Isadora, hoping that she wasn't upset. She tried to soften her voice as she explained why Isadora would be left behind. "The kitten would miss you so much if you went with me, and the trip is long and not something you'd find terribly exciting, I fear. Besides, Harvey will need your help with milking those cows."

"And squirt the cats?"

Amanda laughed. "*Ja*, and squirting milk at the cats."

Isadora seemed to consider this, her face scrunched up as she thought. "You come back?"

"Of course!" It broke Amanda's heart that Isadora asked such a question. That was the one fear Amanda had when, the previous night, she'd decided that she needed to find Alejandro. With so much turmoil in Isadora's short life, Amanda did not want to add more. "I love you so much, Izzie. And I will always come back!"

Satisfied, Isadora nodded her head. "Go help Papi," she said in her soft, childish voice with its heavy Brazilian accent.

"*Danke*, Izzie," Amanda said as she leaned over and kissed the side of her head. "He needs me so."

After breakfast, Amanda quickly cleaned the dishes before they went outside for their morning walk. They walked down the driveway, Amanda holding her hand and pointing out the different birds that flew overhead. When they saw a blue jay, Isadora made Amanda stop so that they could watch it until it flew away.

"You like the blue jay, then?"

Isadora nodded. "Blue."

Amanda smiled. Blue had become Isadora's favorite color. She wanted only blue dresses and slept under a blue crocheted blanket that she had found in a dresser in Lizzie's room. "Oh, *ja*, blue is pretty."

As they walked back down the lane, Amanda spotted Anna already in the garden. With a long hoe in her hand, Anna sifted through the dirt, ridding it of any weeds.

"You should let me do that, Anna!" How many times had she told Anna to let her and Isadora deal with the garden? Amanda wondered, knowing the answer: too many.

With a broad smile, Anna set the hoe against the fence. "Oh, I don't mind none," she said, glancing up at the sky. "It's cool enough yet. Besides, I'm pregnant, Amanda, not disabled." When Amanda didn't respond to her sister's teasing comment, Anna looked at her and asked, "Is everything alright?"

Amanda stood in the grass and let Isadora lean against her legs. "I need to ask a favor of you, Anna," she asked as Isadora placed her bare feet upon Amanda's.

"Anything, Schwester."

Taking a deep breath, Amanda met her sister's concerned gaze. Oh, how she didn't want to leave Pennsylvania, but she knew that there was only one way to resolve the problem with Alejandro. "I need to go to Alejandro," she said at last, "and, as much as I hate to admit it, I don't think it would be good to bring Izzie."

When Isadora looked up at the mention of her name, Amanda placed her hands on the child's shoulders and began to lift her by her arms so that Isadora's feet moved at the same time. Suddenly, giggling, Isadora paid more attention to what Amanda was doing than the adult conversation.

"Everything all right, then, Amanda?"

The concerned look on her sister's face touched Amanda. After everything that the family had been through, so many changes in the past few years—and few of them positive—it was good to know the caring bond was still there. "Yes and no," Amanda admitted. "It's difficult to explain."

Anna sighed. "I can believe that to be true. I don't pretend to understand all of the Englische world that you are experiencing. But I take your leaving to mean that you will work things out with him, *ja?*"

Amanda nodded her head. "I'll need to go to Miami first and then over to Europe."

Anna made a face at the mention of Europe. "Oh, Amanda," she said in a low voice. "Aren't you scared, even just a little?"

The truth was that Amanda hadn't given much thought to being afraid. Whether it was due to having so much on her mind or all of the travel she had already done with Alejandro, flying to Europe was not nearly as daunting a thought to her as it probably was to her sister. In all likelihood, her sister would never fly in an airplane. No bishop in any *g'may* permitted baptized church members the freedom to travel by air.

"I reckon I'm more scared of not going, Anna," Amanda said.

Her sister reached over and touched her arm, waiting until Amanda looked up and met her gaze. Anna smiled as if trying to alleviate any misgivings that Amanda felt. "*Ja, vell,* don't worry none. We'll all take right *gut* care of our Izzie. Right, Izzie? Lots of chocolate chip and sugar cookies for you!" Anna said as she leaned over and tickled Isadora under the chin. Both of them laughed, and Amanda felt a little better, knowing that her family's love and willingness to care for her daughter was genuine and heartfelt.

As they walked back toward the house, Izzie spotted the orange kitten, and with a delighted squeal, she ran after it. Anna took the opportunity to ask, "How long will you be gone, then?"

"If everything goes well, five weeks."

"And then?" Anna asked.

Amanda took a deep breath and looked around the farm. She took in the sight of birds fluttering by the bird feeder, fighting over food. In the distance, the cows mooed as they moseyed out of the dairy barn and into the big turnout fields.

"That's the unknown, Anna," Amanda admitted. "I just don't have an answer to that question." She watched as Isadora squatted on the ground, using a piece of baling twine to play with the kitten.

Once again, Anna tried to sound optimistic. "Just remember that God has a plan for all of us, and his plan will always be the right one."

They continued walking in silence, Anna with her hand on her expanding abdomen and Amanda lost in her own thoughts. Whatever God's plan was for her, it was becoming more difficult to know what exactly he wanted her to do. She knew that she needed to go to Alejandro, but she felt conflicted about leaving Isadora. Torn between the two people she loved so much, she had to make a decision that would be right for all of them. While leaving Isadora behind would certainly hurt Amanda, not going to Alejandro would hurt them both.

Standing in the two-story foyer of the condominium in Miami, her small suitcase by her feet, Amanda looked around in wonder at the room: white marble floors, the beautiful curved staircase, the crystal chandelier, and the round table with the vase of fresh flowers. It didn't surprise Amanda that she felt like a stranger in her own home. She had spent more time away from it than in it since her marriage to Alejandro. Still, she had memories of the condominium, which slowly came back to her as she approached the staircase. After kicking off her shoes, she ascended the steps.

The door to the bedroom she shared with Alejandro was open. She did not linger in the doorway, but entered with mild curiosity at the furnishings. The white comforter on the bed reminded her of waking in Alejandro's arms. The chair by the window reminded her of the night she had a sunburn and sat watching the party unfold on the rooftop patio. The mirror where Alejandro had stood behind her on their wedding night, his hands on her shoulders as he gazed at her reflection, easing her fears before he made her his true wife in the eyes of the Lord.

For a moment, she felt overwhelmed by the memories. Her chest lifted and fell rapidly as she began to breathe faster, her heart pounding and her blood pulsating. The bed called to her and she moved toward it, sitting on the edge near his pillow. She let her fingers move toward it, tracing the place where she imagined his head would rest if he had slept there the previous night.

"Amanda?"

Startled, she looked up at the sound of her name, spoken in such a casual manner by their housekeeper. Señora Perez stood in the doorway, her head tilted to the side as she studied Amanda.

"Oh!" Amanda stood up and rushed to the housekeeper. "I'm so sorry. I hope I didn't frighten you." She gave Señora Perez a warm hug. "I didn't know how to contact you to tell you I was coming."

The housekeeper stepped back, a small smile on her lips. "You are staying?"

*That* is a great question, Amanda thought.

The previous day, she had tried to call Dali, hoping that she might answer the phone to help her book a flight to Miami. After her fifth attempt, Amanda had given up on her and tried her second option: Harvey. While he had never flown before, he had traveled by bus recently and found the flight schedule using a friend's computer.

"I don't have a computer," she had replied.

"True," Harvey responded. "But you have that there phone, don't you? I've never done it myself, but I know people use the fancier ones like it's a small computer."

After Amanda returned to the house to fetch the phone, Jonas had come upon them.

Curious to see them huddled together staring at the cell phone, he wandered over to inquire further.

"What are you looking at there?" he asked as he approached.

Amanda did her best to hide her frustration. "I need to get back to Miami, but I don't know how to get a ticket for a plane."

"Oh, *ja*?" He scratched the back of his neck. "Mayhaps I can help you, then. My younger *bruder* had one of those things, and he used it to look up stuff on the Internet."

To Amanda's surprise, it took Jonas only a few minutes to figure out how to use her phone to retrieve the phone number for American Airlines. Once she had called the airlines, booking the flight from Philadelphia to Miami had been relatively easy. But as Amanda contemplated Señora Perez's question, she knew she needed help to fly to another country.

To begin with, she didn't even know what country Alejandro was currently in. And then there were all the issues with international travel, including exchanging currencies and different languages. When she was on the South American tour, other people took care of these arrangements. And of course, she had been with someone the entire trip. Even when she returned with Isadora, Dali had accompanied her. The only person Amanda knew who could help her was Dali, so it was problematic that, for some reason, her former personal assistant wouldn't take her phone calls.

Amanda looked at Señora Perez and shook her head. "No, I'm not staying. I need to find Alejandro, but I don't know where he is or how to get to him. Dali isn't answering my phone calls." She glanced down at the phone in her hand. If only she could get through to Dali. Perhaps, she thought, if she used a different cell phone to contact her. "Do you think . . ."

Amanda stopped talking, and Señora Perez watched her with curiosity. She coaxed her to finish the question. "*¿Qué, niña?*"

"I need to use your cell phone. Would that be alright?"

Señora Perez gave her a questioning look, but did not say anything. She reached into her pocket and withdrew her phone, handing it over to Amanda. "Everything is good, *sí*?"

Amanda bit her lower lip and took the phone. Clutching it to her chest, she shook her head. "No, no it's not, Señora Perez. But I'm trying to make everything good."

The older woman seemed to contemplate Amanda's response, a studious expression on her face. After what seemed like an eternity, Señora Perez nodded her head. "He is not himself when you are not with him," she said in a soft voice. "He needs you." She paused before adding, "He loves you."

Amanda caught her breath as tears welled in her eyes. As much as she knew that he loved her, she needed to hear it. The memory of his gentle caresses and sweet words whispered in her ears was simply not enough. She needed more affirmation from other people to convince her that the upcoming journey had a final, and favorable, destination.

"He is in Europe now and you are going to him, *sí*?"

"*Sí*, I am," Amanda responded. "And that's why I need your phone. To make some phone calls."

"*Bien*. Take your time. I'll be downstairs in the kitchen making you something to eat when you are finished." She gave Amanda an encouraging smile as she backed out of the room, shutting the door so that Amanda could have her privacy.

Dali answered on the fourth ring.

"Dali, don't hang up," Amanda spoke quickly into the phone.

"Amanda?"

"Yes, it's me."

There was a long silence on the other end of the phone. The surprise in Dali's voice was undeniable. As Amanda suspected, Dali had been avoiding her calls on purpose.

"I . . . I need your help," Amanda said at last.

"I no longer work for you." The dryness of her tone said more than her words.

"But you can still help me, Dali. I beg of you."

Another long pause.

"Please, Dali. I need to get to Alejandro, and you are the one person who can help me." Amanda leaned against the window, the phone pressed to her ear.

On the other end of the phone there was some shuffling, and Amanda realized Dali was not alone. Someone else was with her. "I can't talk right now, Amanda."

"Dali, please!"

Her former assistant sighed. "You left Miami, Amanda. I told you not to do that. You didn't tell me where you were or when you were coming back. You didn't return my phone calls. Do you realize what type of damage control I had to do? I had to cancel appointment after appointment—appointments that I pulled strings to arrange on such short notice! Not to mention the other people I upset by not granting them appointments. Do you know what your actions did to my reputation?"

"I . . ."

Amanda wasn't certain how to respond. She hadn't realized that her departure from Miami and her weeks in Pennsylvania had impacted Dali in such a way. It just wasn't something Amanda had ever considered. Her experience with working among the Englische was more than just limited: it had been nonexistent prior to meeting Alejandro. And she certainly had not known anything about the music industry. From Alejandro she had learned that it was a cutthroat and dark world where people used each other, not caring who they hurt in the process. She knew that women often used their bodies to attract attention. And she knew that for every person who made it, there were tens of thousands—maybe even hundreds of thousands!—who did not.

Even more important was the fact that many musicians lacked the business acumen to keep the money they actually made. Record labels were renowned for creating contracts to entice aspiring artists to sign with them and offering attractive advances that, more often than not, could never be recouped. Between the cost of paying back advances, managers, and lawyers, many would-be stars often found themselves bankrupt, the dream of success within the music industry conflicting harshly with the reality.

But Amanda had never thought about the music industry outside of what she'd gathered from talking with Alejandro or the bits and pieces she overheard in his meetings with Geoffrey. Now she realized that by leaving for Lancaster with Isadora and not returning Dali's phone calls, she, too, had unknowingly contributed to the backstabbing dark side of the entertainment world.

"I didn't know," she admitted meekly.

"I didn't think so," Dali responded, a sharpness to her voice that startled Amanda.

"Please, Dali," Amanda begged. "I want to fix this. I *must* fix this."

Dali sighed into the other end of the phone. There was a long pause, and Amanda heard the sound of a door being shut and the squeak of a chair. She suspected that Dali had gone into her office so that they could continue the conversation in private.

"What exactly do you want, Amanda?" Dali said at last.

"I . . . I want to know where he is or how to get to him."

When Dali laughed this time, there was no mirth in it. "How to get to him? If he doesn't want someone reaching him, they don't. It's as simple as that. I can't help you, Amanda. Why don't you just contact him yourself?"

Amanda cringed at the question. She didn't want to share her personal information with anyone, especially someone outside of her family. However, she suspected she owed that much to Dali. After all, as Dali had pointed out, Amanda's choices had affected her assistant's life, too. It was something Amanda had not even considered before this phone conversation. Suddenly, she felt a heavy weight on her chest, and she saw images of the different people who had come in to and out of her life over the past year: Mike, Maria, Stedman, Dali. While the reasons they no longer worked for Alejandro were different, there was one common thread throughout their disappearances from Alejandro's life: Amanda.

Amanda shook her head and pleaded one last time. "He left me, Dali, but I think for the wrong reasons. And I need to make this right. Please help me," Amanda whispered as she sank down into the chair. "I'm so sorry for everything. Truly I am."

This time, the long stretch of silence was followed by a more compassionate tone of voice. "I imagine you are," Dali said. It sounded as if Dali had opened a drawer, probably in her desk. She ruffled through some papers, and apparently finding whatever she sought, she cleared her throat. "Fine, Amanda. I will make the arrangements for you."

For a moment, Amanda thought she had not heard Dali correctly, especially after just learning how her actions and lack of experience had upset her former assistant. She had truly feared that Dali would not help her. But hearing Dali agree to help was music to Amanda's ears. "*Danke!* Oh, *danke,* Dali!"

"Now, hold on a minute. This comes with a price."

Amanda frowned. "A price?"

"I will organize your tickets and arrange for you to have an agenda and escort. But you have to promise that you'll do everything that is asked of you. Is that clear?"

If agreeing to Dali's demands could bring her back to Alejandro, Amanda would agree to anything, even going to the moon. "Yes, yes, that's clear. Anything and everything you want," she responded, meaning every word.

A drawer shut and more papers shuffled in the background. "Good. Now let me go. I have company."

As Amanda hung up the phone, she realized how little she knew about her assistant. Who was her company? A boyfriend? A husband? Friends or family? She had never really inquired about Dali on a personal level. Dali had a stoic wall around her, but still, to not even have inquired about such things? Amanda felt ashamed as she held Señora Perez's phone in her hand. She leaned her head back. How could she have not seen it before? While there were people trying to tear her and Alejandro apart, there had been people who had tried to keep them together. The only problem was that she'd recognized the former and ignored the latter.

It was time, she realized, to make amends and correct the wrongs of her recent past.

She vowed to start immediately.

Alejandro walked off the set, accepting the towel that one of the stagehands handed him. A group of women lingered on the side, and Alejandro felt a hand on his arm. When he looked down, he saw one of the gofers who worked for Geoffrey.

"Geoffrey said you should go meet those women," the young man said. "Friends of the CEO of Movistar?"

Alejandro nodded and tossed his damp towel to him. "I'm on it," he said while approaching the women. They smiled as he did, each one dressed to the nines with tall stilettos and form-fitting dresses that showed off their curvaceous bodies.

"*¡Ay, qué rica!*" Alejandro said as he sidled up to them, Viper in full gear. He let his eyes rove over their bodies and stood by each one while their friends took photos. He even planted a chaste kiss on their cheeks, lingering just long enough so that each one felt a connection. Then he excused himself and continued toward his dressing room.

He needed a shower. A hot shower to dull the aches in his back and thighs. During his concerts he gave it everything, throwing himself full force into his performance and dancing with the troupe of girls. After a few weeks without performing, his body told him that he hadn't been prepared from a physical perspective.

That, however, was something he kept hidden from the audience. "Alejandro!"

Inwardly, he groaned when he heard Rochelle, one of the numerous assistants on his payroll, run up to him.

"There are some men in the greenroom Geoffrey wants you to meet," she said.

"*Ay, mami*. I really want to change first."

But Rochelle gave him a look—*the* look. If Geoffrey wanted to see him immediately after a show, it had to be important. Sighing, Alejandro acquiesced and turned away from his dressing room.

Three men wearing black slacks with custom-made shirts and expensive shoes greeted him when he entered the room where VIPs and staff often congregated backstage. There was always plenty of food and drink available so that they could watch the concert from the monitors. Most of the greenrooms were fairly sterile, furnished with simple furniture and chairs without fancy decor. The one in Madrid was no different.

"Viper!" The larger of the three men stepped forward and shook his hand. "Victor Byrne, Vice President of Vantage Studios."

Alejandro accepted the handshake. *"Mucho gusto."*

Victor introduced the other two men, but Alejandro already knew that he'd never remember their names. That was Geoffrey's job. Besides, Alejandro suspected that the important man was apparently the one standing before him. "Geoffrey was kind enough to spend some time with us during the show."

Geoffrey appeared and immediately jumped into the conversation. "Victor's over here from New York. Apparently, they'd like to discuss a movie."

"Oh, *sí?*" His curiosity piqued, he considered Victor with more interest. Movies were one of the many untapped areas where he wanted to bring the Viper brand.

"We'd like to film your concert and have it in the movie. It's an action film being shot in Los Angeles right now. We were going to use an actor to re-create the concert scene, but Danny here"—he paused and looked over at one of the other men—"suggested we consider an alternative."

Nodding his head, Alejandro motioned to Rochelle to fetch him some water. "Keep talking . . . ," he instructed Victor.

"They'd like you to go to New York to meet their team and discuss details in three weeks."

"Ah!" He accepted the proffered bottle of cold water from his assistant, pausing to thank her with a simple nod of his head.

Geoffrey waited for Alejandro to down half of the bottle. "You have time just before Prague," he said.

Twisting the cap back onto the bottle, Alejandro handed it back to Rochelle. "Leave any information about the movie with Geoffrey," he said to Victor. "And I'll see you in New York, *sí?*" Slapping Geoffrey on the arm, he gave him a tired smile and started to leave the room, more interested in a shower than a script.

"One more thing," Victor said before Alejandro left. "We'd like to invite you to the Whitney Art Gala. You and your wife, of course. Your manager says it's the same week. We'll put you up at the Peninsula while you're in the city."

Alejandro stiffened at the mention of Amanda. He glanced at Geoffrey and lifted one eyebrow, an unspoken communication that while Victor Byrne might know what the public wanted, he clearly didn't know what the public knew: Amanda was not with him. Such a slip meant they hadn't done their research. They'd be easier to negotiate with come contract time.

"Coordinate with G," he said and managed to walk through the door without further interruption.

# Chapter Five

The itinerary that Dali handed to her was not exactly what Amanda had expected. It listed times, names, and addresses. Amanda scanned it, noting that there was no mention of a hotel, so that she could freshen up after the plane arrived in the morning, and that London's O2 arena, where Alejandro was performing that night, was listed at the very end of the schedule.

"What is this?" Amanda asked as she set the piece of paper onto her lap.

Dali stood before her, her arms crossed over her chest and a stern look on her face. "It's your itinerary."

"Well, I reckon I can see that," Amanda said, glancing through the list of items on the document once again. "Why am I meeting with all of these people? You have me arriving in London at six in the morning and meeting with a radio show, news program, and press people? And then what's this?" She moved the paper onto the table and pointed at an item. "A lunch meeting? But I don't know these people!" She stared at Dali, a look of bewilderment on her face. "I . . . I just don't understand this."

Dali hadn't been in the apartment for more than ten minutes and already she had a dissatisfied look on her face. Her stern expression seemed to peer through Amanda. While Dali had never really been a warm and fuzzy type of person—more of a get-down-to-business woman—she now seemed even more indifferent to Amanda. The blank expression on her face indicated as much.

"Your unexpected departure from the tour cost me a lot, Amanda," Dali said slowly. "People were counting on you to show up for interviews, to make appearances. When you backed out, I lost a lot of credibility from people in the business. You need to give a little back in order to receive, I'm afraid."

Amanda pursed her lips and read through the itinerary once again. If she had hoped to surprise Alejandro, it was clearly not part of Dali's plan. Certainly someone would hear that she was arriving in London. The paparazzi would be tipped off, for sure and certain. She'd be alone in the airport to deal with them, a few airport security guards possibly assigned to escort her to a waiting car. The first stop was a morning radio show where she would be interviewed live during morning rush hour. The second stop was a women's TV talk show. The third stop was a lunch meeting with a children's hospital. Her final meetings were back-to-back interviews at the hotel with two reporters. By the time she would finally catch up with Alejandro, it would be just before the evening concert—if she was lucky. That was not the ideal timing for a heart-to-heart discussion.

"Can't any of these be pushed back, Dali?" She tapped her fingers against the paper on the table. "I mean . . . that's a long day and with the travel and time delay . . ."

"Take it or leave it, Amanda."

Startled by the sternness of Dali's voice, Amanda looked up and studied her once again.

"You said you'd do anything and everything that I put on the itin-erary." Dali leaned forward and tapped her finger on the paper. "You owe me this much."

"He'll know I'm coming," Amanda said.

"He'll find out anyway." Dali brushed some imaginary lint from her sleeve. Clearly, she did not empathize with Amanda's concerns. "They always do. There are no secrets in this business."

With a sigh, Amanda studied the itinerary one more time. She would leave that evening at five o'clock on British Airways and arrive in London a little before seven in the morning with VIP access to customs so that she could make her first interview at eight o'clock. With no sleep and no way to freshen up, Amanda would get off the plane and her day would begin. From the looks of it, Dali had ensured it wouldn't stop until after the concert.

"How did you schedule all of these so quickly?" Amanda flipped over the page and gasped. "And you have more meetings for the fol-lowing day? More interviews?" She looked up and stared at Dali. "Shouldn't I be concentrating on my marriage, not publicity?"

Dali looked as if she might roll her eyes. "Amanda," she said in a soft voice. "Publicity is what will save your marriage."

"Publicity." Amanda merely repeated the word. She had no idea what Dali meant by that statement.

"Yes, publicity."

A promise was a promise, Amanda told herself. "Well, I see that my time in London will be busy. And Cardiff? Where is that?"

"Same. United Kingdom."

"Ah." She felt ignorant for not having known that. "Right. And Manchester?"

"Same."

"Birmingham?"

"Amanda . . . please." The exasperation in Dali's voice caused Amanda to ask no further questions regarding the itinerary.

Since she could only presume that Birmingham was also in the United Kingdom, she accepted it as a positive note: at least there would be less travel, which meant more time for Amanda to be alone with Alejandro and time to work through their problems and come to a better understanding of what changes needed to be addressed.

"How on earth did you make all of these appointments, Dali?" Not even twenty-four hours had passed since Amanda had called Dali. Now she stood before her with a complete itinerary: times, appointments, transportation. Everything was arranged as if Dali had planned this trip for months.

In typical Dali fashion, she gave her an exasperated look. "Really, Amanda?" This time, she did roll her eyes. "This is what I *do*, Amanda. I have my contacts."

"And they will get me into the venue that night? To see Alejandro?"

Dali nodded. "*Sí*, Amanda. And I have spoken to several people who will try to keep him from learning of your arrival."

Amanda's heart lifted.

In her mind, she saw the scene unfold: she would walk into the Meet and Greet session that he did with his fans, waiting in the back. She knew that he would be too busy greeting the people who lined up, waiting for that moment, those few seconds in his presence, to give him a hug and take a photo with him. Hundreds of dollars spent for one photo with Viper. The waste of money boggled her mind, but she knew that the fans did not mind spending it. Afterward, they would share the memory with their friends and family, and they would live on a mental high about how they had, for just those few seconds, been in Viper's arms. And for Alejandro, he would secure lifelong Viper fans who would talk about him for years to come and purchase all of his music.

Alejandro had once told her giving away free photos cost dearly. Now she understood better what he meant.

"Now," Dali said, clapping her hands together. "We need to get you packed. You'll need a lot of outfits, Amanda, and we need you looking your sharpest for these interviews. Without Jeremy, we'll need to shift through your current wardrobe. Once there, I'm sure someone will help you. But in the meantime we have to work with what you have."

Together they went upstairs and entered the bedroom adjacent to Alejandro's, the room that she had slept in when she first arrived in Miami before they were married. Now she used it mostly as a dressing room. After having spent three weeks on her parents' farm, where there were only simple hooks on the wall for hanging clothes, the large walk-in closet felt even bigger to Amanda. The bright lights and rows of skirts, blouses, dresses, and shoes overwhelmed her. Dali, however, merely exhaled and shook her head.

Once again, Amanda wondered about Dali's personal life. The rows upon rows of clothing and shoes probably seemed as excessive to her as they did to Amanda, but in the life of a celebrity, it was necessary.

"Well," Dali said after walking along one row, pausing to touch a piece of clothing every few feet. "At least some of these still have their tags on."

"Is that good?"

Dali glanced at her over her shoulder. "Yes, that means you haven't worn them yet. We can't have you showing up in the same outfits, can we now?"

That never made sense to Amanda, especially when Alejandro usually wore black slacks and a black silk shirt. Still, he, too, had a closetful of clothing, most of it black and, in Amanda's opinion, too similar in style. She never understood why he needed such a large wardrobe; everything looked the same.

"If you say so," Amanda said meekly. She sat down on the settee in the middle of the room, watching as Dali pulled out outfits to assess them. A few she set aside while the rest she put back.

When a pile of clothing hung on the dressing rack, Dali stepped back and surveyed it. "That should get you through the first two days."

"Two days?" Amanda almost laughed. "That's enough for a week!"

Again, Dali cast a disapproving look at Amanda. "Everything and anything, remember?"

Amanda sighed and slouched on the settee. "Everything and anything, *ja.*"

Security had to escort Amanda through the airport in Miami because too many people had recognized her. Given that few people knew she had arrived in Miami the previous day, Amanda could only wonder if Dali had tipped off the media. It had been a while since she'd encountered a mob scene of paparazzi of such magnitude, and while she knew too well that crowds begat crowds, her suspicions remained that Dali's hand was behind the enormity of it.

"Step aside!" one of the security guards said, sticking out his arm to push someone away. The young woman stumbled and fell into another person, who immediately shoved back. When a security guard started to grab the woman, Amanda stopped walking and reached for his arm.

"Don't," she said. "It wasn't her fault."

The flash of cameras blinded her, but Amanda spent a moment talking to the woman.

"Are you all right, then?"

The young woman, who looked to be no more than seventeen, had dirty blonde hair in a loose bun on the top of her head and a white T-shirt with a band's name on it. She nodded her head as if starstruck.

Quickly, Amanda tried to think what Alejandro would do. All too well she remembered being chastised in Miami when she paused to take a photo with a young man outside of the dance studio. No one was around to reprimand her this time. So, with a soft smile, Amanda heard herself asking, "Would you like a photo?"

The reaction from the girl startled Amanda. She began to cry, tears filling her eyes and falling down her cheeks. She covered her face with her hands and could barely move to stand next to Amanda.

"Thank you. Oh, thank you!" the young woman gushed, reaching for Amanda's hands. "You have no idea how much I love you!"

Placing her arm around the girl's waist, Amanda posed while she took a selfie. Then Amanda gave her a soft hug and whispered, "Be careful" into her ear.

"I will. Thank you, Amanda."

The glow on the girl's face lit up Amanda's heart.

"Are you going to Europe?" someone called out.

"Are you meeting up with Viper?"

"Is it true you are getting divorced?"

Amanda ignored the questions, waved to the gathered crowd, and let the security guards whisk her through the TSA security checkpoint without having to wait in line.

Long after she passed through the body scanner and had been escorted to the gate, she found herself still thinking about that young woman and how easily she had told Amanda that she loved her. In America, Viper's fans (and even people who didn't care for him) were so quick to express their emotions. Amanda was not from a world where the word *love* rolled so easily off anyone's tongue. Fans loved Viper. Fans loved Amanda. Fans seemed to love just about anyone who stood in the spotlight.

Yet her experience in South America had been completely different. The South American women cared little for Amanda. Their focus was on one thing and only one thing: Viper. In fact, while the US fans practically demanded Amanda's presence at the VIP Meet and Greets, Amanda merely stood in the shadows in South America. It made Amanda wonder what that said about the cultures of the different countries. It also made her wonder what she would face in Europe.

After clearing security, Amanda was escorted onto the British Airways flight by the guards so that she wouldn't have to wait with the other passengers. She wasn't surprised to find herself seated by the window in first class. She left on her sunglasses so that she could avoid the curious eyes of the passengers boarding. To her relief, the passengers in business and economy class entered the plane through another door toward the middle of the aircraft.

It wasn't just that she didn't want to speak to people. She needed to focus on what was in store for her over the next few days. She felt as if her nerves were on fire, pulsating throughout her body. If a year ago anyone had told her that she would be sitting on a plane by herself, about to fly across the Atlantic Ocean to a country she had barely heard about to reconcile with her husband, she'd never have believed them.

And then there was that: reconciliation.

Just thinking the word stung more than anything else.

She knew Alejandro loved her. There was no denying the intensity of the passion that they felt. At least on her part. It was simply inconceivable that Alejandro might feel differently now. Which brought her to the problem: If two people loved each other, why were they apart to begin with?

In her world, marriage was forever. Wives supported and obeyed their husbands, and husbands simply did not walk out on their wives. Yet Alejandro was not from her world, a world that she had voluntarily left to be with him. She had much to learn about living in the Englische world, and she realized that she had taken much for granted, not least of all marriage. But did adopting his Englische lifestyle mean she had to forgo her Amish values? It was a thought she had not considered before the South American tour.

Alejandro had warned her that it would be much different from the US tour. He had mentioned that there was a stronger emphasis on sexuality in South America, whereas the US fans, although sometimes flirtatious, were more interested in a quick hug and a selfie photo.

Despite his warnings, Amanda had not been properly prepared for *his* reaction to those South American women. After all, there was no denying the fact that the women were beautiful . . . stunning . . . and dripping with desire for her husband. To see her husband whisper in their ears or pose with his hands on their bodies had not helped matters.

In hindsight, she knew that he had only been playing a part, giving the fans what they wanted and letting them believe what they thought they knew. *Keeping my eye on the goal,* he once told her. Amanda knew that she should have been more attuned to the role that he was playing as Viper instead of feeling personally inferior to the women.

Then, of course, there had been that disastrous vacation at the house in Argentina. If only Enrique and his entourage of scantily clad women in bikinis with overly tanned bodies had stayed away. That time was meant for Alejandro and Amanda to reconnect and rekindle the passion that had bought them together. Even with Isadora as a new addition to their family, Amanda had felt strongly that the time alone would have been the balm to soothe the open wounds.

Only they didn't get that time.

Now she was going to do everything in her power to make time so that she and Alejandro could be a team once more.

She shut her eyes and imagined dancing on the stage with him, all of Stedman's hard work having paid off, enough so that she could keep up with Alejandro when he serenaded her for the fans. She thought of the dressing rooms with racks of clothing, most of them sparkling and beautiful, garments that she hadn't even known existed before she met Alejandro. And she remembered the VIP Meet and Greets when they were able to interact with the fans before the show. Just the look of joy on their faces as they stood next to Viper was enough for Amanda to realize how much he touched their lives. She tried to not think about how she felt when the attention was on her. To do so would be vain, and she still felt uncomfortable being alone in the limelight.

\*\*\*

As Dali had promised, someone was waiting for Amanda when she departed the plane. A woman wearing a navy-blue dress with a simple gold belt and a friendly smile walked up to Amanda and introduced herself as Charlotte.

"Mrs. Diaz," she said. Her straight blonde hair framed her heart-shaped face and made her dark eyes appear doe-like. "I trust your flight was uneventful?"

It took a moment for Amanda to decipher what Charlotte had said. Her accent sounded strange, with each word perfectly enunciated and clipped at the end.

"The flight?" Amanda nodded. "*Ja*, it was good. Long but good."

"Brilliant," Charlotte said, reaching out to take Amanda's carry-on suitcase. "We have a tight schedule today." The way she said *schedule* required Amanda to translate the word in her head. "So we best carry on, hadn't we? They'll be time for you to freshen up at the radio station, but I'd prefer to get you there in case we get caught up in traffic. Follow me, please."

Without another word, she began to walk away from Amanda. Not knowing what else to do, Amanda followed her.

"I've received your itinerary and have the logistics worked out, Mrs. Diaz, but it's going to be a bit on the hectic side."

As Amanda followed the woman, she noticed that, unlike the airports in South America or even in the United States, there were no crowds or mob scenes. A few younger people did double takes, nudging the person beside them, but no one approached or followed her.

"Come, let's get you through customs so we can get to the car," Charlotte said as she led Amanda to the front of a special line in customs. "You have quite the busy day, don't you?"

Amanda felt more comfortable with Charlotte helping to guide her. Being in a foreign country without knowing anyone felt daunting. Although the people dressed similarly to the Englischers in America, there was still something different about them. As she walked past the long line at customs, she wasn't certain whether the individuals were American or English. What she did recognize was the look of disdain from many of them, apparently unhappy that she was able to bypass the line and hurry through the process of having her passport stamped.

Less than forty minutes later, Amanda found herself being led into a seven-story building with the words "Capital Radio London" emblazoned on it.

"Here we are," Charlotte said as she signed in with security. "Do you need to use the loo before we go upstairs?"

"The what?"

"The loo." Charlotte tried to explain with a soft smile. "The water closet?"

"I don't need water, thank you," Amanda replied.

Charlotte laughed. "The toilet, Amanda. To freshen up a bit. They'll want to take photos of you."

Amanda bit her lower lip and nodded. She felt naive and unsophisticated in this strange country where cars drove on the wrong side of the road and people spoke with a peculiar accent that, at times, she simply did not understand. They even had different words for things. If she could only get to Alejandro, she knew she'd feel better . . . safer.

Amanda splashed cold water on her face and used a paper towel to dab at her skin. She felt weary, her body weak and exhausted. Sleeping on the plane had come in short spurts, and there would be no time for a nap at the hotel. She didn't even know which hotel Alejandro was staying at. As she looked at her reflection in the mirror, she realized that she didn't even know what Alejandro's reaction to her unexpected arrival would be.

When she exited the ladies' room, Charlotte was already in action, talking to two men dressed in casual clothing. One of them wore a hat that read "Reloaded" across the front.

"There she is!" Charlotte waved Amanda over to join them. "Amanda, this is Will and his assistant, Jon, who will walk you through the questions in advance. I'm leaving you in his capable hands, but I'll be waiting down here for when you're finished."

The thought of being left alone with Will, whoever he was, did not thrill Amanda. But she had done radio interviews before with Alejandro. Speaking into the big microphone did not intimidate her. Being alone, however, did. She worried that she might say the wrong thing when she answered their questions. While she'd get to see the questions before the show went live, even that level of preparation did not erase her discomfort. When Alejandro was by her side, she knew he was there to take over if anything went wrong. Without him, she had only herself to rely on.

Fifteen minutes later she was sitting in the studio, earphones covering her ears and the black microphone before her face. The DJ was a young man with brown hair that was brushed back from his forehead. His smile helped put her at ease, and since she knew the questions already, she felt a strange sense of comfort.

"It's just like a dialogue," the DJ told her. His accent was not as heavy as Charlotte's, and Amanda found that she could understand him better.

The song that was playing faded away, and the light on the studio wall that read "Live" turned on.

"I'm sitting in the studio with a very special guest," the DJ said into his microphone, giving a friendly wink to Amanda. "Anyone in London who is breathing knows that Viper is in town. His concerts are sold out and Capital XTRA is the only station with tickets, which we're giving out throughout the day. But today we have a surprise guest, Amanda Diaz, the most famous Amish woman in the world!"

Amanda took a sharp intake of air. She detested that description, which continued to creep into the media.

"Amanda made national headlines last year when Viper hit her with his car in New York City. Since then, the world of music has been fascinated with this lovely woman who captured Viper's heart and hand." He gave a short pause. "Amanda, I understand that you just flew into London from Miami."

When he stopped talking, she knew that was her cue to respond. "I did, *ja*."

"You must be tired, I imagine."

"I didn't sleep very well on the plane, so I am tired." She pursed her lips, trying to think of something exciting to say. Her mind flickered back to Alejandro when he did interviews. "But I'm excited about being here in London," she said, trying to make her voice sound more enthusiastic than she felt. "It's a lovely city. A far cry from the home where I grew up."

"A farm, correct?"

"*Ja*, a farm." She glanced at the DJ and he raised his eyebrows, still smiling at her. "An Amish farm, I'm sure you heard."

He nodded his head. "We Brits aren't too familiar with the Amish. At least not until we began learning more about you. Is it true that you don't have electricity and plumbing?"

That question had not been on the sheet that Will's assistant reviewed with her, and it caught her off guard. She found herself laughing. "No plumbing? Is that what people think, then?"

"So plumbing is good, electricity bad?"

"The Amish don't categorize things like that," she started to explain. "It's not good versus bad. It's more simple versus worldly. Worldly things take us away from honoring God and being a family. Imagine how nice the world would be if everyone shunned worldly things."

"Such as . . . ?"

Amanda cringed. She had done the one thing that she hadn't wanted to do: talk herself into a corner where she wasn't certain of the correct answer. *"Vell . . . ,"* she started, trying to think of a good example. "Let's start with pride. Pride separates people from each other, creates a barrier between individuals. The Amish live simply, not focusing on building or buying bigger houses or cars. To do so would be showing pride. The Amish do not try to better themselves over other people. Instead, we try to work together and help each other without expecting any gratitude beyond knowing we have followed God's word."

The DJ frowned. "So, thanking people demonstrates pride?"

Again, she laughed. "Oh no, that's not it. It's the *expectation* of being thanked."

"I see. So what if I were to say thank you for coming on to our show?"

She was beginning to relax. "If you did, I would say you're welcome!"

This time, the DJ laughed.

"Now, you flew into London this morning. The last we heard, you were at your parents' farm with Viper's daughter."

She made a soft sound in her throat. This was also not one of the questions Will had reviewed with her.

"How shocking was that, Amanda, to suddenly have a child thrown into your care?"

With questioning eyes, she stared at the DJ. Why had he strayed from the questions? She didn't want to answer anything about Isadora. And she didn't want to answer anything personal about Alejandro. But as the seconds of silence grew, she knew she had to respond somehow.

"I . . . I was surprised, *ja*, but I truly love our daughter. In fact, I left her in the care of my *schwester* . . . sister, I mean . . . and I miss her terribly," she said with as much composure as she could muster.

"Why are you here, then? There are an awful lot of stories floating around, Amanda. Do you care to set the record straight?"

"I don't read those stories," she said truthfully. "But I'm here to support my husband on his European tour."

"No divorce plans?"

Amanda gasped. "Is that what people are saying? No! And I don't care to answer any more questions about my marriage."

The DJ gave her the thumbs-up as he moved on to another topic. But Amanda's cheeks burned, and she took several deep breaths before she could continue the interview. The rest of the questions proved to be more benign, focusing on her favorite memory of the South American tour, which country she was looking forward to visiting in Europe, and how she felt about the changes in her life.

When the interview was over, Amanda quickly stood and removed her earphones, setting them down on the chair where she had been sitting. She said nothing to the DJ, avoiding eye contact with him.

"Brilliant!" he said. "Spot-on, my dear."

She remained silent.

"The listeners will eat that up, Amanda. You're a natural."

"I'd like to leave now," she said at last.

He frowned. "You're upset? About that one question?"

Hating the anger that swelled inside her chest, Amanda tried to remain composed. Words escaped her, and she was afraid to open her mouth for fear of saying something that was not kind.

"Hey," he said, reaching out to lightly touch her arm. "Those were the questions that your assistant sent to me this morning."

Stunned, Amanda stared at him. "This morning?"

He nodded his head. "Just about ten minutes before you arrived. She told me that these were the new questions and topics to discuss."

Dali? Dali had done this?

"I see," Amanda said. "I reckon I was just caught off guard. Personal relationships, whether good or not so good, are not something that the Amish discuss with others."

The DJ nodded his head. "I'm sorry, Amanda. I meant no offense."

The door opened and Will motioned toward Amanda. "We need a few photographs, and then Charlotte says you have another appointment."

Amanda forced a soft, forgiving smile for the disc jockey, realizing that her anger should be directed at its source, not at him. *"Danke,"* she managed to say before she turned to follow Will out of the studio.

Alejandro stood in his dressing room, fixing his red tie as he looked in the mirror. After three days in Spain and two in Portugal, he felt a sense of relief to be in England for an extended period. There was something about the English fans that appealed to him. Their loyalty matched any of the Spanish-speaking countries and, in some cases, surpassed them. Yet they weren't pushy, invading his personal space. It was always a refreshing change.

Someone knocked at his door, and Alejandro frowned. This was his time to regroup and focus on his meetings before the concert. He had been quite clear when he'd told his team he didn't want to be disturbed. Someone had decided not to follow his directive, and that did not sit well with him.

He ignored the interruption until it was repeated.

Frustrated, he stormed over to the door and flung it open. "I told you no interruptions, G!" Despite his irritation, he left the door open for Geoffrey to step inside while he finished getting dressed. Back in front of the mirror, he ran his hands through his hair, fixing the way it draped over his forehead

"How's the crowd?" he asked.

"Sold out. You know that."

Alejandro nodded. Sometimes he just liked to hear the words: sold out. The O2 arena in London. He didn't think he could ever get tired of hearing those two words. He redirected his attention to his tie; it didn't look right. With a quick tug, he pulled it off and tossed it onto the counter. "Hand me that black tie."

Geoffrey did as he was instructed. He stood there for a moment, watching as Viper began to thread the tie under his collar. For the English audiences, he liked to dress a bit more formally than at his other concerts. They seemed to appreciate a more stoic look, unlike the South American cities, where it was preferred he be more casual and outgoing.

"And the reporters? They are here?"

Geoffrey nodded. "Waiting to interview you before the concert starts." He paused for a long moment before he added, "And she is here."

"Who's she?" he asked as he adjusted his tie.

"Amanda."

At the sound of her name, Alejandro paused for just a few seconds, his gaze never moving away from his reflection in the mirror. Amanda? In London? He tried to wrap his head around such a concept. He needed to remain calm. How was it possible for Amanda to get from Lancaster County, Pennsylvania, to London, England? With no resources or experience traveling, outside of the trips they'd taken together, Amanda would certainly not know how to book an international trip. She probably didn't even have his tour information.

Dali.

He knew at once that Dali must have helped her.

He returned to the business of dressing, straightening the sleeves of his black shirt and adjusting his cuff links. "And you learned of this how?" he said, his voice even and calm.

"She's been giving interviews all day, and I understand that she's on her way to the arena."

He tried to not react and remain neutral. Inside, however, he wasn't certain how he felt. Almost three weeks had gone by since he'd left her in Lancaster. Not once had she tried to reach out to him. For his part, he had thrown himself into work: filming a video in Los Angeles, meeting with companies in New York, signing the Movistar deal in Madrid. But at night, when he finally found the courage to retire to his empty bedroom, he thought of her.

Now she was here in London?

He hadn't expected that from her. If something was wrong, he would have heard. That meant only one thing: she wanted something. He wanted something, too. It had been a long and lonely few weeks for him since she'd left midtour in South America. He had to consider his options and prepare himself mentally for seeing her. Geoffrey's warning gave him the time to think about how to best handle this situation.

"*Gracias*, Geoffrey," he said, finally turning around from the mirror. He hardened his gaze as he met Geoffrey's eyes. "Is the Meet and Greet set up? And are the reporters here for the preshow interviews?"

He ignored the look in his manager's eyes, the one that questioned his ability to raise a wall that kept him from displaying his emotions. That invisible barrier was the only way Alejandro could protect himself. That was something he had learned long ago.

# Chapter Six

By the time she arrived at the arena, Amanda was behind schedule. Dali's schedule, she reminded herself. Not mine. Had she been able to sidestep Dali's brutal schedule, she would have confronted Alejandro at the hotel at his most vulnerable: when he was waking up.

Now the vulnerabilities were all hers. The delay in meeting with him heightened the feeling of butterflies in her stomach. The only blessing in disguise was that Dali's schedule had kept her busy with people fussing over her hair and makeup before interviews and crowding around her constantly asking if she was comfortable.

After the last interview with an entertainment reporter, Amanda had to practically beg Charlotte for just a few minutes in the ladies' room to freshen up. A few minutes to think, a few minutes to let her mind get caught up on everything that had happened. Since the previous evening when she had left Miami, two guards escorting her through Miami International Airport and whisking her through security, Amanda hadn't had time to think.

Or rather it was that she'd had too much time to think, but everything she'd thought unraveled when she stumbled off the airplane and into the care of Charlotte.

With a huff and a puff, the previously accommodating Charlotte had crossed her arms over her chest and retorted, "Go on, then! The loo's over there. But be snappy about it. We don't have time to fanny about!"

Amanda had stood at the sink and stared at herself in the mirror. Somehow, she did not look tired. She suspected multiple touch-ups of makeup and fussing by hair stylists had hidden the layers of weariness she felt. She didn't know what she would say to Alejandro or how he would react. With so many appointments and so much media buzz, she knew it was highly unlikely that he had not heard of her arrival in London. She could only pray that he did not turn her away. Just the thought of that reaction made her feel nauseated again.

"What am I doing here?" she mumbled to herself in the mirror. "I must be *ferhoodled* for sure and certain."

Someone banged on the outer door.

"Amanda! Stop lollygagging, and let's get going. We're going to hit that traffic, and it will all go to pot!"

Between the heavy English accent and the strange words she used, Amanda wasn't certain what Charlotte was yelling to her through the locked door.

Traffic had delayed the last interview, and Charlotte barely let Amanda freshen up again before the hired car arrived to take them to their final destination for the day: the O2 arena in London. As they approached the large dome, Amanda leaned forward in the seat to peer at it. White with lighted poles sticking out, it was perhaps larger than any other arena she'd been to with Alejandro. She suspected its imposing appearance might be partly because of the lack of tall buildings in the near vicinity, but she was still impressed with its size.

As the driver passed through the external security checks, Amanda began to tremble. Her heart raced and her palms felt clammy. She was exhausted, both mentally and physically. Yet adrenaline coursed through her veins, giving her new energy. What would Alejandro say when he saw her? How would he react? She had prayed during most of the flight that the coldness with which he'd left her would have vanished, replaced by the love that she knew he felt for her. Still, she couldn't help but worry. If she was wrong and he maintained that icy front, she wouldn't know what to do.

She looked over at Charlotte, who, as always, was focused on her cell phone.

"Charlotte."

The woman looked up when Amanda said her name.

"Do I look all right?"

Charlotte smiled, but it was a distant smile, not one of real caring or compassion. "You look lovely, Amanda."

"I'm tired."

"I bet you are."

"But do I look tired?"

Charlotte gave a soft laugh. "No, Amanda. You do not."

Satisfied, Amanda sat back and stared out the window, praying that God would help her do the right things over the next few hours.

Two security guards stopped the car near the secured entrance to the underground. A man walked forward and opened the door, reaching out his hand for Amanda to take.

"We've been expecting you!" he said in a cheery voice. "The bloody traffic got you?"

"Bloody traffic?"

Charlotte popped out of the car and grabbed Amanda's arm. "Yes, the traffic was horrendous," she said, giving the man a stern look. "Let's get going."

The man led them through a series of doors, pausing at different checkpoints to display his credentials. Several people looked up when they saw Amanda being led down the corridors toward the stage area. She thought she saw a few people sneak a photo with their smartphones. But she didn't care. In just a few minutes, she would see

Alejandro. She had hoped to talk with him before the concert. Now, she assumed she'd have to wait until afterward. At least she was fairly certain he would not have too many time-consuming commitments following the show. They could talk things out, and this time he could not walk away from her. She only prayed that he did not shut her out.

As she followed Charlotte and the man, Amanda rubbed her hands on the sides of her simple cream-colored dress. With her hair pulled back and her skin golden brown from working outside, Amanda felt different from the last time she had been backstage. She recognized several workers from the previous tour, and they nodded their heads in acknowledgment. Although she couldn't remember their names, that was something she would correct.

Geoffrey saw her first. He hesitated, just a moment, before motioning for her to come join him on the wing of the stage. She left Charlotte's side and walked over to Geoffrey, worried that people were watching her. But when she glanced around, everyone was too busy with their jobs to be paying any attention to her.

"Amanda," Geoffrey said and leaned forward to give her a quick hug and kiss on the cheek. "It's good to see you."

His warm greeting did little to set her at ease.

"It's been a long day," she said as she looked around, her nerves on edge. The noise of the crowd was louder than the noise from the music onstage. The opening act. Alejandro wasn't onstage yet, and they would need at least thirty minutes to change the sets.

"You flew in this morning?"

She nodded her head. "*Ja*, this morning."

She looked around, taking in the activity and organized chaos that surrounded them. She peeked at the audience and saw the arena packed with fans, some anxiously awaiting Viper's appearance while others took the opportunity to leave their seats to purchase refreshments or visit the restroom. She did not see Alejandro. "Where . . . where is he?" she asked, hating the way her voice sounded so unsteady.

Geoffrey hesitated before responding. His pause caused her to look at him.

A moment of panic washed over her. "What is it?"

"He knows you're here," Geoffrey said in a matter-of-fact tone.

She swallowed. Was that good or bad? "I . . . I'm not surprised. Dali arranged so many appointments for me."

A man dressed in jeans and a black T-shirt walked up to Geoffrey and handed him a clipboard with some papers on it. Geoffrey scanned the three pages, nodded his head, and handed it back. "Alejandro should be just wrapping up the Meet and Greet."

Of course, she thought, he would be attending the beloved sessions where fans paid money to spend thirty seconds in his presence. In the past, he had liked meeting with his fans and it seemed to put him in a good mood. Now, since she hadn't considered exactly how to approach him, she wondered if meeting him outside the Meet and Greet area might be a good idea.

During the flight over to London, Amanda had thought through a dozen different scenarios. She had wanted to catch him before the show began when he was alone, perhaps reviewing the set list or having just finished the sound check. She had imagined that he would see her standing in the wings of the stage. He would stop what he was doing and walk toward her, surprised by her presence. She worried over his reaction. Would he be cold and standoffish or would he be angry? But she had known that she needed to explain herself in person to win him over. That was why she had traveled so far just to be reunited with him.

Of course, Dali had ruined any of Amanda's preconceived reunion scenarios by arranging all of those appointments beforehand. And Charlotte. Teaming Amanda up with Charlotte had been another exhausting surprise. Her mind seemed to move as fast as her body. Several times throughout the day, Amanda had wondered how anyone could have so much energy and be on the constant go like Charlotte.

Now that Alejandro knew she'd arrived in London, all Amanda's previous scenarios were moot. Her losing the element of surprise had certainly given him the upper hand; he'd had time to prepare for her arrival. Amanda had no idea what to expect when she saw him. Rather than put it off, Amanda decided it was best to just get it over with.

"Might I go to him there?" she asked.

To her surprise, Geoffrey shook his head and glanced at his phone. It was a nervous tic acquired by many of the people who worked for Alejandro. She could never tell if they were checking the time or looking for new messages. In this case, it must have been the time, for he slid his phone into his back pocket and looked at her. "He instructed me to take you to the greenroom."

*Instructed.* The word sent a shiver down her spine. It sounded cold and calculated, a reminder that he was in charge and she was in his territory. Not only did he know she was there, but he already had a plan for how their first meeting would play out. *That* was something she hadn't considered.

"I see."

She followed Geoffrey off the stage and down a narrow corridor to the greenroom, where people gathered to watch the concert and eat the catered food and drink provided by the venue as part of Viper's rider. Amanda had learned every performer had different demands on their riders, but, apparently, Viper's played it straightforward, not demanding special accommodations for himself or his crew, with the exception of the brand of vodka that Alejandro preferred. She wasn't surprised to walk into the room and find it already filled with strangers who mingled among each other while sampling the food and partaking of the bottled beer that lined a linen-covered table.

"Make yourself comfortable," Geoffrey said as he guided her into the room. He didn't stay, but left her standing just inside the doorway.

And then she was on her own.

It took a second for the conversations to fade. First one person noticed her standing there and then a second person glanced in her direction. Amanda stood in the doorway, uncertain what to say or do. Although she recognized none of these people, they clearly recognized her. She glanced at the television screen, startled to see Enrique performing. She had not known that he was Viper's opening act on the European tour. The idea of seeing him again made her feel unwell.

When she turned her attention away from the television screen, everyone was still staring at her in silence. Just as she took a deep breath and garnered enough courage to walk into the room, she felt a strong hand press her shoulder.

"Ah, there she is!"

Alejandro tightened his grip on her and guided her into the room. If he hadn't been holding her so firmly, Amanda knew her knees would have given out. She tried to turn and look at him, but he was focused on the gathering in the room.

"My Princesa!" he said cheerfully, his voice sounding as if they had never been separated. "She has arrived just in time!"

The people smiled, their eyes flickering between the two of them. Amanda started to open her mouth, wanting to say something to him, but Alejandro kept his hand upon her shoulder as he concentrated on greeting the people in the room. Most of them were from the press, and Alejandro glided his way through them, shaking hands and introducing them to his wife as if not a day had passed since they'd been together. The natural ease with which Alejandro moved among the people, Amanda held tightly at his left side, confused Amanda. Was this it? she wondered. Was reuniting with Alejandro that simple?

"Are you enjoying London, Amanda?" asked a woman in a gray dress with a thick black belt.

"It's . . . it's quite nice," she heard herself say. She couldn't keep herself from looking at Alejandro. "So far."

Alejandro gave Amanda's shoulder a slight squeeze as he answered the woman. "She's only just arrived. She'll see much more tomorrow, *sí*?"

Swallowing her trepidation, Amanda forced herself to smile. The casual air with which he had greeted her might have initially caught her off guard, but she had traveled with Alejandro long enough to know what he was doing: playing the part of their image. Two can play at that game, she told herself.

"*Ja*, tomorrow Alejandro has promised to take me sightseeing," she said, hoping that her voice sounded more confident than she felt. "It will be right *gut* to spend some time together, won't it, Alejandro?"

He had no choice. The group of people, especially the reporters, waited for his response. Amanda stood beside him, her face turned upward toward Alejandro until he had no other option but to look at her, his blue eyes meeting her brown ones for the first time. In the seconds that passed, no one else stood in the room. They were alone, standing side by side. There was a hunger in his expression, an element of excitement that suddenly caused his eyes to light up. He dropped his gaze from her eyes to her lips, and then she saw him tense his jaw.

"*Sí*, Princesa," he replied, his voice suddenly low and husky. "But first we have much catching up to do, *sí*?" His eyes met hers once again. "*Mucho.*"

If the color had drained from her cheeks before, now she knew they flushed pink. From the way that he lifted his eyebrow and slightly pursed his lips, she knew he had felt the same trepidation over seeing her as she had felt. The intensity of his look, so full of longing and desire, caused the feeling of weakness to return to her knees. But just as quickly as that look was there, it disappeared, and he returned to being Viper, his focus on the business at hand.

He talked with everyone in the room, spending at least one minute in private discussion with each person, keeping Amanda at his side the entire time. And then, when he had just fifteen minutes before he needed to be onstage, his hand slipped down from her shoulder and grasped her hand. As his fingers entwined with hers, she glanced up at him, her large brown eyes searching his face. But he did not look at her.

"Enjoy the show, *sí?*" he said to the people as he backed out of the room, taking Amanda with him.

Once outside in the corridor, he walked briskly toward his dressing room. She felt the grip on her hand tighten as she struggled to keep up. Someone stopped him and asked a question in Spanish. Alejandro replied and then continued toward the room.

After he opened the door, he pushed her inside, a bit more roughly than she anticipated. She turned around in time to see him shut and lock the door behind him. He stood there, studying her in silence. She wondered what he was thinking and was just about to speak when he lifted a finger and said, "Shh."

Startled, she stood and waited, for what she did not know.

He took three steps, each one slow and calculated. He walked around her in a steady manner. When he stood before her again, he reached out his hand and brushed a stray strand of hair away from her cheek.

"You came here," he said, his words slow and even. "To London."

She felt her heart racing, especially when he let his fingers linger by her neck, gently caressing her skin. "*Ja*, I did."

His eyes traveled down her body, that look of desire returning. He turned away from her and walked toward the sofa, leaning against the back of it. "That is a long trip, Amanda."

"*Ja*, it is," she said, her voice faltering.

He made a noise deep within his throat. He crossed his arms before his chest and continued to study her. If she wondered what he was thinking, he did not torture her curiosity for long. "Why?"

His question took her by surprise. "Why what?"

"Why, Amanda," he said, a dark shadow seeming to cover his face, "did you make such a long trip?"

"I . . ." She hadn't expected that question. Wasn't it obvious to him? If not, would her answer be enough? She knew it would take only one word from Alejandro for security to rush into the room, and Princesa or no Princesa, they would escort her out of the O2 arena in London, take her back to Heathrow Airport, and put her on the next plane scheduled for the United States. The truth, she thought. Simply tell him the truth. "I came because I love you," she whispered.

He shut his eyes and, after a moment, slowly nodded his head. But he did not speak. He just stood there, eyes closed with a deep, thoughtful expression on his face.

When she realized he wasn't going to respond, she took a step forward and, reaching out, grasped his hand. "Alejandro?"

At once he opened his eyes and moved forward, so quickly that she fell backward. He reached out, wrapping his free hand around her waist, and pulled her forward so that she pressed against him as his mouth sought hers. As he kissed her, he moved toward the wall, pushing her backward with his body until she could move no farther. Only then did he let his lips leave hers and trail a soft, gentle line down the length of her neck.

"Amanda," he murmured into her ear, her name rolling off his tongue with his Cuban accent: *Aman-tha.* His warm breath on her neck and the light pressure of his lips against her skin sent a familiar sensation through her body.

Oh, how she had longed for such a greeting! She shut her eyes and enjoyed the gentle kisses that he bestowed upon her. She could smell his cologne, so musky and so . . . him! She breathed in deeply, trying to remember the last time that she had inhaled Alejandro. Feeling his hand holding her waist while his hips pressed against hers made her give a soft sigh of contentment.

When his lips left her skin, she opened her eyes, partially surprised to see him staring at her, his blue eyes looking back and forth as he seemed to study everything about her face. "I forgot how beautiful you are," he whispered.

She blushed.

"I forgot many things, it seems, except for one thing: the reason I left without you."

Stunned, Amanda frowned. Had she heard him correctly? She raised her hands to press against his chest, trying to put some distance between them. "What did you say?"

He kept her pinned against the wall, his strength blocking her from escaping. With his face just inches from hers, he leaned forward so that his forehead touched hers. "It is not good that you came, Amanda," he said in a low, sultry voice, his words conflicting with the fire in his eyes. She knew that reaction only too well. Knowing that she had only one opportunity to win him over, she raised her hand and placed it against his cheek. He leaned against it, his hips still pressed against hers to keep her from moving away. But she had no intentions of going anywhere.

"*Nee*, Alejandro. It is very good that I came," she countered in a soft voice. "How could I not?"

"*Ay*, Amanda," he murmured. "You do not belong here."

She let her hand fall so that she gently brushed her fingertips down his neck and to his shoulder. "There is nowhere else that I belong more than here," she said. "With you."

He kissed her once again, only this time his lips were not soft and gentle but probing and passionate. She responded to his passion, letting her arms wrap around his neck, her fingers entwining with his thick hair. He tugged gently at her lower lip as he pulled away, his eyes holding her gaze. "What you do to me. What you make me *want* to do to you." And then he lifted his hands, placing them atop hers so that he could free himself from her embrace. "But not now. I must perform. We will continue this particular discussion later, *sí*?"

Alejandro did not wait for her response. He brushed his lips against her forehead and released her from his hold.

"I'll see that Geoffrey arranges for a car to take you to the hotel," he said abruptly, moving toward the rack of clothes so that he could switch into a fresh outfit.

"No."

He paused and looked over his shoulder at her. *"¿Qué?"*

"I said no."

Now it was his turn to be stunned. He walked back toward her. "No what?"

"No," she repeated firmly. "I will not go back to the hotel."

He almost laughed. "No?"

"Simply no." She paused, hesitating after her response. She felt uncomfortable standing up to him, but she knew that, unless she did, she would not win this battle. "I . . . I am staying here, and I am watching your show," she said, lifting her chin just enough so that he knew she would not be persuaded otherwise. "When you are ready to return to the hotel, I will go with you. That is what I want to do. As your wife and your partner. I will not leave you again and"—she swallowed as she said the words she had practiced over and over again in her head—"and you can't make me."

He crossed his arms over his chest and looked at her with an expression of great amusement. That only made her more determined.

"I'm not an object, Alejandro. I'm not a possession that can be left behind or called for at will."

"I did not call for you."

She felt anger swell inside her, and she hated the feeling. Anger was an emotion she had never experienced in her life, not until she'd met Alejandro. Anger made her feel far removed from God. It made her think things that forced her to pray for forgiveness later. Right now, the anger she felt took over her words.

"I am well aware of that fact, Alejandro!" she snapped. "You left me with no discussion, no choice. You made the decision that I should stay there, and once you left, you never looked back. Do you know how that made me feel? Waiting each day and praying each night for a phone call or a letter . . . something . . . to explain to me why you decided I should not be by your side?"

He raised an eyebrow, watching her as she vented the frustration of the previous weeks without him.

"It was a horrible feeling, let me assure you!" Her voice had risen just enough that she had to take a breath, willing herself to regain her composure. "And I am determined to show you that my place is by your side, no matter how you feel. So, no, I will not return to the hotel, unaccompanied by my husband. I will see this evening through"—she paused before she quickly added—"and every other evening through as a true wife should be: beside her husband and not cast away!"

He seemed to assess her, mulling over her words. She prayed that she had not gone too far. She had never spoken so sharply to anyone; the feeling of anger brought her immediate regret.

He smiled, the one corner of his mouth lifting just a touch. "Who is this woman? So fiery and outspoken?" he asked in a mocking tone. "Where is my Princesa?"

"She is right here," Amanda replied as she spread her arms out to her sides, "standing before you, and she is not going to leave your side again—not by your choice or by hers. I have a purpose, Alejandro. And that purpose is to be with you and to help you! To love you and support you!"

Someone knocked at the door. "Five minutes, Viper!"

"*¡Sí, sí!*" he called out, sounding irritated.

"I am not leaving," she whispered.

"*Ay,* Amanda," he said as he started to unbutton his shirt, exposing his chest. "I must get ready."

Brazenly, Amanda took a step toward him and reached out, helping him with each button, her fingers brushing against his bare skin. Show or no show, she was not going to let her husband brush her off without realizing that she, too, had a say about their relationship. She would not let the media plant seeds in his mind that created a divide between them. Instead, she wanted to plant another seed in his mind: that together they were more powerful than apart.

She looked up at him as she slid her hands under the shirt and gently pushed it back over his shoulders, guiding it down his arms and letting it fall to the floor. Her fingers ran up his arms, gently pausing to trace the outline of a tattoo on his upper arm. She leaned forward and brushed her lips against it before she looked up at him.

"See?" she asked in a soft voice. "How useful I can be . . ."

He made a noise deep in his throat and grabbed her wrist with an intensity that she hadn't expected but that she did not find unpleasant. "Show me, Amanda," he purred as he guided her toward the sofa in the back of the dressing room. He lowered her onto it and hovered just above her. "Show me just how useful you will be."

Despite the unanswered knocks at the door, they both knew this was one concert that would be starting late. For once, neither of them cared.

# Chapter Seven

The vibration of her cell phone woke her well before she was ready to abandon her sleep. She sat up and rubbed at her eyes before reaching for the phone on the nightstand. She silenced it with one quick touch of her finger and held the device to her ear. *"Ja?"*

"Amanda! You need to get up!"

She blinked and tried to focus on the digital clock on the dresser across from the bed. Six o'clock. "It's six!" she said to Charlotte in a sleepy voice.

"And your driver is coming to fetch you in thirty minutes. Chop-chop, my dear."

"Chop-chop?"

Charlotte laughed as if it were the middle of the day. "Hurry up. I'll meet you at the studio."

Studio? Amanda hung up the phone. She glanced over at Alejandro, who slept undisturbed by the short conversation. The white sheet hung over his bare arm, covering his waist but not his chest. Fighting the urge to curl up next to him and wrap her arms around his warm body was too much, so she succumbed to it. When her hands touched his flesh, she felt him shift and reach for her arm, holding it tightly against his body.

She pressed her cheek against his shoulder and, shutting her eyes, inhaled the musky scent that belonged to her husband. She felt a flutter in her stomach as she remembered the events of the previous night, from their lovemaking in the dressing room to the concert where she watched Alejandro perform for the thousands of adoring fans to the way he'd left the stage and walked directly to her, ignoring the onslaught of people wanting to take photos with him or celebrate his first night in London.

Even Enrique.

She shuddered when she remembered Enrique's reaction to seeing her backstage. He must have spied her standing in the wings, watching Alejandro singing and dancing, the glow of love still on her face. She hadn't known that he was watching her until he sidled up behind her and ran his finger along the nape of her neck.

When she jumped at his touch and spun around, Enrique had laughed. *"¡Ay, qué linda!"* he had said. She knew enough Spanish to know Alejandro would not appreciate such a comment—and spoken in such a way—to his wife. "Why am I not surprised?"

Amanda stiffened her back and responded with a short, "I don't know. Why aren't you surprised, Enrique?"

She had never been a fan of Enrique, especially after that week in Argentina. He brought out the worst in Alejandro and didn't seem to care that she was bothered by his harmful influence. Instead, he seemed to enjoy it.

He had merely chuckled at her retort and started singing something in Spanish, his eyes on her as he meandered away toward a group of English women with special badges hanging around their necks, standing behind a barrier waiting to meet him.

She had quickly forgotten about Enrique as she returned her attention to Viper, watching him dance and sing for the audience. The way he moved, each step so carefully choreographed and practiced that it became a natural extension of him, fascinated her. After all of her practice sessions with Stedman in Miami, and then dancing alongside Alejandro at some of the tour dates in South America, she still could not believe how beautifully Alejandro moved in time with the music.

And then the show was over. He performed his encore, bowing once to the crowd before the lights went black and two white pyrotechnics exploded. When the lights went back on, Viper was gone from the stage.

Amanda had waited for him, and when he appeared from behind the set, he wiped at his face and neck with a clean white towel. Handing it to a young girl standing nearby, Alejandro shrugged off anyone waiting to speak to him. Instead, he directed his attention to her and only her.

"*Ven,* Princesa,*"* he had said as he took her hand. "We have much to discuss, no?"

She accepted his hand but shook her head. "We have nothing to discuss tonight," she said in a soft voice, her eyes never leaving his. "But we have much to do."

She had heard that noise once again, a primal sound from deep within his throat. He waved away anyone who came near as he pulled her toward him, not caring if people saw him kiss her. "Then let's get started," he whispered as he kissed her neck once again.

Now, six hours later, only three during which she'd slept, Amanda felt the warmth of his bare skin against hers and wished that she could stay there, awake but holding on to him. Just to feel him near her, to listen to his breathing, to know that he was by her side. That was all that she wanted. But she had made a promise to Dali: everything and anything. With Charlotte assigned to see that promise through, Amanda knew she could not disappoint Dali again.

She started to pull away, but his hold on her tightened.

"Umm . . . ," he groaned, rolling over to pull her close to him. "Tell me it's early and we have time to sleep, Amanda."

"It's early, Alejandro, and *you* have time to sleep," she said, placing a soft kiss on his chest. She ran a finger along one of his tattoos, tracing the outline. He reached for her hand and tried to hold her tight, something that she knew would end in a battle of time: her desire to stay with him versus her commitment to whatever Dali had scheduled for her. "Oh, Alejandro," she said. "I can't. I have to go."

"Go?" He brought her hand to his mouth and brushed his lips against her fingertips. "*¿A dónde vas, mi amor?* You are in London and you are with me. You have nothing to go to."

Amanda smiled to herself, her fingers tingling from his kisses. "Dali seems to think otherwise, Alejandro."

"Dali?" He frowned and, after releasing her hand, raised his arm to his forehead. "What has Dali done now?"

Amanda stroked his arm and leaned forward, planting a soft kiss on his lips before she slid out from underneath the sheets and stood beside the bed. She stretched her arms and, once again, rubbed her eyes. "I don't rightly know, Alejandro," she admitted. "But she helped me get here, so I promised I would do what she asked. Anything and everything."

He laughed and watched her as she strolled toward the bathroom for a quick shower. "*¿Sí?* Dali made you promise that?"

She flicked on the lights in the bathroom, still amazed at the grandeur that greeted her. Marble floors and walls with chic round sinks and stainless steel faucets. The large glass shower had lights that ran along the molding and created a subtle ambiance. "*Ja*, she wasn't very happy with me, I fear." She leaned into the shower to turn on the water. Within seconds, steam clouded the mirrors.

By the time she stepped into the shower, she was hardly surprised to see Alejandro leaning against the open glass door and watching her.

"You blush, Princesa?" he asked, chuckling as she tried to cover her body. He leaned his head against the wall, his eyes never leaving hers. "After last night, you should have nothing left to blush about."

"Alejandro!"

He laughed as she threw a wet washcloth at him. "Take your shower, and I'll see about getting you some coffee. A little caffeine might help you through Dali's schedule of revenge."

The heat of the water revived her and, despite the three hours of sleep, she told herself that she could get through this day. If nothing else, the memory of being back in Alejandro's arms would be enough to keep the adrenaline coursing through her body. She'd attend to Dali's schedule, and then make her way to the arena in time for Alejandro's sound check and preshow meetings. Tomorrow was Sunday and certainly Dali had nothing scheduled for her then. She could sleep in and relax with Alejandro, perhaps even take in some of the sights in London before his evening concert.

He brought her a white mug of coffee as she dried her hair with a plush towel. "The elixir of life," he said and winked at her.

"Is that how you do it?" she asked, accepting the mug. She held it in both of her hands as she lifted it to her lips. "Umm, that's nice and strong."

"Coffee helps," he said. "I think it's mostly mind over matter, Amanda. You just decide that you are going to get through the day. Just live life large, Princesa."

She looked at him over the rim of the coffee mug. "Live life large?"

He shrugged. "That's the best you get from me at six o'clock in the morning."

She started to laugh, and he reached out for the fold of her robe. She set down the coffee mug in time so that it didn't spill. He wrapped his arms around her, one hand pushing her long, wet hair away from her face.

"You are so beautiful, Amanda," he said, his voice hoarse. "I most certainly forgot how much your beauty captivates me." He shut his eyes for a second and gave a soft groan. "*Ay*, Amanda, the one thing that will drive me through this day is knowing it will end here in this hotel suite with you in that bed. Mine. Just mine."

She lowered her eyes, worried that he would tease her again about the color that flooded her cheeks.

But he didn't. Instead, he placed a finger under her chin and tilted her head so that she had no choice but to meet his gaze. "And after tonight, Amanda, we still must talk, *sí*? There is much to discuss about our future."

"Future?" She nearly choked on the word. A wave of panic washed over her. "This is our future. Here. Now." She paused and gave him a look of determination. "Together."

He gave her a casual shrug. "*Sí*, that is what I would like to believe, Amanda. But we must consider the reality of life, not just the illusions of love."

She backed away from him. "The reality of life? Alejandro, what are you saying?"

"Later, Amanda."

He started to turn away, but she couldn't leave such a statement dangling between them. She reached out for his arm and stopped him. "Alejandro," she said in a firm voice. "Not later. Now."

He raised an eyebrow, glancing down at her hand on his arm and then into her face. *"Ay, chiquita,"* he said. "This is something new, *sí*? Defiance and willfulness. It was charming last night." He slid his arm from her grasp. "Today, I'm not so sure."

Amanda set her mouth in a firm line. "I'm not trying to be defiant or willful, Alejandro."

"You are not convincing me of that."

She almost rolled her eyes but stopped herself. The truth was that his words had startled her, and she knew that she could not survive the day with panic dwelling in the core of her heart. She needed to eliminate any doubt in his mind about their future and her resolve to stay by his side. After the initial greeting he'd given her the previous night, she could only suspect that he was building a wall to protect not just himself but also her. She was determined to break down that wall even if she had to do it one stone at a time.

"Are you telling me that you do not love me, Alejandro?"

"I would never say something that is so absolutely untrue."

"Then what are you saying? That you do not want to be with me?"

He reached for her coffee mug. "Another untruth," he said as he drank the coffee.

"Then why would you push me away?"

"*Ay*, Amanda!" He rubbed his forehead. She sensed his frustration, and while she wished she could quell it, she knew that she couldn't do it at the expense of their small family.

"Do not push me away," she said as she moved toward him. "I came here to be with you, Alejandro, because I love you. And you just said you love me, too." He did not react when she stood before him, her toes brushing against his bare feet. "So the reality of life is not an illusion of love, but it is the power of love." She stood on her tippy-toes and kissed his shoulder. "And we have that power, Alejandro," she whispered.

"¡Dios *mío!*" He pressed his chin against the top of her head as he embraced her, his body relaxing as he gently rubbed her back through the robe she wore. "Why do you have to do that?"

She allowed herself to smile, even though he could not see.

"You'll be late," he said at last, releasing her from his arms. "I'm eager to hear what Dali has in store for you today. You can surprise me with the details tonight, *sí?*"

"Over dinner?" she asked.

He considered her request and then nodded his head slowly. "*Sí*, Amanda. Over dinner. But after the concert." He picked up her coffee mug one more time, finishing most of it. "Now get dressed and make your appointments." When she turned toward the mirror, he stood there for a long moment, watching as she quickly twisted her damp hair into her signature bun. She glanced in the mirror, and when he saw her, he said, "If it is only the power of love that we need, Princesa, that is the one thing we most certainly have."

After he left the bathroom, she shut her eyes and said a silent prayer of gratitude.

With only a few minutes left to get ready, Amanda could not dwell on their conversation. But his words lingered in her mind. The fact that they were in agreement over how much they loved each other gave Amanda all the hope she needed. Surely her trip to Europe had been part of God's plan to help the two of them cross the chasm that had appeared so suddenly during the South American tour.

If Amanda had suspected it the previous day, after today, she needed no further proof that Charlotte was a bundle of never-ending energy. She guided Amanda through the day, shuttling her from one appointment to the next. Everything ran smoothly, from the waiting coffee at the first appointment to the chilled bottled of Voss water at the second.

It occurred to Amanda that Charlotte's connection to Dali ran deeper than she suspected. She wondered how Charlotte had dropped everything so quickly to accommodate Amanda's last-minute trip to London and how Dali had scheduled so many interviews on such short notice.

"How did Dali make all these appointments so quickly?" she asked Charlotte as they rode from the second appointment, a television interview, to her third appointment, lunch with an advertising company. It was something that Amanda had wondered the previous day but hadn't thought to ask Charlotte. Now that she felt a little more comfortable with the woman, she did not hesitate.

Charlotte glanced up from her cell phone, a puzzled expression on her face. "You aren't serious, are you?"

Charlotte's response surprised Amanda. She had thought her question had been straightforward and simple. "Why, *ja*, I am serious."

When Charlotte started laughing, Amanda felt her patience wearing thin.

"I'm sorry," Charlotte said, stopping herself before Amanda could say anything. "I wouldn't have believed it!"

"Believed what?"

"Oh, Amanda," Charlotte said, leaning toward her. "Dali had only to lift the phone to call me, and I had people lining up to meet with you."

"*You* made these appointments?" That thought hadn't crossed her mind. And then it dawned on Amanda that Dali was no longer her personal assistant. She wasn't being paid to help her—something that she intended to correct as soon as she could. However, there was a new twist to the story. She realized Charlotte was not just a personal guide for her during their short time in London.

"I did indeed." Charlotte leaned back and dug through her handbag to retrieve some lip gloss. She motioned toward Amanda to do the same. "We're almost there."

"Why would you go to so much trouble?"

This time, Charlotte did not laugh. "Amanda, arranging these meetings helps my professional career. My credibility just skyrocketed. Now, the people I'm introducing you to over lunch are different. They're not interested in interviewing you. They're interested in hiring you."

"Hiring me?" The idea seemed farcical to her. "Whatever for?"

Her question was met with silence. Charlotte stared at her, a stunned expression on her face. "You really don't know, do you?"

"Charlotte!" Amanda's patience had come to the end. "Please. Explain to me what it is that I am supposed to know!"

"You're a *brand*, Amanda. That means you have a voice and that voice is worth money. A lot of money." Her eyes flashed as she spoke. "That's what these people want. They want to hire your voice."

Amanda frowned. "My voice? To do what?"

"Over the past six months," Charlotte said, with an edge to her voice that indicated her own patience was wearing thin, "you've become the one woman that companies want to hire to promote their products, endorse their companies, adorn their magazine covers. You want to know what you're doing here? This is only the beginning. I have you scheduled for meetings in Paris, Zürich, Bern, even Stockholm."

Stunned, Amanda blinked and felt the color drain from her cheeks. "I don't even know where those places are!"

"That's why I'm with you."

"You're traveling with me?"

This time, Charlotte rolled her eyes. "Amanda, I'm your publicist. Who do you think was arranging meetings for you? Those interviews? That was just the tip of the iceberg, my dear. We were testing the waters before we went full swing. Now the fun begins and Amanda Diaz can be heard, not just as the wife of an international pop star but as an individual in her own right and with her own voice. Based on the response from investors and organizations, I wouldn't be surprised to see you pulling in eight figures over the next fiscal year." She glanced out the front window and leaned forward to give instructions to the driver. "Over here. This is fine."

The driver pulled over, and without missing a beat, Charlotte exited the car, holding the door open for Amanda. She could barely force herself out of the car; her mind was still reeling with the information that Charlotte had just shared with her. She had overheard enough conversations between Alejandro and Geoffrey discussing revenue to understand what eight figures meant. What she couldn't understand was why. Why would anyone want to pay her that much money to talk about a product?

As she followed Charlotte into the restaurant, several people recognized her and quickly withdrew their phones to snap her picture. One young woman ran up to her and, in a nervous voice, asked if Amanda might take a photo with her. Forcing a smile, Amanda nodded her head and stood next to her while she held out her cell phone to take the picture.

Charlotte stood at the door, impatiently waiting. She tapped her foot and glanced at her phone to check the time. "Come now, Amanda," she said. "We have a tight schedule."

The other young women surrounding her requested the same photo, and Amanda ignored Charlotte and stood beside the women, smiling for their pictures. When the group was satisfied, Amanda hurried to join Charlotte.

"Dali warned me about that," Charlotte said in a terse tone. "We'll let it slide this time, but let's not make a habit of that."

"I don't understand something," Amanda said as Charlotte led her to the front of the restaurant, where a man in a black suit immediately escorted them toward a table of three women already seated. "If my brand is worth so much, doesn't that mean it's because of the fans?"

"What's your point, Amanda?"

"*Ja, vell*, if this brand that you keep talking about is because of the fans, mayhaps I should not stop interacting with them? Maybe that's what makes the fans like the brand."

Charlotte stopped walking and turned to look at her. Behind Charlotte's shoulder, Amanda could see the three women at the table standing, waiting expectantly and most likely wondering why their guests had stopped.

"I'm your publicist, Amanda, and I will help build this brand, linking you to the best of the best. But I can't have you questioning me. Is that clear?"

Amanda thought for a moment and, just as Charlotte started to turn, apparently considering the conversation over, said, "*Nee*, I won't agree to that. If someone wants to take a photo with me, if that makes them happy and I can do it, I will do it."

Charlotte's mouth opened, clearly surprised at Amanda's refusal to comply with her request.

Amanda managed to smile in the direction of the women waiting for them at the table, even as she lowered her voice and said, "That is, I reckon, my brand. Wouldn't you agree? Accessibility to the public."

Then, without another word to Charlotte, Amanda walked around her publicist and headed to the table where the oldest of the three women greeted her, introducing her to the other two ladies and then inviting her to sit down. As Amanda did, her hands folded in her lap, Charlotte joined them, a warm smile on her face and her professional demeanor restored. Amanda let Charlotte run the rest of the meeting, listening to their discussion and nodding her head when needed, absorbing everything so that she could ask Alejandro to explain it to her later. But in the back of her mind she realized she had learned an important lesson over the past twenty-four hours: with power came options.

Like Alejandro had told her many times, advice would come to her from many directions. Clearly, this Charlotte woman had her own interests in mind, and not necessarily Amanda's. While Amanda didn't quite understand who Charlotte—or Dali, for that matter—was working for, she did understand she needed to adopt a critical eye in evaluating what she was being told and what she accepted as truth.

Alejandro sat in the back of the hotel restaurant, his team assembled and occupying three tables. Geoffrey sat across from Alejandro with several manila folders in front of him. As Geoffrey shuffled through the papers, Alejandro drummed his fingers against the side of the table.

"Why is it that Europeans don't drink water?" he asked, looking around the room for the waitress.

Geoffrey glanced over at the next table and motioned to one of the men, who immediately stood up to get Alejandro more water.

"I want you to look at these companies," Geoffrey said. "This one is from Japan."

Alejandro took the papers that Geoffrey handed to him and glanced through them. He studied a diagram and frowned, clearly unimpressed. "These numbers are going in the wrong direction," he said. "I don't want to endorse a company that is foundering. I'm not here to save companies, but to make money. That means we align with winners, not losers." He tossed the papers back at Geoffrey. "Next?"

"You might want to reconsider," Geoffrey said. "There are whispers of a merger."

Bored, Alejandro shook his head. "Next?"

Geoffrey sighed and retrieved the next file. "Energy drink company. They want to meet up with you in Las Vegas. I can schedule that meeting to coincide with your weeklong stint in September, but they'd like to move ahead sooner."

Alejandro rolled his eyes. "Energy drinks are cliché."

"Hey, they've doubled in revenue in just four years. An alliance would help them break into the Latino market and help you cross over into mainstream."

"I'm already in the mainstream. What about that technology company?" Alejandro said, snapping his fingers as he tried to remember its name. "Unidad Tech?" The waitress came over and placed a pitcher of ice water on the table. Without saying anything, he reached for it and refilled his glass. "That's got potential to hit the Latino market. It's a no-brainer, *sí*? The name alone signifies unity among Latinos."

Geoffrey made some notes on a document and set it aside. "I'll look into it."

"What's next?"

"Paperwork," Geoffrey said. "The lawyers sent me the contracts for the award ceremony, as well as the Christmas concert tour. Everything is finalized. Just sign where they have Post-it notes." He handed the file to Alejandro and slid a pen across the table, watching patiently as Alejandro glanced through the documents and, satisfied, scribbled his name where indicated.

When he was finished, Alejandro looked at one of the men seated at the other table and motioned for him. Immediately, the man joined them, taking the chair next to Geoffrey.

"What did you arrange with Celinda?"

The man sat up straighter in the chair and cleared his throat. "Willing to fly into Paris, Stockholm, and Zürich. The other dates present a conflict."

Alejandro looked over at Geoffrey. "What do you think? Will that work?"

"We can make it work."

For the first time during their meeting, Alejandro smiled. "That's the attitude! Make it work." He leaned back and eyeballed his tour manager, who sat at another table. "You hear that, *papo?*"

"*Sí, sí,*" Eddie said casually, not intimidated by Alejandro's mocking reprimand.

Returning his attention to Geoffrey, Alejandro nodded his head. "That's short notice for Celinda to get to Paris," he said. "Two weeks?"

"Two weeks."

"*¡Ay!*" He drank from his glass. "Arrange some free time with her and Amanda, *sí?*"

Geoffrey gave him an askew glance. "Does that mean that she'll be traveling for the rest of the tour?"

Alejandro looked at his phone, ignoring Geoffrey's question. "It's almost three. I have things to do. The car is coming at four thirty, *sí?*" He stood up and glanced around the quiet restaurant. Other than his entourage of staff and security, there were only two tables occupied.

"And arrange something for tomorrow, some tour or something that I can take Amanda to see. Just the two of us," he said as he started to walk away. He nodded at the waitress and exited the restaurant. He needed some time alone, time to plan his late-night dinner with Amanda and time to think about everything that had happened in the past twenty-four hours.

What a difference a day made.

# Chapter Eight

He held her elbow and guided her down the sidewalk to the door of the tall building. A doorman dressed in a gray overcoat and wearing a black cap welcomed them. He pulled open the door and gestured for them to step into the lobby. Amanda walked ahead of Alejandro through the doorway and then paused, taking a moment to look around until he caught up to her.

A large aquarium with colorful tropical fish caught her attention. She wandered over to it, gazing at the fish that swam back and forth, some larger than others but each individually magnificent. It was almost three stories high and made of glass so that the outdoor lighting helped illuminate it.

"Beautiful, *sí?*" Alejandro stood next to her for a minute, his hand around her waist.

"I've never seen such a thing!" she gasped. "It's breathtaking."

His grip tightened, and as he started to move, she accompanied him. "The night is young, Princesa. There are many breathtaking things to see."

They walked across the brown marble floor to the escalators, which took them to the mezzanine.

"This is a fairly new building," Alejandro explained. "I believe just four or five years old."

"It reminds me of New York."

He smiled. "*Sí*, that it does."

The elevators were at the top of the escalator.

"Have you been here before?" she asked as they waited for the elevator doors to open.

He shook his head. "I wanted to experience something new with you."

And new it was.

The elevator rose quickly up the forty floors to reach the top of the building. Amanda gasped when she realized that they were riding on the outside of the building in an elevator made of glass. She stepped backward into Alejandro, steadying herself by grabbing his arm.

She felt queasy as it rose and hid her face against his shoulder, a gesture that made him laugh.

"You are afraid of heights?"

"Oh! I can't even look!"

He teased her by putting his arms on her shoulders and turning her around so that she had no choice but to look outside. Still, he held her with her back against his chest and his arms protectively wrapped around her. "It's beautiful, *sí*? The lights of London. Even at this hour, the city breathes life."

She tried to shut her eyes, but found that she couldn't. Her curiosity was too great to miss such an amazing, if terrifying, experience.

When the elevator finally stopped and the doors opened, she almost didn't want to step into the restaurant. He waited patiently for her, his hand holding the door so that it didn't shut prematurely.

If she had been impressed by the aquarium in the lobby and the glass-walled elevator, the restaurant outshone both of them.

Located at the top of the Heron Tower, the entire floor was made of windows, allowing an almost undisturbed 360-degree view of the city. With the lights of the city beneath them, the view was as magnificent as any other that she had seen.

"Good evening, Mr. Diaz," a man greeted him. "Mrs. Diaz. We have your table waiting for you. The best view of the city for a very special couple. Follow me, please."

Amanda glanced at Alejandro as he winked at her, motioning with his head that she should follow the man.

Their table faced the windows, the semicircular booth permitting both of them to enjoy the view. Amanda slid in first and made room for Alejandro. When he sat next to her, he rested his one hand on the table and the other on her knee. Several of the patrons at the other tables glanced in their direction, and Amanda saw the distinct and now so familiar motion of someone trying to capture their photo.

"I've already selected our menu," Alejandro said, either oblivious to or ignoring the stir that their appearance caused in the restaurant. "You do not mind?"

She shook her head, letting her gaze wander to the window.

"You had a busy day?"

She nodded and returned her gaze to the even more breathtaking view: her husband. "I did, *ja*. I did not realize that Charlotte is an employee. A publicist." When he didn't respond, she continued. "And I was under the impression Dali no longer worked for you. I don't quite understand."

Alejandro lifted an eyebrow when he looked at her. "Dali might no longer be *your* personal assistant, Amanda, a situation we can discuss changing, but she certainly still works for me."

His words surprised her. "But . . . ?"

"You look so confused," he said with a soft laugh. "You thought I fired her when you disappeared, *sí*?" He shook his head. "*Ay*, Princesa, a better assistant never existed! I merely reassigned her to work on another project."

Project, she thought, the word tasting cold and unwelcoming. Was that what he thought she was? A project? She wanted to comment but kept her thoughts to herself. The last thing she wanted to do was start an argument when things seemed to be going so well.

The waiter returned to the table, carrying a silver tray that held a bottle and two glasses. Without interrupting them, he quietly set two tall flutes on the table, and after uncorking the champagne, he poured some into each glass. The bubbles rose to the top of the golden liquid, and despite her aversion to alcohol, she lifted her glass when Alejandro held his out to tap against hers.

"*Salud, mi amor.*" He sipped the champagne and shut his eyes for a moment, enjoying the taste. "*¡Qué refresco!*"

Curiosity got the best of her, so she tasted it. It was dry and fruity with a lightness that wasn't entirely unpleasant.

"Now, Princesa," Alejandro said. "Tell me, as I have yet to ask, how is Isadora doing?"

It dawned on Amanda that she, too, had easily slipped back into her role with Alejandro and without Isadora. She felt guilty that she hadn't spoken to Isadora more frequently, but it was hard to connect with her family. Whenever Amanda called, no one answered, and despite her numerous voice messages, she had received only one return phone call from Anna. Her anticipation of a phone call reminded her of the weeks that had passed as she stared at that cell phone, wishing and praying that Alejandro would call. Now she wished and prayed for the same thing, but from Anna and Isadora.

"Isadora seems fine, Alejandro, and adjusting well," Amanda answered him. "At least that's what Anna told me the last time I spoke to her. But I have not called the farm today."

"She's in good hands with your family. I would not worry." He paused and took another sip of his champagne. "Now, what is your plan, Amanda, in regard to Isadora?"

"I should think we'd discuss that together," she replied a little too quickly. She softened her tone with a smile.

He seemed to consider what she had said, undecided whether she was being sincere or sharp with him. Apparently, he settled for sincere. "*Sí*, we should discuss this together. I would, however, ask that you update me on her. You are closer to the child than I."

She couldn't argue with his comment. So, after a moment's hesitation to collect her thoughts, she began to eagerly share with him all that she could about Isadora: her grasp of the English language, her joy at living on the farm, and her love for Anna and Lizzie. At one point, Amanda found herself gushing as she spoke, laughing as she told him how Izzie liked to squirt milk into the mouths of the cats and how she had a particular fondness for the small orange kitten.

He listened to her, nodding his head as she spoke. But Amanda got the distinct feeling that her stories about his daughter were not stirring him in the same way that they moved her.

"I'm hearing that you feel the farm is a good environment for her," he said when she finally finished. He'd picked at his appetizer while she was talking. "That is true, *sí*?"

"I . . ." Amanda swallowed as she looked at Alejandro. "I don't know what is good for her, Alejandro," she admitted slowly. "Is it better for her to be with us or on the farm? Is it better for her if I stayed on the farm without you? Is it better for her to travel with us and have a person tend to her?" Amanda felt overwhelmed at the thought that one decision could change the outcome of her marriage and Izzie's future. "This is not a decision that I can make. She is, after all, your daughter."

Her answer seemed to catch him off guard. "Our daughter," he replied as he pushed his appetizer plate away although he had not finished eating it. Wiping at his mouth with the white linen napkin, he glanced at the waiter and pointed to his drink, indicating he wanted another. "I think we need time before deciding anything, *sí*? At least as far as it pertains to Isadora. Right now, I think we can agree that the farm is the best place for her—we know that she's in a safe and protected environment."

Slowly, Amanda nodded her head. It hurt for Amanda to admit it, but she knew that Alejandro was right: the farm was the best place for their child. Pulling Isadora from the farm would set back the five-year-old, especially if doing so meant constant traveling and living in hotels. No, having Isadora on the road with them was not an option. And, as Amanda had already told Alejandro, she would not leave him again.

"Now, about you," he said. "Where is your safe and protected environment, Princesa?"

It was the very question she had been pondering for the past three weeks since he'd left her at the farm.

Oh, how she wished she could have it all: a home, Isadora, and Alejandro. But with his dedication to his career, something he had warned her about long before they married, she knew that if she wanted Alejandro, travel was part of the package. Settling down into a quiet life similar to the one in which she had been raised was impossible. She thought of a sentiment from Ecclesiastes that her mother had often quoted: *with much wisdom came great disappointment.* How true, Amanda told herself. The more she learned of the Englische world, the more she found herself straddling the fence between two very different pastures: one had hay and the other grain, but neither had both.

She took a deep breath and raised her eyes to look at him. "With you, Alejandro. My safe and protected place is with you."

He considered her response, his fingers pressed together and slightly covering his mouth. "Then those are two of the things we can agree on this evening, *sí?*" he finally said.

"Are there more?" she asked.

Once again, he took his time responding. His eyes never left hers; his silence began to unnerve her. After several seconds, she glanced at a nearby table, worried that people were paying attention to their conversation. No one seemed to notice them. Without people staring at them or taking their photos, Amanda finally felt as if they were a regular couple. She looked back at Alejandro as he drummed his fingers on the white linen tablecloth, still contemplating her. Finally, one eyebrow lifting just slightly in that alluring way of his, Alejandro said, "The media has been insinuating things, Amanda, photos and stories about you and Harvey," he said without any hesitation or even a blink of his blue eyes. "I need to know if there is any truth to the speculation."

She gasped, taken aback by his statement. "Alejandro! That's ridiculous!"

He remained silent as he continued studying her reaction.

"You of all people know the media!" she chastised, her heart beating rapidly at the shock of her husband questioning her loyalty to her marriage vows. "You yourself have been the victim of their fabricated and deceiving stories!"

Alejandro held up his hand for her to calm herself. "All things considered, I'm of the same mindset, Amanda."

She waited for him to finish saying what was on his mind. All too well she remembered how the bishop had visited the farm, delivering those horrid tabloid stories and photos. As if that had not been humiliating enough, to think that people thought she might have been intimate with Harvey made it even worse! People's willingness to believe the worst in others made Amanda question the civility left in the world, even among the Amish.

"But it did make me question whether or not your true happiness remains in Lititz. Perhaps with another man," Alejandro said.

"Oh, Alejandro!" She couldn't contain herself. Leaning forward, she touched his arm. She could feel his muscles through the soft fabric of his black shirt. "How can you say such a thing?" She lowered her voice. "After last night? In your dressing room? In the hotel?" Forcing herself to remain calm, she managed to smile as she lowered her eyelids. She knew she needed to remain calm. To show her irritation that he could even hint at such a thing would not go over well with Alejandro. "There is no one who could show me happiness like that, Alejandro."

She felt his muscles twitch under her hand.

"And there are other things to consider," she continued.

He raised an eyebrow. "*¿Sí?* What other things?"

She ran her finger along the bottom of her champagne glass. "All of these interviews and meetings . . . well, I have a lot to learn and mayhaps there are ways I can help you." She pursed her lips and lifted the champagne glass to her mouth, pausing to look at him over the rim of the glass. "But I would need your guidance, Alejandro."

"*Claro.*"

What she left unsaid was her thoughts about her lunch meeting. The three women were executives at a major advertising company. They represented companies that made products ranging from cosmetics to technology. Amanda had listened to them talk, understanding only half of what they said, committing to nothing. The one thing she did understand, however, was that the public's fascination with her and Alejandro's relationship was transforming into something else— something bigger. She didn't fully understand what, exactly, but she suspected that it had something to do with Dali's cryptic comment about publicity saving their marriage.

Regardless of her thoughts about that meeting, the public, or Dali's comment, Amanda felt confident, at least for the moment, that Alejandro would not send her back to the farm out of fear that he was doing her more harm than good. She wasn't certain when she had first begun realizing that Alejandro felt the most comfortable when he was in control. Perhaps it was when he left her in Lititz. Or perhaps it went as far back as when she left him in South America. He had lost control, even if only for a few weeks. In order to regain it, he had left. Somewhere between the bishop's visit and when she found herself in his arms on the sofa of his dressing room, Amanda had realized the importance of ensuring that Alejandro felt secure in his role as head of their family.

In many ways, it was no different from her parents' relationship. Her father had always had the ultimate authority on the farm. Her mother deferred to Elias in all decisions. However, now that she was older, Amanda realized that her mother often guided her father to make the decisions she felt were the most appropriate. While Amanda now recognized the sacrifices her mother had to make in order to make room for Elias's authority, the reward had been a long and happy marriage. Amanda would happily make the same sacrifices to obtain that same reward.

Her thoughts were interrupted when she felt Alejandro take her hand and raise it to his lips. The soft pressure of his lips against the back of her hand as his blue eyes stared into hers provoked a shiver throughout her body. He let his lips linger just above her skin, never once removing his eyes from hers.

"I . . ." She could barely speak, the intensity of his gaze distracting her thoughts.

"*¿Qué, Princesa?*" he breathed.

"I . . . I could just stay like this for the rest of my life," she gushed in a whisper. Immediately, she felt the awkwardness of her words. Would he understand what she meant? What she felt? "It's just that . . ." She paused, swallowing, as his gaze never wavered. "*Ja, vell* . . . having you gaze at me . . . with your eyes looking at me like that . . ." She bit her lower lip and felt a tightness in her chest. Everything inside her felt on fire, as if sparks of energy and life coursed through her veins. "If I could only feel this moment again and again, I would be just fine, Alejandro."

In one fluid movement, he released her hand so that he could reach out and brush his fingertips across her cheek, trailing them gently down her neck and then her back. He pulled her closer and bent forward to kiss her. It was a tender kiss that lingered longer in her mind than on her lips. When he pulled back, still holding her close to him, the corner of his mouth lifted in a half smile. His fingers pressed into the small of her back, and she felt her back arch, just a little, at his touch.

"*Qué rica,*" he purred.

She tilted her head and gave him a coy smile. "I hear you say that to your fans, Alejandro," she quipped. "Tell me how you mean it differently when you say it to me."

She watched as he caught his breath at her words. His spine stiffened and she felt him struggle to respond. He was uncomfortable, but not in a bad way. She realized, perhaps for the first time, the magnitude of the power she held over him, even if she didn't fully understand that power. To be truthful, she had only wanted his love. Now, however, she recognized the fact that his love for her truly gave her a power, one that she knew better than to trifle with.

"You are so beautiful, Amanda," he said at last. "Inside and out. What a rare treasure you are. You give love on so many different levels, while most people only consider one: themselves." He reached for his drink and took a long, slow sip. "I asked you where your safe and protected home is. You never asked me."

Amanda gave him an innocent look. "Where is it?"

Alejandro shut his eyes and inhaled, his chest rising as he did so. "With you. Only with you."

She tried to hide her smile.

A noise escaped his throat. When he opened his eyes, for once, he looked away from her. Scanning the room as he spoke, his voice sounded hoarse and emotional. "When you are not with me, I feel as though the world is ending, that I live second to second. When you are with me, the world disappears and I find that I can finally live again." His fingers tapped the side of his glass in the rapid-fire motion Amanda knew meant he was anxious. "I cannot breathe when you are not with me, Amanda. Leaving you in Lancaster was the hardest thing that I've ever done . . . perhaps second only to allowing myself to love you."

"Allowing yourself?" she repeated, uncertain what he meant.

"*Sí*, Amanda." He returned his full attention to her. "I have changed since I met you. My life is no longer all about the music. Music has always been my life, the one thing that kept me grounded. Now I have something I just might love more than that: you." Once again, he lifted his glass, but this time, he did not drink from it. "The question is whether my love for you will keep me grounded or rip my roots from the very ground in which they are planted."

It was her turn to look away. A young woman at a table nearby caught her eye and Amanda gave a discreet smile, immediately noticing how the woman's facial expression changed from curiosity to delight.

"I reckon that's a choice for you to make," she said nonchalantly to Alejandro. "There is nothing that I would do purposefully to unground you."

"Of that, I am aware," he said.

"Mayhaps you need to remember that when you feel as though your roots are being ripped." She turned her head and faced him. "Mayhaps you need to trust more in your faith, Alejandro. God should come first," she said. "He will help you stay grounded."

Their conversation was interrupted when two servers approached their table to set down their plates of food. The waiter returned and assessed the dishes before nodding to the other two servers to be excused. "Everything is as it should be," he declared. "May I fetch you another drink?"

Alejandro shook his head and waved his hand once over the top of his glass.

"Bon appétit," the waiter said and backed away from the table, giving them their privacy once again.

For a few minutes, they ate in silence. Amanda wondered if she had offended Alejandro with her comment about God. While he had been raised Catholic and his mother seemed religious, she knew that he was very private about it. He rarely spoke about God or his feelings toward religion. With the exception of his telling her about Saint

Barbara when he'd first stayed at the farm, he usually avoided discussions that involved faith and God. He'd even reacted negatively to the influence of the Amish religion on Isadora when he'd joined her at the farm after South America. She wondered if her comment crossed an unspoken line.

"Alejandro? I'm sorry if I spoke out of line."

He set down his fork and wiped his mouth with the linen napkin. Only when he placed it back on his lap did he speak. "You did not, Amanda." He leaned back in the booth and studied her for a minute. "You spoke from your heart, and I appreciate that. I keep my religion close to my heart, not my tongue."

"Why is that?" she asked, genuinely curious. It was a discussion they'd never had before.

"You don't understand, Amanda," he said, his voice tinged with a touch of irritation. "My life has not been easy. When I was younger and we struggled just to eat, my mother, she prayed every morning and night. But I didn't see where God was helping us. Fighting for survival without help from the Church or community . . . it made me wonder where her God was. Why wasn't he taking care of us?"

"Oh, Alejandro . . ."

He held up his hand, thwarting her rebuttal to his words. "I fought just to stay alive, Amanda. I fought to sing in clubs, fought because I sang in clubs, fought to get ahead, and I still fight to stay ahead. Everything that I did and that I have today? It is because of me, not God. I have learned how to be grounded and focused because of me."

She caught her breath. "Are you saying you don't . . ." She couldn't even finish the sentence.

"Believe in God? No, no, that is not what I'm saying," Alejandro said quickly. "It has taken a lot for me to keep my faith in God. But today I realize that it was the struggles I faced that made me the man I am today. Whether or not I felt God was there, he did not abandon me." He paused at the word *abandon*, and she wondered if he thought of Isadora. "But I do not have faith the struggle is over. If anything, he tested me to see if I could do it, *sí?* And I do not know if that test is over." He paused, looking at her. "When you left me in Argentina, I knew that God was testing me once again. When I came back to Lititz for you, I saw you on the farm, so happy and full of life. I thought God was testing me, but I did not have the faith in myself, never mind God. I thought you would be better there. With your family and with your God."

She shook her head, unable to respond to his confession.

"I saw Isadora and how she thrived under your care and in that environment. That was not something I could provide either of you. I left for your own good, not mine, Amanda." He took a deep breath and exhaled. "I figured this was just one more obstacle thrown in my path."

"How could you think such a thing? That we'd be better off with my family?"

He shrugged. "When your life is based on clawing your way to the top, you experience a lot of collateral damage along the way. My broken heart would be just one more thing in a long line of self-destruction. I always told myself to guard it, my heart. You broke through that barrier, and I figured this was the consequence."

Amanda reached across the table and took his hand in hers. "Please, Alejandro, you must know that God has wonderful plans for you. He would never harm you."

A small laugh escaped his lips. "Ah, *sí,* Jeremiah 29:11. I know that verse well."

"And do you believe it?"

Alejandro tilted his head, watching her with his blue eyes. "I didn't, but I do now."

"What changed your mind, Alejandro?"

The corner of his mouth lifted, just a touch of a smile. "When I heard you were in London, Amanda. That is when I realized that his faith in me was stronger than my faith in him. I just need to believe more. Harder." He raised her hand to his mouth, staring at her over the top of her hand. "And I will, as long as you are by my side, Amanda. You make me want to believe." He pressed his lips against her skin.

She lowered her eyes to hide the welling up of tears that threatened to fall down her cheeks. Too many people were watching them, and she knew that if she cried, whether they were tears of joy or pain, it would make its way to the media. For once, she wanted to enjoy this moment without the world speculating about its meaning. There were some things she wanted to keep to herself. The words Alejandro had just spoken to her and the way he had just made her feel were two of them.

# Chapter Nine

Standing in the center of the courtyard, Amanda turned in a slow circle, staring at the amazing buildings that surrounded her. Many of the thick stone walls were covered with moss, especially those on the north side, near the tall corner tower. From her vantage point in the center of the courtyard, she could see the buildings that jutted out from the eastern wall. She had never before seen such beautiful buildings. In fact, she never paid much attention to architecture. In Lancaster, farmhouses were just that: houses. Simple in their design, the focus was on the kitchen, which was always large enough for the family to be together. But the residential buildings of Warwick Castle were designed to impress people through the ostentatious display of wealth. With tall windows and exquisite detail to moldings and pillars and ironwork, the castle's living quarters were like nothing Amanda had ever imagined.

"It's magnificent," she said.

Alejandro put his hand on her waist and guided her toward the Great Hall entrance. "You are finally where you belong, no?"

She glanced at him, confused by his question.

He laughed at her expression. "A princess inside a castle!"

The joy in his voice made her laugh with him. "I hadn't thought of that," she said, letting him hold her arm as they walked through an archway and entered the building.

Once inside, Amanda stopped and caught her breath. She took in the brown-and-cream marble floor, the high vaulted ceilings, and the arched doors at the far end. Over the doors hung the large horns of an animal and an arch made of long wooden poles, each with a pointed tip at the end.

"What are those?" she whispered to Alejandro.

"Lances," he answered. "Weapons used in war, Princesa."

She shuddered at the thought.

Along the walls were displays of armor. As she walked along the cordoned-off section, she studied each piece as if to memorize them. The shiny metal looked hot and heavy to her. She couldn't imagine people wearing the armor, let alone fighting in it.

"Such a sad thing, war," she said when she stopped in front of the smallest suit of armor. It was clearly made to fit a child.

Alejandro shrugged. "Without war, there can be no peace."

"I don't believe that," she retorted.

He squeezed her waist, just a little, and smiled. "You are the great optimist, *sí?*"

She made a face at him.

"Think, Amanda," he said as they continued walking. "Has there ever been a time when people were not fighting? Even in the Bible there are wars, some of them sanctioned by God, no?" He pointed to some weapons on the wall. "Wherever there is peace, there will always be someone who desires to take it away."

"Why?"

Again, he shrugged. "They don't agree with it. They want to be in charge. They believe something different. There are many reasons, Princesa."

He took her elbow in his hand, guiding her through another doorway. Several people noticed them, a few taking quick photos with their phones. A group of Americans came right up to ask if they might take a photo. Before Alejandro could decline the request, Amanda smiled and stood in the middle of the group, leaving space for Alejandro to join them. She could tell from the stiffness of his smile that he was unhappy at the disruption during their private time.

No sooner had the first group thanked them than another crowd moved closer with the same request. Amanda continued to smile, demonstrating her willingness to pose with the fans even though she knew she'd get an earful later.

"That's enough now," Alejandro said when two more groups approached. "I'm trying to enjoy the day with my lovely wife."

Amanda reached for his hand and entwined her fingers with his. She looked up at him, a smile on her lips. "One more for these people," she said in a quiet voice. "They'd be so disappointed."

He groaned and rolled his eyes. "For you, Princesa," he said.

Five minutes and four more photographs later, Alejandro put his foot down. Taking her hand, he led her along the rest of the tour.

"You shouldn't encourage it," he warned her. "Not in public, Amanda."

"Why ever not?" She frowned. "Everyone keeps telling me that, but I don't understand why."

He glanced over his shoulder to make certain that they weren't being followed. "Remember Lititz? When you had the broken leg? Remember how the mob materialized so quickly?"

She swallowed and nodded her head. How could she forget being shoved to the side and falling to the ground as the crowd surrounded Alejandro? "*Ja*, I do."

"You grant one photo to this person, and then ten more show up. You feel guilty, you pose with those ten people, and then twenty more show up. At what point do you stop, Amanda? If you do not, you eventually put yourself at risk."

He stopped in front of a massive painting on the wall, admiring the piece of art. "Look at this painting, *mi amor.*"

Standing beside him, she peered at the painting of a man on a large white horse riding through an arched doorway. On foot was a man draped in a red cape who seemed to greet him, while on the other side of the painting, tucked into the shadows, was a crown fit only for a king.

"It's almost as magnificent as this room," she said. "Such attention to detail, don't you think? Painting is truly a God-given talent, I think."

Alejandro smiled at her comment. He reached for her hand and tucked it into the crook of his arm as he guided her through the room. "This was the State Dining Room," he said. "Such beautiful woodwork on the ceiling, *sí?*" He pointed upward and she followed his gaze. The ceiling was covered in an intricate design of moldings painted in gold. She had never seen something so ornately beautiful.

"People lived like this while so many suffered from hunger?"

"It happens today, too, Amanda," he replied slowly. "Look at us. We are not living in poverty, *mi amor.*"

She stared at him, horrified. "I had not thought of it that way!"

Prior to meeting Alejandro, she'd had limited exposure to the Englische, although she'd understood from the beginning that Alejandro lived an atypical lifestyle. Yet she had not given it much thought. The condominium in Miami was beautiful, as was the apartment in Los Angeles. But she had nothing to compare it to. She had no sense of how their lifestyle compared to others, although she knew it was not reflective of the average Englische household.

"I see your wheels turning," he said in a lighthearted tone. "I give plenty to charity, Amanda, especially in the Latino communities. Relax."

They wandered through the rest of the living quarters and state-rooms, pausing several times to admire paintings and statues. In one room, Alejandro pointed out three portraits. One was of a robust man wearing a flat-top hat. His face appeared bloated to Amanda, and she wasn't particularly impressed with him from a physical perspective. When she learned he'd been the king of England, she could hardly believe it.

"And this was his second wife." Alejandro pointed to another portrait. "Anne Boleyn. After a few years, he had her beheaded."

"Be-what?"

Alejandro's mouth quivered as he tried not to laugh. "Beheaded."

"You mean . . . ?" She couldn't even finish the sentence. "Oh help! How awful!"

"She must have been a very bad wife, *sí*?" he teased as she playfully slapped at his arm.

"You know a lot about this place," she said as they kept moving through the castle.

He stopped in front of a window and stared outside at the gardens. "I like history," he said. "Particularly European history during the medieval times."

This was something new that Amanda was learning about her husband. She stood next to him on her tippy-toes, leaning her chin on his shoulder. From where they stood, she could see outside the windows onto the expansive gardens. Everything was neatly manicured and meticulously maintained. "How beautiful," she whispered.

"Makes you think of your parents' farm, *sí*?"

"I wonder if Lizzie is outside right now," she said with a sigh. "Maybe she's helping Anna with the garden."

"I thought you'd say that," he said, turning his head to press his lips against her cheek. "When we fly back to New York for that gala, I'll arrange a visit."

"Oh, Alejandro!" Amanda put her arms around his waist and hugged him. He had told her about the art gala in New York City, the one that they had been invited to by the vice president of a movie studio. But she had never imagined that Alejandro would offer to make a short stop to visit Isadora. "That would be *wunderbar!*"

"Just know, Princesa, it will be a very short visit. While you are excited now, leaving after such a short visit can be more painful than no visit at all," he warned her. "No tears or feelings of guilt, *sí?*"

She nodded her head in agreement, although she suspected that, when they had to leave Isadora behind once again, no amount of preparation on his part would stop her from crying and feeling guilt.

They strolled down a circular staircase and exited the castle. Alejandro walked beside Amanda as they headed toward the gardens. Unlike the gardens that Amanda grew, these gardens were all flowers, not vegetables. Different areas were dedicated to one particular type of flower, often separated by pebble-strewn walkways with benches and fountains.

Alejandro sat down on a bench, and Amanda cozied up next to him.

"It is so beautiful here," she gushed. "I never knew places like this existed!"

He smiled and tucked her hand into the crook of his arm. "The world's an amazing place, Princesa. You have yet to see Africa or Asia or even Israel."

She gasped. "Israel! Have you been there, then?"

He nodded. "And so will you. We have a concert in Tel Aviv in the fall."

"Oh, Alejandro! Will we . . . ?" She paused, not wanting to ask anything of him.

But he read her mind. "You wish to see Jerusalem, *sí?*" When she nodded with a sheepish look on her face, he laughed. "But of course, Princesa. How could I possibly take you to Tel Aviv and not spend time exploring that magnificent country?"

The moment of excitement passed as Amanda realized that if they were traveling to Israel, there would be other countries on the schedule. That meant another season of constant travel. "Where else are you scheduled to perform this autumn?" she asked, apprehensive about his answer.

"Singapore, Tokyo, Shanghai, and then down to Australia for two weeks." When she didn't respond right away, he leaned over and pressed his arm against hers. *"¿Qué*, Amanda?"

"Nothing, Alejandro."

But he saw through her feeble attempt to brush over her concerns. "Amanda . . ."

She didn't want to say anything to dampen his mood. They had, after all, only just gotten past the pain from the South American tour. Now she was traveling with him through Europe, committed to making their marriage work, however unconventional it was.

"I don't know where many of those places are," she finally said.

"Ah. *Sí. Claro.*" He raised her hand to his lips. "Such wonders you will see," he whispered as he brushed his lips against her skin. "But none as beautiful as you are to me."

She felt a shiver rush through her body, and she shut her eyes. Wherever these places were—Singapore, Tokyo, Shanghai, Australia—all that mattered was that she woke each morning with Alejandro. Whatever country they visited and whatever hotel they slept in, that was her castle—a fortress of love and safety found only in the protection of his arms.

"Ah, the Princesa is still here?"

Amanda cringed when she heard Enrique walk up behind her. It had been such a lovely day. The last thing she wanted was for Enrique to ruin it. Just hearing his voice made her think back to that week spent on the ranch in Argentina. The way he moved between women, not caring who they were or what they wanted as long as he got what he wanted, made her feel sick.

"I've asked you before, Enrique: please don't call me that," she said as politely as she could. She hated when Enrique used Alejandro's nickname for her, mockery dripping from his voice.

But Enrique wasn't one to care about what she thought, their dislike for each other increasingly apparent: hers because she disagreed with his lifestyle, and his because she didn't swoon over him. "Alright then, A-man-da," he said, enunciating her name. "I'm surprised you are still here, seeing how you ran from the last tour." He leaned toward her. "You missed some good times in Mexico. Spain too, for that matter."

She felt her body tense at his insinuation.

He stood too close to her, invading her personal space, so she moved away from him. This only caused him to step closer and reach out to touch her neck.

She spun around and slapped at his hand.

He backed away, holding up his hands as if to proclaim his innocence. "There was a fly . . ."

She narrowed her eyes, knowing full well that there had been no fly or anything else on her neck. "Don't touch me!" she said as forcefully as she could.

Before he could respond, Alejandro walked into the room. He leaned over and kissed Amanda's cheek.

"¡Che, Enrique!" Alejandro knocked Enrique in the arm in a playful gesture that Amanda almost wished was not. "You ready for tonight?"

Amanda walked away from the two of them to the table full of food. She grabbed a paper plate and filled it with salad. Dealing with Enrique was not something she wished upon anyone. She couldn't understand why so many women were attracted to him. She supposed he was attractive—on the outside, anyway. But knowing how he thought about and behaved toward women made him most unattractive on the inside—at least to Amanda.

"There you are!"

Amanda froze at Charlotte's voice.

"Where have you been? I've been calling your cell for thirty minutes!"

Amanda turned around, a guilty look on her face. She had forgotten her phone in the hotel room. Now that she was reunited with Alejandro, she had frankly forgotten about Charlotte.

"I'm sorry," Amanda said.

"Well, I've found you now." Charlotte reached for her arm. "Put that down. You can eat later. I have two people waiting to interview you."

"Now? The concert is starting in less than an hour."

A disapproving frown crossed Charlotte's face. "That's the best time for an interview, Amanda!" she snapped, clearly irritated that she had to explain this. "You know that the backstage buzz always makes them write more positive interviews. Come on now."

With a sigh, she put down her plate. She had forgotten how hard it was to get a meal while on the road. Between the travel, concerts, and meetings, there was no regular eating schedule, that was for sure and certain. It was no wonder she felt so fatigued—especially with Charlotte making sure she was on the go all day long and Alejandro keeping her up well into the night. While Amanda loathed the former, she longed for even more of the latter.

"I found her!" Charlotte sang out as she led Amanda into a space adjoining the greenroom. A woman and a man stood up to greet them as they entered. It amazed Amanda how Charlotte could switch so quickly between being fierce and tough when things did not go her way to being upbeat and cheerful when they did. "Amanda, these people are here from *On Tour* magazine."

Amanda extended her hand. "It's nice to meet you."

They each shook her hand. When she sat down, they followed her example.

"*On Tour* magazine," Amanda said. "I'm not familiar with it." She ignored the scowl that Charlotte sent in her direction.

The woman, who'd introduced herself as Marilyn Downes, quickly handed her a copy of the magazine. "We're based out of the UK but distribute throughout Europe."

"I see," Amanda said, leafing through the magazine.

"How are you enjoying England?"

Amanda gave a soft smile. "It's lovely, really. Alejandro took me to Warwick Castle today. Just amazing. I've never seen anything like it."

"Do you mind if I take some photos while you two talk?" the man asked.

"Of course not," Amanda responded and made certain to remain composed and aware of how she sat. Posture, her former dance instructor had told her, is everything. Stedman had spent two entire days working with her on just that, making her practice keeping her shoulders down and elongating her neck. She vowed to never give anyone reason to give her "posture" lessons again.

Marilyn glanced down at the notepad on her lap. "We'd love to hear about your travels, Amanda. But also about how it feels to be so far away from home."

Fighting the urge to squirm, Amanda kept her hands folded in her lap and her legs crossed at the ankle and under the seat. "By home, I trust you mean my parents' farm, *ja*?" Marilyn nodded. "*Vell*, I'm glad to be back with Alejandro, but I do miss the farm." Another scowl from Charlotte, and she wondered what she could have said wrong. She tried to expand on her answer. "Obviously, it is very different to be traveling so much. I'd never really traveled before."

Marilyn raised an eyebrow. "But you were traveling through New York when you met Viper, correct?"

Amanda nodded. "*Ja*, I was. I was returning from Ohio. My *schwester* and I were visiting family and then returning home by train. It went through New York City."

"But that is much different from traveling to so many countries, wouldn't you say?"

"Of course!" Amanda smiled and gave a little laugh. "I didn't even know some of these countries existed."

At Amanda's comment, Marilyn frowned. "Amish aren't big on geography?"

Amanda kept smiling as she pondered an appropriate response. She didn't want to say anything that would make the Amish look even more insulated than the media portrayed them. "I suppose that the district leaders see little purpose in learning about so many different countries that their people will never visit," she said at last.

Her response seemed to placate Marilyn, who continued on to her next question. "What's been your favorite country so far?"

That was an easy question. While South America was beautiful, the different architecture and the culture fascinating to her, Amanda had not enjoyed the permissive culture. "It's nice to be in England. I can understand the language and everyone has been very kind to me."

"And the castle?"

Amanda nodded. "Of course. That was quite special to see."

"Your life certainly has changed a lot over the past year."

Another easy question, although Marilyn stated it as a fact. "*Ja*, it has."

"Any regrets?"

Too many, she thought. Not being there for her parents when her father had a stroke. Not having faith in Alejandro when his former manager leaked photos of Viper with Maria in the Los Angeles apartment. Not staying with Alejandro in South America when she couldn't take the pressure of juggling Isadora with the crazy life of being on tour. Not being able to stay with Isadora when she needed to fix her relationship with Alejandro. *"Nee,"* she said at last. "No regrets."

Marilyn wrote something down on her pad of paper while the man snapped some photos. Amanda did her best to ignore his camera, feeling uncomfortable with how close he got to her to take the pictures. "You just arrived in London earlier this week. For someone who hasn't traveled too often, at least alone, that's quite a journey!"

"It was a little scary," Amanda admitted. The truth was that when she traveled with Alejandro, she often forgot she was thirty thousand feet in the air. Traveling alone, however, made her far too aware of the fact that she was in an aircraft and not on the ground. "I don't know that I'll ever get used to flying. Seems unnatural to me. God would have given us wings if he meant for us to fly."

Marilyn laughed, but Charlotte rolled her eyes and glanced at her phone.

"Still," continued Amanda, "I wanted to be with my husband. So missing him took precedence over my fears, I reckon."

"I'll say."

The interview was interrupted when Alejandro walked into the room. His presence immediately took over, for which Amanda was grateful. She was tired of the interviews. Dali and Charlotte were over-scheduling her, and so many of the reporters asked the same questions so that Amanda felt as if she were a parrot, repeating herself over and over again. She tried to be more like Alejandro, who always responded as if it were the first time he'd heard those questions, even though she knew better.

"You are interviewing my Princesa? She is delightful, *sí?*" He sat down next to her, sliding his arm across the back of the sofa so that it rested just above her shoulders.

Marilyn nodded. "As expected," she said. "It's no wonder the world loves her."

Amanda blushed and the photographer quickly snapped a photograph.

"Does that bother you, Amanda?" Marilyn asked.

"The world does not know me," Amanda said honestly. "I don't know how they can love someone they do not know."

She ignored Charlotte's scowl as well as Marilyn's and Alejandro's soft laughs.

"It's true," Amanda continued. "I'm just a person, no different from anyone else. I have good qualities as well as not so good qualities."

"I'd like to see one!" Alejandro teased.

"No one is perfect," Amanda chastised him gently. "We can only strive to do the best we can to mirror Jesus, loving our neighbor as well as honoring God above all others." Even as she said the words, she realized she'd already failed that miserably. She would need to pray for more tolerance when it came to Enrique, a "neighbor" she found very difficult to like, never mind love.

"You performed in South America," Marilyn said, changing the subject as she referenced her notepad once again. "Why not on this tour?"

Amanda glanced at Alejandro. She didn't have an answer for this one.

"I'm sure we'll get Amanda onstage a few times," he responded with a sly wink in her direction. "In fact, we have quite a few surprises along the way during this tour."

*That* was news to Amanda.

"You come from very different backgrounds," Marilyn said. "I think it's clear that people are fascinated by the very obvious passion you share for each other. Where does that come from?"

Amanda waited for Alejandro to respond. When he didn't, she looked at him. He lifted one eyebrow. "*Sí*, Amanda, where does that come from?" he asked, teasing her with a half smile playing on his lips.

"I . . ." She stumbled over her words, searching for the right response.

No one had ever asked her this question, and she wasn't certain what to say. How could she explain the way they had met and how he made her feel? How could she possibly share the way her body felt on fire the day that he had danced with her in the *grossdaadihaus*? Or how her heart raced faster than ever before when he returned to Lititz to retrieve her when the paparazzi refused to leave her parents' farm? Or the night he proposed to her on board his yacht? Or the way he had so tenderly made love to her on their wedding night, making her his true wife in the eyes of the Lord?

"I would never question God's plans," she said at last. "This is what he wants, for sure and certain. He led us to each other, literally putting me in the path of Alejandro's car. Why, just a minute earlier or later, we never would have met!" She glanced at Alejandro, her eyes searching his. "How fortunate for us that the accident happened. Before we met, we were lost apart, but now that we are together, we are found." She paused, still looking at Alejandro. She felt a wave of electricity through her body, knowing she spoke the truth. "The passion? It is God given, and no one has the right to take it from us."

He leaned over and slowly gave her a tender kiss on her cheek. "Mmm . . . I'll second that," he murmured. "*Qué deliciosa* response, Princesa."

Marilyn smiled, watching the two of them as they shared a moment. The photographer continued taking photos.

Reluctantly, Alejandro tore his eyes away from hers first. "I suppose you should like some other photos and to speak with some of the stage crew, *sí*? Amanda and I must get ready," he said. He stood up, reaching for Amanda's hand and ignoring Charlotte's eyes, which bulged as she struggled to maintain her composure. Clearly, this abrupt departure was not a planned part of the interview. Alejandro tried to hide his smile as he leaned over to her and whispered, "Take them to see Geoffrey and Eddie, Charlotte."

He led Amanda out of the room and down the corridor to his dressing room.

"We still have another hour or so, Alejandro," she said, trying to keep up with his long strides. "I think she had some more questions for us."

At the door, he turned to her, using his free hand to push it open. "Enough questions," he said, that oh-so-familiar look in his eyes.

"What are you doing . . . ?"

When he reached out for her arm, she felt warmth course through her veins. Just his touch was enough to cause her heart to race. Being near him when he looked at her that way, his expression full of longing and passion, made her realize how much control he had over her. It was a feeling she did not resent.

Gently, he pulled her inside the room and shut the door behind her, making certain to lock it. For a moment, he leaned against the door, his head bent forward so that she could barely see his eyes taking her in. He reached up and undid his tie. "Amanda," he said, his voice heavy with desire. "You cannot talk about passion, Princesa, and not expect me to react."

She blushed and backed away from him. "That wasn't my intention."

"And that makes it even more powerful," he murmured. "Your intentions are always so honest, so pure." He pulled her toward him, his one hand holding her close while the other hand worked expertly at the zipper to her dress. The soft noise of it sliding open gave her goose bumps.

As her dress slid from her shoulders, with Alejandro's gentle help, she shut her eyes and felt the air caress her bare skin. She knew that her cheeks flushed, anticipating his touch and waiting for him to pull her into his arms.

"You were talking with Enrique earlier," he whispered. "I saw him touch you."

Amanda froze.

"I told him to never do that again." He lowered his lips to her bare shoulder. "No one touches you but me, Princesa. You. Are. Mine." He raised his lips to hers, crushing her against him as he kissed her mouth, her body pressed against his. When he lifted his lips, he whispered one word as he lowered her onto the sofa, cradling her in his arms. "Mine."

# Chapter Ten

"You're the royalty of rap!"

Amanda watched the television screen with her eyes focused on one image: herself. In the video, she was seated in a chair, being interviewed by a reporter. It had been taped earlier that morning and then played during the morning news program. The interviewer, a young man with blond hair and a big smile, had come up with the nomenclature, and social media had been buzzing with it all day. The video segment had gone viral within hours.

Charlotte paused the video, giving Amanda a minute to study the screen. "Your reaction, Amanda," Charlotte said. "Spot-on!"

The interview had taken place the previous week in London, and Charlotte had recorded it so that they could watch it later at the arena in Manchester. Now, in the privacy of her own dressing room, Amanda stood in a white silk bathrobe, her makeup and hair finished, and watched the recording.

"Is that something they are actually calling us?" Amanda asked, her large doe-like eyes not leaving the monitor. "The royalty of rap?"

Charlotte coughed into her hand in an overly dramatic way. "In the UK, royalty is as good as it gets these days. They used to be inaccessible, these royals of ours. But that changed in the eighties with Princess Diana and continues today with her son's marriage to a commoner. Accessibility, Amanda. That's what it's about!"

Amanda couldn't help frowning a little as she fought the urge to remind Charlotte that the concept of accessibility had been her own. It was a demand she'd made when Charlotte insisted that she not waste time taking photos with fans. After much arguing on the part of Charlotte, and much ignoring on the part of Amanda, they'd finally come to an impasse. As Amanda was rapidly learning, there was powerful truth to her mother's adage about a wise man silencing his tongue while a fool's tongue ran wild.

"Now look at your reaction here," Charlotte said as she pointed to the screen. "When the reporter said that to you, you maintained your composure, that regal presence, not even batting an eye." Charlotte glanced over her shoulder at Amanda and smiled. "You're becoming a master of hiding your emotions on-screen."

Amanda did not look away from the television screen. "Not hiding," she said in a neutral tone. "Handling."

Charlotte grinned at Amanda's correction. "Smashing! I like that!"

Earlier that week, Alejandro had performed in Cardiff before traveling to Manchester for the Thursday and Friday night concerts. After the concert that evening, the crew would tear down the set and move it to the next location: Birmingham. Alejandro and Amanda had little time for themselves, especially with Alejandro working on a new album during the day. With a four-day break between Birmingham and Paris, Alejandro had arranged for them to fly to Los Angeles. Geoffrey had scheduled a meeting with the people at the recording label as well as time at the studio to discuss his next music video.

In the meantime, Charlotte continued to keep Amanda busy, meeting with her daily to discuss possible endorsement opportunities as well as scheduling meetings with very important "posh" people. Amanda had begun to dread the meetings, knowing that happy-go-lucky Charlotte often turned into an angry, irritated, and complaining Charlotte when things did not go her way. Somewhere between the two polar extremes of her personality was a brilliant woman who knew her line of business better than anyone else Amanda had met.

"Why did they start calling us that?" Amanda asked.

When Charlotte pressed her lips together, Amanda feared an outburst. To her surprise, Charlotte remained calm. "You remember at Warwick Castle? A photo of the two of you went viral. You saw it: the one of you admiring the portraits of Henry the Eighth, Anne Boleyn, and their daughter Elizabeth. Someone commented that you two were the royalty of rap and the phrase went viral. You Americans might have everything, but you don't have a royal family."

To Amanda, none of this made sense. Why a photo of her and Alejandro looking at portraits would be of any interest to anyone was beyond her. "What's so great about a royal family?"

"History, my dear. History."

"Well, I reckon I just don't understand that."

Charlotte set down the remote control and started going through her files. "It's quite simple. Many wars have been fought by people wanting to be the king or even queen of England, Amanda. It's really no different from the music industry. People are willing to do just about anything to be on top of the charts and in demand by the fans. All of that leads to where you are today, sitting here with a list of companies that want to pay you to endorse their companies or products. The money isn't necessarily in the music, my dear. It's in the professional connections made by the music."

Amanda scratched the back of her neck and leaned into the sofa cushion. "That's all too complicated for me, Charlotte."

For a moment, Charlotte stopped fussing with her papers and looked at Amanda. "Yes, I imagine it is," she said in a kind voice. "All of these people are fighting to be where you are: in the spotlight. Yet all you care about is Alejandro." She seemed to think for a moment. "Perhaps that's one of the reasons so many people adore you."

"I care about more than Alejandro," Amanda interjected. She didn't want to point out that she'd taken Isadora away from Alejandro and brought her first to Miami and then to Lancaster. "God, Isadora, my family, my friends . . ."

Charlotte returned her attention to the papers in her hand. "In this business, there are no such things as friends."

"That's not true!" Amanda could tell Charlotte's mood was beginning to sour, but she continued anyway, hoping to snap Charlotte out of it. "Why, I consider Celinda a friend and she's a successful singer, *ja*? And as much as I'm not particularly fond of him, Enrique is Alejandro's friend."

Charlotte scoffed. "I take back my comment that people adore you because you seem to only care about Alejandro." She gathered her things and stood up. "I see now it's your innocence that they adore. Blind innocence."

Rolling her eyes as Charlotte left the dressing room, Amanda glanced at the television screen and thought back to that interview. Royalty was not how she wanted to be referenced by the public or the media. God did not want people to be superior to others in any regard. As for the royal families that felt they were born superior, just because of their bloodline, it sounded far too much like vanity—and therefore a sin—for Amanda's comfort.

Yet she couldn't help but think back to the day that Alejandro took her to Warwick Castle. Such opulence and finery was clearly for someone who gave little thought to others. She wondered how many poor people could have benefited from the money that had been invested in building and decorating such a castle. Even today, millions of dollars went into maintaining that castle for the public to visit.

Not even ten minutes had passed when she heard a familiar rap at her door: Alejandro. He always knocked in the same way, with three sharp taps. Smiling, she hurried across the room to open the door.

"Princesa!" He leaned over and kissed her right cheek. She glanced over his shoulder and saw three young men standing behind him. "I want you to meet some friends of mine."

With Charlotte's words about there being no friends in the music industry still lingering in the air, Amanda smiled cautiously and stood a step behind Alejandro. He introduced each of them, but she had never heard any of their names before. Two of the men were English, and one was Irish. They played in an all-male band that was breaking international records for hits and popularity.

The three stood just inside the doorway. The shortest one, blond with a crooked smile, stepped forward to shake her hand. His accent was so strange she suspected he was the one from Ireland. The other two men were taller, one a bit willowy with large green eyes and a thick shock of wavy black hair. When he smiled, he looked like a mischievous little boy. The third man had a short-cropped haircut and dark-brown eyes. His baby face made Amanda think of her late brother, Aaron.

"Pleasure to meet you, ma'am," the one with striking green eyes said as he reached forward to shake her hand.

She liked his accent, so different from Charlotte's. It sounded more country and less polished. Amanda took his hand and shook it, but said nothing.

"Princesa, we're talking about some collaboration," Alejandro said, wrapping his arm around her in a loving embrace. "A song and music video."

"Oh?" She tried to sound interested but failed to understand why Alejandro had brought them to meet her.

"With you in it, too."

"Me?" She practically squeaked out the word. "Oh, I can't sing!"

All four men laughed, and Alejandro pulled her closer to his side to kiss the top of her head. The way his eyes sparkled made her flush. "Just the video, *mi amor*. You can do that, *sí*?"

"You mean like acting? Like the video you shot in Los Angeles last autumn?"

The memory of the video shoot still haunted her whenever she thought about it. Seeing Alejandro nuzzling the neck of another woman, his hands on her body while he looked at her with such longing, had pained Amanda. Later, he had explained it was just acting. While she thought that sounded like a lie, he had convinced her it wasn't. And when she finally had viewed the finished video, Amanda found that the producer had included a clip of her with a tear rolling down her face while watching that scene being taped. She hadn't been happy about that.

"*Sí, sí*, like that." He leaned over and whispered in her ear, "Only it will be you in my arms, Princesa, and when I hold you and touch you, I will not be acting."

From the snicker on the face of the green-eyed man, Amanda knew he'd overheard Alejandro. She suspected that was what Alejandro wanted. Accordingly, she smiled and glanced away demurely, knowing that was the response he wanted from her.

After a few more minutes, Geoffrey joined them and urged Alejandro to get ready. The crew had finished the stage change between Enrique's and Alejandro's sets. "If you hurry," Geoffrey said, "the show might actually start on time for once."

After Geoffrey led the visitors away, Amanda turned to Alejandro. "Who are they?"

"Members of the most popular band in history, *mi amor*," he said as he quickly changed his shirt.

"They look awfully young."

He laughed. "*Sí*, Princesa, they *are* awfully young. Two of them are just twenty-one years old. One is nineteen. The Irish one, I think."

"So young to be so famous, don't you think?"

He grunted a response, which she took to be a noncommittal agreement with her statement.

"What is the song about?" she asked as she leaned against the wall, watching him as he looked through the rack of clothes.

"Love," he responded as he pushed aside a few hangers of clothing. "Is there anything else worth singing about?"

She thought about that for a minute. At church, they sang about God and Jesus. They sang about pain and suffering. Many of their hymns were written by Anabaptists, who were captured, tortured, and jailed by the Catholics during the initial Lutheran movement. For hundreds of years, the Anabaptists had been persecuted simply because they chose to question the organized Church. Yet even though many of these songs were not love songs—at least not in the way Alejandro meant—at their core was a love of God.

"I suppose you have a point," she said, noticing how he took off his shirt.

She eyed his dark skin with the tattoos that covered parts of his well-defined chest muscles and upper arms. All of them were a dark-blue ink, each one having some special meaning to Alejandro. While she never had been partial to tattoos, thinking the Englischers rather strange to want to permanently mar their bodies, she found Alejandro's tattoos fascinating.

But when he turned to grab something from the counter behind him, she noticed something different.

"Alejandro, is that a new tattoo?"

She pushed off from the wall and walked toward him. He glanced over his shoulder at her, pausing before he slipped on his fresh shirt. Across his shoulder blade, she saw that he had, indeed, acquired a new tattoo. Three words: *Amanda "Princesa" Diaz.*

She stood behind him and traced the lettering with her finger. "When did you get this?"

"You like?"

It was written in script with the word *Princesa* larger than the other two. *Amanda* was above and *Diaz* on the bottom. She let her finger remain on his shoulder, just barely touching his skin, and then, as if to answer him, she leaned forward and gently kissed it.

He turned around and wrapped his arms around her waist, pulling her toward him as he looked down into her face. "Where will you put your first tattoo?" he teased.

She tried not to smile.

"Here?" he asked, kissing her neck. "Or here?" he asked, kissing the top of her shoulder. He lifted her arm and kissed her wrist. "Or here?"

She could hide it no longer. Smiling, she pulled her hand free and placed it over her chest. "Here," she said. "You are already tattooed, Alejandro, inside of my heart."

His eyes lit up as he pulled her closer, their legs and hips pressed together, as he playfully growled and nibbled her ear. "You show me that tattoo later, *sí*? And if I can't see it, I'm going to draw tattoos all over your body."

She laughed at him, her hands around his neck, feeling the heat of his skin under her touch. He smelled musky and masculine, already energized and in full Viper mode after the sound check, preshow interviews, and Meet and Greet. In just a few minutes, he would leave her to go perform and she would watch him from the greenroom, knowing that afterward, when they retired to their hotel, she would get him all to herself.

While he finished getting ready, Amanda excused herself, leaving him so that she could try to call Anna. With the time difference, she figured it was about four o'clock in the afternoon back in Lititz. Jonas and Harvey would be outside in the dairy barn, milking the cows, Lizzie and Anna would be preparing supper, and Isadora would be seated on the bench at the table, her small legs swinging as she colored.

Perhaps, Amanda thought, Anna would have the cell phone with her in the kitchen.

She walked into the greenroom, pleasantly surprised to see that it was empty with the exception of a man who was refreshing the assortment of food that had been set out. Amanda curled up on the leather sofa with her phone and dialed the number.

Anna answered the phone on the fifth ring. "Hello?" She sounded as if she were singing the word. Amanda couldn't help but smile to herself at the sound of her sister's Pennsylvania Dutch accent.

"Anna? It's me, Amanda!"

"Oh, Amanda!" Anna must have held the phone away from her ear. "Mamm! Izzie! It's Amanda!" she called out. There was a scurry of movement in the background, and Amanda could imagine that her mother now stood beside Anna so that they could both listen to the phone. "How are you, Amanda?"

"Right *gut*," she answered, realizing that she had slipped into her old self, the Amish woman who sang her own words, the last syllable usually ending in a higher pitch than the others. "How's my Izzie doing?"

"Mammi 'Manda!"

Amanda laughed as she heard Isadora in the background and realized that she, too, was listening to the conversation. "Izzie! Are you being a good girl, then, for Anna?"

"Mammi Anna makes cookies!"

Mammi Anna? Amanda felt a moment of surprise at hearing Isadora refer to Anna as her mother. But just as soon as she felt that emotion bordering on jealousy, Amanda forced herself to appreciate the goodness behind it. Isadora was happy and being taken care of, not missing Amanda because she was loved by her family. She could not begrudge Anna or Isadora that relationship; it was good for everyone in the family.

"*Ja, vell*, not before dinner, you hear me now?"

Isadora giggled and must have handed the phone back to Anna.

"Oh, she loves those cookies, Amanda," Anna said cheerfully. "We bake them every afternoon!"

"Do you now?" Amanda smiled, knowing the joy of baking cookies with her own mother from years past. "Just make certain she's having her vegetables, too!" They both laughed. It felt good to hear her sister's voice. "How are Mamm and Daed?"

"Oh, just about as right as rain," Anna replied. "Mamm, anyway. Daed's about the same. Won't try to talk none at all and barely eats."

"Ach! Keep on him. He needs his strength, Anna." Something new to worry about, Amanda thought. "And you? How are you and the *boppli*?"

Cheerful Anna returned, laughing again. "Still jumping around inside of me. It's such a blessing to feel it move."

She felt happy for her sister but still wondered when she'd get the opportunity to experience the joy of life growing within her. She thought back to Alejandro's reaction when, before the South American tour, she had learned she was not pregnant. While she had felt distress, he had looked relieved—a reaction that had disappointed Amanda. That had been before Isadora entered their life. She could only imagine how he would react now. As he had told her, his life on the road did not accommodate an expanding family. While she could certainly join him, she'd have to leave a baby behind with a nanny, and that was something Amanda wouldn't consider.

The guilt of leaving Isadora with Anna still lingered in her mind. Both Anna and Lizzie had reassured her that Isadora was young enough to adapt and adjust. Whenever Amanda spoke with her stepdaughter on the telephone, it was more than apparent that Isadora seemed perfectly content to remain behind on the farm. However, that did nothing to erase the self-reproach and shame she felt over leaving the child in order to save her marriage. Even more important, she missed Isadora, with her large chocolate-brown eyes and angelic smile. Hearing Isadora's voice only intensified those feelings.

After she hung up the phone, Amanda glanced at the television screen and saw that Viper was onstage. He wore white pants and a black shirt with three buttons open. With his sunglasses on, the only sign of his emotions was the broad smile on his face as he sang. Occasionally, he would walk over to one of his dancers and stand behind her, his hand on her hip as she bent over, pulling her toward him. Amanda shut her eyes and looked away, disliking the implied intimacy between the two of them.

"Look who it is! The Princesa!"

Amanda opened her eyes to look in the direction of the voice. Enrique had entered the room with three women by his side. He had his arm around the waist of a tall blonde who wore a sleeveless blue dress and black platform high heels. Her long hair hung down her back with the exception on one thick strand that hung over her bare shoulder.

The women were tall, thin, and glamorous, their faces covered in heavy makeup and bright lipstick. Amanda watched them as Enrique lead them sauntering across the room to the table of drinks. He poured each of them a drink that was clear—vodka, from the smell of it. He lifted a glass and looked at Amanda, as if to ask her if she wanted one. Amanda turned her head.

When he chuckled under his breath, she started to get up to leave the room.

"*¡Ay!* What's this? We come to see you and you leave?" Enrique gestured to the sofa for the women to sit down. After pouring himself a drink, he joined them, making certain that he sat between the blonde and Amanda.

"I want you to meet my friends," he said, putting his arm around Amanda's shoulder. She shrugged it off and he laughed. "The Princesa is an ice princess, *sí?*"

The three women laughed at his joke, regardless of its poor taste.

"I should go watch from the wings," Amanda said. But Enrique reached for her wrist and held it. "Let go of me."

He didn't. Instead, he pulled her back down so that she was beside him once again. "I asked you to meet my good friends, Princesa."

"Do not call me that," she said again, her voice firm, eyes narrowing. If she hadn't liked Enrique before, she despised him now. His tone was far too sharp, and his grip on her wrist too tight.

"Why not?" He held his hands out before him and glanced at the three women. "Everyone else does!"

She glared at him. "That's not the same thing."

Several more people entered the room, mostly the men who made up Enrique's entourage. His "yes men," as Alejandro called them. With so many people in the room, she found it even harder to get away from Enrique.

"Now, this is . . ." Enrique pointed to one of the brunettes. "What's your name again?"

Whatever name she gave, Amanda didn't understand it. She suspected Enrique hadn't either. But he likely didn't care.

"And her friend . . ." He paused, giving the other brunette a chance to respond.

"Barbara."

He snapped his fingers. "That's right. Barbara!" One of his friends walked past and Enrique gave him a high five. "And my very good friend, Monica." He looked at her. "It's Monica, sí?"

The blonde woman nodded.

Amanda felt awful. There was a queasiness building in her stomach. Was this how Alejandro had behaved in the past? Had he been so callous and uncaring that he didn't even know the names of the women he selected to be his nightly lovers? She saw Enrique reach out and caress the blonde's neck, a gesture that Alejandro did to Amanda when they were alone and occasionally when they weren't. It was an intimate gesture and spoke of something much more than a one-night stand. While Enrique played it off as if he meant it, Amanda knew that, come morning, his very good friend Monica would be nothing more than a memory of Manchester, England.

"I have to leave," Amanda said once again and this time successfully stood up.

"You don't want to join our party, Princesa?"

She glanced over her shoulder at him, giving him a look of disdain and disgust. His eyes were large and dilated, making her wonder if he had been partying in private before he entered the room with tonight's newly acquired friends.

"There is always room for a fourth," Enrique said, gesturing to the three other women.

"You're repulsive," she heard herself say and immediately wished she had thought before speaking. She saw anger flash in his dark eyes. If the three women heard her, they gave no indication. The entourage of men, however, laughed, a few of them making encouraging noises, as if urging Enrique to respond.

Without waiting for Enrique to say another word to her, Amanda hurried out of the room, making her way through the throngs of people hanging out in the corridor and the stage wings. She wanted to find Geoffrey, knowing she'd feel safe with him. When she got close to the side of the stage, she noticed that Geoffrey was standing with the three men Alejandro had introduced her to earlier.

Safe enough, she thought, and walked over to join them.

The tall young man with the big green eyes and curly black hair that swept over his forehead smiled as she approached. He stepped aside to make room for her.

Geoffrey seemed surprised to see Amanda standing there. When he gave her a quizzical look, she merely said, "Enrique's in the green-room," and he nodded his head, understanding the unspoken.

"You are enjoying England, ma'am?" Green Eyes said to her.

"Oh, *ja*, it's quite nice. So much history."

He smiled. "A bit of a far cry from where you come from, I must say."

She liked how he spoke. "I reckon so. Our farms only go back to the 1700s!"

He laughed, a joyful sound, and his eyes crinkled. "I meant the touring."

"Oh." She blushed, feeling naive, even next to this man who was about her age but clearly more worldly. "That too, *ja*."

He leaned over and she caught the scent of cologne on his shirt. He smelled fresh and clean, like laundry that had just been brought in from the clothesline on a sunny day. She decided that she liked him, and then he said, "I come from a small town, too, you know?"

She wasn't certain if she was supposed to answer that. She knew better than to admit that she had no idea who he was and had already forgotten his name. "I did not, *nee*."

He nodded. "This is all a bit new for us lads, too. What a difference a few years can make, eh?"

"You haven't been singing long, then?"

He laughed again. "I was going to take over my dad's shop in town. But I entered a singing contest. One of those reality shows?" When she shook her head, indicating that she didn't know what that meant, he smiled even bigger. "I lost."

"Oh? I'm sorry."

Once again, he leaned in close and whispered, "Don't be. Look where I am now." He winked at her and smiled again. "Sometimes losing is winning."

Geoffrey interrupted their discussion. "Amanda, do you want me to have someone take you back to the hotel?"

She shook her head. The loud music from the stage stopped, and the audience began cheering and screaming. The eruption of noise distracted her from the men, and she wandered away so that she could watch Alejandro. He stood on the edge of the stage, one arm reaching over his head as he stared into the audience. From her past experience on the stage with him, Amanda knew all too well what he saw: masses of people cheering for him. With all of the bright lights, it was hard to see much beyond the stage unless someone had turned on the main lights in the arena. At this moment, they were on.

For several drawn-out seconds, Alejandro stood there, absorbing the adoration of his fans. Amanda smiled as she watched him, wondering if he knew that his biggest fan stood in the wings, her hands clasped in front of her and her heart beating rapidly. As if reading her mind, he turned and looked in her direction. He reached up to pull back his sunglasses and met her gaze before he raised his hand to his lips and blew her a kiss.

The crowd knew who was standing there, so they began to shout and cheer even louder. Viper laughed and waved to her to come join him, a gesture that incited the audience to even louder decibels of screaming. She began to hear them chanting her name, and she felt the color flooding her cheeks.

Green Eyes walked over to her and crooked his arm, offering it to her. "Let's see if we can blow the roof off the house, shall we?"

The other two men flanked her other side, and surrounded by the three members of one of the most popular and influential bands in the world, Amanda found herself being escorted onto the stage. There was a moment of hesitation as the audience realized that their beloved Princesa was not alone but accompanied by Britain's own celebrities. The noise was deafening and caught Amanda off guard. She knew that the cameras were displaying their images on the massive screens overhead so that the fans even in the far seats could see. Surely they saw how inflamed her cheeks were.

Once Green Eyes passed her over to Alejandro, he took a step back and joined his fellow band members. Alejandro escorted Amanda to the front of the stage and let the audience have their moment of adoration. She lifted her arm and waved, feeling uncomfortable but not wanting to disappoint Alejandro.

Behind her, the three men were still standing there, waving to the crowds, when music suddenly began to play. It was a song that Amanda had not heard before, and based on the beat, it clearly was not a song that Viper sang. Suddenly, she realized that Green Eyes and his band members now held microphones and were singing one of their songs, with Viper joining them. She wasn't certain what to do, but Viper guided her, taking her hand as he sang and danced across the stage. She tried to follow him, but before she could, Green Eyes took her hand and pulled her away from Viper. It was his turn to sing and dance with her. And then it was the next one's turn and then the next one. She laughed when she realized that the song was about friends fighting over the same girl.

The crowd drowned out the music while the blond Irishman laughed as he bumped into Green Eyes. Their playful interactions reminded her of the kittens that Isadora loved so much. The three young men teased each other as they danced, ruffling each other's hair and stepping in front of each other.

It dawned on Amanda how their rapid rise to fame was so different from Alejandro's years of struggling to find success within the world of music. From nothing to something, the young men had risen quicker than most artists in the industry. Yet, unlike Enrique and Alejandro, they rose to success together, which allowed them to enjoy it as a team instead of in isolation. No wonder Green Eyes had told her not to feel bad that he had lost the reality show. From that experience, he had met these other young men and rocketed to fame.

She had never considered that Viper's world was unique to Alejandro. However, as the song ended and the three young men surrounded her, waving to the audience as they led her off the stage, she realized that her previous conception was naive. Celinda, Justin, Enrique . . . they were all unique individuals and experienced fame in completely different ways. There was no one-size-fits-all formula for success.

"Blinding!" Green Eyes said to her, a grin on his face that indicated how pleased he was with the response. "That just about takes the biscuit!"

The Irishman winked at her. "They'll go on about that for a while, eh?"

She smiled but said nothing. Between their strange accents and foreign expressions, she wasn't entirely certain what they meant.

Geoffrey motioned for them to join him. Amanda, however, stayed where she was, watching as her husband continued performing for the audience. She was starting to understand what Charlotte had said to her earlier that day. There could be no real friendships within the industry because everyone was after the same thing: success. If one artist had it, another thousand people wanted it. Yet in the upper echelon of artists who made it, they had to work together in order to maintain their success.

Such a fine line to walk, she thought as she watched her husband—as Viper—sidle up to one of the dancers, gyrating his hips against hers while his hands roamed her body. For once, Amanda found it did not bother her . . . at least not as much as usual. The audience got what the audience wanted. As long as he came home to her each night, Amanda decided that giving the audience their fix of Viper was a sacrifice she was willing to make.

# Chapter Eleven

"*¡Che, Amanda!*"

She looked up from where she sat backstage reading a magazine. She was surprised to see Enrique approach her and immediately felt herself put up an invisible wall. The way he sauntered toward her, shoulders slouched forward and his eyelids semi-drooped over his dark eyes, his hands in his front pockets, reminded her of a predator approaching its prey. He was cold and calculating, someone that Amanda knew was worth giving a wide berth at all times. Even though Alejandro had warned him not to touch her again after catching Enrique brushing his fingers against her neck, he continued to find ways to get under her skin.

"Alejandro sent me to look for you," he said. He casually crossed his arms over his chest as he stood before her, covering up his red flannel shirt, which was unbuttoned far too low for Amanda's comfort. Unlike Alejandro, Enrique took a more casual approach to his wardrobe, preferring jeans and boots to suits and ties. Coupled with his bad-boy reputation—not to mention what she had personally witnessed—his informal and rugged appearance made him seem all the more threatening to Amanda.

"Oh?" She shut the magazine, leaving it on her seat as she stood up. "Whatever for?"

"He's meeting with some journalists. He asked me to walk you over to the Meet and Greet area. Said he'd find you there."

Amanda stared at him, wondering if he was telling the truth. There were half a dozen people that Alejandro would have sent over to escort her to the Meet and Greet. She highly doubted Enrique was one of them. Alejandro knew how she felt about him. She made a mental note to ask Alejandro about it later.

"*Danke*, Enrique, but don't bother yourself," she said in as friendly a tone as she could muster. She wanted to love her neighbor, to see something redeeming in Enrique, but she felt blind to anything that might change her opinion. "I see Geoffrey over there. I'm sure he can take me."

Without giving Enrique a chance to respond, she called out to Geoffrey and began walking toward him.

She couldn't wait to return to Los Angeles after the show that night, even if it was only for four days. She wanted some time away from the crew and the fans, the music and the interviews. While Alejandro worked, she could catch up on some quiet time for herself. And when they flew to Paris on Thursday, Celinda would be waiting there, and Amanda certainly welcomed some female companionship while on the tour.

She slipped through the curtain at the back of the room where the Meet and Greet was taking place. Normally, she waited for Alejandro so that Viper and his Princesa could enter together, but the crew member Geoffrey had asked to escort her to the room was unaware of that. And because Enrique had mentioned that Alejandro would meet her there, Amanda wasn't certain if her husband had already arrived.

There was a moment's pause as the people waiting to meet Viper realized that Amanda had entered the room. Quietly, Amanda began to approach the fans, smiling as recognition slowly crossed their faces and their questioning expressions turned to enthusiastic joy.

"Hello," she said to a girl in her late teens. "I'm Amanda."

The girl grinned. "Oh, we know who you are!"

Amanda gave a small laugh at herself. "I reckon that's true. I don't always remember that."

As she circulated the room, meeting the people and taking photos with them, she suddenly realized that, in many ways, this was her God-assigned ministry. In an industry where sex, alcohol, and drugs were so prominent, Amanda represented the other side, a godly righteousness that was clearly a better role model for the fans. By taming Viper and by remaining true to herself, Amanda was working God's plan to help show people that they could live any lifestyle and still honor him. That realization made her even more determined to focus on exhibiting as much patience as she could when it came to Enrique.

The people in the room were so focused on her, their eyes wide and bright with smiles plastered on their faces, that no one realized that Alejandro had entered the room. Amanda saw him first, standing in the doorway, his arms crossed over his chest and an amused smile on his lips. She stopped and turned toward him, waiting in deference for the fans to observe that their beloved Viper had arrived. When no one noticed his entrance, Amanda quickly crossed the room to join him. Immediately, the crowd followed her, Viper's staff directing them to stand single file in a line to take a photograph with him.

Alejandro lifted his sunglasses and watched Amanda, his eyes bright and full of mischief, as she stood by his side. "Ah, mi Princesa," he said and leaned over to kiss her cheek. Removing the sunglasses, he slid them into the front pocket of his black trousers. "They are here to see you, not me, *sí*?"

While Amanda still didn't understand the public's fascination with her, she also never wanted Alejandro to feel that she garnered too much attention from the fans. If Alejandro's goal was to be the top entertainer in the world, hers was to support his efforts in achieving that goal.

"I'm so sorry! I thought you were already here when I entered the room!" she gushed in a low voice so that no one could overhear. But Alejandro merely laughed and hugged her to his side.

"*Qué bien,*" he whispered into her ear. "You are becoming more comfortable with the fans. *Me gusta.* Besides, they adore you." When he released her, he added, "As do I."

For the next thirty minutes, Amanda stood by Alejandro's side as he greeted his fans and posed for the photographers who would later upload the photographs to the Internet for the fans to download. What seemed like such a long time ago, back in Miami, her former dance instructor, Stedman, had taught her to practice her smile and positioning so that in each photo her eyes were open, her smile sincere, and her posture flattering. She had thought it was a silly thing to have to learn, but over time she'd come to appreciate the lessons.

"I just love you, Princesa," a teenage girl gushed when it was her turn to pose with the two celebrities. "You inspire me so much."

Amanda glanced at Alejandro, worried that so much attention directed toward her and not him would bother him. But she quickly saw that he was more than pleased with the fans fawning over her. "*Danke,*" she said in a soft voice, uncertain what else to say.

"I want to move to America and live on an Amish farm one day," the girl continued. "It would be such an adventure!"

"Oh help!" Amanda laughed at that comment. "I don't know about the adventure part. A lot of hard work, though."

"*You* did it. And look at you now."

The photographer motioned for them to pose, so Amanda stood next to the girl, her arm lightly around the fan's waist. Alejandro stood on the other side and gave his "photo smile," as Amanda had come to call it. When the photographer signaled that he had the photo, one of the crew assigned to help at the Meet and Greets motioned for the girl to move along. But the girl paused and, before Amanda knew it, had wrapped her arms around Amanda in a warm hug.

"Thank you for being there for us," she said before being escorted to the other side of the room.

Amanda watched as the girl paused once to stare at her over her shoulder. Amanda smiled at her before turning her attention to the next fan.

Later, as they walked back through the corridor toward the other side of the arena, Amanda touched Alejandro's arm. "What did she mean, that girl? That I am there for them?"

Alejandro kept the same pace, hurrying to change his shirt before the show. With so much activity beforehand, he always liked to put on fresh clothing before going onstage. Besides giving him a moment to decompress from preshow interviews and meeting fans, that time alone in the dressing room was one of the few times of the evening when he was not surrounded by hordes of people. "The social media?" He glanced at his phone to check the time.

"Social media? You mean the reporters and paparazzi?"

He shook his head. "You interact with them on social media," he stated.

"I do what?"

Alejandro glanced at her. "Instagram. Twitter. Facebook. All of the social media. You have your own accounts and interact with them."

"I do?" She frowned. This was news to her. She wasn't even familiar with the media he'd mentioned. "Alejandro, I have no idea what you are talking about."

"Later, Princesa." They were just outside of the dressing room. "Remind me on the plane, *sí*? I want to get changed for the concert." He raised her hand to his lips, kissed it, and with a quick smile, disappeared into his dressing room.

\*\*\*

When the concert ended and the cheers of the fans still echoed in the arena, Alejandro hurried offstage and, without pausing at the dressing room, hurried over to Amanda.

"*¿Listo,* Princesa?"

Two security guards and Geoffrey approached them, Geoffrey gesturing to the corridor. They wasted no time exiting the arena before the entrance reserved for the crew and talent became a mob scene. Outside there was a car ready to take them to the Birmingham airport, where a private plane waited to take them back to the United States. They would fly to Chicago to refuel and then continue their flight. It would be a long night, over fifteen hours of travel. By the time they arrived in Los Angeles, it would be six in the morning.

Amanda tried to figure it out on a piece of paper as they sat in the plane on the tarmac. How was it possible to leave Birmingham, England, at 11:30 p.m. on Saturday, travel for fifteen hours, and arrive in Los Angeles at . . . six in the morning?

Alejandro laughed as she scribbled out her numbers and tried to figure it out once again.

The flight attendant handed him a drink, and he took a long sip. "You forget the time changes, *sí?*" he said, pointing to her numbers.

"Oh, bother!" She pushed the piece of paper away. "And I thought we had it rough growing up with fast time and slow time!"

He raised an eyebrow, silently questioning her.

"Amish don't follow the Englischers' daylight savings time. So we go to church an hour earlier during fast time, at least if you consider the time change."

Shaking his head, he took another sip of his drink. "Sounds confusing."

"It was, *ja.*"

Just before the door to the plane was about to shut, Carlos hurried on board, followed by Paolo, Andres, and Eddie. The men nodded to Amanda, and as they passed by Alejandro, each slapped his raised hand.

Carlos made a comment in Spanish, and Alejandro laughed before the four men took their seats toward the back of the plane. While Amanda wasn't surprised that Eddie and Andres joined Alejandro on the private plane, she was curious about Paolo and Carlos. Most of the other members of his team had other travel arrangements; however, since she had met them in Miami before the South American tour, they seemed to be regulars in Alejandro's inner circle.

Giving up on trying to figure out the time differences, Amanda shoved aside her notepad. After buckling her seat belt, she stared out the window at the darkness that engulfed them. In the distance, she could see the city lights and realized that by the time they arrived in Los Angeles, the people of Birmingham would be enjoying their Sunday off, the concert just a fading memory for most of those who had attended.

After the plane took off and the pilot reached cruising altitude, Alejandro unfastened his seat belt and stood up. He stretched before walking down the aisle and sitting on the sofa in the center of the plane. "Amanda, you want to go lie down in the back?" he asked her. "It's going to be a long flight. Sleep makes it go faster, *sí*?"

She shook her head, wanting to hold off sleep for a while.

"Tell me, Alejandro," she said, moving to join him on the sofa. "What did you mean about the social media?"

"Ah, *sí*. Social media." He put his arm around her neck and pulled her next to him so that her head rested on his shoulder. "Dali has a team of people managing your social media accounts."

This was news to her. While she knew what social media was—Alejandro had shown her several of his different accounts—she certainly did not have her own. "What do you mean 'managing my social media accounts'?"

If she sounded alarmed, Alejandro made no indication that he noticed. Instead, he responded casually, "She monitors the people who post photos and status updates to your accounts on a daily basis.

Sometimes they even reply to your fans." He glanced over at Geoffrey. "What is her social currency, G?"

"Five million," he said.

Alejandro nodded. "*Sí*, that's right. Five million."

None of this made any sense to Amanda. "Five million what?"

"Followers. People who follow you on the different social media applications."

"That sounds like a lot of people," she commented. "I didn't even know I had any accounts."

He laughed at her. "*Sí*, Princesa, five million is a lot. Especially when you consider that they just started your accounts less than two months ago."

Why hadn't she known about this? Vaguely, she remembered the one fan who'd asked her for a "follow" on Twitter. At the time, Amanda hadn't really understood what the fan meant. She suspected it had something to do with the cell phone, and Amanda had merely sidestepped the question by explaining she did not have her phone with her at the moment. Now she was learning that Dali had created accounts for her on the social media sites and had hired other people to manage them?

"Why am I not managing those accounts?" Amanda asked.

Alejandro shook his head. "*Ay*, Princesa! It's too time-consuming. Let others handle it. They know what they're doing. It's their job." He leaned his head back and shut his eyes. "You have more important things to do."

But she wasn't so certain. If interacting with the fans was part of her brand image, she wasn't all that comfortable with complete strangers posting on her behalf. She wanted to see these social media applications and understand better what it was that the people posing as her were posting. "I don't want to sound quarrelsome," she started, "but I think I should know what this is about, Alejandro."

"*Sí, sí*, if you insist," he said with a sigh. "When we're in Los Angeles, Dali can show you, *sí*?"

"Dali will be there?"

He nodded. "I asked her to meet with you and discuss your brand strategy, what you'll be doing over the next year."

Brand strategy? Year? She frowned, trying to understand when, exactly, she had become a product. Was this the way that all celebrities thought? Or did most of them merely morph into the person that the public made them? Either way, she didn't like it. "This sounds so . . . so cold," she said. "So detached from reality. I'm a person, Alejandro, not a brand."

He held her closer, his arm warm against her skin. "This is true, Amanda, but there's only so much one person can do when five million people—and counting—want a piece of you."

"How many people follow you, Alejandro?"

"G?" he called out. "Social currency for Viper?"

"Sixty million," Geoffrey replied without a moment's hesitation.

Amanda caught her breath. "Sixty million! Why, that must be everyone in the country!"

Both Alejandro and Geoffrey laughed.

"*Ay*, Princesa, not by a long shot, I'm afraid. Besides, that's international, *mi amor*. When I reach one hundred million"—he pointed his finger in the air as if to punctuate the number—"then I will be happy."

Geoffrey moved over to the leather chair and opened a manila folder. "Before you fall asleep, Alejandro . . ." Alejandro groaned. "The label wants the final documents signed for your next album. They're getting anxious."

"Let them get anxious!" But he gently moved Amanda so that he could sit up. She scooted down the sofa and watched as Alejandro got back into business mode. "What is it they want? What's the sticking point for the delay?"

Geoffrey glanced at Amanda.

She took that as a hint that she should leave. Standing up, she placed her hand on Alejandro's shoulder. "I'll go into the back room and let you talk," she said. But before she could withdraw her hand, Alejandro took hold of it. She looked at him, wondering why he wanted her to stay when Geoffrey clearly wanted her to go.

"You should stay, Amanda," he said. "You should hear what the label wants."

She sat back down, curious as to why she would have any interest—and why he would *think* she might have interest—in what his record label company wanted.

Geoffrey began flipping through a pile of papers until he found the document he wanted. "Here it is," he said and handed it to Alejandro. "The number of promotional interviews, concert appearances, and merchandising points are the main issues right now. Everything else is manageable."

Alejandro took the paper and looked it over before handing it to Amanda.

"I don't know anything about that," she said, refusing to take the paper. "I don't even understand what he just said. Besides, it's your decision."

"Not when it's about you, Amanda."

"Me?" She stared at him for a moment and then took the paper from his hands. "What on earth?" Her eyes scanned the document and tried to make sense of the information. But there were words she could not understand: *points, back end, rights, licensing.* She placed the paper on her lap and looked at Alejandro for an explanation.

"They want to include you in the contract, Amanda," he said point-blank. "The next album will not be just Viper but will include Princesa."

"For what purpose?"

"For touring and promotions. They also want to license your image for merchandising. T-shirts, jewelry, cups, posters, you name it. If I sign this contract, you would be obligated to show up at every concert and appearance, including any television and interviews that they set up. You'd be given a very specific role, perhaps not onstage this time," he said in a calm, even tone.

"What on earth . . . ?" She was stunned and picked up the paper again. "What would my role be, then?"

This time, Geoffrey spoke up. "Right now, they are exploring options, but they are leaning toward having you be the conduit to Viper."

Amanda glanced at Alejandro.

"Let me explain it to you this way," Geoffrey said as he leaned forward, his elbows on his knees. "When the fans line up outside of the hotel or studios or wherever Viper is to attend, you would be the one to meet the fans and pick a few people to give tickets for the show. Front row tickets. At the concerts, your security team would escort you through the crowds, meeting the fans—the very thing you love doing the most, right?—and selecting a few to come backstage with you to meet Viper and watch the concert."

"I see."

Alejandro touched her knee. When she looked at him, he picked up where Geoffrey left off. "It's what you like to do, *sí*? And it will create a new, different level of energy at these events. When people see the Princesa at these events, you'll be more than just someone who stands next to them and smiles for a camera. You are the doorway to living a dream that so many of them don't even know to dream."

"I . . . I think it's best if you decide for me, Alejandro," she said reluctantly. "Whatever you want from me, you know I will do."

Immediately, she thought back to South America, the one time she had not done what he had wanted her to do. Instead, she'd left, tired of the travel and the women who threw themselves at her husband, not to mention her husband's change in attitude after Isadora became their responsibility. And what about Isadora? Could she just leave her in Lititz with her family indefinitely? Was that fair to Isadora? To her family? To herself?

If she agreed to what the record label requested, from a legal perspective she would have no choice but to do everything the record label wanted. There would be no last-minute flights from Argentina to return home to Miami or Lititz just because she felt like it. If she agreed to this, she would be an employee with responsibilities to not just Alejandro and his fans but to the record company.

"You have time to think about it, Amanda," Alejandro said.

"Actually, no, she doesn't," Geoffrey contradicted. "We've been sitting on this since Mexico. As I said, they're getting—"

"Anxious." Alejandro finished the sentence for him. *"Sí, sí, comprendo."* He sounded irritated. "She needs to understand what they want from her, G. I will not have her sign something blind." He stood up, a scowl on his face. "Now, I'm going to sleep for a while. I'm suddenly more tired than I thought." He headed toward the back of the plane, where there was a small private cabin with a bed and private washroom. He paused at the doorway and turned back, staring at Amanda. "You are coming, no?"

Obediently, she rose from the sofa and handed the paper to Geoffrey. Then, she followed Alejandro into the bedroom.

She shut the door behind herself and looked around the room. Alejandro unbuttoned his shirt and slid his arms free, tossing the shirt on a small chair next to the door. He was frustrated, that much she could tell. She bit her lower lip and tried to decide how best to approach him so that he would forget his bad mood.

She walked toward him, reaching out to help him unbuckle his belt. "Alejandro, you know that I trust you. If you want me to do this," she said and looked up at him, "I'll do it. I just don't understand the wording in that document."

He was silent for a moment as he watched Amanda struggle to remove his belt from the loops of his pants. She could tell from the way his breathing slowed down that his mind was shifting from his irritation with Geoffrey to focusing on her. He reached his hand up to rub her shoulder, his finger trailing down her arm.

"I suppose I just worry about Isadora," she said as she freed the belt and gently placed it on the chair with his shirt. Before unbuttoning his pants, she let her hands brush across his chest. She wondered if she would ever lose the feeling of wonder and excitement she felt whenever she touched him. His skin seemed to ignite her longing, and she felt that familiar yearning to be with him as a wife should be with a husband. "But I worry about you, too," she added as she lowered her hands to his pants, starting to unbutton them.

He grabbed her hands and held them for a second.

Once again, she looked up, searching his eyes.

He pushed her back onto the mattress and stood at the edge of the bed. The shadow of his razor stubble covering his cheeks and chin plus the furrow in his brow made him more handsome than ever. Amanda reached her hand out for him to take. She pulled him toward her and moved onto the bed to give him room. He crawled over her, one knee on either side of her legs, his hands by her head.

"You worry about me, *sí?*"

"*Sí,*" she said.

"You worry about many people."

She nodded her head, never once breaking his gaze.

"Who worries about you, Princesa?"

"You."

It was his turn to nod. "*Correcto.* I worry about you." He shifted his weight and placed one of his hands on her leg, gently moving it higher and pushing up her black skirt. "I worry about you all the time, Princesa."

"All the time?" When he nodded, she bit the corner of her lip. "That's a lot."

"*Sí,*" he breathed, his eyes beginning to droop as he leaned back and pulled her into a sitting position. He tugged at her blouse, pulling it over her head and throwing it onto the floor. "So very much." He wrapped one arm around her, practically scooping her against his chest, and lowered her back onto the bed. "I worry about you. About making you happy. About pleasing you."

She shut her eyes as she felt his hands touching her bare skin. "Pleasing me . . . ," she echoed.

"I want to please you now," he murmured, his breath hot on her neck.

"Yes," she whispered.

His lips met hers, and as they kissed, their bodies pressed together at thirty-thousand-feet altitude. The plane headed west while Alejandro and Amanda forgot about everything for just long enough to remember what was most important: each other.

# Chapter Twelve

The four men sat in the business meeting, each one wearing slacks and a collared shirt, and stared at her as she sat next to Alejandro, Geoffrey, and Alejandro's lawyer. Amanda felt small and insignificant, still jet-lagged and weary from the plane flight over from England. With the eight-hour time difference, she barely knew whether it was morning or evening. All she knew was that her body wanted sleep.

Ever since they'd arrived that morning, they had been on the go. Although they stopped at the apartment to freshen up and the bed beckoned to her, Amanda kept her complaints about being so weary to herself. She knew that Alejandro kept a full schedule and arriving in Los Angeles meant meeting after meeting for the few days they were there.

The fast pace with which Alejandro moved continued to amaze Amanda. A few cups of coffee or a quick shower was all he needed to bypass sleep.

"People say that they want to live?" he had said to her as he stepped out of the shower shortly after they'd arrived at their LA apartment. "I say just wake up!"

She wished that she had that energy. Her body felt worn out and battered. She had slept most of the way from Birmingham to Chicago. When she awoke, it was to Alejandro gently rubbing her bare shoulder and whispering for her to prepare for the landing at the airport. They would need to go through customs prior to boarding for the final leg of the flight into Los Angeles International Airport.

Somehow she had found the energy to get dressed. When she stepped outside the cabin door, she saw Alejandro seated at a table, his laptop before him and scattered papers on the table. It dawned on her that while she had slept on the plane, he had been working.

It was almost seven in the morning when they finally arrived at their apartment, and by eight o'clock they'd left in a black SUV for his first meeting of the day at the recording studio to listen to his latest tracks. Many of the songs had been recorded in hotels while Alejandro was traveling in South America and Europe. The song mixer had pieced together the different elements and finally had some product for him to listen to. Amanda had gone along—both to keep him company and to avoid crawling into bed, where she feared she might sleep so soundly she would never wake up.

By two in the afternoon, Amanda sat in the large conference room at the record label's management offices, feeling out of place in the plush black leather chair. Around the table sat a group of men, most of them wearing suits, although a few wore slacks and crisp button-down shirts. The men looked at her as if assessing or studying her. Several times she saw one of the men scribble something on a piece of paper and slide it to one of his colleagues. Amanda did not doubt the note was about her. Their obvious—and poor!—attempt at secrecy made her wish she'd never arisen from the bed on the plane. Besides being tired from traveling and the time difference, she felt as though she were on display, a feeling she disliked.

"We need more time to discuss the contract," Alejandro's lawyer said. "At this time, you're asking for more than we can commit."

One man, who'd been introduced to her as Richard Gray, tapped his pen against the side of the table, still staring at Amanda. He leaned back in his chair and shook his head, his eyes narrowing as he tore away his gaze to address Alejandro. "No," he stated in a level voice with a sharp edge to it. "That's just not good enough, Viper."

"What do you mean, Richard, that it's 'not good enough'?" Alejandro said, leaning forward in his seat, the leather chair squeaking under his weight.

Out of the corner of her eye, Amanda saw Geoffrey touch Alejandro's leg under the table. Alejandro leaned back in his chair, but his eyes still shot daggers at the man. It had been a hostile meeting so far, and despite her best attempts to understand why, she hadn't been able to follow the discussions over the past hour. Several times her mind wandered back to Pennsylvania as the men on the other side of the table droned on about points and reach and other terms she didn't quite comprehend.

This time, it was the man sitting to the left of Richard who spoke up. "It's been several months since the revisions to the original contract were sent over. We need an answer now before the entire negotiations are thrown out and we start all over again."

To Amanda's amazement, Alejandro's lawyer cleared his throat and spoke. "Since that time, her value has increased. These numbers are no longer acceptable." He pushed a file folder across the table toward Richard Gray and, as he did so, a piece of paper slid out of the side. Amanda knew it was a page from the contract that she had seen the previous night.

She looked at Alejandro, wanting to ask him what the lawyer meant. This was the first time she'd heard anything about value increasing or unacceptable numbers. But Alejandro stared straight ahead, his eyes riveted on Richard Gray.

"So it's about more money, is that it?" The man seated next to Gray said, ignoring the folder that was now in no-man's land.

"Easy, Eric," Richard said. For a long second, as he tapped his pen on the side of his notepad, he seemed to contemplate Alejandro. "What we are offering for the promotions and merchandise is more than any other label would give." His gaze swept from Alejandro to Amanda and then back again. "You've done a lot of business with us, Viper. To bail out now over percentages . . ."

Alejandro shrugged. "Either you get less or you get none, you decide."

Another man mumbled something under his breath to Richard, and Amanda realized that it was probably better that she hadn't heard him.

"I don't believe this," Eric said as he leaned back in his chair. He tossed his pen onto the table and ran his fingers through his thinning hair. "We're offering almost five million dollars for something she's already doing! This is ridiculous!"

Alejandro did not look impressed. "Be that as it may, if you want exclusivity—and someone will, Eric, you know that—then we want more points for Amanda."

"Three months, Viper," Eric snapped. "Three months of waiting and now this? More delays at the eleventh hour?" He glared across the table at Amanda. "Is this your doing?"

She caught her breath at the viciousness of the words, but Alejandro was faster, lunging across the table at Eric. His chair tipped backward as he grabbed the shirt of the stunned man and pulled him forward, not caring that Geoffrey was tugging at his arm. With his face just inches from the other man's, Alejandro lowered his voice to what Amanda knew was a very dangerous level and hissed through clenched teeth, "You want to play, *chico*? You need to cock back and reload! Aim it in a different direction. That's my wife, you hear!"

"Let go of me!"

Immediately, Amanda stood up and reached for Alejandro's arm. "Please, Alejandro. Stop!" She felt the reluctance in her husband as he loosened his hold on the lawyer and shoved him back into his seat. "It's not worth it," Amanda continued. "Frankly, while I do not pretend to understand all that is asked of me in that contract"—she pointed to the file folder—"I do know this is not a company I wish to be associated with."

When Alejandro sat back down, she kept standing and turned to look at both Eric and Richard Gray.

"I will do whatever my husband asks of me," she said calmly, "as long as it is not with someone as ungodly as either of you."

From somewhere within, she found the courage to step around the chair and walk to the door, not looking back as she exited the room, shutting the door behind her. Uncertain what to do, or where to go, she merely sat down in one of the chairs in the outer room. Her heart beat rapidly as she found herself feeling anger well up inside her chest. How dare that man accuse her of trying to manipulate the contract! She didn't understand any of this, and she certainly didn't care one bit about the money. What she did care about was respect, and clearly that man did not have any for her or for Alejandro.

She waited for what seemed like an eternity, her mind reeling as she realized how horrible the people were that Alejandro had to deal with. Such an ugly industry, she thought with a heavy heart. Surely God must weep when he looked down upon his creations and saw such black hearts within them.

Finally, the door opened and Geoffrey stepped into the waiting area. He walked over to her and knelt down, taking her hands in his. "Amanda, will you come back into the conference room?" he said.

She shook her head, fighting the urge to cry. If Alejandro had sent Geoffrey to her and not come himself, certainly he was angry. She simply could not go back into that room.

"Listen to me," Geoffrey said in an even tone. "They are willing to negotiate."

"I don't want to be obliged to people like that," she whispered so that the woman at the desk didn't hear. "They are not nice people."

Geoffrey did not argue with her. "No, Amanda, they are not nice people. But they are rich people, rich people with power." He glanced over his shoulder at the closed door. "And I do not believe there are many people who would stand up to them and walk out of a room like you just did. They are willing to up the ante."

"What does that mean?"

"It means they are willing to pay you, Amanda, just for doing what you love to do."

She tried to understand what he was telling her. Such an amount of money was unheard of, at least in the world in which she'd grown up. "For interacting with fans? For giving out free tickets and doing interviews? That just doesn't sound right, Geoffrey. It's too much money and wasteful." She wiped at her eyes, hoping he didn't see her tears. "And it still doesn't make them people that I'd like to be associated with."

He stood up, still holding her hands. "Come, Amanda. This is what Alejandro wants," he said. "Think of what you can do with so much money. You can help people all around the world."

She hadn't thought of it that way. "It wouldn't be my money," she said slowly. "It's Alejandro's, too."

Geoffrey nodded. "True, but it's because of you. He'll let you do what you want with it. Start a school for children. Help the needy. Whatever you want."

How could she tell Geoffrey that, while that sounded good, all she really wanted was to be with Alejandro and raise his child. She wanted a life with the man she loved, and she wanted to be a mother to Isadora. Nothing in that contract spoke of anything that related to her role as wife and stepmother. Instead, it focused on one thing: increasing their revenue as it related to Viper.

Still, if this was something that Alejandro wanted, she knew she could not refuse.

"I won't go back into that room," she said. "But I will agree to whatever Alejandro wants." He was, after all, her husband and head of their small household. Who was she to go against God's command when he told his people: *Wives, submit yourselves unto your own husbands, as unto the Lord. For the husband is the head of the wife, even as Christ is the head of the church: and he is the saviour of the body. Therefore as the church is subject unto Christ, so let the wives be to their own husbands in every thing.*

Geoffrey nodded his head and gently patted her hands before releasing them. "Sit here then, Amanda. I'll go back and speak to them."

As the door shut behind Geoffrey, Amanda did her best to ignore the inquisitive stares of the woman behind the desk. A tear fell on her cheek, so Amanda wiped it away, angry with herself for having permitted herself to react in such a way. Whether or not she was right in standing up to the men, she knew better than to speak in such a sharp manner to anyone. How many times had her mother instructed her to be quick to listen and slow to respond? But seeing Alejandro defend her and lunge at that man had upset Amanda almost as much as hearing the awful man's words. It was a side of Alejandro she had never witnessed. And the man, that Richard Gray, had no right to speak to her in such a manner. While Amanda increasingly understood how ugly the music industry was, she certainly did not have to subject herself to such ugliness.

Twenty minutes later, the door opened again and Alejandro stepped into the waiting room. He looked at her and grimaced, crossing the room toward her. "You are all right, Amanda?" he said. "You've been crying, *sí*?"

She nodded her head and then shook it, uncertain what to say to him. "I . . . I'm so sorry," she finally said, looking up at him through tear-filled eyes. "I didn't mean to ruin your meeting. I just couldn't sit there with that man a moment longer."

Alejandro chuckled and pulled her to her feet. He wrapped his arms around her and gently rocked her back and forth. "You did the right thing, Amanda. And they are willing to sign a very lucrative marketing contract for the rights to use your name and image. Six and a half million dollars, to be exact."

For a moment, she didn't believe that she had heard him properly. She pulled away from him in shock. "What?"

"*Sí, mi amor*. Over six million dollars because of you!"

"Six and a half million dollars? Just for using my name?"

Laughing at the stunned expression on her face, Alejandro tried to explain it to her. "All of these concerts, the fans want merchandise. Richard will contract out to merchandise providers, Amanda, and they'll create products to sell at the concerts as well as online. Posters, shirts, princess crowns, anything that people will buy with your name or image on it! We'll get back-end points on sales. He's also talking about a perfume and cosmetic line. It's an unprecedented deal, Amanda!"

She could scarcely believe what he was saying. "This is just so unreal," she said. "I don't understand any of this."

He laughed and held her in his arms. "*Ay, mi amor*, that's what makes you so beautiful!" He picked her up and twirled her around. "Beautiful and rich, *sí*?"

When he set her back down on her feet, she noticed how happy he was. She wanted to tell him that money mattered nothing to her. Whether they paid her six dollars or six million dollars, she really did not care. But instead she said, "If this is what you want, then I am glad. I just trust you will tell me what I need to do to honor this agreement."

"Just keep being you," Alejandro said, placing both of his hands on her cheeks and leaning down to kiss her lips. "That's all anyone is asking of you."

The only thing she wanted was some time at the beach, to feel the warm sand under her feet and to watch the waves as they pulsated against the shoreline.

They had slept late that morning and would leave for Paris the next evening. Their time in Los Angeles had been limited, and with so much activity, it had flown by far too fast. Before he left the apartment, Alejandro had promised to bring her to the beach in the afternoon after he met with his team at the recording studio.

But by four o'clock, she still hadn't heard from him. Sitting out on the balcony, Amanda had her Kindle on her lap and was reading the Bible. The sun was still shining brightly, but the air was cooling down. Earlier, when she'd gone for a walk after lunch, it had bordered on hot. While she didn't mind it, especially with no humidity, she much preferred the cooler air.

From inside the open sliding door, she heard her cell phone. Setting her Kindle on the small table by her chaise lounge, she hurried inside to fetch it. Two texts: one from Alejandro and one from Celinda. She looked at Alejandro's first:

```
Sent a car to bring you to Marina del
Rey. Meet you there to watch the sunset
over Malibu.
V.
```

She read the text twice, a smile on her lips. Even if he was running late, his thoughtfulness made her happy. Quickly, she hurried into the bedroom to change into a sundress and tossed a sweater over her arm. When the sun went down, the air could get chilly in Los Angeles, even in the late spring.

The drive from the apartment to Marina del Rey took longer than she anticipated. Santa Monica Boulevard was congested with rush-hour traffic, although, from what Amanda had seen on her few trips to Los Angeles, there weren't many times it *wasn't* congested. After forty minutes, the car pulled into a marina and stopped at the edge of the parking lot.

Amanda looked around, wondering why the driver had brought her there. Was this where Alejandro was meeting her?

There were several large boats tied to the end of the docks, one that reminded her of Alejandro's yacht in Miami. As the driver opened the car door, she could hear a strange barking noise coming from the water. When she looked in that direction, the driver merely said, "Seals."

"Amanda!"

She heard someone calling her name and turned her head in that direction. A crowd was on the back of a boat, which was not as big as Alejandro's yacht but large enough to accommodate at least twenty people. For a second, Amanda hesitated. She did not recognize anyone on the boat and worried that someone may have recognized her. But when the crowd parted and she saw Alejandro walking toward the back of the boat, she felt better—even though she was disappointed he was not alone.

He jumped from the boat to the dock and hurried to meet her as she carefully moved down a sloped walkway from the parking lot toward him. At the bottom of the walkway he greeted her with a warm kiss that tasted of rum. "There's my Princesa!" he said with a happy smile on his face. "Come, *mi amor*. Meet my friends."

Immediately, caution lights went off inside her head. As Charlotte had forewarned her, she now knew that in the music industry, there was no such thing as friends. The men wore khaki shorts and polo shirts while most of the women were in short sundresses, with the exception of one who wore a skirt with a bikini top.

Why on earth would Alejandro think that any of these people were his friends? Amanda had never met them, and as he introduced her to them, she realized she had never heard of them either.

No sooner had she boarded the boat and started meeting his so-called friends than the boat began to leave the dock and motor a painfully slow five miles per hour, heading away from the marina into the narrow inlet that led to the open sea. Amanda glanced at the front of the boat, wondering where the captain was going to take them. Knowing Alejandro, it would be some wonderful place that she had never even known existed. She just wished they could experience it alone.

As the boat began to move through the channel, Amanda walked along the deck toward the bow of the boat. She could hear music playing from the boat's stern and knew that the men and women were dancing. But Amanda preferred to stand at the bow and watch the reflection of the sun on the water as the boat cut toward the wide-open ocean.

"Amanda! Look!" Alejandro found her at the front of the boat and pointed toward the shoreline. Three seals played in the waves, dipping their heads out of the water before disappearing, their tails slapping against the surface.

"Oh! How beautiful!" she gasped. "I heard them earlier, but how very special to see them!"

He chuckled at her and put his arm around her neck. "How very special to see you so happy, Princesa."

She leaned her head back against his shoulder. "Look how the sun just sits so perfectly over the horizon," she said. Then, pointing, she asked, "What is that mountain?"

"¿Dónde?" He squinted and lowered his sunglasses to peer at the place where she pointed. "Ah, sí! That is Malibu, Princesa. It's a beautiful place. I will take you there on our next trip to Los Angeles. Such an amazing beach, and the restaurants!" He kissed his fingertips. *"¡Ay, qué rico!"*

She wanted to ask when that would be and whether Isadora would be with them. The apartment was not as large as their condominium in Miami, but Amanda could easily convert one of the spare bedrooms into a special place for Isadora.

"Come, Princesa," Alejandro said at last. "Let's go mingle with the people."

"Who are they?"

He shrugged. "People."

"Just people?" she asked him incredulously. "How do you know them?"

"From the label. Two of them are singers I've recorded songs with in the past. One is my LA sound engineer. The rest are their friends." He pulled his sunglasses down over his nose so that he could have eye contact with her. "It's good to mingle with people sometimes, Amanda. You never know when you might need them."

He took her hand and led her to the back of the boat. As she had suspected, several women were dancing to the music while the men lingered around the outdoor bar, drinking beer from bottles. When Alejandro approached them, the group parted to make way for him while someone handed him a beer.

She stood nearby, watching as Alejandro conversed with them. She marveled at how he managed to move so swiftly and smoothly through a group of people, talking and laughing with them despite not really knowing them. He made them feel as if they were the most important people in the world. Perhaps, at that moment, they were, she thought.

With a deep breath she set her shoulders and decided she, too, would do the same. Emulating Alejandro would take her out of her comfort zone, but she needed to try. Standing on the sidelines was doing nothing to help him or her.

"I'd like a water, please," she said to the bartender. The person next to her turned and smiled. Amanda took the opportunity to strike up a conversation. "The weather tonight is simply magnificent, *ja*?"

"It's always magnificent in Los Angeles," the woman replied cheerfully.

"So you are from here, then?"

It was the right question because the woman began to talk about how long she had lived in Los Angeles, where she had moved from, and what she did for a living. Amanda found that just by asking a few questions, the woman continued talking, her eyes lighting up and her facial expressions animated. More people began to loosen up and join them, all of them vying for Amanda's attention as they eagerly began to monopolize her.

She felt him behind her, his body pressed against hers as he wrapped his arm around her chest. He leaned forward, his cheek against the side of her head. "*Mi* Princesa. She holds court, *sí*?"

Several people laughed, and while Amanda didn't quite understand what he meant, she smiled to be polite.

"I want everybody to raise their glasses," Alejandro said. No one questioned his demand. When everyone's arms were lifted, Alejandro did the same. "Let's make a toast! To Amanda Diaz!" Everyone cheered as they looked at her. Uncomfortable with the attention, she felt her cheeks grow hot. "Not only is she my wife, but she is now part of the Viper marketing team!" More cheers.

He gave her a hug, his arms holding her tight, and then he lifted her in the air, his arms holding her as if she weighed no more than a feather.

"*¡Ay, Princesa!*" he said. "I'm so proud of you!" He let her slide down his body until her chest was pressed against his before he leaned into her, his lips seeking hers, not caring that other people were nearby and watching.

His display of affection warmed her heart but did little to make her feel more comfortable. Pride, she thought, is a sin. Yet, for some reason, it didn't *feel* sinful to her. Didn't Proverbs state that *her children arise up, and call her blessed; her husband also, and he praiseth her.* Praise and pride, so closely linked. She didn't know where the one stopped and the other began. In order to give the former, one had to have a little of the latter.

For the next hour, as the sun set behind the mountains of Malibu, the party continued. Amanda stayed by Alejandro as much as possible while still mingling with his "friends." But as the bottom of the sun disappeared and the boat turned around toward the marina, she found herself mentally exhausted from being so tuned in to the people around her. She didn't know how Alejandro managed to keep up his positive energy for so long every day. All she wanted was to get off the boat, return to the apartment, and enjoy a nice quiet evening at home with her husband.

From the look on Alejandro's face, she doubted that was going to happen. And, to her further disappointment, she realized there wouldn't be any time in the schedule to visit the beach.

# Chapter Thirteen

"There's something about him that I just don't care for," Amanda confided in Celinda.

They sat outside of a Paris cafe under an overhang, which protected them from the sun. Two security guards stood nearby while a table of Parisians paid little attention to them, regardless of whether they recognized the two women.

"Enrique?" Celinda said and laughed, dismissing Amanda's concerns with a wave of her hand. "He's all talk, Amanda. Perfectly harmless."

"I'm not so certain about that," Amanda replied. She remembered far too well how, when they were in Argentina, Enrique had surrounded himself with beautiful women wearing skimpy bathing suits. What was supposed to be a relaxing week for just her and Alejandro had turned into a twenty-four-hour party for everyone—everyone, that is, except Amanda.

Celinda sighed as she reached for her glass of white wine. "There are far more dangerous people out there, Amanda. You're fortunate to have Alejandro's protection."

"You have Justin's," Amanda pointed out.

Celinda shrugged. "Do I? Do I really?" Her chocolate-brown eyes peered at Amanda from beneath long black eyelashes. There was something wholesome about Celinda, and Amanda was glad they had managed to catch up on the tour. "When I needed him the most, he left me. And why?"

Amanda knew the stories that had circulated in the tabloids, but she also knew that tabloid stories were often far from the truth. So she remained silent.

"He's on tour, Amanda," Celinda said at last. "An unattached Justin sells more than a committed one. I feel like a rubber band the way he pulls and releases me." She shook her head, a strand of her thick dark hair falling over her cheek. Absentmindedly, she pushed it away. "I see the stories about him, the photos. He's just twenty-one, Amanda. I'm well aware that he's out with other women." The casual way that Celinda admitted it made Amanda wonder if her friend was holding back something, perhaps denying how she truly felt about Justin Bell's infidelity, which had, ultimately, led to the dissolution of their relationship.

"You don't know that," Amanda said, but she didn't sound very convincing, even to herself.

Celinda laughed again. "Yes, yes I do. That's the nature of the entertainment industry. Fidelity is as rare as successful marriages in this business!"

Amanda found nothing humorous about what Celinda said. She, too, had worried that Alejandro had been unfaithful to her. The media's portrayal of Alejandro with Maria had convinced Amanda that he'd slept with another woman. Yet the media was wrong: Alejandro had never strayed. Even in South America, Amanda never questioned whether Alejandro had remained true to his wedding vows, even after she had departed and returned to her parents' farm.

"Besides," Celinda said in a more somber tone, "he's not currently the darling of the social media world right now anyway."

Amanda tilted her head, trying to understand what Celinda meant.

"I mean that his antics in South America . . . Brazil, in particular . . . have not won over many fans. And now he's touring on the West Coast, trying to clean up his image. I heard he's even teamed up with some underage YouTuber whose only talent is that he looks like Justin. I suppose that's fair though," Celinda said. "The kid exploited his resemblance to Justin to gain millions of followers, and now Justin is exploiting him to appeal to the younger teenybopper audiences." She laughed and shook her head. "It serves both of them right!"

Amanda didn't like what she was hearing. When she'd met Justin and Celinda last year in Los Angeles, they were the hot couple, featured in every tabloid and on every entertainment show. With their tumultuous relationship always front-page news, even the die-hard Justin fans sympathized with Celinda's heartache. But Amanda did not remember him that way. He had seemed attentive and abundantly affectionate to Celinda. The demise of what had appeared a storybook romance made Amanda even more determined to stay in tune with Alejandro's moods and needs.

"Do you miss him?"

Celinda shrugged in a noncommittal way. "At times, yes."

"So what happens now?"

"With Justin and me?" She laughed. "Oh, Amanda, you're so refreshing to be with! I'm so glad I can spend this time with you. You're like a breath of fresh air."

Amanda didn't respond, not quite certain what to make of Celinda's comment.

Taking Amanda's silence for confusion, Celinda leaned forward. "He'll be back. He just needs some time to experience life. He's young. Younger than I am."

"He's the same age as me," Amanda commented.

Celinda waved her hand dismissively. "Oh Lord, Amanda! You are light-years ahead of everyone in this industry!" She laughed once again, the sound joyful and friendly. "The way you work the media and the public . . . why, you're more in demand than I am!"

Amanda panicked when she heard that. "Oh!" she gasped. "That's not true!"

"Yes. It is true," Celinda said, picking up her drink. "And that's OK. If it has to be anyone, I'm glad it's you." She took a sip and glanced over Amanda's shoulder in the direction of the street. She nodded her head. When Amanda looked, she saw a small crowd starting to gather, trying to peer inside. "Word has spread, my dear."

"Word?"

Slipping on her sunglasses, Celinda glanced around to make certain no one could overhear. "Fans. They're outside the door."

Amanda checked in the direction of the door and noticed the gathering. "Oh help."

"Shall we have some fun, Amanda?" Celinda teased. "Play with the fans a little?"

"Play? How?"

Celinda gestured toward the back of the cafe. "We can leave through the back and see how long it takes for them to catch on. Then we can hurry down the street and visit some shops. When the word spreads, we'll see how quickly it takes for the street to shut down and police to be called."

That didn't seem like much fun to Amanda; she could only imagine what Alejandro would say when he learned about it. The sparkle in Celinda's eyes and the smile on her lips told her that this was not the first time Celinda had played such a game.

"That boy band from London can shut down a street in ten minutes," Celinda said. "Let's give the security guards a run for their money."

Celinda threw some euros onto the table and gathered her purse. Amanda followed her, casting an uneasy look over her shoulder at the window where the fans had gathered. In just a few minutes, the crowd had doubled in size. A fan frenzy, Alejandro called it. While Celinda thought of the mobs as fun, Alejandro always warned Amanda that they were dangerous. Now Amanda was following Celinda right into the heart of creating a mob scene.

They slipped out the back door of the cafe and headed toward the Champs-Élysées, one of the fanciest shopping streets in Paris, according to Celinda. The tree-lined avenue hosted hotels and stores, many of them frequented by the rich and famous. Amanda followed Celinda down the sidewalk, ignoring the few turned heads that recognized her. She felt her pulse quicken, wondering if the crowd from the cafe had realized that the two young women had slipped out the back. When she heard noises behind them, Amanda knew that the impromptu group of fans had figured it out and were following them.

"Look!" Celinda said, reaching for Amanda's hand. "Louis Vuitton!" She pulled Amanda with her as she crossed the street. "I could use a new outfit!"

Amanda glanced over her shoulder and saw the crowd following them. While Amanda wasn't certain if the street would be shut down, she certainly suspected they'd need a police escort to return to the hotel.

Once inside the store, Celinda moved toward the back of the building while Amanda lingered at the front, amazed by the marble floors and high vaulted ceilings. It reminded her of Cartier in Beverly Hills, but it was larger. Fancy shoes on glass shelves lined the walls, and farther from the doors were displays of cocktail purses and evening clutches, most of them embellished with crystals. Nothing in New York City or Los Angeles compared to the opulence of the store.

"*Bonjour, mademoiselle,*" a saleswoman said as she approached Amanda. "*Pourrais-je vous aider?*"

Amanda didn't understand and merely shook her head.

Before the woman could translate, something distracted her and she glanced over Amanda's shoulder. The expression on her face changed as she took a step toward the front windows. "What in the world?" she said in English. "Why are there so many people?"

The store's security guard mumbled something in French; the saleswoman turned to look first at Amanda and then to Celinda. After a quick back and forth, she gestured toward the front door and the security guard nodded, locking it shut against the crowd that had gathered. Amanda suddenly realized what was happening. A mass of young women stood outside, pressing together and trying to shoot photos through the window. From the looks of it, over a hundred people stood out there, waiting and hoping to meet Amanda and Celinda. Amanda walked toward the window and paused, lifting her hand to press it gently against the glass.

Immediately, the women on the other side of the glass began to scream, a few with tears of joy streaming down their cheeks while others continued shooting pictures.

"What are you doing?"

Amanda turned around to face the saleswoman, only partially surprised to see the angry expression on her face.

"Do not entice them!" the woman snapped. "We will have to call the police to disperse them."

As soon as she said that, Amanda heard the sound of an approaching police car. Apparently, someone else had alerted the authorities about the unexpected crush of fans blocking the sidewalk and spilling into the street. Simultaneously, Amanda's phone vibrated. She dug into her handbag and withdrew it. Alejandro had texted her:

```
Do NOT leave that building.
I have sent security to pick you up.
V.
```

She didn't need to guess how he knew so quickly: without doubt, social media was abuzz and someone on his payroll had noticed photos, most likely with the hashtag #parisprincesa. She shouldn't have been surprised. That hashtag had been hitting the top trending tags on different social media platforms even before Alejandro and Amanda had arrived in Paris. However, knowing that his day had just been interrupted, she immediately felt guilty. She should have known better than to leave the cafe without security. How many times had he warned her about the danger of crowds surrounding her in public? She knew that she'd have to confess that she had created this willingly. Without a doubt, he'd be angry with her.

```
I'm sorry.
A.
```

That would suffice for now, she thought. She'd apologize later when she could explain exactly what had happened. If nothing else, it was a lesson well learned and, except for the blocked traffic on the Champs-Élysées, there was little harm done.

From the back of the store, Celinda came bounding toward Amanda and, seeing the throng of people, stopped short. "Oh!" She took a step closer to the windows and lifted her hand to wave. The fans responded with more cheers and banging on the doors.

"Please. You must stop!"

Ignoring the irate saleswoman, Celinda stepped away from the window on her own accord. She cringed, looking as surprised as Amanda felt. "Oops," Celinda said under her breath. "I didn't count on that."

"On what?"

"Beating the boy band so fast! Where did all these people come from?" Once again, she gazed over her shoulder toward the window. Flashing lights could be seen and the crowd started to move, the police trying to force their way through the people. "I can only imagine Justin's response to this media circus," she said, more to herself than to Amanda. "Celinda and Princesa, shutting down the Champs-Élysées!"

Amanda didn't respond. While she repeatedly professed to not understand people's fascination with celebrities, she knew that she was finally seeing firsthand how dangerous fame could be. As horrible as the situation looked, with police trying to disperse the crowd and Alejandro sending security to rescue her and Celinda, there was a positive side. The fans were thrilled to see them, the social media was buzzing with photos, and the Louis Vuitton store would be front and center in all of the magazines—not that they needed the publicity.

The staff at the store paced back and forth, speaking rapid-fire French, a language neither Amanda nor Celinda understood. Amanda figured it was probably better that way. She couldn't imagine they were saying anything particularly kind about being trapped in their own store. A few other customers lingered in the back, bewildered by the two celebrities as they waited for security to arrive and escort them to safety.

It took at least twenty minutes for the police to get a car in front of the building. As they waited for the officers to make a path through the crowd so that Amanda and Celinda could exit the store, Amanda glanced down at her phone. She had two messages: one from Charlotte and another from Alejandro.

```
Your social media is exploding, my
dear. Brilliant!
~Char
```

Amanda rolled her eyes. Charlotte would see only the publicity opportunities. Knowing her, she'd be after Louis Vuitton for an advertising campaign.

She deleted Charlotte's message and looked at Alejandro's, feeling guilty once again when she read it:

```
Be careful leaving the building.
I'm waiting for you at the hotel.
V.
```

Certainly he had cut short his meetings to wait for her at the Hotel George V. While it was only just a short walk from the shop, Amanda knew that the crowds would continue to delay their departure, even with police and security.

An officer rapped at the door and motioned for the two women to exit the building. Amanda followed Celinda, pausing just a moment to apologize to the staff at the store. Then she walked through the door and along the safe passage created by a line of police officers. No sooner had they darted into the backseat of the black Bentley than police sirens sounded and the car slowly moved through the crowd.

Celinda covered her mouth and stared at Amanda. "That probably wasn't the best idea," she admitted. "I'm so sorry."

Amanda shook her head. She could have said no to Celinda, but she hadn't wanted to disappoint her friend. Even more to the point, Amanda had to admit that there was some part of her that wanted to test the boundaries of her fame. She couldn't deny that she felt a sense of excitement when she realized how popular she was with so many people.

"I'm sorry, too," Amanda admitted. "I think I have become far more worldly and accustomed to too much attention. It's not *gut*."

Celinda laughed. She leaned over and nudged Amanda with her shoulder. "Oh please, Amanda. You are the least worldly and vain person I have ever met! You sacrifice enough for your fans. There are times when you can stop to enjoy it a bit, no?"

If only Amanda was enjoying it. Being with Alejandro was enough excitement for any person. It was the extra commotion—the travel and hordes of fans and media scrutiny—that Amanda didn't want. She just wanted to be with Alejandro, but she knew that it was a package deal. To have Alejandro, she needed to sacrifice so many other parts of herself: her family, Isadora, even a steady home. She also had to sacrifice her freedom. This was just another example of something that Amanda could no longer do: visit a store sans security to extricate her.

"Alejandro will be angry, for sure and certain," Amanda said at last, turning to look out the window as she anticipated his reaction.

She didn't have to wait long. As soon as the car pulled up in front of the Hotel George V, the door was opened and both of the women were quickly whisked past a waiting crowd and into the hotel. Alejandro stood in the lobby, flanked by Andres and two other men Amanda didn't recognize.

"Princesa!" He hurried away from the men when he saw her walk through the door. "What happened?" He addressed the question to Celinda. "You shouldn't be unattended. You know that something like this can happen."

Celinda apologized. "It was my fault, Viper."

Amanda glanced at her. She didn't want her friend to take the blame for her. "*Nee*, Alejandro, I knew, too. I should have come back here instead of going to the store."

If she thought he was going to be angry, she was immediately surprised. Instead of being upset with her, he led her over to Andres. "Amanda, if I am not with you, you'll go with these two men." He motioned to them. "They will travel with us and be assigned to you alone. We cannot risk having you injured by these mobs, whether on the streets or at a venue."

She nodded her head, still feeling guilty for having put so many people through so much trouble. If vanity was a sin, she had sinned deeply that day.

Before the concert that evening, Amanda sat in the greenroom. She was waiting until security came to fetch her. It was the first night she would be wandering the floor, taking photos with fans and selecting a few to move up to the front of the stage. After the afternoon's episode at Louis Vuitton, her stylist, Jeremy, had arranged for her to wear a simple white

Louis Vuitton dress with a gold belt that matched her shoes. With her hair fixed in a low bun and her makeup fresh and perfect, Amanda knew that she looked the very princess the public wanted to see.

"*¡Ay,* Princesa!"

She looked up and smiled as Alejandro walked into the room. He reached down for her hand and gently pulled her to her feet. Holding her at arm's length, he gestured for her to turn around. When she did, he whistled.

"*¡Ay caramba,* Princesa!* I am quite positive that Louis Vuitton will sell out this dress, no? A kind way to thank them for your mischief this afternoon."

Amanda blushed and looked away, still ashamed of herself.

He gave a soft laugh and put his finger under her chin, forcing her to look up. "Mischief or not, it was a smart publicity move, Amanda. Reckless but smart."

Part of her wanted to tell him that Celinda had come up with the idea, but she didn't want to point the finger of blame at anyone else. She was an adult and knew what she was doing.

The day's events had, however, made her wonder about Celinda's loyalty to her. Once things had calmed down, it hadn't taken Amanda long to realize Celinda had encouraged the mob scene more to capture Justin's attention than to play with their fans. She also realized that Celinda wanted to be aligned with her, showing the public that they were close friends, casually shopping in Paris in the afternoon before the concert.

She felt as if Celinda had used her and that did not sit well with Amanda.

"Forget about it, Amanda," Alejandro said softly. "I know you feel bad. I can read it in your face, *mi amor.*"

Do not cry, she told herself. If she cried, she'd have to go back to makeup, and that was something Amanda did not want to do.

"What is it?" he persisted when she pressed her lips together and blinked her eyes. "What is troubling you?"

She shook her head. "I . . . I feel so different, Alejandro. It's just not like me to do things like that."

Placing his hands on her shoulders, he knelt down and stared into her face. "Look at me," he demanded in a caring tone. "Amanda."

She did as she was told and lifted her eyes to meet his, shining a bright blue.

"You feel different, *sí*," he said. "You *are* different. You are no longer that naive Amish girl who crossed the street in New York City without looking both ways. But that does not make you a bad person, Amanda. It makes you a different person—and I love that person, whether you are shutting down streets in Paris or curled up in my arms in the early-morning hours."

"I don't want to be different," she whispered.

He raised one eyebrow and tilted his head as he looked at her. "What you want and what you get are sometimes two different things, *sí*? Living this life is bound to change you. You cannot travel from city to city, living in hotels and surrounded by an entourage that protects you from the vultures wanting pieces of you, without changing. Accept it as part of God's plan for you, Amanda. This is what he wants for you, and for us."

None of that made sense to her. How could God want this for her? It was so far removed from everything she had learned during her twenty years before she met Alejandro. Now, in just one year, she had left her family and community, traveled the world, married a rap star, and become a celebrity in her own right. How any of that fit into God's plan was beyond her comprehension.

"I see you thinking," Alejandro said. "Let it go, Amanda. Look for the good and forget the bad. That is the only way you will remain sane."

Andres, the head of the security team, leaned through the open door and motioned to Amanda. *"¿Listo?"* he asked.

Amanda nodded. She started to walk toward the door, but Alejandro stopped her, pausing to gently kiss her forehead.

"I am proud of you, Amanda," he said. "Now, go make a difference in the lives of some people."

Obediently, she followed Andres to the corridor that led to the floor. There were several security guards standing at the closed doors. When Andres approached, the guards stepped aside, one of them pushing open the door. It took a moment for Amanda to adjust to the level of noise on the arena floor. It was deafening to hear the people in that grand space. When the fans closest to the door recognized her, the screaming intensified into a wave that roared throughout the stadium.

"Princesa! Princesa!"

Amanda followed Andres onto the floor while another security guard walked behind her, ensuring that no one grabbed her from behind. The crowd opened up before her, spreading like the Red Sea. But as she walked, it filled in behind her, the throngs of people trying to crush each other to get to Amanda. The security for the stadium maintained crowd control as Amanda moved down the aisles between the sections of seats.

One young girl who looked to be no older than fourteen began to cry as Amanda paused in front of her. She was not French; that much was clear. With her ginger hair and freckled face she looked more Irish. When she spoke, she had a thick accent Amanda could not identify.

"I can't believe it's you!" the girl sobbed, her shoulders heaving under the weight of her emotion.

Amanda gave a soft laugh. "And you cry over that?"

The girl tried to calm down but failed. An older woman behind the girl placed a hand on her shoulder to help calm her.

"What's your name?" Amanda asked, barely able to hear above the screaming fans around her. Several held their arms out, desperate to just touch Amanda. Between Andres, his team, and the venue's own security team, Amanda knew she did not have to worry.

"Lucille."

"Lucille," Amanda repeated. "That's a lovely name." She paused and glanced over her shoulder at Andres. He gave a nod of his head, and Amanda turned back to the bewildered girl. "Lucille, I would like you to come with me."

The girl stopped crying and looked up at her with confusion in her eyes. "What?"

"Come with me." Amanda held out her hand as Andres stepped aside so that Lucille could climb over the barricade that separated Amanda from the rest of the crowd. "You will watch the show tonight in a special place, *ja?*"

The girl looked around wildly, not believing what she was hearing. "But . . . my mother . . ."

Amanda gestured to the woman with her. "She can come, too."

The rest of the people in the area began screaming for Amanda to pick them, too. But as Alejandro and Geoffrey had trained her (and Charlotte reinforced), Amanda merely smiled and waited for Lucille to take her hand. She could not select everyone, but she could select one or two who would never forget the night Princesa took them out of the crowd and brought them backstage.

She continued walking through the fans, Lucille and her mother behind her. She paused at several places so that she could stand next to people who wanted a photo of her. With Andres and the rest of security nearby, she did not fear the crowd. Instead, just as Alejandro predicted, she felt an overwhelming sense of joy as she talked to the audience. Many of them cried; others just jumped up and down screaming. A few gushed their gratitude to her, telling her that she had made a positive impact on their lives. Amanda did not have much time to talk with each of them, but she thanked anyone who took a photo with her and then let Andres guide her across the rest of the floor.

When they came to the other side of the arena, Andres rapped on a door and it opened, letting them slip through into the backstage.

Lucille and her mother stood there, their mouths hanging open as if they did not believe their good fortune. One of the guards motioned for them to follow Amanda, who was immediately surrounded by a team of people to touch up her makeup and her hair as she walked.

"Lucille," Amanda said at last, turning to reach for the girl's hand. "Come walk beside me. Tell me about what made you cry."

The young girl blinked her eyes and swallowed, accepting Amanda's hand and walking beside her. "I . . . I don't know why I cried," she admitted. "I've just wanted to meet you forever."

Amanda gave a soft laugh. "Your forever must not be very long, then. Last year at this time, I was just an Amish girl visiting family in Ohio."

The young girl smiled nervously. "You are different from the other celebrities," the girl said. "You care about your fans. Really care!"

Amanda nodded. "*Ja*, I do. But I do not consider myself a celebrity. I'm just a person. Like you."

"Oh, you are nothing like me!" the girl gushed. "You are so beautiful and so kind. I wish I could be just like you."

Amanda frowned. "You are beautiful," Amanda said. "And I imagine you are kind, too. But beauty is in the eye of the beholder, Lucille, and kindness is something you must work on every day. I know that I do, that's for sure and certain."

The mother spoke up. "You have no idea what this means to Lucille," she said.

Amanda gave a wistful smile. "I'm sure I do not."

"She has issues at school, you see."

"Mom!"

Amanda glanced from one to the other. She saw a desperation in the eyes of the mother that was countered by the humiliation in the eyes of her daughter. Immediately, Amanda understood what must have happened. Even in the Amish community, the teenagers often socialized in groups. While bullying was rare among the Amish, it wasn't completely unheard of.

They stopped in front of the greenroom, and Amanda gestured for them to step inside. She let them get a cold beverage before she sat down on the sofa.

"Lucille, I want to tell you a story," Amanda said. "I had issues, too. Not at school though. But in my church. They did not treat me well after the paparazzi came to the farm and the bishop wanted me to leave my family." She paused and glanced at the mother, who smiled in appreciation of Amanda's story. "I felt very alone, Lucille. Mayhaps just like you feel sometimes, *ja*?"

Reluctantly, Lucille nodded.

"*Ja*, I thought so," Amanda said tenderly. "Feeling different or feeling alone is never fun, is it? But you need to stand up for yourself and take back the control in your life. If I had not done that, I'd still be on a farm in Ohio and not married to Alejandro. And I certainly would not be sitting here with you."

The girl lit up and nodded her head.

"Now, I must go for a few moments." She looked over her shoulder at the security men. "Security will make certain you have everything you need, and they will escort you to meet Viper before the show starts. Then one of these men will escort you to front-row seats just before the opening act starts." She leaned forward and hugged Lucille. "Make certain that you give them your social media information so I can follow you, *ja*?"

Lucille gasped and looked at her mother.

Amanda did not wait for a response. She stood up and started to shake hands with the mother. But the mother also gave her a hug.

"Thank you, Princesa. You have no idea what you have just done for my daughter."

Amanda pulled back and peered into the mother's face. "*Ja*, I think I do," she said. "Probably the same thing that Alejandro did for me." She gave the mother a soft smile. "Good luck with Lucille."

Andres stood outside the door to escort her from the room, just as Enrique walked by. He glanced over her shoulder and saw the girl sitting there with her mother.

"What have we here?" he said, curious.

"My personal guest, Enrique," she heard herself say in a voice that sounded stronger than she felt when she was around him.

"Oh, *sí*?" He gave her a grin and walked around her into the room.

Amanda took a deep breath and turned back, giving Andres a look that implored him to keep an eye on Enrique. Even though Andres did not respond, she knew he understood her. She needed to go change her dress before the VIP Meet and Greet and did not want to leave Lucille and her mother alone with Enrique, even for a few minutes.

To her surprise, Enrique merely posed for a photo with the girl before grabbing a cold beer from the beverage table. He untwisted the top and tossed it across the room at the garbage can but missed. A few other people walked into the room, one of them a reporter, who immediately sat next to Amanda's guests and began speaking with them. Satisfied that they were safe from Enrique's roguish ways, Amanda retreated to her dressing room, where her small team of people would help her dress and fix her makeup before meeting more fans.

# Chapter Fourteen

In the morning, Amanda woke early to find that Alejandro was not beside her. Curious, she slid out from beneath the sheets and quietly padded across the room. The double doors to their bedroom were shut to the outer living area. She had just started to open them when she heard voices on the other side of the doors. Geoffrey, Eddie, and Carlos were talking with Alejandro. She glanced over her shoulder and saw that it was not quite eight o'clock. She couldn't imagine what was so important they would already be meeting at such an early hour, at least for them.

She hurried to the bathroom to get changed and fix her hair before joining the men.

"Ten-percent increase overnight," Eddie said, handing Alejandro a piece of paper. "The numbers are printed here for each of the social media outlets." He pointed to a line on the paper. "Check out the chatter numbers on Twitter."

Amanda crossed the room and placed her hand on Alejandro's shoulder.

He looked up at her and gave her a quick smile.

"So early," she said. "Everything alright, then?"

He nodded, gesturing for her to sit in the empty chair beside him. Then he motioned for Carlos to bring her a coffee.

"Reviewing the impact on social media from your interaction with the crowd last night, Amanda."

"From last night?"

He nodded and slid the paper across the table so that she could look at it. "Almost half a million new followers added to your social currency."

She stifled a yawn. Social media. Social currency. It seemed like that was all she heard about it. She looked down the rows and columns on the paper; the names and numbers looked like a foreign language to her. "Is that good?"

Alejandro laughed at her innocent question. "*Sí*, Amanda, very good."

Eddie glanced down at another folder in his hands. "And two entertainment stations contacted your guys in Miami last night requesting interviews about her."

"Only two?" Alejandro lifted an eyebrow as though he was disappointed with that news. To her surprise, he said, "Deny both of them. That will up the interest for an exclusive."

Amanda pushed the paper back to Alejandro as Carlos set down a mug of coffee for her. She gave him a quick smile of appreciation and lifted it to her lips, enjoying the feeling of the warm liquid sliding down her throat. Only when she set down the mug again did she trust her voice. "All from walking through the floor and taking that girl backstage?"

"*Sí*, Amanda. That was just brilliant."

She didn't see what was so brilliant about it, but she was glad they were pleased.

Geoffrey must have sensed her lack of comprehension, for he tried to break it down for her. "You see, the larger your presence, the more powerful your combined social currency."

"Oh?"

"For marketing, Amanda. New people to reach for promoting products: concerts, albums, merch."

She still didn't get it. "If Viper has such a big following, wouldn't my interacting with his fans mean that those new followers are only a subset of his?"

Alejandro looked at her with curiosity. "Go on," he encouraged.

"I mean, they love Viper, attend a concert, and find Princesa because of him, *ja?*" She felt ridiculous referring to herself as Princesa, but had come to understand that these meetings, which usually took place on airplanes or during long rides in buses, were about marketing products, not people. When it came to Viper and Princesa, it was the image that people bought into and wanted to connect with, not the real people behind it. "Mayhaps reaching new people would be more meaningful if you introduce them to the real product: Viper."

Geoffrey glanced at Alejandro before he responded. "What do you have in mind?"

She shrugged. "*Vell*, back in Lititz, when I lived there, I always had a garden. If I have one garden plot and I invite someone else to plant in it, I still only produce the same amount of vegetables, even if they are working that section, *ja?* It doesn't really help me. Oh, mayhaps I have less work because they are doing some of that, but I also have less reward, *ja?* Now, if I expand the garden plot and let that person plant there, in the previously unplanted section, we increased the production of the crops. Mayhaps we need to expand the garden plot, if that's what is so important. Reaching new people, I mean."

"Interesting," Alejandro said slowly. "Princesa does appeal to many different audiences."

She nodded. "That girl last night . . . her mother brought her to the concert, *ja?* But is the mother part of your audience? Maybe reach out to the mothers who are struggling with their *dochders*, like this mother was struggling." She realized that the three men were staring at her and suddenly she felt self-conscious, worrying she had said too much. She reached for her mug. "Mayhaps that's a silly thing to say," she said, wishing that she had not spoken out loud.

Alejandro leaned forward. "No, no. You might have something there. Those mothers come with their children to the concerts, *sí*? But they do not care about the music. If we gave them something to care about, that would expand our audience. Perhaps a private meeting with Princesa before the concert?"

She almost choked on her coffee. "What?"

Alejandro ignored her stunned expression and continued talking to Geoffrey. "Special tickets to talk with her backstage and then seating in the first ten rows."

Amanda's mouth fell open. "Talk with me? About what?"

"Simplicity. Self-esteem."

Immediately, she shook her head. She couldn't imagine that she would have anything important to share with these girls. "Oh no, that's not for me. I can't do that."

Geoffrey dismissed her concerns by saying, "Princesa, you are already doing that. You just don't realize it."

But she remained firm. "*Nee*, Alejandro. I cannot talk to these people about that. Please don't ask me to do that."

Alejandro ignored her plea. "Think of school visits. These young girls have such low self-esteem. They need an ambassador of goodwill to help them realize their worth."

Eddie nodded his head in agreement. "The younger women . . . the girls . . . they have poor self-image."

Geoffrey gave a harsh laugh. "And how." He glanced at Amanda. "They need a role model, Amanda."

Now it was Alejandro's turn. "And they already adore you, *mi amor*. Now we must find ways to capitalize on it to expand our other products. Cross marketing, *sí*?"

Amanda groaned and sank back into her chair.

Eddie tried to hide a smile while Alejandro laughed at her reaction. "You should have stayed in bed, *sí?* Waited for me to wake you up," he said, leaning over to put his arm around her shoulders and pulling her toward him. He kissed her temple and gave her a gentle squeeze as he whispered, "Now you will know better next time."

She blushed and lowered her eyes, too aware that the other men were laughing at her embarrassment.

The door opened and Enrique entered. He wore the same clothes from the previous night; they had all gone clubbing. His hair looked disheveled and, even indoors, he wore his sunglasses. "Yolo!" he said cheerfully and made a beeline for the coffee. "You ready to record, Viper?"

Alejandro released Amanda and his cheerful demeanor changed to irritation. "Walk of shame, *chico?*"

Enrique laughed to himself, downing one cup of black coffee before pouring himself another one. "Shame or glory: depends on how you look at it."

Alejandro glanced at his watch. "It's after eight o'clock." If there was one thing that riled up Alejandro, it was tardiness. Amanda sensed his frustration and lowered her gaze away from Enrique and his bedraggled appearance.

"I'm on Parisian time, man. Eight o'clock means eight thirty, nine!" When he pulled off his sunglasses, it was clear from his glazed and bloodshot eyes that he'd stayed out partying long after Alejandro and Amanda had left last night. "Besides, I didn't want to be rude to my company."

That's it, Amanda thought, disgusted with Alejandro's colleague. How Alejandro put up with him was a mystery to her, although she reminded herself that, at one time, Alejandro had been no different. Amanda stood up, not wanting to stay in his presence. Gloating over his previous night's conquest was Enrique's specialty, and not something she wanted to be privy to. "Mayhaps I'll see if Celinda's up for breakfast downstairs, *ja?*"

At the mention of Celinda's name, Enrique laughed once again. "She's not. I can personally attest to that."

For a moment, Amanda felt as if the floor fell out from beneath her feet. She remembered seeing Celinda and Enrique dancing when she'd left with Alejandro. With so many people together, Amanda hadn't given it a second thought, although some of their moves on the dance floor were provocative and a little too sensual for Amanda's taste.

She refused to give him the satisfaction of knowing his insinuation bothered her. Without another word, she walked to the bedroom, eager to leave the presence of a man who still stunk from last night's sins.

As she shut the door, she heard Alejandro scolding him. "Come on, *papito*. Why you gotta be like that with her?"

Enrique responded with another laugh. If he answered, she didn't care to know how. She sat down at the chair by the window, focusing her attention on the street below, where regular people walked down the sidewalks on their way to regular jobs, oblivious to the fact that they were being watched by the very woman who graced the cover of the morning paper. It was better that way, she thought. Watching them gave her a sense of reality, an escape from *"la vida loca"* that she had not only married into but of which she was now a contracted member.

If anyone needed role models, she thought angrily, it wasn't the people walking in the streets below but many of the very people they looked up to, that was for sure and certain.

When she finally saw Celinda, it was backstage at the arena as they prepared for the evening show. Celinda breezed into the room, practically floating on air as she headed to the table set up with food.

When she saw Amanda, she smiled, grabbed a soft drink, and hurried over to plop down on the sofa beside her.

"What'd you do today?"

"Alejandro took me to the Notre-Dame Cathedral and for a walk along the Seine. And you?" Amanda tried to sound neutral, knowing that Celinda's choices would be judged by someone far more important than herself.

Celinda gave a little shrug. "Not much. Stayed in bed most of the day."

They were interrupted by some of the crew members, who barely greeted them as they hurried to grab some food before it disappeared.

"Paris is beautiful," Amanda said. "Did you know that during World War II the townspeople took the stained-glass windows out of the cathedral piece by piece so they wouldn't be damaged?"

Celinda glanced at the door behind Amanda as she responded. "I did not."

"*Ja*, and the statues on the inside. Why, they are just the most beautiful things I've ever seen . . ." She hesitated as she thought back to the opulence of the cathedral. "*Nee*, the paintings were beautiful, too. *Ach*, I don't think I can decide between the two of them!" she declared, tossing her hands in the air.

Laughing at her, Celinda leaned her head back and shut her eyes. "I'll have to take your word for it. I'm too tired to do just about anything right now."

Amanda wanted to remind her that she had just said she spent the day in bed, but she didn't want to pry. Besides, it was Celinda's choice to stay out too late the previous night and to waste a perfectly fine late-spring day in Paris. As for Amanda, she was glad that she had not missed seeing the cathedral.

One of the stagehands walked into the room. "Celinda, a change in the set list tonight," he said and handed her a piece of paper.

"Tonight?" She groaned. "They expect me to actually remember a new set list? Just when I was used to the other set list." Her eyes scanned the paper and a smile crossed her lips as color rose to her cheeks.

Amanda couldn't help but wonder what type of change would bring such a reaction.

Celinda looked over at Amanda and, with a girlish giggle, handed her the paper. Amanda scanned it but couldn't immediately see what was different. Then, on her second look, she saw the big change: Celinda would be performing two songs with Enrique, one of them a song called "Loving You Last Night." Disgusted, Amanda handed the paper back to her friend.

"I got together with him last night," Celinda whispered.

*So I figured,* Amanda wanted to say. But she reminded herself that it was not up to her to judge others.

"He's really not as bad as you think," Celinda gushed, her hands clenched together and pressed under her chin.

Amanda wanted to warn Celinda that he was much worse than what she'd originally thought. His inference to having slept with Celinda that morning was crude and inappropriate. It was bad enough that he engaged in such reckless behavior, but there was no excuse for sharing the story with other people.

"I thought you loved Justin," Amanda said at last.

"Why, of course I love him!" Celinda responded hastily. "But we're apart now, and a little Enrique-dating-Celinda news being leaked to the Shiny Sheet or onto social media would not necessarily be a bad thing, Amanda."

Amanda couldn't imagine loving one man and sleeping with another. She said a quick prayer, thanking God that she would never be in such a situation. While she may have become more worldly, she still had her morals.

# Chapter Fifteen

The car had barely stopped when Amanda opened the door and jumped out. She had been counting down the days, waiting for their return to Lititz. Despite her daily phone calls to her family, she often had to leave messages for Anna, who did not always carry the phone with her or sometimes forgot to charge it. Based on the lack of returned calls, Amanda suspected she didn't check the voice mail too often either. But on the few occasions when Amanda had managed to talk to Isadora, her heart felt as if it broke all over again.

The door to the house opened and Anna stepped outside, Isadora running out behind her. Her little feet, devoid of shoes, ran as fast as they could to Amanda.

Kneeling down, Amanda opened her arms and welcomed her stepdaughter into a warm embrace. The scent of lavender drifted to Amanda's nose and she smiled. Isadora's little arms around her neck clung tightly, as if Amanda might disappear if she let go.

"Mammi 'Manda!" Isadora cried out, still clinging to her.

"Izzie! How much I have missed you!" Carefully, she peeled Isadora's arms away from her neck and held her hands. "You look so big! You must have grown almost as tall as Jonas!"

Isadora giggled at Amanda's teasing and jumped into her arms once again.

"Now, let's greet your *papi, ja*? He's eager to see you, too." Amanda wasn't certain if *eager* was the correct word. *Apprehensive* might have been more appropriate. But she wanted this to be a positive visit. She stood up and, holding Isadora's hand, walked back toward the car.

Alejandro stood outside of their rented car, his sunglasses hiding his eyes. During the past four weeks, Alejandro had not once inquired about Isadora unless Amanda mentioned that she'd spoken with her or Anna. Only then did he ask about her well-being. Amanda continually noted the lack of enthusiasm whenever her name was mentioned.

Now, as Amanda approached him with their daughter, she felt anxious. How would he react to her? While she knew that it was unrealistic to expect a warm reception from him, Amanda hoped there was some melting of the icy feelings he displayed toward her—especially now that Amanda had reassured him that, no matter what, he still came first in her life.

"Izzie, say hello to your *papi*," Amanda coaxed.

The child looked at him, her eyes taking in his larger-than-life frame, and then she moved behind Amanda's legs.

He appeared completely out of his comfort zone. For a moment, Amanda felt a wave of sympathy for him. He hadn't asked for the responsibility of this child. But then she reminded herself, as Stedman had told her, it took two to tango. Alejandro was Isadora's father and he had agreed to take over her care. Amanda tucked any inkling of sympathy for him into the back of her mind.

Knowing that Alejandro had brought her to Lititz only because she wanted to see Isadora and her family, she tried to be understanding. But it was also high time he stepped up to his role as the child's father.

"Go on now, Izzie," Amanda said. "Give your *papi* a hug, *ja*?" Amanda gently guided Isadora toward Alejandro.

To his credit, he knelt down before the child and removed his sunglasses, leveling his gaze at her. Amanda could tell that he was struggling, trying to figure out how to talk with the girl. This remarkable man who had risen from the streets of Miami to international stardom, this man who could walk into a room and, without saying a word, capture everyone's attention and respect, was brought to his knees when it came to his child. It struck Amanda as an unfortunate situation, but she was proud that he was at least attempting to make a connection.

"You are doing well, *sí?*" he asked at last.

Isadora stood before him, one hand on his knee and the other behind her back. She swung her hips a little so that her skirt moved, just a touch. Just as Alejandro struggled, Amanda suspected Isadora was also nervous. This man who she had only heard about for the first five years of her life, and then finally met under the worst of circumstances, was larger than life. If he took away Amanda's breath with his charisma and presence, surely he intimidated Isadora.

Amanda knelt down behind Isadora and placed her hands on her stepdaughter's hips. With Amanda behind her, Isadora appeared to feel more confident and she nodded her head.

"What's this I've heard about an orange kitten?"

Amanda smiled at him over Isadora's head. The question was just the right thing to ask. Immediately, Isadora became animated and began telling Alejandro about her kitten. Within seconds, she grabbed Amanda's hand and pulled her toward the outbuilding. Amanda paused to reach for Alejandro's hand, and while he still looked uncomfortable, he followed them as they searched for the object of Isadora's affection.

It was asleep on top of a pile of hay bales, its tail hanging over the side as it lay on its back, one paw over its ear. Isadora climbed up the stack of hay and pulled the kitten onto her lap. It had grown over the past five weeks and was no longer small and meek. Instead, it was gangly and much more confident about being held on Isadora's lap.

Alejandro reached out and scratched at the kitten's ear. "She's a nice kitten, *sí?*"

Isadora smiled at him. *"Ja!"*

He raised one eyebrow in a perfect arch and looked at Amanda.

"Oh, I imagine you found a right *gut* name for her!" Amanda said, ignoring Alejandro's unspoken question about his daughter using Pennsylvania Dutch.

"Katie," Isadora responded. "Her name is Katie."

Amanda smiled. "Clever girl!" When Alejandro questioned her with his eyes, Amanda explained, "Kitten in Dutch is *katje*. Now she has a Katie Cat."

He didn't seem as impressed as Amanda was, but he nodded his head regardless.

"Well, she's a nice kitten, Isadora," he said and then, his interest in the cat and his child maxed out, he took a deep breath and looked around. "You should visit with your family, Amanda. I need to make a few phone calls."

Isadora sat on the hay bale, the kitten draped over her lap, and looked up at the two of them. She didn't seem disturbed by her father changing the subject from the kitten to work. Instead, she set the kitten beside her and jumped down. Reaching for Amanda's hand, she waited patiently to walk beside her toward the house, her bare feet padding across the driveway without any attention to loose rocks or gravel.

Inside the house, Amanda took a moment to greet her sister, mother, and father. Her father seemed thinner than when she had left and his eyes looked dull. Amanda wanted to ask her mother about how he was doing, but she knew better than to say anything about his condition in front of him. Instead, she sat down in the chair next to her father's wheelchair and opened her arms for Isadora to climb onto her lap.

"Oh, it's right *gut* to be home!" Amanda gushed. "Mamm, Daed, the things I have seen! Why, I don't think I could explain them if I had two lifetimes to live!"

Her sister pulled over a kitchen chair and sat next to her. Her stomach protruded, and to Amanda, she looked as if she were ready to give birth, although Anna still had three months left. "It sure does sound"—Anna searched for the appropriate word—"interesting."

"In England, they drive their cars on the wrong side of the road! Can you imagine? And they have castles that are older than this country and decorated so beautifully. It just is something you can't even imagine exists until you see it."

Anna leaned forward. "Castles?"

Amanda nodded. "Just magnificent buildings, Anna. Just like those books we used to sneak-read at the doctor's office!"

Anna laughed and Lizzie gave them a disapproving look. "You two thought I didn't know you read those books, but I did!"

"Only they aren't white castles, Anna, but made of big, huge stones. It's a wonder any man could move those stones, especially the ones high up on the walls and towers."

Isadora leaned her head back onto Amanda's shoulder. "Princesses?"

Now it was Amanda's turn to laugh. "*Nee*, Izzie. No princesses in these castles."

The little girl thought for a moment and then said, "You were there. You are a princess. Papi said so."

The color rose to her cheeks and Amanda gave her a warm hug. "Clever girl," she said for the second time in less than an hour. "Your *papi* just calls me that, Izzie. I'm not any more a princess than you are a horse!"

After giggling at Amanda's comment, Isadora reached up and stroked Amanda's cheek. "Tell more, Mammi 'Manda," she insisted.

"Well, let's see," Amanda said thoughtfully. "We spent three weeks in England and then flew to Los Angeles." She glanced at her sister. "That's California. And last week we were in Paris, France."

"Where is that?" Anna asked.

"Europe. It's beautiful with old buildings and large churches. My friend Celinda was there, and we were able to visit some places together. The Notre-Dame Cathedral. Oh, it was just overwhelming how beautiful it is."

Lizzie frowned. "Is that safe, Amanda? Wandering around these strange places?"

She laughed. "Of course it is, Mamm! It's a different country but still civilized! Besides, Alejandro sends us with security. He'd never let anything happen to us." She ignored the look her mother gave her at that comment. "When we leave here, we'll visit Prague and Zürich. Oh, and Vienna!"

Lizzie clucked her tongue and shook her head. "Such travel you do, Amanda! It can't be good to move from one place to another so much."

Amanda wrapped her arms around Isadora and held her close to her chest. "Now, Mamm! The only bad thing about it is that this little one cannot be with us."

"Why not, Mammi?"

Amanda hugged her tighter. "I told you before: you couldn't bring your Katie Cat with you. She'd miss you so much, and I think you would miss her, too."

"Oh *ja*!" Isadora said. "I forgot."

Amanda smiled and kissed the top of Isadora's head. "I'm impressed with how much she is speaking," she said, directing the comment to her sister. "You must really be working with her, *ja*?"

"Nonstop," Lizzie answered for Anna. "Both of us. In fact, we have Isadora reading to Elias twice a day. Don't we now, Elias?" She leaned over and placed her hand on Elias's arm. "You like hearing Isadora read, don't you?"

"Reading!" Amanda repeated the word. "Why, that's *wunderbar!* Izzie, what are you reading to Elias?"

Without being asked to, Isadora jumped down from Amanda's lap and ran across the floor toward a basket with some toys in it. She pulled out a picture book and carried it back to Amanda. "I read to you," she said, leaning against her leg with the book placed on Amanda's lap. Immediately, Amanda recognized the book. It was one that she used to read to her brother, Aaron: a simple ABC book with different pictures of animals and objects associated with each letter of the alphabet.

"Apple . . . Ant . . ." Isadora pointed to each object as she said the word. She looked up at Amanda as if seeking approval and expecting something from her.

"That's very good." Amanda smiled and pointed to the apple. "What color is the apple?"

"Red!"

Amanda laughed at her enthusiastic reply. It was a game that Amanda and Anna had played with Aaron when he was just a little younger than Isadora. Because he had grown up speaking Pennsylvania Dutch, it was an easy way to help him learn English before he went to school. Each item was pointed to and then questions were asked in order to expand Aaron's vocabulary and sentence structure. Clearly, Anna and Lizzie played the same game with Isadora.

"What does the ant want?" Amanda asked.

"Food!"

"That's correct. It wants your food!"

Isadora took back the book and walked over to Elias. She crawled onto his lap and leaned her back against his chest. She began to do the same reading exercise, but this time, she played it with Elias.

"Butterfly . . . Butter . . . Barn . . . ," she said as she pointed to each item. "What color is the butterfly?" she asked Elias and, after waiting for a few long, silent seconds, she nodded her head. "*Ja*, it is blue."

Amanda glanced at Anna, who merely watched the little girl reading to Elias, love in her eyes. Despite how painful it was for Amanda to be apart from Isadora, watching her interactions with the rest of her family made it obvious that the decision had been the right one.

After they'd listened to Isadora read to Elias for fifteen minutes, Lizzie brought over glasses of lemonade. "Anna said you are only staying two days, *ja*?"

Amanda accepted the lemonade. "*Danke*, Mamm. *Ja*, just two days. We have a fund-raiser in New York and then fly to Prague on Friday morning."

"I see." There was a distant and disappointed look in her mother's face. Over the few weeks Amanda had been away, her mother looked as if she had aged ten years.

"What's wrong, Mamm?" she asked, leaning forward to touch her mother's leg. "Tell me. Please."

When Lizzie did not respond, Anna answered for their mother. "It hasn't rained in a while. The crops aren't growing properly," she said in a somber voice. Then, after a brief hesitation, she whispered, "And Daed isn't doing so well."

Amanda glanced over at her father. He did look gaunt—she had noticed that right away. But now as she looked closely at him, she saw his sunken eyes and pronounced cheekbones. His arms seemed weak, resting meekly on the arms of the wheelchair, and he stared at nothing, his eyes devoid of any spark that resembled his former self.

Amanda looked back at her sister. "Is Daed getting fresh air?"

Anna shook her head. "He barely eats and doesn't want to go outside at all."

That was not like her father. Even when he suffered the stroke, Elias still wanted to be outdoors. "Does he go outside with Jonas and Harvey when they milk?"

Silence. Anna exchanged a look with Lizzie, a silent conversation exchanged between them.

"What is it?" Amanda asked. Neither one of them spoke. "Mamm? Tell me."

Amanda waited for their response, knowing that whatever they had kept from her was too painful for words. And it certainly did not bode well for the family.

With a deep sigh, Anna's shoulders drooped as she finally admitted the truth. "Harvey no longer works here."

Amanda tried to catch herself before reacting to the news. Harvey no longer worked at the farm? Surely that meant that Jonas was doing all of the work by himself, a merciless feat that Elias had tried to perform on his own after Aaron passed away. Despite her father's insistence that he could do it, Amanda finally had stepped in to help. Now, without Elias's help and with Anna pregnant, it was no wonder everyone looked tired and drawn. Between milking cows, growing crops, and tending to the animals—never mind the regular house chores—it was too much for them to manage.

The realization that her mother and sister had kept this from her on purpose made her wonder about the circumstances surrounding Harvey's absence. "When did this happen?"

"Shortly after you left," Lizzie said as Anna looked at the floor, avoiding eye contact with Amanda.

She didn't need to ask the question to know the answer. Without doubt, Harvey's departure from the farm had not been voluntary. Whether it was a result of the tabloids gossiping about the relationship between her and Harvey or because Alejandro wanted the man gone, Amanda did not know. She wasn't certain she wanted to find out, either. Then she remembered Stedman, and how he'd been fired as her dance instructor from the South American tour when Alejandro thought he was becoming too friendly with her.

"I see."

Neither Anna nor Lizzie commented further, and Amanda did not press them. She knew that she would have to confront Alejandro—surely he knew the truth—but she did not want to do so until a more appropriate time. This was not that time.

Isadora leaned on Anna's leg and looked up at her with big eyes. "Tell Mammi 'Manda about the cookies!" she insisted.

Anna laughed and gave Isadora a quick hug. "Oh, *ja*! The cookie frolic on Wednesday! Mayhaps she will come with us!"

"A cookie frolic?" Oh, the memories that came back to her at the mere mention of a cookie frolic! Amanda smiled to herself, despite the pangs of homesickness. How she missed the fun gatherings, kitchens filled with laughing women and hungry children, all the while delicious food was being cooked in the oven. "For who?"

"For the people who lost their homes in the wildfires out in California," Anna said. "The Mennonites are having an auction next weekend. It's a shame you'll miss that. They're always so much fun."

Amanda sighed. "We'll be leaving for New York City on Wednesday. I would have loved to go to the frolic."

Isadora made a sad face, but Anna shrugged her shoulders. "Mayhaps next time."

But Amanda suspected that there would be no next time. She had signed that contract with Alejandro, so now she was committed to helping him when he traveled. And judging by the last six months, travel was all that Alejandro would do in the near future. She knew his schedule for the next few months was nothing more than a string of hotel stays and concerts with some meetings and photo shoots thrown in. He recorded his new songs in hotels and conducted most of his business with Geoffrey and the rest of his entourage from his private plane and buses. She would be beside him with no time to fly home to

Lancaster to visit with her family or attend cookie frolics to help those in need.

And, of course, Isadora staying in Lancaster was still an issue. What had been a temporary solution could not be a permanent one. Yet Alejandro and Amanda had not discussed how to fit his daughter into their lives. While Amanda originally disapproved of having a nanny take care of Isadora, she was beginning to realize that a nanny was the only way to keep Isadora with them. Despite how well the child was flourishing under the care of Anna, Amanda was having doubts. Not only did she miss her stepdaughter, she knew that Isadora needed to have a relationship with her father and that meant a life on the road. Other children adapted, she reminded herself, as she tried to convince herself that it was in Isadora's best interest, not just her own.

Frustrated, she abruptly stood up and made her apologies. "I best go take a nap," she said. "The flight was long, and I'm starting to feel poorly."

To her delight, Isadora insisted on coming with her, sliding her hand into Amanda's. But the gesture made Amanda feel even unhappier with the situation at large. Seeing Isadora and watching her read to her stepgrandfather made Amanda long to be a part of the child's life. She would miss so much if Isadora did not travel with them—but she feared what Isadora would miss if she did.

When Amanda lay down on the bed, the five-year-old crawled up next to her and snuggled against her body, one arm tossed around Amanda's neck. To feel Isadora pressed against her, listening to the gentle sound of her stepdaughter's soft breathing as sleep overtook the little girl, made Amanda feel as if she were home for the first time in weeks. Yet it was a bittersweet feeling for she realized she only had forty-eight hours to enjoy it.

Holding her stepdaughter, Amanda shut her eyes and followed Isadora's example, letting sleep overtake her for an early-evening nap.

\*\*\*

Two hours later, Amanda stirred, feeling as though someone were watching her. Her eyes fluttered open, and it took her a minute to place where, exactly, she was. The room felt familiar but it certainly was not a hotel. The peace and quiet was marked only by the sounds of birds singing outside the window as she realized she was not in London or Paris, or even Los Angeles. She was, instead, back in Lititz on her parents' farm, the sun starting to set outside the window.

When she finally realized where she was, she remembered that Isadora was with her. The child had rolled over and had one arm flung over the top of her head as she napped. Amanda smiled and reached for her, pulling her closer to her chest. She breathed in the lavender scent that lingered on Isadora's hair, and she smiled.

"*Ay, Princesa,*" Alejandro said in a soft voice. "You are so beautiful sleeping there with Isadora."

She turned her head, unaware that Alejandro had been leaning against the back wall, watching her. Careful to not disturb Isadora, Amanda quietly released her and moved off the bed. She gave him a lazy smile, wanting to stretch so that the lingering effects of her jet lag might dissipate, but she knew that would not be ladylike. Instead, she reached for his hand and let him pull her to her feet.

She pressed her head against his shoulder and stood like that for a long minute. Finally, she pulled back and looked up at him. "Did you get everything finished that you needed to, then?"

He nodded his head and, glancing over her shoulder at Isadora, motioned her toward the other room.

Quietly, they walked into the living area, Amanda careful to shut the door behind them so that they wouldn't disturb Isadora.

"You feel better now, *sí?*" he asked when she turned around and faced him.

Nodding her head, she smiled once again. "My family must think I'm terribly lazy, sleeping like that after just arriving."

"*Ay*, no." He shook his head. "It's the middle of the night for you, Princesa." He glanced at his phone to check the time. "Almost two in the morning or so."

She frowned. "I never should have napped." One thing that she had learned quickly: traveling through different time zones drained her of energy, but no amount of sleep changed that. Once the plane landed, it was better to continue on with the day and ignore the bone-tired weariness that plagued her body. While she had thought Dali via Charlotte was punishing her after her flight to London, in hindsight she recognized the wisdom they had bestowed upon her by having her leave the airport and immediately begin her day.

"You will not sleep well tonight, I fear," he admitted.

"What time is it?"

He glanced at his phone. "Almost eight."

"Oh! We've missed supper! You must be hungry." She glanced back at the bedroom door. "And Izzie didn't eat."

"You are so nurturing when you are here." A soft smile crossed his lips. He walked toward her and ran his hand up her arm. "I like it."

She tried not to smile as he leaned down and nuzzled her neck, his lips soft against her skin. "You do?"

"*Sí, mi amor,*" he breathed. "You are a good wife."

She noticed he did not say she was also a good mother, and a wave of guilt washed over her. She tried to shake off the feeling, but it clung to her. Legally, Isadora was as much her daughter as she was Alejandro's.

"Did you see Jonas?" she asked.

"*Sí, sí,* I helped him with the milking," Alejandro said.

Surprised, she pulled away from him. "In your travel clothes? You should have changed. That's so much work for the two of you."

Instead of answering, he sighed and changed the subject. "I suppose you heard about Harvey, *sí*?"

Amanda pressed her lips together and said nothing.

"I didn't want to worry you, Amanda."

"Did he leave on his own or . . . ?"

Alejandro contemplated his answer. "I did not encourage him to stay, Amanda, but I did not ask him to leave, no," he said.

"Then why did he leave?"

"The tabloids, Amanda," Alejandro admitted. "There were questions raised at his church, and he felt it best to leave the job."

She shut her eyes and inhaled deeply. Amanda knew all too well the pain inflicted by the tabloids and their vicious stories, which frequently were not true. But she also recognized that the tabloids served a purpose. The stories published therein kept the public demanding more by keeping the actors' and singers' names in front of the public. In fact, Amanda realized that without the tabloids, she would not have heard from Alejandro again after he left Lancaster last summer. After all, it was the paparazzi that drove him back to fetch her.

"He was collateral damage, Amanda, and I am truly sorry for that," Alejandro said.

She understood what Alejandro meant; she just didn't like hearing it. Had she not stood up to the paparazzi, she, too, would have been collateral damage—her life ruined just so that people could see a photo of her in the papers. "What now, Alejandro?"

"Jonas told me that it is too hard to get someone to work here."

"Oh, Alejandro!" That was bad news indeed. How could Jonas manage the entire farm by himself? With Lizzie tending to Elias and Anna tending to Isadora, there was no one else to help him. And when Anna had her baby, Lizzie would have to help out with the newborn as well as with Elias's care so that Anna could help her husband with the farmwork. "All because of the paparazzi?"

"There is also a tour that comes by the farm now," Alejandro commented slowly. "A bus tour."

"No!"

He nodded emotionlessly. "You are not just royalty in Europe, it appears, Princesa."

"A bus tour . . ." She shook her head. Why would people pay money to simply ride past her parents' farm? "That's so silly!"

"Not to the tourists," he said in a solemn tone. "To them, you are a true princess, Amanda. They want to catch a glimpse of your life. Why do you think the record label wanted you so much? You do not sing, Princesa. But Viper and Princesa are a package deal now. The fans are coming now for you just as much as for me."

She gasped. "That's not true!"

"*Sí*, Amanda. It is," he responded. "And that's all right. There is no cause for alarm, Amanda. It is good."

But it wasn't good and she knew that. A woman was supposed to support her husband: *wives, submit yourselves unto your own husbands, as unto the Lord.* No man would want a woman who usurped his authority. She had never wanted fame. All she wanted was Alejandro. From the moment he had visited her in the hospital last summer, serving her lobster for the first time, she had known that he was the most remarkable of men. When he returned to Lancaster with her, she fell in love with him while dancing in his arms in this very room. Now, just a year later, he was sharing the spotlight with her, both onstage and off.

How was it possible for so much to have happened in just one year? she wondered in amazement.

"What will we do for the farm?" she asked, changing the subject back to what was most important.

He shrugged. "I do not know, Amanda."

That scared her because Alejandro always seemed to have an answer for all situations, no matter how big or small. "Jonas cannot run this farm without help."

"*Sí, sí*, I understand that."

"If only the church district would help," she mumbled. While the bishop had eased up tremendously on her, he had not gone out of his way to help the family. Nor did he push the community to assist the Beilers during their time of need.

"I would not worry too much, Amanda. Not yet. Jonas is young, and he will do fine for a while. I will find another farmhand for them."

How could she explain to him that it wasn't that easy? Other Amish and Mennonite men would not want to subject themselves to the barrage of paparazzi that continued lingering around the farm. As for Englischers, there weren't many young men in the area who had experience farming, unless they already worked on their parents' farm. "It's just not that easy."

Alejandro took a deep breath and sighed. "Then, if need be, I will help them financially."

She shook her head. "*Nee*, Alejandro. You've helped enough by hiring Harvey. Besides, Jonas and Anna will never accept financial help. Not while they can work. They barely took any money to care for Izzie when I offered it. Besides, they pay into Amish Aid. The community should be helping them."

"So be it, then." His response seemed out of character for him. "Remember that Jonas and Anna are both here, Amanda. When you came home to take care of the farm, it was only you until Harvey showed up. They will struggle, but at the end of the day, they will be fine." He reached his arm out toward her, motioning with his hand that she come closer to him. "Now, as for you and I," he said when she stepped into his arms, "we, too, will be fine. A good night's sleep with my wife beside me is all I want."

"And your daughter, too?"

He glanced toward the bedroom door and sighed, his hands rubbing her back as he held her. "With Isadora? That wasn't exactly what I originally had in mind."

She blushed. "You are insatiable."

"And you make me deliciously ravenous!" He stroked the back of her neck with his thumb. "But if you want Isadora to sleep with you, then I will not say no." She started to say something, but he held up his finger. "On one condition!"

She tried not to smile.

"No questions, Princesa," he said, placing his finger against her lips. "Just follow me."

# Chapter Sixteen

When Amanda awoke, the bed was empty. Neither Isadora nor Alejandro were beside her. For a long moment, she stared at the ceiling, taking deep breaths as she tried to shake sleep from her body and mind.

She remembered the previous night and smiled to herself, shutting her eyes as she remembered Alejandro's gentle lovemaking to her in the upstairs guest room. Later, when they quietly stole back downstairs, Amanda had slipped into bed and wrapped her arms around Isadora, holding her tight to her chest while the little girl slept. When Alejandro joined her, he casually tossed his arm over both of them, and the small family slept that way without interruption.

Until now.

From the other side of the closed bedroom door, Amanda could hear the faint sound of voices. Curious, she slid out from beneath the sheet and padded across the floor. Carefully, she cracked the door just enough so that she could peer outside. Alejandro stood by the stove wearing black gym pants and a white sleeveless shirt. Beside him on the counter sat Isadora, her legs dangling over the edge and swinging as she watched him.

"Now, your aunt might make the best pancakes, but I make the best scrambled eggs," Alejandro said as he used a spatula to move the eggs in the pan. "The secret is in the wrist, *sí*? You have to beat them just right before you cook them."

"Mammi 'Manda makes the best pancakes," Isadora corrected him. "It's Mammi Anna who makes the best scrambled eggs."

Alejandro glanced at her. "I see. I got it backwards. Well, we shall see about that, Isadora. Just wait until you taste these eggs."

Isadora didn't look convinced. "And don't forget the toast. It's not breakfast without toast. That's what Jonas says."

"Oh, does he?" Alejandro looked around the room. "I don't see a toaster."

She pointed to the oven.

"Ah."

Amanda shut the door, pressing her hand against the doorframe, and smiled. She had hoped and prayed for this moment—the moment when Isadora and Alejandro might find a connection, a way to break down the icy barrier that time and distance had created. This morning, God had answered her prayers.

She changed out of her nightgown and put on a plain, simple dress. It felt refreshing to not worry about makeup or what outfit to wear. She hadn't felt so free in months. The constant scrutiny of the public and the media forced her to consult with fashion designers and stylists on an almost daily basis. To say she hated those meetings would be putting it mildly.

After she pinned back her hair into a loose bun, she opened the door. Both Alejandro and Isadora looked up and greeted her with big smiles.

"Princesa!" Alejandro called out.

"Mammi 'Manda!" Isadora jumped down from the counter while Alejandro reached out to grab her arm so that she didn't fall. After steadying herself, Isadora ran across the room and hugged Amanda.

"What a greeting!" she said cheerfully to Isadora. "And what a sight!" She directed this last comment to Alejandro. "Why, I don't recall ever seeing you cook before!"

He carried the plates to the table and set them down. "There are many things you do not know about me, Princesa," he said with a wink. "The fun part of the journey is discovering them. Like last night, *sí*?"

She widened her eyes and gave him a fierce look, which only made him laugh.

Isadora sat down and waited for her parents to join her. Then she folded her hands and lowered her head in silent prayer. Alejandro glanced across the table at Amanda, lifting his eyebrow in an unspoken question. He had not been happy that Isadora so rapidly adopted the Amish way of life. Now, as she prayed with her hands folded before her, it appeared that she was adopting the Amish religion, too.

After they prayed over their breakfast, Isadora picked up her fork and scooped up some scrambled eggs. She ate them and seemed to consider how they tasted. Amanda watched her reaction and did her best not to smile.

"What do you think, Isadora?" Alejandro asked.

"I reckon they are *gut*, but they are not the best," she said, which caused Amanda to laugh.

Alejandro tried to not laugh with her. "*¿Sí?* Just *gut*? Not the best?"

Isadora shook her head. "You need cheese," she said in a matter-of-fact tone.

At that, Alejandro could no longer contain himself and started laughing with Amanda. "Cheese, *sí*? I shall remember that for next time," he said in a solemn voice.

Satisfied, Isadora continued eating her breakfast and hummed a soft tune, one that Amanda recognized from her youth. She watched Isadora and thought back to her own childhood, sitting at the table with her sister and brother, the small family enjoying each other's company as they talked, sang, or simply prayed.

The realization dawned on her that moments like this would be the exception, not the rule, in her future. Breakfast was usually a cup of coffee and a pastry before the meetings began. Lunch was almost always on the run, eaten at a restaurant. And dinner? They tended to eat late at night—either room service at the hotel or late-night meals out, which Alejandro's assistants arranged for them.

There was very little home cooking and even less family time.

"Izzie has a cookie frolic tomorrow," Amanda said to break the silence. She wanted to enjoy the moment of normalcy as long as she could.

"*¿Sí?*" Alejandro looked at Isadora. "That will be fun."

Isadora nodded her head and then asked Amanda, "You come, too?"

Amanda shook her head. "*Nee*, Izzie. I have to leave with your *papi*."

Alejandro remained silent. He took another bite of his eggs before pushing the plate away from him and leaning back. "I will help Jonas today, Amanda. I suppose you will spend the day with your family."

The perfect day, she thought. She knew that Alejandro didn't mind laboring in the fields or helping with the dairy. He enjoyed manual labor, finding it a refreshing change from the hustle and bustle of his day-to-day life. As for Amanda, she looked forward to working with Isadora in the garden and helping to bake bread with her sister. She also wanted to visit with her father and perhaps get him outside for some fresh air. They would have supper with the rest of the family before leaving in the morning on Wednesday. The lingering reminder of them leaving so soon was the only black spot in her day.

In the early afternoon, Amanda worked with Isadora in the garden. The plants grew well, despite the lack of rain, but so did the weeds. Amanda gave Isadora the task of filling a bucket with as many weeds as she could. "Whoever gets the most can choose what type of cookies we bake later today, *ja*?"

"Oh!" Isadora's face lit up. "Sugar cookies!"

"Chocolate chip cookies!" Amanda retorted.

"Sugar! I win."

Amanda laughed at Isadora's confidence. "We'll see about that."

They worked in silence, Isadora determined to win and Amanda determined to enjoy the feeling of dirt on her hands and the sun on her face. The heat from the sun didn't bother her, even when she felt beads of perspiration on the back of her neck. She pushed herself, working as hard as she could so that she felt full of each moment. Once they left for New York City in the morning, she would not be able to garden again. Not for a long while, anyway. They would continue their tour of Europe and visit Miami for a brief stay before returning to the road for more summer concerts in the United States.

Then the cycle would continue.

She heard the door of the house open and shut. Glancing over her shoulder, she saw Anna walking across the grass, carrying a pitcher of lemonade and several plastic glasses.

"Oh my!" Anna said as she approached them. "Why, look how much you've weeded, Isadora!"

The little girl beamed at the praise.

"*Kum* now. I've something cold for you to drink," Anna commanded and Isadora reluctantly left her bucket of weeds.

Accepting the cup of lemonade, Amanda smiled her appreciation at her sister's thoughtfulness. As she lifted it to her lips, she turned to let her eyes scan the fields behind the dairy barn. She could see Jonas and Alejandro working in the fields, cutting hay. Alejandro stood at the front of the smaller cutter, driving two Belgian mules down the rows while Jonas drove alongside him with another team of mules and the larger cutter. Twice the manpower meant half the time spent on the task.

"That's a beautiful sight," Amanda said wistfully. She hadn't meant to say it out loud. When she realized that she had, she glanced away. But Anna had heard her.

"Amanda, if you wish to stay here, why don't you tell him?"

She shook her head at her sister. "*Nee*, Schwester, I've made my choice. My place is with my husband." Besides, she wanted to confide, I signed a contract and, with it, lost the right to return. She knew she could never tell her sister—it would sound as if she, too, had gotten caught up in the game of fame. Chasing front covers of magazines and headline stories on the entertainment channels was not her main interest. No, all she wanted was to be with Alejandro and to contribute to his life.

Unfortunately, that meant sacrificing the part of her that kept her grounded.

"What if he stayed with you?"

Amanda looked up, startled by Anna's question. "Whatever would give you the idea he would do such a thing?"

Her sister shrugged her shoulders. "He seems happy when he is here. Usually, anyway."

"He's happy on the road, too. Working."

"*Ja*, I can see that." Anna rubbed her enlarged stomach and glanced in the direction of the two men working in the field. "But he can work here, too. Besides, how much money can one person need?"

Amanda followed Anna's gaze. As she watched her husband and brother-in-law, she knew she saw a much different scenario from what her sister perceived. Alejandro found happiness here in Lititz, Pennsylvania, because it was an escape from the journey, not a final destination. He worked hard—not for the money but because he was a businessman. In his own way, he was a steward of the earth, too, only his crop was not hay or corn but people. He wanted to leave the world a better place by helping to inspire people and to provide opportunities for education for immigrant children in Miami. It was the side of Viper that only Amanda seemed to truly appreciate. Few others—regardless of whether they were fans, media, or music industry executives—looked deeper than the man on the stage, dancing and singing for their entertainment.

Clearly, Anna saw something different. Amanda suspected she saw what she wanted to see, the only future that she knew: a future of living and working on a farm. Anna simply could not imagine any other life, mostly because she had never experienced it. When Anna saw Alejandro's happiness working alongside Jonas, she translated that into thinking that he valued the same life outcome as the Amish: worshipping God, living plain, and working the land. No. Anna knew nothing of Alejandro's euphoria when he performed onstage or interacted with fans. And she clearly did not know about his new focus on expanding the Viper brand along with Princesa's.

"And what will you do when you have a *boppli*?" Anna asked.

A baby? Amanda swung her head around, startled from her thoughts by the question her sister posed. "I . . . I hadn't thought about that."

Anna raised an eyebrow at her, giving her one of those older sister looks. "Oh, Amanda, how transparent is your lie! You disappoint me." She leaned down and whispered something to Isadora, who grinned and immediately ran toward the barn. Clearly, Anna wanted some privacy to continue this discussion with Amanda. It was a conversation that Amanda did not want to have.

"I really don't care to talk about this," Amanda said.

"You've been married for how long? Seven months? Eight months?" Anna kept a steady gaze on her sister, waiting for a response that never came.

"Eight months," she admitted slowly.

Anna spread her hands over her midsection as if to make a point.

"Anna . . . ," Amanda began to say in defense of her lack of pregnancy.

Anna, however, interrupted her and blurted out the question that was on her mind. "Have you and Alejandro decided against children?

For you know that God wants us to be fruitful and multiply. Thwarting a life from forming is just as bad as stopping one from developing."

Amanda knew what her sister inferred. Birth control was simply not something that Amish women used. If anything, some women tracked their cycles and avoided days in the middle when they were most likely to be ovulating. But even that practice was frowned upon and, if suspected, might result in a stern lecture from the bishop.

Just the insinuation caused the color to rise to Amanda's cheeks as she quickly responded, "*Nee!* I would never do that!"

For a moment Anna studied her reaction, as if deciding whether Amanda was speaking the truth. Finally, she appeared to accept her sister's response. "*Vell* then, after eight months, mayhaps you might want to wonder at that, Amanda. Even if you wouldn't use such sinful methods, have you considered that he might?"

Amanda's mouth opened to respond in defense of her husband, but she quickly shut it.

"I've heard tell that men can take care of having *bopplis* with a single doctor's visit," Anna said in a low voice. "Mayhaps he did after Isadora was born. Have you thought of that, Amanda?"

She shook her head. "He wouldn't have done that and not told me, Anna. He was just as disappointed as I was when I found out I wasn't pregnant before the South American tour." Deep down, however, she remembered his reaction was rather nonchalant, seeming more disappointed for her than for the nonexistent baby. In fact, he seemed rather unconcerned about her not being pregnant.

Anna gave Amanda an if-you-say-so look.

"I mean, *ja*, he's Englische, but he would never do such a thing. He's an honorable man!" Yet it crossed Amanda's mind that while he might be honorable to her, he had not been honorable enough to truly take care of Isadora until his unwanted, illegitimate child was thrust upon them. Was it possible that he could have gotten a vasectomy and not told her? The thought niggled at her, and after Anna left her to bring the rest of the lemonade to Jonas and Alejandro, Amanda found that she could barely think straight as she worked in the garden, letting sugar cookies win over chocolate chip cookies without even trying.

"What time is the car picking us up?" Amanda asked Alejandro in the morning as she made pancakes for breakfast.

He stood at the door, looking at the fields through the glass panes. Once again, he wore simple black workout pants and a tight sleeveless shirt. With a coffee mug in his hand and his brown hair swooping over his forehead, he looked relaxed. "Hmm," he said under his breath. "To go or not to go."

She lifted the frying pan off the stove and set it aside before walking over to him. She leaned against him, looking over his shoulder to follow his gaze out the window. When she put her one arm around his chest, he held on to it with his free hand.

"What is that supposed to mean, Alejandro?" she asked in a soft voice. "You have appointments."

"*Sí*, I know." He gave a mirthless laugh. "Oh, how I know."

She planted a gentle kiss on his bare shoulder. "You must go."

"But you do not."

She swallowed. This was not a discussion she wanted to have. Not again. "*Nee*, Alejandro, you are wrong. Wherever you go, so shall I."

He leaned his head back, his razor stubble tickling her cheek. "Spoken like my Princesa, *sí*?" For a long moment, he remained silent. She wondered what he was thinking but knew enough about her husband to remain quiet. If it was something he wished to share with her, he would in his own time. She didn't have to wait long. "You will miss the cookie frolic," he said.

"*Ja*, I will. But Izzie won't."

He nodded his head and fell silent again.

"She is happy here, Alejandro. As much as that hurts my heart, it also makes me happy. For her."

"What do we do with her, Amanda? She can't stay here forever. She needs schooling and stability."

Amanda took a deep breath. She had dreaded this conversation, despite knowing that it was long overdue. "It's almost summer, Alejandro. You have to finish the European tour, and then you have summer concerts in America. Mayhaps this is her home."

"*¡Ay, Dios!*" he mumbled and set the coffee mug on the counter. "And have her raised Amish?"

Amanda turned her body so that she could watch him as he began to pace the floor. "Why not? It is not a bad life for her, and certainly better than what she had before."

"It's abandoning her!"

"That was already done, Alejandro," she said in a compassionate but firm voice, a reminder that his involvement in Isadora's life had begun only a few months before. "Leaving her here *is* caring for her. It's stability and simplicity, both of which she will benefit from."

He lifted his hand to his head, one arm tucked under his elbow. "Amanda, it just doesn't feel right."

Amanda crossed the room and wrapped her arms around him. "Mayhaps what doesn't feel right to us is right for *her.*"

He embraced her, but only lightly. His heart was not in it. Although she suspected he knew she was correct, he was uncomfortable with the solution. Amanda understood why. She loved Isadora and wanted nothing more than to mother her. But the child needed a home and family. It was not something Amanda and Alejandro could give her. Dragging the five-year-old around the world, leaving her care in the hands of a hired nanny while they worked for most of the day and well into the night, was not an ideal situation for any of them.

"Mammi! Papi!"

They both looked up at the same time to see Isadora holding the handrail and then clambering down the stairs, her bare feet making a soft noise against the wooden steps. "Today's the cookie frolic!" With a big smile, she ran across the room and wrapped her arms around Amanda's legs. "More sugar cookies!"

Laughing at her enthusiasm, Amanda knelt down before her. "Is that the first thing you thought of this morning? Why, I reckon you might turn into a sugar cookie before the day is out!"

Isadora giggled.

"Now, go set the table, please. I made pancakes for breakfast."

Isadora jumped up and down. "Pancakes!" she shouted and then ran to push a chair from the table over to the counter so that she could climb up to fetch the plates.

Amanda smiled as she watched Isadora, her heart swelling with joy but breaking at the same time. She glanced over at Alejandro and saw that he, too, was studying his daughter, a mixture of interest and regret in his expression. Amanda couldn't help but think back to what Anna had suggested the previous day. Was it possible that Alejandro knew Isadora was his only chance at having a child? She felt a wave of anxiety wash over her at the thought. A future without experiencing the joy of giving birth to her own baby as well as having a houseful of children was simply not something she had ever considered.

*** 

Alejandro waited patiently for Amanda to say her good-byes to her family. With hugs and promises to write as much as she could, Amanda couldn't help but linger. Especially when it came to Isadora.

Amanda knelt before the little girl and smoothed the front of her rumpled dress, brushing off a few stray strands of hay that Isadora must have collected when she was playing in the barn earlier that morning. "You take care of Katie Cat, *ja?*"

Isadora stood by Anna's side, holding on to her hand, which she swung back and forth. "*Ja*, Mammi 'Manda."

"And you be a big girl and help Mammi Anna, too," Amanda said, glancing up at Anna. As her sister began her final trimester, and with the weather turning warmer, Amanda knew that Anna would need as much help as she could get.

"And weed the garden for sugar cookies!" Isadora exclaimed happily.

"That's a right *gut* girl," Amanda said, fighting back the urge to cry. She wrapped Isadora in her arms and hugged her, trying to memorize the feeling of the little girl's body pressed against hers. It would be weeks before they would return. Amanda didn't know which hurt more—the fact that they would be away for so long or that it did not seem to concern Isadora.

Amanda stood up and faced her mother. "You'll write, too, *ja*?"

"Now how do you reckon I'd get a letter to you?" Lizzie said, frowning.

"Just mail it to the address I left you. They forward all of Viper's mail to wherever he is going." Amanda ignored how her mother cringed when she used Alejandro's stage name.

"Well, I reckon I can try," Lizzie reluctantly agreed. But when Amanda gave her mother a hug, she felt her hold on a little tighter than usual and knew her mother would certainly write to her. Her feigned ignorance at not knowing how to send a letter to Europe was just a facade to cover up her worry for Amanda as she prepared to leave, once again, with Alejandro.

Amanda walked over to her father's wheelchair and knelt down. She reached for his hand and raised her voice. "Daed! I'm leaving now."

He looked at her and tried to speak.

"You need some water, Daed?" She glanced at Anna, who quickly brought her a glass of water with a straw in it.

"Here you go, Daed," Amanda said as she lifted it to his parched lips. At first, he struggled to sip it, but Amanda waited patiently. "You need to do those exercises that the therapist tells you to do. I know that you can do better."

He mumbled something that she couldn't understand.

"I'll see you in a few weeks, *ja*? And you'll be much better then. But only if you listen to that therapist!" She wagged her finger at him in a playful gesture.

"Safe"—Elias managed to say—"travels."

Amanda smiled at him, fighting the urge to cry. She gave him a hug and pressed her lips against his cheek. "I love you, Daed," she whispered, knowing that it was one of the few times she had expressed such an emotion to any of her family members. Showing people love was much more important than simply using the words, but she didn't know how else to communicate to him how she felt. With his inability to talk, it had been hard to connect with him over the past two days.

"Amanda," Alejandro said, glancing at his phone. "I want to beat the traffic getting into the city, *mi amor*."

Taking a deep breath, Amanda gave Anna a last good-bye, hugging her tight. "Take care of Izzie," she whispered. "And yourself."

Anna laughed. "Oh, don't you worry about a thing, Amanda. Isadora and I have our cookie frolic in a little bit, and we have more than enough to keep ourselves busy, don't we now?" She addressed Isadora with this last part. To Amanda's relief, Isadora grinned and nodded her head.

As she walked out of the house to follow Alejandro to the rental car, she remembered how he had warned her that short visits almost always ended with pain and regret upon leaving. Vowing to keep her emotions in check, she waved only one time as Alejandro drove out of the driveway. But she kept her eyes on the side mirror, watching as her small family slowly disappeared from her sight.

# Chapter Seventeen

Walking into the Pierre hotel in New York City, Amanda caught her breath and reached for Alejandro's hand. He glanced up from his smartphone at her touch and followed her gaze of wonder at the lobby. The black-and-white-tiled floor shone with a perfect reflection of the crystal chandelier. The tray ceiling, trimmed with fine molding painted in gold, made the room feel bigger and brighter than most of the lobbies at hotels in which she'd stayed. Tall vases filled with fresh flowers seemed to enchant from every vacant corner and tabletop in the lobby, and the sweet fragrance of roses and lilies permeated throughout the room.

"There are castles in New York, too, *sí*?" Alejandro teased.

The other guests who lingered in the small clusters of chairs barely looked up at Alejandro and Amanda, too involved in their own lives to care about anyone else's. For once, Amanda didn't have to worry about people invading their privacy or stealing her photo when she wasn't looking.

When the bellhop left them at the Tata Suite, Amanda quickly walked to the window. From the thirty-ninth floor of the hotel, the windows provided sweeping views over Central Park as well as the surrounding city. She pressed her hand against the glass, trying to steady the queasy feeling in the core of her stomach.

"You like?"

She looked at him. "The view is exquisite, Alejandro."

He smirked, trying to suppress his smile. "But . . ."

"It's so high up!"

He laughed and walked over to the small minibar, which looked more like a desk to Amanda. "That it is, Princesa." He opened the hidden refrigerator and pulled out a cold beer, gesturing to Amanda to see if she wanted anything.

"Mayhaps a water," she said, and when he handed her a bottle of sparkling water, she gave him a soft smile. *"Danke."*

"You can freshen up before our dinner tonight, Amanda. Tomorrow I only have a few appointments, but you'll be meeting up with Jeremy to finalize your dress for the gala tomorrow night."

She wandered through the expansive suite on the thirty-ninth floor of the Pierre Hotel, taking in the dining area with its floor-to-ceiling windows before she headed down the hallway toward the bedroom. She was surprised to see two bedrooms, one with two twins and the other with a king bed. She couldn't imagine many people brought their children to such a fancy hotel.

"The bathroom has a large bathtub," she said when she rejoined Alejandro in the sitting area before the gas fireplace. "With windows!"

"And . . . ?"

Amanda made a face. "Why, who would take a bath in there! The whole city could see you!"

He shook his head, amused at her response. *"Ay*, Princesa, you never cease to amaze me." He took a long swig of his beer and smacked his lips together. "Ah. *¡Qué refresco!*" Then, setting the beer on the table, he withdrew his smartphone from his pocket and sank down onto the sofa. His fingers moved over the touchscreen as he started to check his messages, stopping for a moment to glance at her. "And, Princesa, I can assure you that before we leave on Friday evening, you will take a bath in that tub."

She gasped and he smiled, turning his attention back to his phone and away from the shocked expression his wife wore.

She felt uncomfortable in the tight, form-fitting off-white gown that Jeremy had picked out for her and, to her dismay, insisted she wear.

"It's Versace, Amanda!" Jeremy exclaimed when she had first tried on the dress and scowled at her reflection in the mirror. With his clipped French accent, he always sounded as though he was talking *at* her instead of *to* her, as if she were a child. "Most women would kill to wear a gown like this." He opened his eyes wide and pressed his hand against his own chest. "*I* would kill to wear this gown."

"It exposes so much skin though," she complained, looking in the mirror.

She could see Jeremy roll his eyes in the reflection in the mirror.

"That's what they want to see!"

"*Ja, vell,* I don't like them seeing it!"

Jeremy put both hands on his hips and stared her down. "You are wearing that dress. It's important that you do, Amanda. And wear it with style and grace! No slouching."

Her mouth fell open, and she wanted to point out that she already had had posture lessons from Stedman earlier in the year. But rather than speak back to him, she remained silent.

Now, as Alejandro guided her along the red carpet to the entrance of the gala, she reminded herself to walk with grace and keep her shoulders straight. The gown flowed onto the carpet behind her, just enough so that she knew she'd be worried all night that someone would step on it. The front of the dress had a slit that went all the way up to the middle of her thigh, and there were patterns of sequins that made it appear as though she were wrapped in the leaves of a graceful vine.

Whether or not she personally cared for the dress, she certainly knew that it was breathtaking, especially after Alejandro's reaction earlier that evening. His eyes had lit up as he pressed his lips together, fighting the urge to say something. Truly, he hadn't needed to say anything. His expression said it all. When he gave her his arm to escort her down to the lobby and out to the limousine that waited for them, he had covered her hand with his and whispered, "*Esplendida*, Princesa," into her ear.

Remembering his warm breath on her neck, she felt the quickening of her pulse and looked at him as they approached an opening on the red carpet. He seemed to read her mind and stopped walking, pausing to meet her gaze. His blue eyes traveled her body from head to toe, and when he met her gaze again, he lifted her hand to his lips, gently kissing her skin.

"Now it is all about you, *mi amor*," he said in a low voice so that no one else could hear. Then, to her surprise, Alejandro released her arm and stepped aside. She looked at him, confused as to why he moved away from her. But as the photographers swarmed in, kneeling before her and snapping photographs while she stood alone in the center of the red carpet, she immediately understood she was expected to pose for the cameras upon entering the gala.

Once she rejoined Alejandro, he smiled and whispered, "Well done, Princesa."

They were stopped once more as they walked up the red-carpeted stairs, this time by photographers who wanted pictures of them together. Amanda stood and gave a wistful smile, the back of her dress draped down two stairs below her, as the photographers took their photo. Alejandro stood beside her with his hands behind his back as he watched her.

"And what, exactly, is this gala for?" Amanda asked once they were inside.

"They sell paintings to raise money for the arts," he said.

"For the arts?"

He nodded to someone who passed by and paused to shake the hand of two other men. "*Sí*, Princesa, the arts. The entertainment industry."

Before she could ask another question, a familiar face approached them.

"Viper! Amanda!"

Justin Bell stood before them, wearing black pants and a black shirt with a gold-and-silver-embroidered jacket. While Alejandro whistled and commented on "his threads," all Amanda could think about was Celinda and Enrique.

"Thought you were in South America, man," Alejandro said as he gave Justin a friendly hug.

"Flew back for this." He glanced at Amanda. "Looking lovely as ever, Mrs. Viper," he said, his boyish charm not lost on her. "Or should I call you Mrs. Royalty of Rap?" He pretended to bow before her, moving his hand in a flourish.

"I'd prefer you didn't," she said, embarrassed at the attention drawn by Justin Bell's dramatic greeting.

With a big smile, he laughed and stood up straight, giving her a quick hug before he turned his attention back to Alejandro. "And you. Thought you were in Europe tearing up the charts."

"*Sí, sí*, same as you, my friend. Flew back between concerts." A man walked by carrying a tray of champagne flutes and Alejandro gestured to him, taking one and giving it to Amanda. She gladly accepted it and lifted it to her lips.

"Been hearing some stories about your tour," Justin said with a teasing tone in his voice that did not mirror the look in his eyes.

Amanda bit her lower lip and wondered how Alejandro would address the unspoken question.

Alejandro, however, did not take the bait. Instead, he shot right back, "*Sí*, and I hear the same about yours."

Justin removed his sunglasses and ran his fingers through his hair, which somehow remained perfectly coiffed. "Aw, Viper, you know the media. They're bound to make anything up."

"Be careful, man," Alejandro warned. "The public can turn on you faster than a dog attack. Some of those stories . . ." He shook his head. "Focus on the goal, *amigo*."

"Aw, you always used to say it's not the destination but the journey!"

Alejandro gave a short laugh. "Not when it comes to your image, *chico*. Don't mess with that."

Apparently tired of that conversation, Justin gave a playful eye roll and turned to wink at Amanda. "Heard you had some company on the tour, eh?"

At first she wasn't certain whom he was addressing: her or Alejandro. She lifted the champagne one more time to her lips, tasting the smooth bubbles against her tongue. But when Alejandro remained silent and she realized that Justin was staring at her, she knew she had no choice but to answer him.

"*Ja*, if you mean Celinda."

The way that Justin's face lit up at the mention of her name told Amanda all that she needed to know. He was still head over heels in love with her. As she realized it, her heart broke for the two of them. With Justin on one continent and Celinda on another, staying together would certainly be hard. But the rumors of what both of them were doing while apart made Amanda realize how fragile relationships were in this industry.

"She doing alright?"

Amanda took a third sip of champagne and nodded her head.

"Thing is . . ." Justin rubbed at the back of his neck, glancing around at a small crowd of people who stood nearby. He nodded his head at one of them before he moved closer to Amanda and lowered his voice. "Been hearing stories, you know? Something about her and that Enrique guy." He made a face and shook his head. "Not good, man." He glanced at Alejandro. "You know what I mean, right?"

Alejandro took a deep breath and gave a stiff shrug. "What I do know is that I don't get involved in that business, Justin." Then he reached over and took Amanda's champagne glass, raising an eyebrow at her as he took a long, slow sip. "It'll go to your head," he whispered to her. "Don't drink it so fast."

Already her head felt as if she were floating just a little. She felt light on her feet and found it easier to smile at people she didn't know. Unlike the previous events she'd been to with Alejandro, events where women openly glared at her and refused to speak with her, Amanda found that she was constantly in the center of a small crowd of people. When Alejandro left her to go mingle with some people he knew, the liquid gold of the champagne gave her the courage to interact with the other guests without him, posing for photos and listening to their stories. She remembered the night in Los Angeles on the yacht, and with the same determination, she focused on the people she interacted with, asking them questions about themselves and making the effort to listen to their responses.

Before she realized it, Alejandro was back at her side to escort her to their table. With a clearer head, thanks to losing the champagne glass, Amanda greeted his return with a warm smile and happily accepted his arm.

"I want to warn you," he said in a low voice but with a broad grin on his lips, acknowledging people he knew as they passed, "that Richard Gray is here and seated at our table."

Amanda almost stopped on the carpet. "That awful man from Los Angeles?" she asked.

"*Sí*, the one and the same," Alejandro answered with a soft chuckle. "The one that is funding your contract, as well as mine, and the one that is, perhaps, the most powerful man in the industry. *Sí*, that one."

"Oh."

"My advice is to pretend that the confrontation never happened. Present him with your most beautiful of smiles and most charming attention."

Amanda sighed. "If I must."

"Oh *sí*, you must," Alejandro said. "You are sitting next to him."

She didn't have time to plead for a new seat, for no sooner had he whispered it than they were standing at the round table draped with golden linens and adorned with tall centerpieces filled with magnificent white flowers. She recognized the man right away and almost stumbled, but Alejandro tightened his hold on her hand.

With more grace than Amanda thought she could muster, she watched as Richard stood up to greet Alejandro.

"You remember Amanda, *sí*?" Alejandro stepped aside as he presented Amanda.

Richard raised his eyebrows, his eyes opening wide as if amused, while he tilted his head and nodded. "Of course," he said pleasantly. "How could I not remember our meeting in Los Angeles?" He leaned forward and kissed her cheek. "I've been hearing nothing but good things, Amanda, from the tour. I'm quite pleased with our"—he hesitated for a long moment, his hand still clutching hers—"investment."

Her mouth felt dry and she glanced at Alejandro, hoping he would guide her in how to respond. But by the amused expression on his face, she knew he had zero intention of doing so. For the second time that evening, Amanda wished she could hide behind the champagne flute that Alejandro had snuck away from her.

"I . . . I'm glad that you are pleased," she managed to say. "It's been quite an interesting few weeks."

Richard nodded. "So I heard. Whatever it is you are doing, keep it up. Social media is exploding, sales are continuing to increase, and the entertainment world is buzzing over this coupling."

She cringed at his word choice, as if they were two animals put together in a cage with the hopes they'd attract more visitors to the zoo.

"And the VMAs, Alejandro," Richard said, returning his attention to him. "They want the two of you to host it."

Alejandro gave a loud shout and, ignoring the people who turned to see who was making such a ruckus, wrapped Amanda in a quick hug. "Now they're getting it!"

"I don't understand what that means . . . ," Amanda said.

Richard leaned over so that she could hear him clearly. "It means that the two of you together are taking the music industry by storm." He gestured to the server. "Champagne for the table and"—he looked at Alejandro—"two vodkas on the rocks."

"The VMAs!" Alejandro could hardly contain his enthusiasm. "Do you realize, Princesa, that you will be the first person to host the music awards who is not a singer or an actor? This is unprecedented. A year ago they barely knew who you were. Now they want us to host the show?"

"So this is *gut*?"

At this, Richard laughed and shook his head. "Is she for real?" he asked.

Amanda detected no malice in his voice.

"Princesa," Alejandro started, "it means they think we can increase ratings in a way that no one else can. It also gives amazing exposure to my music. So, *sí*, it's a very good thing!"

The champagne arrived at the table. As Richard handed her a glass, the server offered champagne to the other people seated at the table.

"Let's make a toast," Richard said, his voice loud enough to capture the attention of several other tables filled with people. "To the Royalty of Rap, Viper and his Princesa!"

Amanda followed Alejandro's example and lifted her glass so that he could touch his glass to hers.

"Cheers, *mi amor*," he said, his eyes sparkling at her as he watched her raise her champagne flute to her lips. "May the reign long continue," he said before leaning over and planting a kiss on Amanda's lips, lingering just long enough for the nearby photographers to snap a picture.

# Chapter Eighteen

Prague. It was a beautiful city with old buildings surrounding a cob-
blestoned town center in which the residents gathered to sit outdoors
drinking coffee or beer while watching horse-drawn carriages pass by
and street performers entertain the crowds with magic tricks. Three-
and four-story buildings surrounded the large public gathering area,
but none surpassed the tall church with the massive astronomical clock.
Each hour it put on a show of the moving figures of the apostles, as
well as other figures. When Amanda learned that the clock dated back
to the early 1400s, she stared at it with renewed amazement—both at
the antiquity of the clock tower and her husband's extensive knowledge
of history.

"You really do enjoy medieval history, *ja?*" she asked, her arm
tucked into his as she walked beside him along the streets.

Her surprise seemed to amuse him, and he smiled mischievously,
raising one eyebrow. "You did not believe me?"

"I just did not know that about you before this tour," she answered
honestly.

"Ah, Princesa," he purred. "There is nothing new under the sun,
therefore we should study the past to understand the future, *sí?*"

She laughed. "Are you quoting Scripture to me now?"

Before he could answer, a burly man with a large camera stood a few yards away from them to take a photo. Realizing that they were being photographed, Amanda looked up in surprise. It didn't take long for a small group of people to begin gathering, staring as Alejandro took her elbow in his hand and they continued walking through the center of town.

"Do they really have to do that?" Despite flying first class, Amanda felt unusually tired and irritable after their trip back to Europe from New York City. The flight had not been direct, and between the change of planes at Heathrow Airport and the throngs of people who recognized them, Amanda found herself resenting the intrusion of the public. While she enjoyed seeing the amazing city of Prague, she was increasingly tired of never having a moment of uninterrupted time with Alejandro, unless, of course, they were locked in their hotel room.

To her surprise, Alejandro seemed unperturbed. He continued walking, ignoring the gawking people who recognized them in the best preserved city of Europe. Several people called out "Viper," so Alejandro responded by lifting his hand and waving in that general direction.

"Do they have to do that?" Alejandro repeated. "I suppose they do. They are, after all, fans, no? That's what fans do."

"Just once," she said. "One day without it would be nice."

Alejandro chuckled at her reaction. "Is this my Princesa, the reigning queen of rap, complaining? The very person who loves to interact with the public?"

"I never said I *love* it."

He stopped walking long enough to cup her chin in his hand and lean down to kiss her lips. "But you do, Princesa. I know you do."

Regardless of her love for talking with Alejandro's fans, Amanda couldn't shake the feeling of being irritated with the constant interruptions from every direction. If it wasn't fans, it was Alejandro's entourage of people who constantly texted, e-mailed, or merely barged in on their time.

For once, they were enjoying a leisurely day before his concert that evening. They were being regular people, even if only for a few hours. She had basked in the luxury of enjoying an outing alone with Alejandro, but she knew it would quickly deteriorate if a mob developed.

But she held her tongue and focused on the little time she had left in Alejandro's company before they were interrupted again.

He gestured toward a restaurant with a heavy wooden overhang that provided some shade from the sun. Without waiting for her response, began to lead her there. "You like the city, *sí*?"

Amanda nodded, trying to relax. "Of course. How could I not?"

It was beautiful, perhaps just as much as Paris. The one difference she had noticed during their short stay was that the people were not as aloof as the Parisians. Until now she had enjoyed that rare privacy.

"It's a special place," he said.

Amanda couldn't agree more. "To think that all of this was here while I was growing up . . . It's amazing, *ja*? Right now, what are Anna and Jonas doing on the farm? Isadora? We are thousands of miles away in a whole different world while they are on the farm and working, birds chirping and flying over the clothesline."

"It's Sunday," he pointed out.

"Then they are at church, sitting on the benches and listening to the hymns. The room is probably stuffy unless someone has mercy and opens the windows," she said.

It seemed like a lifetime ago that she had been one of them, spending three hours worshipping God through the slow chant-like singing of the Ausbund hymns. She could almost hear the voices lifting together as they slowly sang each line in harmony, one hymn taking thirty minutes or more to complete just the first few verses.

"I reckon I understand why the bishops allow so little access to the world," she said aloud, her mind wandering.

She couldn't imagine her sister visiting such a place as Prague and then being able to return unchanged to Lititz. In just one year, Amanda had changed so much, and now understood far more about the world and how it operated outside the confines of the Amish community. To return to such a plain and simple lifestyle would be difficult, indeed. But she did not regret leaving. After all, the choice had been hers and hers alone. In some ways, she had forced the issue by reaching out to Alejandro through the media when the bishop wanted to send her away. Had she not reached out to Alejandro, the paparazzi would have eventually lost interest and moved on to something else. She hadn't realized that then, but hindsight provided clarity on the situation.

"There is a saying from a philosopher," Alejandro commented, "that no man can step into the same river twice, for the river has changed as has the man."

She had to think about that for a moment. It was true that rivers were constantly moving and the water never stayed in one place. But the man? Perhaps the knowledge that the river was wet or a rock slippery changed the man?

"That's quite a profound saying," she admitted. "I reckon if the river is life, the constant motion of it changes a person from one day to the next, *ja*?"

He nodded as they sat down at the outdoor table that overlooked the Old Town Square. He motioned to the server to bring them coffee. "And how quickly it changes, no?"

She saw him glance over the top of his sunglasses toward the street. When he grimaced, she knew that if she turned around, she would see a crowd gathering. He sighed and leaned back in the chair, rubbing at his temples. It was frustrating to always be "on."

"How many?"

He shrugged. "Twenty?"

But crowds grew, and Amanda suspected that by the time they finished their coffee there would be twice that many people standing outside. Of course, she knew that was the name of the game. They had to remain on, talking quietly and smiling to each other, presenting the face of the Royalty of Rap to the public instead of simply being themselves. And when the time came to leave, they'd have to exit through a back door in order to escape the crush of their adoring public.

Yes, she thought, no one can step into the same river twice.

Backstage at Prague's O2 arena, Amanda was surprised to see Enrique and Celinda sitting together in the greenroom, her legs gently brushing against his. Enrique's arm lay across the back of the sofa, not touching Celinda but definitely hinting at more intimacy than just colleagues. Amanda was about to back out of the room when Celinda spotted her.

"Amanda!" She leaned forward and patted the chair next to her. "Come listen to this idea!"

That was the last thing Amanda wanted to do. However, she did not want to be rude to her friend.

"Where did you go today?" Celinda asked as Amanda sat down.

"Old Town Square," she answered, avoiding Enrique's invasive stare. "And you?"

Celinda glanced at Enrique and smiled, a smile that said more than Amanda wanted to hear. Amanda ignored the look Enrique gave Celinda in return. "Oh, this and that. I've been to Prague before, so it was nice to sleep in late and then grab a bite to eat near the Lennon Wall."

"Lennon Wall?"

"It's a long wall of graffiti near the Grand Priory Square," Celinda explained. "All for John Lennon." When Amanda still wore a blank expression, Celinda laughed. "He was one of the Beatles, a famous rock band from the sixties."

"Oh."

"Well, anyway," Celinda said, moving to a new topic. "We leave Prague tonight and go straight to Vienna. We have all day tomorrow to do whatever we want in Vienna. So we were thinking that the four of us could go see Schönbrunn Palace. I hear it's lovely and almost rivals Versailles. Enrique arranged for a videographer to film us!" She laughed and clapped her hands, leaning backward into Enrique's shoulder. "Enrique and Alejandro can use the footage for their new video! Wouldn't that be fun? Just random real video, not that structured stuff that the studios make us do."

Amanda had forgotten that Enrique and Alejandro planned on recording a song together. She suspected that Alejandro hadn't spoken about it recently because he knew how uncomfortable she was around Enrique. And, truthfully, Amanda was looking forward to a lazy morning at the hotel, catching up on her correspondence and enjoying a quiet, relaxing day. Walking around a large palace with tons of tourists in the summer heat was not something she considered fun. She'd had enough of palaces and castles in England and France, anyway. The opulence of the royal families was something that did little to appease her dislike for the media's nickname for her and Alejandro. Filming at Schönbrunn Palace would only add more fuel to the fire of being called the Royalty of Rap.

"I reckon I should check with Alejandro," she responded at last.

Enrique pursed his lips as he studied her, his eyes moving from her face to other parts of her body. Just one more black mark against his name, she thought as she crossed her arms over her chest. "*¡Sí, claro!*" Enrique said in a mocking voice. "Since Viper arranged the film crew to meet us there, his answer will most likely be yes, *sí?*"

Celinda playfully slapped him on the shoulder. "And here I thought you were so clever!"

"When did he schedule this?" Amanda asked, hoping her voice hid her irritation.

Enrique shrugged. "Maybe five weeks ago?"

So that explained it, she thought. He had scheduled it prior to her arrival in Europe. She wondered if agreeing to this video was part of their contract with the label. Probably not, she told herself, since Alejandro had scheduled the shoot before she'd signed the contract.

Someone leaned around the open door and said, "Sound check, guys."

Enrique rolled his eyes and slid his arm away from Celinda. "Like it's even needed," he mumbled, but loud enough for the man to hear. "It always works fine, *sí*?" He reached down to help Celinda to her feet. Amanda noticed the glow in her friend's eyes when she placed her hand in Enrique's and stood, brushing her arm against his side so that he had to steady her.

Amanda followed them to the stage and then walked out onto the floor. She saw Alejandro talking with the sound engineer in the back. Not wanting to disturb him, she wandered up the aisle and sat a few rows away.

"No, no," Alejandro said. He wore a short-sleeved shirt that exposed his tattoos and his muscular forearms. He leaned over and pointed to something on a monitor. "Too much bass, man. It drowns out the vocals."

The engineer nodded and twisted some dials, adjusting the different sounds.

Amanda watched, amazed at how Alejandro knew about the different aspects of the equipment. At every concert he oversaw the setup of the stage and tested the different speakers. Amanda had long ago noticed that Enrique left all of that to his own crew, who tended to defer to Alejandro. It struck Amanda that as much as Alejandro had been a playboy like Enrique at one time in his life, his attention to the professional side of the business had far exceeded anyone else's on these tours. Despite his not having gone to college, he was, without doubt, the most intelligent man she'd ever met.

"When did you sneak over there, Princesa?" he asked while walking over to where she sat, leaving the engineer to finish correcting the sound levels.

"Just a few minutes ago." She stood up and let him pull her toward him, his hands on her waist. "I was watching you," she said flirtatiously.

"Oh, sí?" Music started to play over the speakers, and Alejandro began to sway to the song. "Like a stalker, sí?"

She swayed with him, his hips pressed against hers. "*Nee*, not a stalker."

"No?"

She lifted her head so that her lips were close to his. "Like a crazy fan."

He shut his eyes and moaned. "Not another one."

She laughed. "The craziest of fans!"

His mouth twitched, so she knew he was trying to hide his smile. "Craziest, eh? Then I shall have to reward you." He kissed her. "But not until later, sí?"

Someone called for him from the stage. He glanced over his shoulder and responded in rapid-fire Spanish.

"Before you go . . ."

He turned back to her. "*¿Sí?*"

"Celinda and Enrique . . . they mentioned something about a video?"

"*¡Sí, sí!*" He lit up at the mention of it. "A play on the whole Royalty of Rap. Brilliant, sí?"

"They seem awfully close these days," she said as if it were just a casual observation.

"Close?" He scratched at the back of his neck as if trying to escape the topic.

"Alejandro," she said, "I don't believe I need to remind you of his reputation. He's not exactly a one-woman kind of man."

Alejandro tossed his head back and laughed. "No, Princesa, that he is not."

She didn't appreciate his reaction and found no humor in the situation. "I don't want to see Celinda hurt, especially after her breakup with Justin."

Alejandro shook his head as he placed both of his hands on her cheeks. "You worry too much," he said. "Remember what happens when you worry." He growled playfully at her before planting a gentle kiss on her lips. "Celinda is stronger and smarter than you give her credit for, *mi amor*. She knows what she is doing. So no more worrying, *sí*?"

She watched as he jogged down the aisle toward the stage. He jumped onto the stage in one fluid motion, not an ounce of struggle.

# Chapter Nineteen

If Amanda had thought the Notre-Dame Cathedral opulent, she couldn't help but gasp in awe at the beauty of Schönbrunn Palace. When their car pulled up to the yellow building on the outskirts of Vienna, Amanda stared out the window, her mouth hanging open. The courtyard, protected by a gated wall, was as wide as the building and deep enough to accommodate two, if not three, more buildings.

"People used to live here?" Amanda asked incredulously.

"*Sí*, Princesa," Alejandro said as he slipped his cell phone into the front pocket of his short-sleeved shirt. He leaned forward and looked through her window. "That is why it is called a palace. The royal family of Vienna lived here."

"It must have been a very large family!"

He laughed and shook his head. "Not by Amish standards."

They pulled up to the small army of cars and trucks already in the side parking lot. Alejandro helped her out of the car, and after she thanked the driver, he guided her toward the courtyard and the main building. Several horse-drawn carriages stood at the ready for anyone willing to spend seventy-five euros for a ride around the grounds. Amanda paused long enough to pet the velvety nose of one of the horses, inhaling the musky equine scent as if trying to store it up inside her brain.

"¿Princesa, *listo?*" he called out when he realized that she no longer walked beside him.

A man that Amanda had never seen before came up to Alejandro and began speaking to him in Spanish. She turned her attention to the massive building before her, which appeared to be three stories high, with the center section rising into a fourth story. It was perfectly symmetrical: the first and third floors had small rectangular windows, exactly on top of each other, only interrupted by the large, arched windows all along the second floor. Six white pillars marked the entrance at the center of the building, where two arched staircases curved upward to the second floor. Directly beneath that section of the building was a breezeway. When Amanda saw a horse and carriage pull through and continue to the other side of the building, she realized that it was likely where the royal family had been picked up and dropped off by their carriages.

"Come, Princesa," Alejandro called out to her. "You can explore later. We only have the Great Gallery for one hour. After that it will be open to the tourists again."

He motioned for her to join him as he ascended the stairs that led to the second floor.

What she thought had been windows turned out to be doors. When they approached the first set, she hesitated and caught her breath.

"Oh help!"

Inside the doorway was a long, wide room, completely empty except for the cameras, lights, and crew that were already set up, waiting for them. Amanda walked into the room, her mouth agape. Opposite each window and door was a mirror of exactly the same size, which reflected the light and gave the illusion that the room was larger and more airy than it really was. Beside each window and mirror were tall, ornate pillars that led upward to two arched ceilings with frescoes painted in each center. She craned her neck to stare at the ceilings, taking in the cream-and-gold molding that framed the frescoes. Layer upon layer of woodwork and rosettes drew her eyes toward the magnificent paintings that loomed above her.

"What is that?" she whispered.

"It's a painting for Maria Theresa," someone said from behind her.

Amanda turned and saw a man dressed in a suit with thick glasses and thinning hair.

"I'm one of the docents here," he explained, his English perfect and without a trace of an accent. "They asked me to stand by in case of questions."

"I see." She looked back at the fresco. "Who was Maria Theresa?"

He smiled and for a moment she wondered if he was mocking her lack of knowledge. "She was the Empress of Vienna in the mid-eighteenth century." The man hesitated and took a quick breath before he continued. "You may know her better as the mother of Marie Antoinette . . . ?"

Amanda shook her head.

"If you've been to Paris and visited the Palace of Versailles, you'll notice that much of the influence in decor there is similar to here at Schönbrunn Palace. One of the reasons for that is because Marie Antoinette grew up here, and after marrying King Louis XVI, she had a hand in decorating Versailles before she was beheaded."

"Beheaded? You mean like . . ." She searched her memory for the name of the woman Alejandro had told her about at Warwick Castle. "Boleyn?"

The man looked as if he wanted to roll his eyes.

"Maria Theresa was the last of the Habsburg line to rule Vienna," he said, changing the subject.

"And she lived here?"

The man nodded. "With her sixteen children."

Amanda's mouth opened. "Sixteen? Why, she had more children than any Amish woman I know!"

She felt a hand on her elbow and heard Alejandro say, "Excuse me" to the man as he directed her toward the back of the room.

*"Mi amor,"* he said with a strained voice. "I need you to help us get through this hour. They are waiting to get you dressed and fix your makeup. Please, Princesa."

Feeling like a rebuked child, she hurried along in the direction that he pointed. As soon as she neared the rear corner, a young woman guided her behind a large screen where Amanda was ordered to change into a pretty cream-colored dress with a tight bodice and full skirt. Two other women helped with the zipper while straightening the bottom. From the other side of the screen, someone called out in German and the older of the women shook her head, gesturing for everyone to hurry up. Amanda felt more hands tugging at the dress before someone took her arm and led her toward the makeup table. Bright lights, little brushes, more words that she couldn't understand. But within fifteen minutes, she was back in the center of the Great Gallery and waiting for Alejandro to join her.

What she hadn't expected was to see Enrique and Celinda emerge, holding hands and laughing from a doorway that Amanda had thought was just a mirror. Celinda wore a dress similar to Amanda's, only it was a different color, one that played up the rich olive tone of her skin. Enrique, for once, was dressed in slacks and a decent shirt. Despite how much she disliked him, Amanda had to admit that, when dressed properly, he was a handsome man.

"Amanda!" Celinda lit up when she saw her and hurried over, leaving Enrique to stand by himself in the center of the room by the fireplace. "You look absolutely divine!" Then, spreading out her hands, Celinda took ahold of her skirt and twirled around. "Aren't these dresses just so fun?" She stopped spinning and the fabric of her dress wrapped around her legs. "They used to wear this style back in those days—isn't that amazing?"

"What days?"

"Oh, the early 1800s, I think. Maybe late 1700s. These are replicas of dresses worn by the Habsburgs."

Celinda didn't have time to explain any further. Alejandro emerged, dressed in all black. Immediately, he was surrounded by several people, each one speaking to him over the other. Within minutes, music was blasting throughout the hall, bright lights flooded the room, and cameras began to roll.

Without needing any direction, Alejandro began singing the song, dancing by himself while Amanda watched. The cameramen filmed from different angles as he sang and danced to the music.

"Girls?"

Amanda looked up and saw that one of the crew members was motioning for her and Celinda to join them in a different corner of the room. It was hard to hear over the music, so Amanda tried to follow the man's directions, two cameras recording every move that she and Celinda made. The recording of the video would be done in stages and then edited together. One hour of filming in the Schönbrunn Palace might amount to thirty seconds of useful material. But she tried to follow their instructions: walking with Celinda through the grand doorway, standing by a fireplace in an adjourning room, gazing out the windows into the courtyard. While Amanda had no idea about the story line of the video, she knew that it had been well thought out and planned in advance.

When the crew was finished filming their pieces, Celinda hurried over to where Alejandro was now singing and dancing with Enrique. Curious, Amanda watched them, too aware of the number of cameras, lights, and people focused on her husband. Amanda wondered how Enrique could have arranged something of this scale, between reserving the Great Gallery and organizing all of the staff. And the dresses? Amanda knew the video shoot was something Alejandro had arranged long before the European tour had started. She remembered that, just recently, he had met with some people in Los Angeles regarding an upcoming video shoot. Certainly something as sophisticated as this was the work of someone with cultured tastes—and that person was certainly not Enrique.

And that meant that, when Enrique had suggested the idea about the photo shoot, he had tried to pass off Alejandro's hard work as his own, perhaps with the sole purpose of impressing Celinda. From the way that Celinda kept looking in his direction and blushing when she caught him watching her, Amanda realized that it had, indeed, worked. His constant quest to impress women so that they might wind up in his bed was just one more reason why she found herself repulsed by the man more and more with each day.

"Do you know about Enrique and Celinda? That they are . . ."

She couldn't even finish asking the question. She had been disgusted with both Enrique's and Celinda's behavior at Schönbrunn Palace. The short amount of time reserved for filming the video had run over for one reason: Enrique and Celinda spent more time flirting with each other than focusing on the directions from the video film team. Amanda saw the way that Celinda looked at Enrique and worried that her friend felt more for him than he did for her. The last thing Amanda wanted to see was Celinda get hurt again, especially after her recent breakup with Justin.

After the photo shoot, Amanda and Alejandro had returned to the hotel. They were both exhausted, and since they didn't have any obligations that evening, Alejandro had no desire to go out in Vienna, even though they only had a short stay in the beautiful city. Silently, Amanda had cheered. She wanted nothing more than to snuggle in bed beside her husband, listening to him catch up on his much-needed sleep while she read from her Kindle. Right now she was in the midst of rereading the book of Proverbs, one of her favorite books in the Bible, especially all of the quotes about wisdom.

Alejandro was already stretched out under the covers, one arm tossed behind his head as he pointed the remote control at the television with his other hand. "There's no news on? *¡Ay, mi madre!*" he mumbled.

"Did you hear me, Alejandro? About Celinda and Enrique?"

He glanced over to where she stood in the doorway of the bathroom, dressed in a silk nightgown and brushing her long hair that she had just unpinned. "*Sí, sí*, I heard you. It's none of my business what either of those two do."

Amanda frowned. "She loves Justin, but she spent the night with Enrique?"

He sighed and tossed the remote onto the comforter. "*¡Ay, Princesa!* Why are you worrying about Celinda? We have our own lives to worry about, no?"

She set down the hairbrush and walked over to the bed. Alejandro moved the sheets back so that she could crawl in next to him. "I know it's her own life," she said as she settled down, her head resting against his shoulder, "but what if . . ."

"What if what?" he asked, his tone clearly indicating his lack of interest in the subject.

"What if she were to . . ." She wanted to ask the question, yet felt embarrassed to even broach the subject. But pregnancy was on her mind. Once again, earlier that morning, she had taken a pregnancy test, eagerly waiting for the window on the little stick to change into a pink plus sign, indicating that she was pregnant. And, once again, it had not.

Alejandro shifted his weight and leaned on his elbow. "*¿Qué,* Amanda? What has you so tongue-tied?" he asked, his attention now more focused on her than on the television.

Reaching out her hand, she traced the outline of one of his tattoos on his upper arms. She loved waking up in the morning to see him sleeping on his side, her name tattooed on his shoulder. It was almost as if he had branded himself to show that she was his and he would always be hers. "They are both young, and what if she were to become with child?"

At this question, Alejandro began to smile, just enough to indicate his amusement.

"I find nothing humorous about my question," Amanda stated. "I'm concerned for my friend."

"*¡Ay, Princesa!*" He reached out and ran his fingers through her hair. "They are adults, and while young, they are well versed in how to avoid getting pregnant."

And there it was, the reminder of Anna's question as to whether Alejandro had done the same: prevented future children.

"You know I'm not familiar with such things," Amanda said slowly, her fingers moving upward from his shoulder to brush along his neck.

He smiled. "*Ja,* I know. I remember well the number of children in the Amish families when we went to church last summer." His eyes narrowed as she continued to touch his skin. "Mmm . . . I always wondered why your parents had such a small family."

"Mamm had several miscarriages after I was born," Amanda stated. She remembered far too well the years of tears with the loss of each pregnancy. "We were surprised when Aaron came along. The doctor didn't think she could carry a baby to term."

Moving his hand from her head, he touched her waist and pulled her toward him so that he could rest his head in her lap. She began to stroke his hair, loving the way that his thick curls twisted around her fingers. He hadn't shaved after his shower, so his razor stubble tickled her leg through her nightgown.

"Alejandro?"

He gave a soft moan, his eyes shut as he relaxed under her gentle caresses. *"¿Qué?"*

"I took another pregnancy test," she said quietly.

His eyes opened and she felt his hold on her waist stiffen. When he didn't respond, she frowned. Shouldn't he have asked her what the results were? Or did he already know? She waited for him to ask, but he didn't.

"Aren't you curious?"

*"Sí . . . "* But he let the word drag out so that she wondered if he truly meant it.

"Then ask me."

He sat up and peered at her with his blue eyes and his jaw tense. "You must have taken it for some reason, Amanda."

"It's been months, Alejandro. Months since I . . ." She paused, uncomfortable talking about her menstruation. "I haven't had it since before I left South America."

His eyebrow arched over his left eye as he continued waiting for her response.

"And it was negative."

"What was negative?" he asked.

"The pregnancy test." When she noticed the relieved look on his face again, she averted her eyes, not wanting him to see her own disappointment that now extended beyond the results of the test to include his reaction.

"I'm sorry, Amanda," he said at last and tried to wrap his arms around her shoulders.

But she slipped out of the bed and away from his touch.

"What is that?" The anger in his voice was instantaneous. She had never shied away from his touch. "I try to comfort you and you walk away?"

"We've been married for eight months, Alejandro." She turned around to face him. "You make love to me almost every day when we are together! Why am I not pregnant?"

He slid his legs over the side of the bed and stood up. His shoulders carried the weight of his irritation as he walked over to grab a water bottle from the ice bucket on the dresser. "I don't know, Amanda." He leaned against the dresser as he uncapped the bottle. "Do not punish me for this."

She did not look away from his steady gaze. "I know how you feel about children, Alejandro. Your career comes first."

"What?" he asked, his harsh tone revealing his irritation at her comment. "That's ridiculous, Amanda!"

She ignored him and continued. "You've also known many women after Isadora's birth. Why don't you have other children?"

"*¡Ay, mi madre!*" He ran his fingers through his hair and looked up at the ceiling. "You want me to have more illegitimate children? You are angry with me because I don't?"

"*Nee*, Alejandro," she responded, trying to soften her tone. "I am, however, curious as to why you don't."

"I am not having this conversation," he muttered to himself, crossing his arms over his chest.

Taking a deep breath, Amanda finally blurted out the question that had been on her mind since leaving Lititz. "Have you done something so you can't have more babies? I . . . I have a right to know."

For a long moment, he simply stared at her, a blank expression on his face. He blinked his eyes and furrowed his eyebrows. Then, just when she thought he might be on the verge of admitting the truth—a truth that she did not want to hear—he surprised her by bursting into a deep, hearty laugh. He set down the water bottle and crossed the room to her, his laughter causing her to feel even worse as she began to tear up.

"Princesa!" he said as he put his hands on her shoulders and bent his knees so that he could look directly into her face. "Is that what you think? *¡Ay, Dios, mamacita!* No, Amanda, I would never do such a thing."

A tear escaped her eye and slowly fell down her cheek. She swiped at it with her one hand.

"As for you, we will see a doctor when we return, *sí?* It will be fine, I'm sure. Most likely the travel and the poor diet of life on the road is affecting your menstruation. Why, you are doing so much; I see how you fall into a deep sleep on the buses and planes. We need to make certain you eat better and more regularly. You'll see," he said, trying to reassure her, his hands rubbing her arms. "You'll feel much better, *sí?*"

She wiped at a tear and looked up at him through watery eyes. "What if that's not it? What if something is wrong?"

Pulling her into his arms, he pressed her head against his shoulder. "Shh," he whispered. "There is nothing wrong."

"But you don't even *want* a baby," she said as she began to sob.

"I never said that!"

She nodded her head, trying to control herself, but her sobs merely turned into soft hiccups—which, to her dismay, only seemed to amuse him even more. "You said we're traveling and that it's too hard to have a baby on tour."

"*Sí,* that is true. But that doesn't mean I don't want one."

"And . . . and look at Isadora!" she managed to say. "I feel as if we've abandoned her, Alejandro."

"*Ay, mi madre,*" he mumbled, pressing his hand against his head. "You said yourself just last week that she is loved and in a much better environment than being dragged from city to city, country to country."

Her tears fell onto his shoulder, and she tried to wipe them away, only to have more tears wet his skin.

"Now, please stop crying, *sí?* It will happen when it happens, *mi amor.* Aren't you the one that always tells me God has a plan for us?"

He moved back and put his hands on either side of her cheeks, staring into her face. "God has one for you, too. And you will have a baby, Amanda. My baby. But only when God decides."

She sniffled and nodded her head, feeling foolish for having confronted him in such a manner.

"Now," he said, a mischievous gleam starting to fill his eyes. "About that comment you made?"

"Which one?" she asked in a soft voice.

He let his hands fall down to take hers and gently guided her back toward the bed. "About making love to you every day . . ."

She blushed and tried to resist him.

"You reminded me we have missed a day. Today."

She gave a soft laugh, a final tear falling from her eyes. "I was just crying!" she protested. "I'm sure I look—"

He placed his finger against her lips to silence her. "Crying or not, you are always beautiful, Princesa. And I don't care if you have tear-streaked cheeks or puffy eyes." She balked at his description, knowing it was true. "What I care about is my promise to you that we will have fun trying to make this baby, Amanda. And after all of that," he said, "so much emotion, I think I know just the way to make good on that promise."

# Chapter Twenty

With Celinda not joining the tour in Zürich or Bern, Amanda felt a new sense of loss. Gone was the only person she considered a friend. There was no one else—certainly not Charlotte—in whom Amanda could confide. Just as Alejandro had once told her, everyone seemed to want something from her. Simply put, she could not trust anyone, and it made for long and lonely days. In those moments, Amanda realized how much she missed Anna and even her mother. However, Amanda forced herself to keep a firm upper lip so that Alejandro would never suspect how homesick she felt.

At least Charlotte had honored her promise to keep Amanda busy in each country on the European tour. Today was the continuation of a photo shoot started in Paris that was a behind-the-scenes look at Amanda's life on the road. This time, the photographer and journalist would accompany Amanda to a high school where she was to be given a tour and meet with students.

The previous day Amanda had done a tour at a different school on the other side of Zürich. If Amanda had originally balked at the idea, she found that it was one of the more enjoyable days on the tour, much better than the repetitive interviews for radio, television, or magazines.

Just hearing the teenagers thanking her for being a role model and providing inspiration in their lives made Amanda realize that, just as Alejandro and Geoffrey had predicted, adopting the role of ambassador of goodwill was something she truly found engaging.

When she awoke the morning of their second day in Zürich, she found she did not dread the schedule as much as she normally did.

Alejandro looked up from his laptop as she walked out of the bedroom, dressed for the day. His eyes drank in her white dress with its slightly revealing V-neck plunge line, the fabric hugging her body in a simple way that showed off her figure without being too provocative. *"Ay, mi madre,"* he said, whistling as she sauntered into the room, pretending to turn around for his inspection.

"You like?"

*"Sí,* Princesa," he said, standing up and approaching her. Wearing just his black gym pants and no shirt, the contrast between the two of them was comical. He reached for her hand and lifted it over her head as she twirled around for him. "Ooh la la, *mi amor!*"

Before she realized what had happened, he pulled her against him. She shouldn't have been surprised. The sultry look in his eyes was all too familiar.

"What time is that appointment, Princesa?" he asked as he started walking her backward with him toward the room she had just left.

"Alejandro!" she protested. "Really, I have to go."

He ignored her pleas and gently pushed her onto the mattress, standing over her as she struggled to sit up. "They will wait for you," he said as he reached down and stroked her neck. "You are, after all, Princesa, the royalty of the rap world."

She gave a little laugh. "I hate that," she said, but her voice faltered and she shut her eyes, forgetting that a car waited for her downstairs and that she would be late for her appointment. His touch on her skin sent a shiver down her spine. Slowly, she responded to the closeness of his body, especially his naked chest. She couldn't help but reach out and touch his stomach, so firm and warm.

He grabbed her hand and her eyes flew open.

"Did I do something wrong?" she asked innocently.

He answered by lowering his body onto hers and pressing his mouth against hers, a kiss filled with such passion it took her breath away. She barely even noticed that he was reaching to pull her dress over her head. By the time she realized what he was doing, the warmth of his body against hers had eliminated any and all further protests.

By the time her phone began to ring, she lay in his arms, basking in the glow of his love. She started to get up in order to retrieve it, but he held her even firmer, his legs entwined with hers. She noticed her dress crumpled in a heap on the floor and quickly tried to figure out what she would wear in its place.

"Don't go, Princesa," he purred into her neck.

"I really must." She kissed his arm as she slowly peeled herself away from his grasp. "And you have things to do today, too."

He rolled over and leaned his head against his hand, watching as she picked up the dress and examined it.

"That was brand-new," she scolded him.

"I'll buy you ten more like it!"

She frowned as she passed the bed, the dress in her hands. "That would be rather wasteful, Alejandro."

He laughed and threw a pillow at her, which she artfully dodged.

Five minutes later and wearing a simple black dress, she hurried into the elevator to meet up with the car. Alejandro insisted that the black dress was more striking, even though she'd wanted to wear the other dress. Charlotte had repeatedly told her that white clothing was a more sophisticated look for her, and it often caught the attention of people at the different places she visited. And today Amanda wanted to be visible since she was trying to raise awareness about the school.

The elevator stopped at a floor and two people entered, an American-looking girl with her mother.

"Oh!" The girl gasped before she tugged at her mother's hand and leaned over to whisper something in her ear.

Amanda tried to hide her smile.

"Excuse me," the girl said nervously. "Are you . . . Princesa?"

"I am Amanda Diaz, *ja*," she responded, silently wishing that the British interviewer had never made the comment about Alejandro and Amanda being the royalty of the rap world. The pet nickname that Alejandro had given her had spread like wildfire. Whenever she heard it, she cringed. "And you are . . . ?"

"Me?"

Amanda laughed. "You, *ja*! What is your name?"

"Julia."

Amanda extended her hand for Julia to shake. "It's very nice to meet you, Julia."

The girl's face lit up as she shook Amanda's hand.

"Would you like a photo, then?" Amanda asked. "Perhaps in the foyer, if that's where you're going. It's much prettier than here." She glanced around the elevator as if to make her point.

"Oh, I would!"

The mother leaned forward. "We're your biggest fans!" She, too, looked as starstruck as her daughter.

Amanda lowered her eyes demurely. "I never quite know what to say to that," she said.

"We follow you on social media, too!" The girl reached for her phone. "Do you think you could . . . ?"

"Follow you?" Amanda made a sad face. "I'm afraid I don't have my phone with me." The truth was that she still had yet to conquer social media. She left that to Dali and Charlotte to delegate to their teams. "But a photo is just as well, then, *ja*?"

Once the elevator doors opened, Amanda found a proper backdrop for her to stand in the middle of the mother and daughter, her head tilted at the perfect angle and her smile just right for the camera. After the camera was handed back to the mother, Amanda bade them good-bye and continued on her way outside. Surely Charlotte would be fuming, that soft, fun side of her disappearing behind her forked-tongue-spitfire side. But Amanda already knew how to handle that.

"Goodness gracious, Amanda! You're half an hour late!" Charlotte scolded Amanda while she ran behind her. "And you are dillydallying in there with who? Fans?"

Amanda shook her head. "Not fans. *Friends.* The very *friends* who make this photo shoot meaningful."

Charlotte mumbled something under her breath, which Amanda ignored as she got into the waiting car.

The photo shoot was scheduled to begin in a downtown Zürich studio and then move to the Augustinerstrasse for more photographs before Amanda headed over to the high school to meet and talk with the students. The photographer from *On Tour* magazine would most likely take thousands of photos throughout the day, with only a handful selected for the magazine article. With any luck, Charlotte informed her, one of her studio photos would be selected to grace the cover.

"There she is!"

Amanda strolled across the classroom, careful to take slow and deliberate steps. After much practice, she had finally mastered how to enter a room in a way that made people pay attention. In this case, it wasn't hard to do, as the students were eagerly waiting to meet with her. She stopped and greeted each student with a warm handshake and kind word before she stood at the front of the classroom and waited for their questions.

The questions were very similar to the ones from the previous day, many of them asking her about her youth growing up in the Amish community and about her life with Viper. As she became more comfortable with the interactions, she began to share more and more of herself with the students.

"What's it like being famous?" one of the students asked.

"Am I?" she answered innocently, to which the students laughed. "I reckon it isn't something I'll ever get used to," she admitted. "After all, it's not like I can sing or paint or even write a book. But I find that I meet the most interesting people each and every day."

"You met Harry in England, didn't you?"

Amanda had to think back. "You mean the young man with green eyes?" Several girls sighed and Amanda knew that's whom they meant. "I did, *ja*. But they are just people, no different from us," she explained. "They, too, enjoy meeting fans and pleasing them, knowing that, at the end of the day, they have made a difference in people's lives." She had been leaning against the desk in the front of the room. Now, she stood up straight and found herself walking, just a little, back and forth in front of the rows of students. "That's why these people do what they do. At least, that's what I've learned. They are people who want to make a difference, but they are just like you. You are just as special as they are."

"They have an awful lot more followers on Snapchat than I do," one teenage boy with blond hair and blue eyes quipped, which caused the others to laugh.

"And what, exactly, does that mean?" Amanda asked in a gentle tone of voice. "I keep wondering about this and asking Alejandro . . . Viper . . . about the meaning of this. Social media? Social currency? Is our value to be measured in numbers or in how we impact change? Be the change that you dream for your future," she said. "Don't leave your future in the hands of others."

Out of the corner of her eye, she saw Marilyn, the journalist for *On Tour* magazine, scribbling furiously on her pad of paper, taking notes on what Amanda was sharing.

"Back in my Amish community," Amanda continued, finding a topic she was much more comfortable discussing, "we shied away from worldliness. I never understood why until I experienced the world of fame. Now I understand why the bishops and the parents wanted to keep the children away from the changing technologies that many of you use on an hourly basis. Worldliness changes you, and like an old philosopher once said, no man can step into the same river twice, for both the man and the river are constantly changing.'"

A young girl seated in the front row raised her hand and, before the teacher could call on her, said, "Heraclitus said something like that."

Amanda made a face. "Mayhaps. I don't know. Alejandro told me that."

The class laughed and Marilyn smiled while the photographer continued taking photos.

"The moral of the story is that you need to find the balance in your own life. Do not look to others to make you feel complete and whole. Do not look to the world for that. For, once you step into the world, you will not return the same person and everything will change, leaving you with new situations to deal with."

By the time she was done talking with the class, Charlotte was tapping her foot and pointing toward her wrist as if she wore a watch.

"Now seriously, Amanda," Charlotte said, an edge to her voice. "An hour? We have another classroom to meet and still need to take photos of you at the arena."

Amanda rolled her eyes. "Please, Charlotte. Which is more important? Talking to these students and making a difference or taking hundreds of photos, from which one might be selected?"

"According to my schedule, both—but only if you stay on task!"

Amanda shook her head and walked away from Charlotte, choosing to follow the school guide into the next classroom. She noticed that Marilyn followed, continuing to write notes on her pad of paper. Amanda hoped that what she had just said to Charlotte was not something that might reflect poorly on her. However, she knew she spoke from the heart, and if she had learned anything over the past year, she knew she could speak no other way—not for Charlotte, and certainly not for the media.

With a smile, she greeted the next class, walking through the line of standing students, meeting each one with a handshake before she stood at the front of the class and began to answer their questions just as she had done in the previous class. Although the questions were the same, her answers were different. After all, as she had just told the other students, even she could not step into the same river twice.

"You invited Enrique to join us?"

She could hardly believe she'd heard Alejandro correctly. Had he truly said those words to her. Enrique Lopez? Of all people?

"Celinda isn't here and he wanted some company," Alejandro explained as he stared in the mirror, fixing his hair, the back still damp from his post-concert shower. He wore a black shirt and white pants, a nice change from his typical all-black outfits that he insisted on wearing in public.

Amanda leaned against the wall as she watched him, her arms crossed over her chest. "*Ja, vell*, I'm sure he can find plenty of company in no time. He always does."

Alejandro glanced in the bathroom mirror at her reflection and she immediately apologized, dropping her hands to her sides and releasing the tension in her shoulders. "I'm sorry. I know I shouldn't feel that way, Alejandro. I just find it so hard to trust a man who has the morals of a scrawny barn tomcat."

She thought she saw him smile at her description.

"Mayhaps you should just go out with him alone, then," she offered.

"No deal." He spun around and grabbed her hand, pulling her into his arms and dipping her backward. With her back bent and her head almost touching the floor, she gave a cry of surprise as she clung to his neck. "What is an evening in Zürich without my Princesa?" He nuzzled at her neck and nibbled at her ear, causing her to squirm and laugh at the ticklish feeling of his razor stubble against her skin. "Wherever one goes . . . ," he teased.

"So goes the other," she finished for him. After he set her upright on her feet, she sighed. "Fine. I'll go. But please don't make me sit near him."

"He's going to be at our table. He's having dinner with us!"

"Now you are really pushing it," she said, wagging a finger at him. "At least don't expect me to be happy about it, especially if he finds some woman to ease his need for company."

Alejandro turned and playfully smacked her bottom. "Go and have some of that champagne I opened. Relax while I finish getting ready."

She stuck her tongue out at him, dodging the hand towel he tossed at her as she escaped the bathroom and wandered into the main area of the suite.

Obediently, she walked over to the bar and took the crystal flute of champagne that he had poured for her earlier. The bubbles climbed to the top and she lifted the glass to her lips, savoring the sweet taste of the drink. With the glass in her hand, she moved to the window and stood there, staring outside at the lights of the city. It was different from the other cities they had traveled to, far less pretty during the daytime, but nighttime masked its drabness in a glow of pretty lights from the buildings, houses, and streets.

She heard the door open and glanced over her shoulder, not surprised to see Enrique saunter into the room. Forcing herself to be pleasant, she greeted him with a simple, "Hello."

"Well, hello to you, too, Princesa," he said as he beelined to the bar for a drink. He bypassed the gentle and smooth champagne to dive right into the vodka. "Imagine my surprise when I was summoned to join the Royalty of Rap's court tonight."

Inwardly, she groaned. She could see exactly how this evening would play out. Already Enrique was starting with her, pushing her buttons in the way that only he knew how. Ignoring him, she turned away to look outside, preferring the beauty of the city to the ugliness that stood on the other side of the room.

"Have you heard from Celinda?" he asked, clearly oblivious to Amanda's discomfort or, if not oblivious, indifferent.

"She's back in Los Angeles," Amanda said in a flat voice, not wanting to offer more information than Enrique needed.

He sighed and plopped himself down onto the sofa. "Such a shame. I was beginning to enjoy her company."

Amanda shut her eyes and counted to ten, wondering how Celinda had seen anything in this man that could have tempted her to think intimacy was a good idea. Just the thought of Alejandro having behaved in such a manner during his wild days made Amanda feel nauseated. She could only calm her anxiety by reminding herself that, unlike Enrique, at least Alejandro seemed to always demonstrate class, even with his female conquests.

It was almost midnight by the time they arrived at the restaurant, which, thanks to Geoffrey, remained open extra late so that they could dine after the concert. For Amanda, the concerts had begun to blend together, becoming a mixture of blurred crowds cheering for her while she wandered through the floor, taking photos with many people and talking with a select few. At some concerts she might pull two or three people to join her backstage, while at other shows she might only pull one.

People had begun to carry signs, begging to be "called to court." While Amanda didn't understand it at first, Geoffrey and Alejandro had told her the people were asking her to select them to come back-stage. She didn't like the comparison to the royal families and feudal systems of the past, especially since it appeared that so many of the royals died violent, horrific deaths. Still, whenever she complained, Alejandro reassured her that it was a compliment.

"Wine, *sí*?" Alejandro gestured for the server. They'd been joined by Geoffrey, Eddie, several other men from his entourage, plus Enrique, so Amanda was hardly surprised when Alejandro ordered four bottles of wine for the table.

Her head spun as everyone talked about numbers: ticket sales, merch sales, social media numbers, trending hashtags. Thankfully, she sat in between Alejandro and Geoffrey, so she wasn't subjected to Enrique's boisterous contributions to the conversation. Once, while Alejandro and Geoffrey were discussing the success of Amanda's first meeting at the high school in Zürich, she caught Enrique staring at her. His steady gaze made her feel uncomfortable, but rather than give in to her feelings, she stared back at him with a cool look until he, not she, turned away.

But as he looked away, she saw something on his face, a dark expression of anger that made her wonder if Alejandro really under-stood just what motivated Enrique. If his past transgressions meant anything, Amanda knew that he was not a man to be trifled with—nor was he a man who took no for an answer.

Amanda had begun to realize that she challenged him in a way few women ever had. And by challenging Enrique Lopez—a man who was used to getting his way—Amanda had not made a new friend in him. Of course, she didn't want him as a friend. But she'd only just realized she most likely didn't want him as an enemy either.

Unfortunately, with Enrique, it was one or the other. From the look on his face, she suspected under which category she fell.

# Chapter Twenty-One

As soon as she entered the hotel suite, Amanda kicked off her high-heeled shoes and pushed them to the side so that Alejandro would not trip over them when he returned. She had thought he might be there already, but the suite was empty. For once, she wasn't going to complain. She needed a few minutes of peace and quiet, time to gather her thoughts and relax.

Starting with the night of the group dinner in Zürich, it had seemed like the past few days blurred together. Between two back-to-back concerts before traveling to Bern, their hotel suite seemed to be constantly filled with people. Even after the concerts, Alejandro had invited his entourage over to party while he recorded lyrics to some new songs. Despite his focus on work, his friends had been noisy and Amanda had hardly slept. She'd sat and watched her husband working some of the time. His attention to detail was so precise and on point that she found it fascinating to observe him. She was also amazed by how much could be done outside of a recording studio.

Today, however, Charlotte had scheduled three interviews and one photo shoot that had run far too long. Amanda needed to sit down, just for a while, to relax even if only for an hour, before the next round of evening activities began.

The sofa beckoned, and she padded across the plush white carpet to stretch out on it. Dropping her purse onto the floor, she sank into the cushions and leaned back. She wanted to shut her eyes but feared falling asleep. If she did, she'd probably sleep for hours. The level of exhaustion that she felt was taking a toll on her, both mentally and physically. She felt ill and couldn't eat. Her stomach bothered her, yet despite drinking bottled water as if she were in a desert, she felt bloated. The irregular, unstructured schedule and constant flying to and from different countries didn't help.

Her cell phone made a noise; groaning, she reached into her handbag to retrieve it.

"Please don't let it be Charlotte," she mumbled to herself.

It wasn't.

Princesa,
Running late. I'll be back in an hour.
Dinner tonight. Just us.
V.

She smiled and tucked the phone under her hip—an hour's respite from noise and energy. It sounded like a little bit of heaven to her, so she let her eyes shut, too aware of their burning from such a long day.

The day had started with a breakfast in her honor at a local children's hospital. While she hadn't minded the breakfast, although she barely ate anything, the tour of the hospital tired her out. She definitely had worn the wrong shoes. And then, of course, when she walked along the cancer floor, where the children were waiting to meet her, her heart broke for the pain and suffering many of them were going through. She made certain to spend a moment with each of the children, a translator nearby in case the Bern children couldn't understand her broken

German. For the most part, the translator was not needed, a fact that delighted all of the officials as well as the children.

Charlotte, however, had begun to tap her foot and glance at the time Amanda was spending with each child.

And that was all it took to cause happy, energetic Charlotte to change into her alter ego—irritated and angry Charlotte. For the rest of the day, Amanda heard nothing but biting remarks and complaints about the chaos caused by the extended visit to the hospital.

Amanda simply ignored her.

Another photo shoot, this time in the center of the small historic section of town, was her last appointment. She changed her clothing into a new designer dress, and two women scurried around her, one touching up her makeup while another one worked on her hair. The photos near the Zytglogge clock tower, a beautiful medieval tower built in the early 1200s, would be used for an advertisement in a tourism magazine. According to Charlotte, they had paid a handsome fee—well into the six-figure range—for the honor of having Princesa entice people to visit their city. The photographers, however, wanted the lighting to be just right as the sun began to set, so they hurried her along and gave her no breaks during the hour that they shot photograph after photograph.

In the morning they were scheduled to travel to Copenhagen before wrapping up the tour with a long weekend, first in Oslo and then Stockholm. Amanda smiled as she realized that they were just a week or so away from returning to the United States and having a degree of normalcy in their lives for a while. Shortly after they returned to the States, they would travel to Los Angeles for Alejandro to review the latest version of his newest music video and Amanda to approve some product concepts designed by Richard Gray's team. Fortunately, there was to be a week of respite. They would then stop at Miami for a few days because Alejandro needed to meet with his Miami-based team, and Amanda would most likely spend some time with his mother,

Alecia. And Alejandro had reassured Amanda that there would be time to spend a few days with her family in Lititz. Amanda was counting down the days until they could return to Pennsylvania. She couldn't wait to see Isadora and soak up her lavender-scented hugs and kisses. And to sit down for a home-cooked meal! Pure heaven.

She must have drifted to sleep for the room was almost dark when she heard the door open. Barely awake, she swung her legs off the sofa and sat up, trying to see where he was.

"Alejandro?"

A flick of a switch and light washed over the room. She blinked at the brightness, her eyes needing a moment to adjust.

"Sorry, Amanda," a too-familiar voice said.

"Enrique?"

If she had been sleepy before, she was wide-awake now. Her body tensed, and she wondered what time it was.

He wandered to the bar and leaned over it for a glass. "Want a drink?"

"What are you doing here?"

He ignored the question and poured himself a vodka straight up. He lifted the glass into the air, gesturing to her. "You sure?" When she didn't answer, he walked over and sat down on the other side of the sofa. Amanda immediately stood up and took a few steps away. "Where's Viper?"

She didn't like him being there, not without Alejandro. She glanced at the window, wondering how long she had slept and when he would arrive. Being alone with Enrique was not something she desired. "Are you supposed to meet him here, then?"

"*Sí*, for the final recording of our song."

Amanda frowned. That didn't make any sense. Alejandro had said they would have dinner alone when he returned. "You must be mistaken," she said. "He's running late from his meetings, and we're to go out tonight. Alone."

If she had hoped he would take the hint, he didn't. Swirling the alcohol in his glass, he lifted it to his lips and took a long, slow drink. "I can wait a bit to see him. We won't have time to finish it in Scandinavia." He glanced at the window, but with the sun down for an hour, the only light to be seen was from the buildings. "Bern's a pretty city, *sí*? It's old. I like that." He looked over at her. "The history. We don't have that in America."

She didn't respond.

"What is it, Princesa—" he started to ask, but Amanda interrupted him.

"Don't call me that." She frowned. "I've told you that at least a dozen times before."

He laughed, standing up and slowly moving toward her. "Why not? The rest of the world does, no?"

As he approached her, she backed away but refused to lower her eyes from his. To do so would show a sign of weakness. "It sounds dirty from your lips."

"As I was starting to ask, what is it, *Amanda*," Enrique said, emphasizing her name, "that you find so unappealing about me?"

She looked away from him, her arms crossed over her chest as if to protect herself.

"Women throw themselves at me, Amanda," he said. "You, however, won't even look at me." He stood in front of her and reached out as if to touch her cheek.

Amanda recoiled, taking a second step backward and continuing to stare directly into his face. "Do not touch me, Enrique."

He closed the distance between them, his eyelids drooping and a lazy smile on his face. "Of all the women in the world, you are the only one who says that."

"I find that very hard to believe," she said, feeling the edge of the counter pressing against her back. She could not move any farther away from him.

"Women find me sexy, Princesa."

She didn't bother to correct him, suddenly realizing that, in all likelihood, the vodka he had just downed in two gulps was not the first, or even second, drink he had consumed that evening. She sensed danger about him and immediately glanced around the room, trying to find a way to put some distance between them.

"Now, why doesn't that apply to you?" He smirked at her. "I wonder if it's because you are married. If so, that's a sorry excuse, Princesa. In this business, everyone cheats."

At that comment, Amanda lashed out at him. "Just because you live for one-night stands does not mean that everyone does that. In fact, just hearing you say that makes you even more repulsive to me, Enrique."

"Repulsive?" He repeated the word, letting it roll off his tongue as if he were tasting it. "That's not what your friend Celinda said about me in Paris, Prague, and—if memory serves me correctly—in Vienna, too," he said. "Now I know why Justin Bell left her. Unlike you, she's a bit too willing to give."

Without thinking, Amanda slapped his cheek. She knew far too well what had transpired between Celinda and Enrique, and to hear him speak of her in such a negative way infuriated her. But as soon as her hand made contact with his face, the noise loud and sharp, her mouth dropped open and the color drained from her cheeks. "Oh, Enrique!" She almost made a move toward him. "I'm so sorry!"

With his head still turned in the direction of the slap, his cheek swelling pink from the contact, he reached up and touched his jaw.

"I . . . I don't know why I did that." There was panic in her voice. She had never struck anyone in her life. Violence was a very serious sin. It went against everything that she had been raised to believe. How could God ever forgive her for striking someone in anger, even if that someone was Enrique? "Please. Are you all right?"

She finally did reach out to touch his face, but he grabbed her wrist and twisted her arm away from him, causing her to cry out in pain.

"Does that hurt? Princesa?" he said, forcing her backward. "¿Sí? Not very nice, is it?"

She pressed her lips together. "You are hurting me, Enrique."

"Maybe that's not a bad thing, Princesa." This time he used a mocking tone when he spoke her nickname. With his body, he pressed her against the bar, standing far too close to her. "If you weren't so coddled, you might find you like it," he hissed into her ear.

"You're disgusting," she managed to say.

"That's not what Celinda said."

Amanda tried to move away as Enrique released her, shoving her so that she stumbled to the floor just as Alejandro walked through the door.

He stood there, just inside the doorway, staring first at Amanda and then Enrique, as if trying to make sense of what he had just witnessed. "What's going on here?"

Amanda scrambled to her feet and hurried over to him. She was too afraid to say anything as she stood next to Alejandro.

He placed his arm around her protectively. "You are hurt?"

She shook her head, but her wrist was already swelling and discolored.

He kissed the side of her head and then gently pushed her behind him. Only then did he begin to approach Enrique.

"You touched my wife?"

Enrique glared at Alejandro. "She attacked me."

"That's not true!" Amanda cried out.

"She hit me," Enrique said, pointing to his face. "For no reason."

Alejandro clenched his teeth, the muscles in his jaw tensing as he tried to assess the situation. Amanda watched, wide-eyed, as Alejandro turned back toward her. "You hit him, Amanda?"

"I . . ."

"Did you hit him?"

She pressed her lips together and nodded her head.

"I told you," Enrique said, mumbling something under his breath in Spanish.

At that moment Alejandro turned around, so quickly and with such force that his fist—making contact with Enrique's jaw in the same place that Amanda had slapped him—sent Enrique backward and into the table by the sofa. The glass shattered and Amanda screamed. Before Enrique could get up, Alejandro leaned over him and grabbed Enrique's shirt, pulling him to his feet.

"I've had just about enough of you," Alejandro said before he shoved Enrique, causing him to fall once again. Hovering over him, Alejandro pointed in his face. "A man does not touch another man's wife!"

"I barely touched her," Enrique said.

"I saw what I saw!" Alejandro bent down and grabbed Enrique, raising his fist once again when Amanda ran forward.

"Stop! That's enough!" She placed her hands on Alejandro's shoulders, hoping to pull him away from Enrique. "Please, no more . . . ," she pleaded.

Alejandro shook her off him, his attention focused completely on Enrique. She could see the anger in Alejandro's eyes as he struck Enrique again. When blood started running out of his nose, Amanda screamed.

The door to the hotel suite burst open and two men rushed into the room, both of them grabbing Alejandro and dragging him away from Enrique. Shortly after, a third man ran into the room and went to Enrique's side.

The men spoke so rapidly in German that she couldn't understand them. It was only when both Alejandro and Enrique were placed into handcuffs that she realized the men who had entered the room were security.

"You can't arrest them!" she cried out, first in English and then in her fractured German. "It's a big misunderstanding!"

She tried to go to Alejandro, but one of the security guards blocked her, placing both of his hands on her shoulders to keep her from moving. Helplessly, she watched as security led Alejandro from the room. Outside the door, she could see more people were gathered in the corridor, mostly security along with hotel personnel. Nowhere did she see anyone from Alejandro's team.

Where was Andres? she thought. And Carlos and Eddie? If only they had been with Alejandro . . .

"You need to go to the hospital," the guard said, redirecting her thoughts. "Get that looked at by a doctor."

"I'm fine," she replied, trying to move away from him once again.

"You're bleeding." The guard pointed to Amanda's head. As Amanda lifted her hand to her temple, she grimaced and looked at her fingertips. Indeed, blood covered her fingers, and she realized she must have hit her head when Enrique shoved her to the floor. She sat down on the sofa and covered her face with her hands just moments before she blacked out.

"We have good news for you!"

Amanda stared at the tall blonde woman standing next to her. "Where am I?"

The woman smiled at her. "University Hospital, Mrs. Diaz. I'm Dr. Helbling."

"Why am I here?" Amanda sat up and looked around. She was in a hospital bed in what looked like a private room. "My husband? Where is he?"

Dr. Helbling shook her head. "I'm sorry, I don't know where he is. You came into the emergency room last evening, Mrs. Diaz. Your wrist needed attention, and you had a severe cut on your head. Are you feeling better? No headache?"

The doctor watched Amanda as she reached up to touch the side of her head and felt a bandage.

"Seven stitches, nothing too bad."

"I need to make a phone call," Amanda said suddenly. She didn't remember anything about coming to the hospital. All she remembered was Alejandro wanting her to call Geoffrey. She hadn't. "How long have I been here?"

The doctor glanced at the clock on the wall. "Not quite six hours. We put you in a private room. The emergency room filled up quickly. Seems you are quite popular, Mrs. Diaz."

Amanda sank back into the pillows and shut her eyes. "I need to get in touch with someone."

"Well, you are being released, if that helps. But before you go, I wanted to let you know that your wrist is only bruised and the baby is fine. We did an ultrasound and everything looks as it should be."

Amanda frowned as she stared at the doctor. Had she misheard her? "I . . . I think you are mistaken. I'm not pregnant."

Dr. Helbling shuffled through some papers on a clipboard, her eyes quickly scanning the documents. "I can assure you, Mrs. Diaz, that you are. I did the ultrasound myself. Looks like you are ten weeks . . . maybe a little further."

Amanda's mind raced. How many pregnancy tests had she taken? Three? Four? All of them had turned up negative. "How is this possible?" she whispered, more to herself than to the doctor. "Not one of my tests said I was pregnant."

The doctor nodded. "Ah yes, the home pregnancy tests. Their reliability is usually impeccable, but whether it was a bad expiration date or a problem administering it, false negatives can occur."

"A problem administering it?" Amanda echoed. "It's just a little stick!"

The doctor gave a soft laugh. "Well, some people don't realize that they have to pull the cap off before they test their urine."

Amanda froze. A cap? She had not considered that she needed to remove the cap before she dipped the stick into her urine sample. She thought backward, mentally trying to calculate where she was ten weeks ago. That was just around the time when Alejandro had visited her at the farm and, after a night of passion, snuck out to leave before dawn crested over the hill.

Only he hadn't left her alone. He had left her with a new life, a life they had created together just hours before he was planning on leaving her.

"Are . . . are you sure?" Amanda asked. A baby, she thought. Her baby with Alejandro. What should have been a moment of joy, learning that she was finally pregnant, was filled with apprehension as she remembered that Alejandro was sitting in a jail cell, probably waiting for Geoffrey to show up, but Amanda had never made the phone call.

The doctor placed her hand on Amanda's arm. She smiled at her and said, "There is a heartbeat, Mrs. Diaz. I can assure you that you are, indeed, pregnant."

Amanda nodded, barely hearing the words the doctor said.

"We'd like to observe you for a little while longer, let you rest. But we will release you later today. So try to get some sleep," Dr. Helbling said as she started to walk to the door. Before leaving the room, however, she paused and looked back at Amanda. "And, by the way, congratulations."

Despite feeling tired and bruised, Amanda hadn't been able to sleep, especially after she couldn't reach Geoffrey, Charlotte, or even Dali. The nurses had promised to keep trying, urging her to sleep, but Amanda's mind kept racing, worrying first about Alejandro and then trying to grasp the news that she was carrying his baby. The two conflicting thoughts held sleep at bay.

Everything had been her fault. She knew she never should have lashed out at Enrique and struck him, letting anger drive her action. Oh, it was true indeed, she thought. *A fool's wrath is presently known: but a prudent man covereth shame.* She had never felt such anger as when Enrique, after weeks of his crude teasing and looks, even his gestures, had made a comment about Celinda. But she could hardly believe that her anger could force her to raise a hand and strike another person.

What has happened to me? she wondered. When had she lost her way from the values of her youth?

And Alejandro. She felt another wave of guilt that her actions had caused him so much trouble. They were supposed to leave that day for the last three concerts. Surely he would not make it in time to catch his flight, if at all. She knew nothing of the court systems in America and even less about those of Europe, if the situation wound up there.

And then she remembered the unexpected news that she was pregnant.

She placed her hands on her midsection, slowly caressing her belly. Over the past few weeks, she had noticed that her clothes were snug, but she attributed it to the travel and not eating properly and so much water retention. Now, as she lay in the hospital bed, she tried to think back to the last time she had had her period. It was before leaving South America. In fact, she had all but forgotten about it, the constant travel and busy schedules distracting her from something so important.

She tried to count backward, but couldn't. Was it possible that she had been pregnant that entire time while they were in Colombia, Brazil, and Argentina? She had been so tired on the farm, but she never thought twice about it. Between Isadora and the chores, not to mention her stress over Alejandro, it was understandable that she was exhausted.

"Amanda!" The door opened and Geoffrey rushed into the room. With his disheveled hair and wrinkled shirt, he appeared worn-out, clearly not having slept through the night. "I came as fast a I could." He glanced down at her and saw her arm. His expression changed. "Are you all right?"

She looked down and saw the large purple bruise that covered her wrist and part of her forearm. "It happened so fast," she started. "I was sleeping and Enrique let himself in. He . . . he said that he was to meet with Alejandro, and he wouldn't leave. He kept asking me questions and . . ." She paused, not wanting to identify her friend, but she needed to tell Geoffrey everything so that he could get Alejandro released. "He said something . . . something disgusting and awful, about Celinda."

Geoffrey's expression changed from worry to irritation. He took a deep breath and began to shake his head.

"I . . ." She could barely say the words. "I acted out of anger and slapped him."

Geoffrey shut his eyes.

"I know that I shouldn't have, and I'm ever so sorry . . ."

"What happened next, Amanda?"

"Enrique . . . he grabbed me and twisted my arm." She saw Geoffrey open his eyes and look down at her wrist. His eyes narrowed as the irritation in his face increased. "He shoved me just as Alejandro walked in and . . . and I don't know what happened. The next thing I knew, Alejandro was on top of Enrique and there was blood and the door burst open with security and . . ." She started crying again. "They just took him away, and there was nothing I could do!" A sob escaped. "And then I . . . I must have passed out."

Geoffrey stopped her by placing his hands on her shoulders and looking into her eyes. "Listen to me, Amanda. I have something I need to tell you."

She blinked, feeling the wetness of tears in her eyes once again. "It's all my fault, isn't it?"

"Amanda, you need to go back home," Geoffrey said. "Your father."

"My . . . my *daed*?" None of this made sense. Too much was happening at once, and she couldn't process it. "What does my *daed* have to do with this?"

Geoffrey told her somberly, "Your father had another stroke. Your sister contacted us, and we've been trying to find you for an hour. You didn't answer your phone or your text, and we couldn't locate Alejandro. Charlotte has arranged a flight for you to leave first thing in the morning. Charlotte will accompany you as far as Zürich. You'll be taking a private plane from Bern to Zürich so that you can make the flight. And Dali has arranged for a car service to fetch you from the airport."

Her father?

Amanda felt numb. To leave in the morning when Alejandro would need her the most? Being unsure how long it would take to resolve Alejandro's situation, Amanda couldn't bear the thought of having to leave without saying good-bye. She was sure he would be angry with her for having caused him so much trouble and disrupting the end of his tour. But she certainly couldn't stay. Her family needed her, and she had to see her father, to help nurse him back to health. And then there was Isadora. With so much change in her recent life, Isadora would be frightened and would need comfort.

"Now, Carlos is going to stay here with you while Eddie and I try to figure out what to do about Alejandro."

Her head felt light and the room seemed to spin. Geoffrey seemed to sense this and gently touched her arm, a gesture intended to reassure her. "You need to try to relax. It's been a bad night for all of us, and you have a long day ahead of you. You take care of *you*, Amanda, and let me take care of Alejandro."

As she leaned back against the pillows, she reached out for his hand. "Promise me you'll make certain that Alejandro is alright," she asked.

"Of course." Geoffrey gave her a small smile that did not erase the worry in his expression. "You just rest and leave Alejandro to me."

She watched as he walked out of the room, gently closing the door behind him. In the darkness of the room, she turned her head to look out the window, the lights of the city the only thing she could see. Somewhere out there, Alejandro was at a police station, maybe even sitting in a cell with other prisoners.

With her hand resting on her stomach, she thought of the life that grew within her. Despite wanting a baby so desperately, Amanda was confronted with just one more worry: Alejandro's reaction to the news.

She shut her eyes and began to pray, begging God to forgive her, to protect Alejandro, and to keep her father safe until she could get home to him.

# Chapter Twenty-Two

Alejandro sat in the chair, staring out the window at the mountain range. He hadn't slept all night, not since he had returned to the hotel and learned that Amanda had left. For several hours, he paced the floor, hoping against hope that she would return. Each time he walked past the broken table, he cringed at the memory of the previous night when he had walked into the room.

He hadn't meant to hurt Enrique. But seeing Enrique—his friend and colleague!—touching her body had sent him into a tailspin of blinding rage. How dare anyone touch his wife?

"You in here, V?"

Alejandro looked up as the door to his suite opened and Geoffrey walked in with Charlotte and Eddie. He motioned for them to sit down, but he returned his gaze to the window.

"Eddie, call someone from downstairs to clean this up," Geoffrey said, his voice sounding irritated.

"What's the damage?" Alejandro asked, his eyes still scanning the mountains. With the sun setting, there was an orange glow on the snowcapped peaks. He wondered how far away they were, and for just a moment, he wished he could go to them—anything to escape the misery of the past twenty-four hours.

"Besides all the fines to get the case thrown out so you don't have to fly back here?"

Alejandro glared at him. "Don't get wise with me, Geoffrey!"

"You have to learn to control your temper."

Alejandro jumped to his feet and thrust a finger at Geoffrey's face. "He was hurting Amanda! For once I believe this was justified!"

Geoffrey held up his hands as if calling a truce. "Calm down, Viper. Don't shoot the messenger."

The publicist jumped into the conversation. "Social media has picked up the story and it's gone viral, especially the photos of you and Enrique being led into the police station. There is one video circulating of you leaving the station but not a lot of interest in that." He shuffled through some papers and glanced at his tablet. "The main focus is on whether or not Enrique and you fought over Amanda, and why. Oh, and there is one story circulating with speculation about who's the father of her baby."

Alejandro rolled his eyes. "That's ridiculous even by tabloid standards! She's not even pregnant!"

Geoffrey cleared his throat and waited until Alejandro looked up.

"What is it, G?" The dark scowl on his face indicated the blackness of his mood. He lowered his head into his hands and mumbled, "I'm not in the mood for games! Just spit it out!"

"Well, I feel a bit awkward having to tell you this." Geoffrey shifted his weight, clearly uncomfortable. "Apparently, she is."

There was a silence in the room, and every pair of eyes was upon him. Alejandro maintained his position, his elbows on his knees and his head in his hands. Only his eyes flickered to Geoffrey's. "What did you say?"

"I . . . uh . . . I said she's pregnant. Ten weeks pregnant, apparently. She told me herself at the hospital."

"Dios *mío,*" he mumbled and shook his head. Pregnant? "And she left? Alone?"

Geoffrey nodded his head. "You know that her father is ill, Alejandro. He's taken a turn for the worse. She had to leave."

He couldn't imagine Amanda traveling alone to return to Lititz. In his mind, he could see her, sitting on the plane with her mind racing in too many directions. She'd be worrying about her father, worrying about the baby, and, most of all, worrying about Alejandro's reaction to the news that, once again, he was to be a father.

"I need to go to her."

Alejandro started to stand up, but Geoffrey placed a firm hand on his shoulder. "Not so fast, my friend. You have a concert tonight. You need to get out there and knock it out of the ballpark."

"And then what?"

"You have Oslo on Thursday and Friday and Stockholm on Saturday and Sunday. The earliest you can get to her is Monday."

Standing up, Alejandro faced Geoffrey. The previous night had been a long one, and there had been far too many questions. By the time a translator had arrived, two hours had passed. Security wouldn't let anyone into the room where Alejandro remained, so he had paced the floor, angry at Enrique and angry at himself.

When security finally let in a translator, Alejandro learned that Amanda had gone to the hospital. But with police now involved, they would not release him to go to her. Instead, he spent the better part of the morning and most of the afternoon sitting alone in a room while Geoffrey and the translator negotiated with the hotel management, security, and the police.

All during that time, Amanda had been alone.

No, he thought. He wouldn't wait until the following week to see Amanda. "That's just not good enough," he said. "I need you to help me do the right thing, Geoffrey. For once, I'm going to do the right thing, and you, *amigo,* are going to help me do it."

Geoffrey shut his eyes and exhaled. He still hadn't changed his clothes from the previous evening, and the stress of the day was more than apparent on his face. When he finally looked at Alejandro, he appeared exhausted. "What, exactly, would you have me do?"

Leveling his eyes so that he met Geoffrey's, Alejandro said the only words that he knew would get him to Lititz in order to support his wife: "Cancel the rest of the tour."

Amanda arrived at the farm almost one full day after she had left Bern. Between two flights and a long car ride from New York's LaGuardia Airport to Lititz, Pennsylvania, she felt bone weary. She hadn't slept on the plane, and her nerves felt shattered from the events of her last day in Switzerland. Now, as the car pulled into the driveway to her parents' farm, she did her best to take a deep breath and try to calm herself.

She didn't know what to expect when she walked into the house. From the looks of the driveway, there were people already there, most likely the bishop and preachers along with several neighbors. If her father's health was failing, they would certainly be there to pray for him. She counted at least six gray-topped buggies in the driveway, three with the horses unhitched, which meant that the people were staying for a while.

"Thank you," she said to the driver as he opened her car door to help her out. She waited for him to fetch her luggage and, despite his protests, took it from him and carried it to the porch.

She set down her luggage before she quietly opened the door and stepped inside the house. She wasn't certain whether the visitors were praying or comforting her mother and sister. However, she didn't want to disturb whatever was happening.

As she passed through the mudroom and into the kitchen, she saw a circle of folding chairs occupied mostly by men in black suits with black hats on their heads. A few had removed their hats, revealing gray hair or, in some cases, balding heads. But all of the men had long beards that covered the front of their chests. Amanda paused in the doorway, recognizing the men as the bishop, deacon, preachers, and a few of the neighbors. In the midst of the men sat her mother, a white handkerchief in her hand as she dabbed at her eyes while the bishop spoke in a low voice to her.

Jonas spotted Amanda before the others did and nudged Anna. "Amanda!"

Everyone on the folding chairs turned to look in her direction. But it was Lizzie's face that Amanda sought.

"Maem," she said. "I came as fast as I could."

Lizzie stood up and slowly walked toward her.

Amanda glanced at the men who still stared at her. She caught sight of the bishop and noticed that he looked at her with sympathy. "Maem? Why is everyone here? Why is no one with Daed?"

"Amanda," Lizzie said.

Just the one word, her name, spoke in such an emotionless tone.

"Where is Daed?" Amanda asked, looking from Lizzie to Anna and then back to her mother. "Is someone sitting with him? He shouldn't be alone!"

"Amanda," Lizzie said again. "Your *daed's* been called home," she said in an even voice that did not mirror the drawn expression on her face or the blotchy patches on her cheeks.

It took Amanda a minute to digest what her mother had just said. "I . . . I don't understand. I just learned that he had another stroke yesterday." She looked from her mother to her sister. "I've been traveling for almost twenty hours to get here . . ."

Anna stepped forward and reached for her sister's hand. "Schwester," she whispered. "He passed just after midnight this morning."

Amanda glanced at the clock and saw the hands frozen on the one and the four. She realized that someone had stopped it, something that only happened if there was a death in a household.

"Oh, Anna!" Amanda cried. "That cannot be!" She turned to look at the gathering of people. It began to make sense. With the church leaders sitting on the chairs, comforting her mother, she should have suspected that her father had died.

"I came as fast as I could," she said in a soft voice, tears starting to fill her eyes.

Anna reached out for Amanda. "I know, Schwester. God had other plans for him."

Letting her tears fall freely, not caring that there were people in the room, Amanda clung to her sister. "I . . . I wanted to be here," she sobbed, holding on to Anna. Despite her sister's attempts to console her, Amanda felt a hollow pain inside her chest as she realized that, as hard as she had tried, she'd arrived too late to say her final good-bye to her father.

# Chapter Twenty-Three

When Alejandro heard the voice of his mother calling up the stairs for him, he shut his eyes.

"Dios *mío*," he mumbled. How had Alecia known that he was in Miami? He could only imagine who her sources were. He had thought that he could get away without having to deal with his mother. After all, he had only stopped at the condominium in between his flights so that he could freshen up.

"*¡Un momento!*" he called out as he tossed the last of his clothing into the suitcase. He wore white linen pants and a black button-down silk shirt. His white jacket hung on a padded hanger by the closet for when he left. In the meantime, he walked across the white carpet in bare feet and headed into the hallway. "I didn't know you were visiting," he said casually as he started to descend the staircase. "To what do I owe this honor?"

She glared at him from the bottom of the stairs. "I don't want your sarcasm, Alejandro!"

"I'm sorry."

For a long moment, she stared at him, studying his reaction as if to assess whether he was being sincere. Enough time passed that she must have decided he was, so she moved onto a new topic. The stern expression on her face told him that this was not a social visit. It never was. There was always something behind her visits.

"Alejandro," she said at last. "I am here to tell you that enough is enough of this business with your wife. It is time for you to be a man and go to her!"

"Mami . . ."

She held up her hand. "*¡Basta!* You will hear me out!"

He folded his arms across his chest and leaned his hip against the banister.

"Amanda is your wife, Alejandro. She is a treasure to be taken care of, not discarded because of a misunderstanding. I stood by and watched you ruin relationship after relationship in the past, fathering a child that you never met, splashing the cover of magazines with woman after woman. And not one of them worthy of more than a short stint in your bed."

He cringed at that comment.

"But when you brought home Amanda, I knew." She shook her finger at him. "And I warned you not to mess up with this one. And right now? You are messing up."

"Mami . . . ," he said, trying to interrupt her again.

"I do not know what happened in South America. I do not know what happened in Pennsylvania. And I do not know what happened in Europe. But I do know that your wife needs you. She lost her father and needs her husband to give her support and love during a difficult time! Not to mention that your own daughter is there! It is time for you to go to your family"—she stopped, just for a second, to give dramatic effect to her words—"the family you chose, *mi hijo*. You chose to marry Amanda, and you chose to make that child. It is time for you to be a man and go to your family."

She paused, and for a second he thought about speaking, but then he saw that look in her eyes, a fierce determination to finish her thoughts.

"You don't know what it was like to raise a child without a father. You don't remember how much I worked just to be able to feed you! Some days I worked three jobs!"

He took a deep breath. "I remember."

"You cannot know what Amanda is feeling, her father passing away and her husband deserting her."

"I did not desert her!"

"She is not with you," his mother said. "You are stronger than her in the ways of the world. You, of all people, could have insisted that she stay with you."

He raised his hand to his head and mumbled under his breath in Spanish. Then he turned to face his mother. "I don't believe this, Mami! You don't know what has gone on."

"I know enough, Alejandro, and I know that you are quick to judge and even quicker to act. But it takes a real man to own up to his mistakes and fix them."

Alejandro shook his head, and after taking the final two steps, he stood before his mother. Placing his hands on her shoulders, he looked her in the face and said, "Stop, Mami! I *am* going to her."

For once, his mother stopped, speechless.

"I am going to my wife, and then I am bringing both her and Isadora home." He glanced over his shoulder at the top of the staircase where Rodriego was already bringing down his suitcase and jacket. "See? I was upstairs packing when you arrived. My plane is waiting to take me to Philadelphia."

He smiled at her, a soft and understanding smile.

"I am owning up to my mistakes, Mami, and I am fixing them," he said. "I know what a treasure I have in Amanda, and I need her by my side."

"You will have to change, Alejandro."

Change. Yes, he would have to change in more ways than he had since meeting Amanda. That was a realization he had made long before he was willing to admit it. He nodded his head. "*Sí, sí.* I understand that, too. I am willing to make the sacrifices to be more of a husband and father." He noticed the harsh look in his mother's face slowly soften as she listened to him. "I am going to her, Mami, to support her, and when I return, both Isadora and Amanda will accompany me."

The visitors seemed to never end. Since eight o'clock in the morning until well after sunset, horses and buggies lined the driveway, young boys tending to them as their owners visited with the Beiler family.

Elias's body, dressed in his Sunday suit, was laid out in a simple pine coffin at the front of the large gathering room. The visitors paid their last respects to him, standing by the coffin and gazing down at the physical remains of a man who now walked with God. Amanda watched as the people prayed over her father. She couldn't help but wonder what they thought. Certainly they felt for his sacrifices: losing his son, losing his daughter, losing his mobility. Amanda wondered if anyone realized that the death of her younger brother, Aaron, had certainly led up to the other two major losses in her father's life.

Not for the first time, Amanda felt guilt that she had not insisted on helping Aaron with the horse on that tragic day of his fatal accident. Perhaps, she thought, if I had helped Aaron, none of this would have happened. But, as usual, she immediately reminded herself that without Aaron's accident, she would have never met and married Alejandro, would not have adopted Isadora, and certainly would not be carrying Alejandro's baby. From tragedy came bittersweet bliss, she told herself.

Isadora tugged at her hand, interrupting Amanda's thoughts. She looked down at her daughter and tried to smile.

"Are you crying again, Mammi?"

Amanda knelt down and took Isadora into her arms. She breathed in the sweet scent of lavender from her freshly washed hair. "No, Izzie. You are here and that makes me feel ever so much better."

"Is Papi coming to say good-bye to Dawdi?"

Amanda shook her head. "*Nee*, Izzie. He is working and very far away. I'm sure that he wants to be here."

She didn't know that to be true, however. She worried about him, wondering what had happened with the security guards and the fight with Enrique. More important, she worried about what he thought about her. Charlotte had arranged her departure, and before she knew it, she was leaving the hospital and on a flight to begin the long journey back to Pennsylvania.

Her phone had not rung once since she arrived: no phone calls, no text messages. After she arrived at the farm, she had checked it once and was surprised that no one had updated her about Alejandro. After that, she found herself caught up in the whirlwind of comforting her family, praying with the church leaders, and now talking with all of the visitors. This wasn't the time or place to be checking her cell phone.

Amanda knew that it would be a busy twenty-four hours. In the morning, there would be a two-hour service in the very room where Elias's coffin rested. Afterward, the horses and buggies would follow the wagon carrying the coffin to the graveyard. Each buggy, marked in chalk with a number, would follow in a prearranged order; Lizzie, Anna, Isadora, and Amanda would be carried in the buggies with the numbers one and two marked on the back.

After one last private viewing of Elias, the family would say good-bye and the men would carry the coffin to the grave, gently lowering it into the ground before taking turns covering it with dirt while the family watched. The family would remain stoic, trying hard not to cry. Elias might have left them, but surely he now walked with God.

Isadora leaned into Amanda's arms, holding her even tighter. "It's all right, Mammi," the little girl said. "I'm here for you."

Amanda shut her eyes, taking the moment to just feel her daughter's embrace. She could hear the people murmuring in the room, speaking softly to each other. She knew that it would be a long two days, but she also knew that she would get through it with the love of her family, the support of the community, and the gift that God had given her in the small child who held on to her neck, trying to return the very comfort that Amanda had given to her.

# Chapter Twenty-Four

She stood at the grave site, staring at the dirt that was piled atop her father's coffin. Despite knowing what the day would bring, no amount of preparation could have prepared her for this moment. Her father was gone. How had this happened? she wondered. How could Daed have been so vibrant and alive just twelve months ago and now he was no more?

She wore her black dress, the only black one she had that wasn't Amish. It fell to her knees instead of her ankles, something that she felt certain others had noticed and probably whispered about on their buggy ride back to the farmhouse for the noon meal.

Amanda hadn't joined them. She wanted to stay for a while with her father so that he did not fear being interred in the ground. Fortunately, Anna had taken Isadora with her and Jonas so that Amanda could have this time alone with her father.

She wished she could have talked to him, to tell him how everything was such a mess in her life: her marriage to Alejandro, her future within the community, even her relationship with Isadora. Everything was in jeopardy, and all because of one mistake. She never should have struck Enrique. That one act, an act committed in anger, had caused problems for Alejandro, both legal and professional. Surely he would be angry with her for creating just one more in a long line of issues, not to mention that she had left so unexpectedly. Hadn't she promised him she would never do that again?

"Oh, Daed," she whispered. "When did this all get to be so hard?"

In many ways, she often wondered what would have happened if she had not gone to Ohio or had not crossed the streets of New York City on that day last summer. She would not have been struck by the car, and she would not have met Alejandro. Instead, she would have returned to Lancaster and continued with her life as an Amish woman. In all likelihood, she would have been courted by a young man and married last autumn with a *boppli* on the way.

She rested her hand on her stomach and sighed.

In the distance, she heard the sound of a car door shutting. At first, she didn't look up. The undertaker was certainly returning to the cemetery to remove the few items that remained, such as the boards that surrounded the grave and the chair he had placed there for one of the older women of the *g'may*.

When the undertaker did not appear, she looked up to see who had arrived. To her surprise, she saw a figure of a man standing against the front gate of the cemetery. He wore a white suit with a black shirt. From the way that he stood there, his hands clasped behind his back as he watched her from behind dark sunglasses, she knew right away who it was.

He had come.

A sob escaped from her throat as she covered her mouth with her hand. Without a moment's pause, she ran toward him, tears streaming down her face.

He didn't move as she approached him, but she didn't care. She threw her arms around his neck and wept into his shoulder. She felt the stiffness in his shoulders and the hesitation in his response. As she continued to cry, her hands clinging to the back of his jacket, he finally began to soften and reached one arm around to hold her. When he did, she clung to him even more.

"Shh, Princesa," he said at last.

"I . . . I didn't . . ." She couldn't speak, for the emotion that welled up in her throat robbed her of the ability to talk. What she wanted to say to him, that nothing had happened with Enrique and that she meant everything she had said to him about giving up her past just to be with him, seemed stuck inside of her.

He exhaled and let his other arm relax enough to console her. "You must calm down," he whispered. "You've been through too much."

"Oh, Alejandro," she cried. "I just love you so much. I want you and only you. Don't you know that?"

With a firm hold on her shoulders, he pulled away and bent down enough so that he could stare into her eyes. She couldn't see his eyes for they were behind his sunglasses. Hesitantly, she reached up and steadied her trembling hand before she gently removed them. His blue eyes met hers.

"*Sí*, Princesa," he said. "I know that." He wiped the tears from her cheek with his thumb. "That is why I am here."

Another wave of tears and sobs racked her shoulders. She fell against him, holding on to his sunglasses in one hand and his shirt in the other. She didn't want to let him go, refusing to release her hold upon him. Instead, she clung to him as if her life depended on it.

"Amanda," he said after giving her a few moments to calm down. "I am sorry about your father."

She sniffled and rubbed at her eyes. When he offered her a handkerchief, she accepted it and dabbed at the tears on her face. "He did not suffer long. For that, we are all thankful."

"Your family? They are strong, yes?"

She nodded her head. "Mamm is holding everything together, much better than I would have expected."

"And you?"

She glanced at him, those blue eyes studying her face. "I . . . I miss him. But he hasn't been himself for a while. Since the stroke." She managed to sigh. "He's with God, so it would be selfish to wish he were still with us, I reckon."

Alejandro nodded his head. "That's a good way to think about it, Amanda."

"How did you hear?"

He lifted an eyebrow as if questioning her inquiry.

"Oh, Dali," Amanda said, answering her own question.

"*Sí*, Dali. And my mother." He paused before he added, "And the media. Everyone knows, Amanda." He spoke slowly, her name rolling off his tongue in that special way: *Aman-tha*.

Amanda was surprised to hear that even the media knew. "How . . . ?"

"You know enough about the media to know that they make it their business, Amanda, to follow everything that affects you."

"And you spoke to your mother?"

He nodded. "*Sí*, Amanda. I saw her. She came to the condo in Miami and told me to come to you."

Something dropped inside her chest. She had thought he had come on his own accord, wanting to comfort her in a time of need as well as to end the stalemate that had become central to their relationship. To think that he had come strictly because his mother told him to do so was a disappointment to Amanda.

"I see," she finally said.

He reached down and put his finger under her chin so that he could tilt her face upward. Peering into her face, his eyes flickered back and forth for just a few seconds. "My bags were already packed when she arrived," he said. "I was already planning to come for you."

"Oh," she breathed.

"And for Isadora," he added in a soft voice. He leaned down and gently pressed his lips against hers, a kiss so tender that she thought she might cry again.

When he pulled back, one arm still encircling her waist, he held her tight against his body. "She is my daughter," he said. "I want to be a part of her life, Amanda. I understand that we are a family now, *sí?* Things must change." He paused. "I am willing to change."

"I don't want you to change," she said, her voice soft and beginning to fill with emotion.

He pressed a finger against her lips to silence her. "It has been one year, Amanda. Over one year that we have been together. Do you not think that both of us have changed during that time? Remember where we were and how far we have come. You talk about not being selfish since your father is with God. That is God's plan, the plan that you always talk about. Would it not be selfish to wish ourselves where we were twelve months ago? Clearly, that is not God's plan."

She shut her eyes, letting his words sink in. He spoke wisely and she appreciated his candor. In the past twelve months, she had lived a lifetime of change, some of it good and some of it not so good. But the one thing she realized was that, through it all, she had lived and she had loved. Alejandro had taught her how to do both.

"And there is something else that was not in God's plan," Alejandro said, bending down once again so that he was at her eye level. "This."

He placed his hand on her small protruding belly and gently rubbed.

She caught her breath and placed her hand atop his. "What do you mean?"

"God did not plan for you to hide this from me," he said in a tender voice. "When, Amanda, were you going to let me know that you are carrying my baby?"

She stumbled over her words. "I'm sorry, Alejandro," she finally said. "I . . . I didn't know."

The look on his face showed his surprise. After all of her concern over getting pregnant, the numerous tests that she had taken, and her recent tears over possibly being infertile, he found her admission as incredulous as she found her pregnancy. "You did not know?"

She shook her head. "I would have told you, Alejandro. I'd never keep that from you."

He pulled her into his arms, holding her tight against his chest. "*Ay,* Princesa," he breathed into her hair. "I cannot believe that we are going to be parents! That I find out from Geoffrey and not you!" He gave a soft laugh and kissed the top of her head.

"You are happy?"

This time, he pulled away from her and frowned. "You ask if I am happy? *¡Claro, mi amor!* This is our baby. Ours."

"But . . ."

He shook his head. "There is no 'but,' Amanda. I told you that things must change. We can spend more time here on the farm. I will slow down with the music, Amanda. I cannot give up everything, but I will not give you up." He paused and took a moment to smile at her. "Or our children. Both of them."

For a long moment, he looked around, his eyes traveling across the landscape until he saw the fresh dirt of the grave that belonged to her father. He took a deep breath and nodded with his head toward that direction. "But we can discuss that more later, Amanda," he said in a solemn voice. "We have much to catch up on. For now, I should pay my respects to your father and then return you to the house, no? People will be wondering where you are."

Parting from her side, he walked to the grave and stood there, his hands clasped before him. For a long while, he was quiet, his head bowed and his eyes closed. When she saw his lips moving, she realized that he was praying, something she had never before witnessed.

"Life is so short," he said when he finally opened his eyes, staring once again at the grave. "What Elias would have given to see his grandchildren born, to watch them grow and to love them."

She felt emotion well in her throat and pressed her lips together, willing herself to not cry.

Alejandro lifted his head and looked into the distance at the surrounding fields that encircled the graveyard. His pensive nature surprised her and she remained silent, waiting for him to collect his thoughts.

At last, he turned to her, his dark hair casting a shadow over his face. But his blue eyes met hers as he said, "I will not miss such things, Amanda. There is much more to life than music and money."

She caught her breath, anticipating what he was thinking.

He took two steps and stood before her. "We will get through this, Amanda. Together. We will get your family situated, even if I have to stay here to help."

"But your concerts . . . ?"

He dismissed her concern with a wave of his hand. "Canceled. All of them until we sort this out. My place, Amanda, is by your side. Just as you said you would never leave me again, I make you this vow that I, too, will be with you through all of this. You are my wife, and you take precedence over everything else." He paused before he added, "You and our children. God did not intend for us to move through life alone. I see that now, although I already knew it . . . deep down, anyway. That is why he sent you to me. He intended you to show me what is important in life: faith, family, love."

Amanda had not thought about this possibility. She always knew that God had led her to Alejandro, but she always thought it was for them to find each other. She had never considered that all of the hardships during the past year—the accident, the paparazzi, the scandals and speculation, even the fight between Alejandro and Enrique—had been part of God's greater plan to bring Alejandro closer to him.

When Alejandro reached for her, gently pulling her into his arms, she pressed her cheek against his shoulder and shut her eyes. They stood like that, Alejandro's chin resting atop her head and Amanda in his embrace, for several minutes. In the distance, they could hear an approaching horse and buggy, the gentle noise of the rattling buggy wheels and the horse's hooves on the road increasing as it neared the graveyard. Neither one of them moved as they listened to the rhythmic sound that sang a song of peace and tranquility that was so much a part of the Amish life.

For the first time, Amanda knew where she belonged. She would no longer straddle a fence between her upbringing among the Amish and the surreal world of fame. She knew that she and Alejandro had come to the same conclusion: the contrasting lifestyles could not coexist. Yet, together, they would create their own world that combined the best of their lives. Everything would be fine.

They had made the choice to be together, to find a way to make it work. It was a choice that would ensure that God's plan was finally fulfilled.

# Epilogue

When the hospital door opened and Alejandro entered the room, Amanda caught her breath at the large bouquet of roses that he carried. Pink. Three dozen pink roses in a large vase with a white bow around it.

"How are you doing?" he asked as he apprehensively approached the bed. "You are feeling better?"

She bit her lip and nodded her head.

For a moment he seemed to consider where to set the roses. The confused expression on his face almost made her smile. She finally pointed to the wide windowsill. After setting them down, he stood for a moment as if uncertain what to say or do.

"I'm so sorry, Princesa," he finally said.

"It's all right," she said, reaching out her hand for him to take. "I understand, Alejandro."

"I should have been here."

At her insistence, he finally approached the bed and took her hand. She moved over, making room for him to sit beside her on the bed. His hand felt warm and clammy, and she realized that he was nervous. She smiled at last, ignoring any pain that she felt. "Did you see her?"

He looked horrified at her question. "*¡Ay,* Amanda, *claro no!*"

She gave a soft laugh at his reaction. "Why ever not? She's your daughter, too!"

"I would never meet her without you!" He rubbed at the back of his neck and glanced around the room. "She is not here?"

Amanda watched him, astonished at how edgy and tense he was. He had only been gone to New York for one night, but the labor pains came too fast for Amanda to deny the inevitable truth that she was having the baby without Alejandro. Señora Perez had hardly been able to contain herself when Amanda came into the kitchen. Isadora had been sitting at the kitchen table, coloring a picture of a farm while the orange cat lounged in a sunbeam on the floor beside her.

"The baby is coming," Amanda had said.

"My sister?" Isadora dropped her crayons and jumped to her feet, the sudden movement scaring the cat into the other room.

Señora Perez, however, began talking rapidly in Spanish and hurrying for the phone. Amanda tried to sit down at the table, but the tightening of her abdomen forced her to stand up until it passed.

"When do I meet my sister?" Isadora asked as she leaned against the table.

"It could be a brother," Amanda pointed out, to which Isadora made a face.

Señora Perez hurried over to Amanda and took her arm. "Walk, Miss Amanda," she insisted. Without questioning her, Amanda did as her housekeeper instructed, well aware that Isadora was following her.

"Mammi!" Isadora cried out as if something had finally dawned on her. "You can't have my sister without Papi here."

Amanda wanted to respond that Alejandro would return the following day, but another pain took her breath away. The baby wasn't due for another two weeks, and after much discussion, Amanda and Alejandro had agreed that it was safe for him to take this one last trip. But life happened and the baby did not want to wait for his return.

It was Alecia who arrived to take her to the hospital. Without Alejandro to support her in the labor room, Amanda insisted that her mother-in-law stay with her for the delivery. Five hours later, a healthy baby girl had been born.

From the look on his face, Amanda knew Alejandro felt guilty about not being there. In hindsight, Amanda suspected that there were benefits to him not being with her. While the actual delivery had not been long and drawn-out, she doubted Alejandro could have handled watching her suffer when the labor pains came closer together, never mind when the time had come for her to push.

"You should call the nurse," Amanda said. "They'll bring her to us."

For a moment Alejandro looked terrified at the thought, but then nodded in agreement. "I'll go tell them," he said. He returned to the room almost immediately, but rather than sit back on the bed, he pulled over a chair.

"Do you remember the first time I met you?" she asked.

He leaned over and brushed her hair from her cheeks. "You were lying on the street just outside of Times Square," he answered. "How could I forget, no?"

She tried not to laugh. "*Nee*, Alejandro. Not when *you* met me, but when *I* met you."

At first, he didn't respond. She watched him, waiting for the moment that he remembered. "Ah! *¡Sí!* The hospital!" He smiled at the memory. "You were so beautiful lying in the bed with your braid hanging over your shoulder."

Amanda could see him relaxing. "You never should have seen me with my hair down, Alejandro!" she teased. "You know that only a husband should see an Amish woman with an uncovered head."

"You are not Amish."

"No," she said. "I am not, not anymore."

He leaned forward and rested his elbows on the edge of the bed so that he could hold her hands. "Tell me, Amanda. Are you doing as well as you look?"

She nodded. "Yes, Alejandro. I am."

"I was so scared." He lowered his head and kissed both of her hands. "So worried about you."

"Your mother was a wonderful help," she said. "And she is bringing Izzie later."

He rolled his eyes. "*¡Ay, mi madre!* She must have sent me a hundred messages!"

This time, Amanda laughed. "She's so excited! It's a good thing, yes?"

He didn't have time to answer for the door opened up. Alejandro jumped to his feet, inadvertently pushing back the chair, the four legs scraping against the floor. While he watched the door, Amanda looked at him. She felt a familiar burning at the corner of her eyes, emotion beginning to well up inside her as she heard the nurse rolling the bassinet into the room. Alejandro's face changed from a look of panic to curiosity, and then, when his eyes fell upon the bundled baby, her cherubic face turned to one side and her mouth puckering as she slept, it changed to awe.

The nurse reached into the bassinet and lifted the baby. She started to hand her to Alejandro, but he immediately took a step backward, shaking his hands in front of him.

Amanda raised her arms and took the baby, holding her protectively against her chest and gazing with adoration into her face. She waited until she felt Alejandro move to her side before she looked up and said, "Meet your daughter, Alejandro. Isn't she beautiful?"

"Dios *mío,*" he murmured, cautiously reaching out to tuck the blanket under the baby's chin. "She is . . ." He stopped talking, just for a moment, and Amanda knew that he was overcome with emotion.

Always the one to try to remain stoic and in control, Alejandro could not avoid being affected by meeting his new daughter. "She is perfect."

"You can hold her," Amanda prodded gently. "She won't break."

He didn't look convinced. "She's so small."

But Amanda insisted, and never one to say no to her, Alejandro took a deep breath, pulled the chair back over to her bedside, and accepted the infant into his arms.

"I am holding her correctly, *sí*?" he whispered.

Amanda leaned over to peer into the baby's face. "She is perfect, isn't she?"

"She is perfect, *sí*. A perfect *princesa*," Alejandro breathed the words and then, glancing up at Amanda, added, "like her mother."

For several minutes, they sat there, staring at the baby in Alejandro's arms. When her mouth made nursing motions, he smiled and laughed to himself. Amanda couldn't help watching Alejandro.

Over the past few months, he had stayed true to his word. He'd cut back on scheduling new obligations while fulfilling those he already had been committed to. Both Amanda and Isadora had traveled alongside him until the autumn, when he traveled to Israel and the Far East. He hadn't wanted her to travel so far into her pregnancy. While Amanda did not want to be separated from him, she'd felt relief that she could relax in Miami with Isadora for the final weeks of her pregnancy.

Now, as she watched him falling in love with their daughter, she realized that she was also witnessing the final evolution of her husband. Viper had completely disappeared, leaving all of Alejandro in her care. Gone was the man who constantly considered what he could get rather than what he could give. He had finally learned how to love someone—other than Amanda and, within the past few months, even Isadora—with complete adoration and selfless abandon.

"What are we going to name her?" Amanda asked.

He looked up as if surprised by her question. "We never settled on names for a girl."

Amanda glanced down at the baby. "You once mentioned a name that we both liked," she said. "It was a name that you said meant wisdom. That is something we have learned to respect since we have met. And it's something I hope we continue to acquire as we raise both of our daughters."

Before he could respond, someone knocked at the door. Without waiting to be invited into the room, Alecia opened the door and walked in with Isadora by her side. The little girl was dressed in a brand-new white dress with ruffles and a pink ribbon tied around her waist, clearly the doing of Alecia. Amanda greeted her daughter with a big smile and open arms, which only incited Isadora to break free from her grandmother and run across the room to lean against the bed for a hug.

"Oh, Izzie!" Amanda said, wrapping her arms around Isadora. "You look beautiful!"

"Now, now," Alejandro warned. "Be careful with Mammi, *sí*?"

Isadora stepped away from the bed, staring at her father. "Abuela told me that I have a sister."

Alecia stepped forward and placed a hand on her granddaughter's shoulder. "Papi is holding your sister." Then, with a gentle push, Alecia urged her forward to see the baby.

Cautiously, she stepped forward, pausing to look at Amanda as if seeking permission. Amanda knew that it took a lot of control on Isadora's part to not rush forward and see the baby. After Elias had passed away, Amanda and Alejandro agreed that Isadora needed to be with them full-time. Shortly after that, Amanda told Isadora that she was going to have a baby brother or sister before Christmas. Since then, not one day had passed that Isadora didn't talk about her future sibling.

Now the moment was here.

Alejandro held the baby in his arms but shifted his weight in the chair so that Isadora could lean against his knee to see.

"Isadora," he said, "I am honored to introduce you to your sister, Sofia Diaz."

She stood on her tippy-toes to see better. Her dark eyes sparkled as she looked at baby Sofia, a hint of a smile crossing her lips. "My sister?" she asked, looking up at Alejandro as if questioning him.

"*Sí*, Princesita. Your sister."

Alecia stood behind Alejandro, her hand proudly resting on his shoulder, and Isadora returned her gaze to Sofia.

Amanda watched them, emotion welling up in her throat. My family, she thought.

And she knew that, no matter what lay ahead in their lives, God would provide for them. He had brought them this far, had shown them the final destination, even if the journey was far from being over.

Together, she thought, we will get through anything as long as we have each other.

# *Glossary*

## *Pennsylvania Dutch*

| | |
|---|---|
| *ach vell* | an expression similar to *oh well* |
| *boppli* | baby |
| Daed, or her *daed* | Father, or her father |
| *danke* | thank you |
| *dochder* | daughter |
| Englische | non-Amish people |
| Englischer | a non-Amish person |
| *fraa* | wife |
| *g'may* | church district |
| *grossdaadihaus* | small house attached to the main dwelling |
| *gut mariye* | good morning |
| *gut nochmidawk* | good afternoon |
| *ja* | yes |
| *kapp* | cap |
| *kinner* | children |
| *kum* | come |
| Mamm, or her *mamm* | Mother, or her mother |
| *nee* | no |
| *schwester* | sister |
| *vell* | well |
| *wunderbar* | wonderful |

# Spanish

| | |
|---|---|
| *ay, mi madre* | an expression; literally *oh, my mother* |
| *buenísimo* | excellent |
| *bueno* | good |
| *buenos días* | a greeting; good day |
| *claro* | of course |
| *dígame* | talk to me |
| Dios *mío* | my God |
| *gracias* | thank you |
| *linda* | pretty |
| *listo* | ready |
| *mamacita* | little mama |
| *mi amor* | my love |
| *mi hija* | my daughter |
| *mi querida* | my dear |
| *pobrecita, probrecito* | an insult, literally "little poor one" or "poor baby" |
| *qué* | what |
| *sí* | yes |
| *vamos* | let's go |
| *ven conmiga* | come with me |

# *About the Author*

The Preiss family emigrated from Europe in 1705, settling in Pennsylvania as part of the area's first wave of Mennonite families. Sarah Price has always respected and honored her ancestors through exploration and research about her family's Anabaptist history and their religion. For over twenty-five years, she has been actively involved in an Amish community in Pennsylvania. The author of over thirty novels, Sarah is finally doing what she always wanted to do: write about the religion and culture that she loves so dearly. For more information, visit her blog at www.sarahpriceauthor.com.